UNCONTROLLABLE DESIRE

Jennara clung to Bramwell in the soft summer darkness, his beard caressing her face, his lips warm and compelling against hers. Nothing was real to her except his firm muscles under her fingers, the exciting heat of his body against hers, the urgent pressure of his mouth. She'd never expected to feel such uncontrollable desire for a man, but Bramwell's embrace ignited a passion she didn't know she possessed. She pressed closer to him, desperate for more.

Jennara struggled to think coherently, to regain control, but Bramwell's touch sapped her will as his hands caressed her. She must end this, but she didn't want to. Jennara wrenched her mouth from his to urge him to stop, but found herself breathing his name instead. *"Bramwell,"* she murmured. *"Oh, Bramwell."*

In answer he brought her hard against him, showing her how badly he wanted her. The realization added fuel to her own inner fire. Why should she stop? Why shouldn't she continue on this exciting journey until she reached the ultimate unknown but oh-so-desirable destination? Why not yield to this insatiable craving and abandon all control?

ZEBRA'S GOT THE ROMANCE
TO SET YOUR HEART AFIRE!

RAGING DESIRE   (2242, $3.75)
by Colleen Faulkner
A wealthy gentleman and officer in General Washington's army, Devon Marsh wasn't meant for the likes of Cassie O'Flynn, an immigrant bond servant. But from the moment their lips first met, Cassie knew she could love no other . . . even if it meant marching into the flames of war to make him hers!

TEXAS TWILIGHT   (2241, $3.75)
by Vivian Vaughan
When handsome Trace Garrett stepped onto the porch of the Santa Clara ranch, he wove a rapturous spell around Clara Ehler's heart. Though Clara planned to sell the spread and move back East, Trace was determined to keep her on the wild Western frontier where she belonged — to share with him the glory and the splendor of the passion-filled TEXAS TWILIGHT.

RENEGADE HEART   (2244, $3.75)
by Marjorie Price
Strong-willed Hannah Hatch resented her imprisonment by Captain Jake Farnsworth, even after the daring Yankee had rescued her from bloodthirsty marauders. And though Jake's rock-hard physique made Hannah tremble with desire, the spirited beauty was nevertheless resolved to exploit her femininity to the fullest and gain her independence from the virile bluecoat.

LOVING CHALLENGE   (2243, $3.75)
by Carol King
When the notorious Captain Dominic Warbrooke burst into Laurette Harker's eighteenth birthday ball, the accomplished beauty challenged the arrogant scoundrel to a duel. But when the captain named her innocence as his stakes, Laurette was terrified she'd not only lose the fight, but her heart as well!

Available wherever paperbacks are sold, or order direct from the Publisher. Send cover price plus 50¢ per copy for mailing and handling to Zebra Books, Dept. 2695, 475 Park Avenue South, New York, N.Y. 10016. Residents of New York, New Jersey and Pennsylvania must include sales tax. DO NOT SEND CASH.

SUNSET TEMPTATION

JANE TOOMBS

ZEBRA BOOKS
KENSINGTON PUBLISHING CORP.

ZEBRA BOOKS

are published by

Kensington Publishing Corp.
475 Park Avenue South
New York, NY 10016

First printing: June, 1989

Printed in the United States of America

Chapter 1

Jennara Gray reined in the pinto and gazed eastward at the wooded bluffs of the Cottonwood River etched dark against a dawn sky tinted pale pink and gold. She imagined the lone figure of the old Dakota medicine man No Cloud as she'd once seen him, silhouetted against the morning sky, paying homage to the coming day. This was going to be a hot day, judging by the already warm breeze teasing her hair—a scorcher, as her father used to say.

Jennara sighed and clucked to Sage, urging him on. Her father had been dead three years last month, and still she missed him. She could almost hear him chuckle at her wasting time by stopping to watch the dawn.

"The sun comes up every day, Jen," he'd tell her, "just as sure as every August in Minnesota will be hot as Hades."

No Cloud had been her father's friend. The Indian medicine man and the white doctor traded information much as physicians might anywhere. No Cloud had taught her almost as much as she'd learned from her father—though sometimes none of it was enough.

Last night had been one of those times. Jennara took a deep breath, trying to find solace in the beauty of the dawn. Even after three years of helping babies come into the world, she mourned the ones who didn't survive birthing. If only she'd realized beforehand that Mrs. Lawson was carrying twins, she might have been able to save both boys instead of only the firstborn.

The grandmother had tried to console her. "My daughter's got one babe to hold, likely that's all she could nurse anyhow, she's so wore down. You done good getting him out alive, hinder-first like he was."

Sage's ears pricked up, ending Jennara's musing as she searched to discover what had attracted the pinto's attention. She tensed when a man eased from behind the trunk of a cottonwood in the grove to her right, but a moment later she recognized him and relaxed, smiling in greeting, slowing her horse. No Cloud had appeared as though evoked by her thoughts of him. He was naked to the waist, as he usually was in summer, and wore only a breechclout and moccasins—he refused to wear white man's clothes. His fur medicine bundle hung at his side.

"Go." No Cloud spoke softly, at the same time motioning for her to keep moving.

Obediently Jennara let up on the reins and Sage ambled on, No Cloud striding along beside the horse as easily as a young brave.

"Great evil comes," he warned, speaking in his limited English.

Jennara was far more fluent in the Dakota tongue than he was in hers, and she stared down at him, wondering why he chose to use English. He wasn't looking at her; his gaze sought something behind them. Involuntarily she half turned in the saddle. Nothing, no one followed her.

"What is this great evil?" she asked, keeping her voice as low as his.

"I paint sign on house. House now safe. You stay inside. No go out for many sleeps. I come tell you when."

"Please tell me *now* what's wrong." Even as Jennara spoke, her scalp tightened with dread as she realized the implications of No Cloud's warning. Did he avoid speaking in his own tongue because he feared being overheard?

No Cloud had complained earlier in the summer that the Great White Father in Washington hadn't kept the promises he'd made when he took away Dakota land and forced the people to live on two reservations, the upper and lower, near Fort Ridgely. Many moons had passed and still the Dakota received no money or supplies, and their children's bellies were shrunken from lack of food.

"They call us *Sioux*." No Cloud always hissed the word. "Enemy name, not name of The People."

Sioux, according to her father, was a French corruption of the Chippewa word for snake. Sioux was what all her white neighbors and the soldiers at nearby Fort Ridgely called No Cloud and his people.

Jennara drew in her breath in apprehension as she looked at the silent old man loping alongside her horse. "Do your warriors ride against the soldiers?" she demanded.

Without glancing at her, without a word, he turned and melted into a thick stand of yellowing reeds along Porcupine Creek. The reeds rattled and clicked against one another in the breeze, but otherwise there wasn't a sound. Jennara opened her mouth to call to him and shut it again. Why weren't birds calling? Insects chirping? Her nape prickled with fear. She'd be a fool to risk a shout. No Cloud wouldn't warn her lightly.

She cast an apprehensive look over her shoulder and kicked Sage into a gallop, heading for the safety of home. The Indians know I'm their friend, she told herself, remembering the Dakota children whose illnesses she'd treated, the brave whose broken leg she'd splinted. I'm no soldier, the warriors won't harm me, she tried to reassure herself.

But if the Dakotas were on the warpath, they wouldn't kill just soldiers. She might still be safe, but what about Susanna and Ronald? Neither had sense enough to come in out of the rain, though her sister was twenty-two and Ronald twenty. The two of them had to be the most impractical pair in Minnesota, if not the entire United States and the Territories. It'd be a chore to keep them inside the house until the uprising was over.

Uprising — a word dreaded by all frontier settlers. *Indians on the warpath*. And most of the soldiers at Fort Ridgely were gone, sent back east last year to fight against the Rebs after President Lincóln had declared war. She urged Sage to go faster.

We'll be all right, the three of us, Jennara assured herself. There was food stored in the cellar, and the water cistern on the roof was full. Even if Dakota warriors rode to the house, No Cloud's medicine signs would turn them back. Susanna and Ronald would be safe with her.

Her nostrils flared as the rising wind brought the acrid stench of something burning. A farmer clearing stubble, she decided firmly, banishing her mental picture of a homestead in flames while war-painted braves danced and yelled outside.

Chimneys rose above the huge maples shading the white-painted, two-story frame house her father had bought from a dispirited settler who was heading back to St. Paul after losing his wife to cholera. Jennara let out the breath she didn't realize she'd been holding as Sage, winding between the trees, approached the rear of the house. Everything was exactly as she'd left it the night before, when she'd been summoned to tend to Mrs. Lawson.

She tied Sage by the barn, planning to unsaddle him and give him a rubdown once she'd alerted Susanna and Ronald. As she climbed the steps to the back door, fatigue overtook her — she'd had little sleep. She would rest after making sure everything they might need was inside the house. As she pulled open the door, she noticed No Cloud's red-painted medicine drawing — the zigzags of lightning, the sun, and his own symbol, the hawk.

Hurrying through the kitchen, she heard footsteps in the parlor. It was early for Susanna to be up. More likely it was Ronald, sketching while waiting for someone to fix him breakfast. He really was most helpless. . . .

Jennara stopped short in the arch between the dining room and the parlor, staring at the tall, dark-haired man glowering at her, a stranger. She hadn't seen his horse—he must have tied it at the front. She wasn't frightened; she'd found strangers in her house before, people who needed her for an illness or a birthing. She started to walk toward him, a question ready on her lips.

The words died unspoken and her step faltered. Though she'd never seen him before, she recognized him. Color flared into her face and her pulse sped alarmingly. Ronald had sketched his man from memory. She remembered gazing, entranced at Ronald's drawing of this face, stern and saturnine except for the glint of amusement in his dark eyes. To her embarrassment, she'd wondered if she'd have been so quick to say no if he, instead of Ronald, had been the man to ask her to be his wife.

She took a deep breath and swallowed, doing her utmost to quell her fears. "Bramwell Sumner, isn't it? From Philadelphia, I believe." Her voice sounded amazingly calm, though her insides churned in turmoil. "You're Ronald's stepbrother."

"You've been expecting me, Miss Gray?" His words were clipped and cold.

"No. That is, I knew Ronald wrote you, but—"

"Then you should have known I'd come." How unlike Ronald he was. Older—thirty or more, she guessed—and dark where Ronald was fair, the brown eyes smoldering with anger, while Ronald's were the guileless blue of a summer day.

There was no hint of friendliness, much less amusement, in the hard angles of his face. Why was he so hostile? she wondered, raising her chin.

Bramwell couldn't look away from the slender woman, her brown hair coming loose from its single thick braid so that wisps framed her oval face. She wore a dark, rather dusty

9

divided skirt and what seemed to be a man's white shirt that was much too large. She gazed defiantly at him from eyes that first looked green, but flared into amber as her temper rose.

He'd known her immediately from the sketch Ronald had sent him, the sketch with "My future wife" scrawled across the bottom.

From the drawing it was obvious why she appealed to Ronald. Seeing her in person, Bramwell was attracted to her himself. Jennara Gray's face was too strong to be called pretty, but it fascinated him, and her level gaze challenged him as it had in the drawing. He'd known he was going to tangle with this frontier woman and he'd looked forward to the chance, anticipating the pleasure of winning.

She'd been clever to predict his arrival and send Ronald away, thinking to outsmart him. He smiled one-sidedly. He'd soon put an end to her maneuvering.

Glancing down in distaste at the paper in his hand, Bramwell suddenly thrust it at Jennara. "Your doing, I presume?"

Jennara grasped the single sheet in nerveless fingers, feeling as though Bramwell Sumner's dark glare had pierced her through and through. Recognizing the writing, she gasped.

"Why, it's from my sister Susanna!" Her back stiffened. "What are you doing with this?"

"Let's dispense with the histrionics. I have the feeling you're already aware of the contents."

Hastily Jennara scanned the note.

Dear Jen,

Ronald has asked me to marry him. We couldn't help falling in love. Please forgive our hurried departure, but we felt it was best for everyone this way. We'll write later from St. Louis.

Your loving baby sister,

Susie.

"Susanna isn't here?" she asked blankly, unable to believe what she'd read. "Ronald's gone?"

"I found no one in the house when I arrived an hour ago." Bramwell's tone was sardonic. "As if you didn't know. Don't deny this is your doing."

"*My* doing?" Bewilderment wrinkled her forehead. "What are you talking about?"

He took a step toward her and the cold fury in his face cautioned her to back away. She ignored the warning and didn't move. She would not be intimidated!

"Along with your sister's letter," he said, "I found your note to her saying you'd been called to a birthing. At first I was puzzled—I imagine you counted on that—but while waiting for your return, I managed to put it all together. Very clever of you, but not quite clever enough."

"You're making no sense." She spoke tartly.

He shrugged. "I fully expect you to deny you staged your sister's elopement with Ronald because you were worried my arrival might ruin your own carefully laid plans to snare a wealthy man. Better she should have him, you decided, than neither of you."

Indignation made her speechless. "I haven't the vaguest notion what you mean," she sputtered after a minute. "Who's wealthy? Certainly not Ronald . . . he hasn't a cent to his name."

Bramwell's gaze was contemptuous.

"Your stepbrother was naked and half-dead when he was brought to me," Jennara protested. "He had nothing. I fought to save his life and feared more than once that I'd lost."

A vision came to her of how pitiful Ronald had looked two months ago—emaciated, sun-blistered, unconscious—when No Cloud had secretly carried him into her house in the dark of night.

"Do you deny that my stepbrother asked you to marry him?"

Jennara gestured impatiently. "I'd helped him, he was

11

grateful. I certainly didn't take Ronald seriously."

"Do you think I'm fool enough to believe your lies?"

Bramwell moved closer, standing over her threateningly. She stood her ground, anger firing her blood.

"I can only think you're mad," she retorted, "raving mad."

His half-smile was as cold as January. "Perhaps your sister *was* a better choice as Ronald's bride—at least she's younger. I understand you're a twenty-nine-year-old spinster. Quite a gap in years between you and Ronald."

Jennara fought against the simmering rage that threatened to break through her rigid control and reduce her to tears. "You've insulted me," she said icily, "and now you seek to humiliate me. I find your company noxious, Mr. Sumner."

She started to whirl away from him, but he grasped her arm.

"How long have they been gone?" he demanded.

"Let me go!" She tried to wrench free but failed.

"Not until you tell me."

"Even if I knew, I wouldn't—" She broke off, her eyes widening as she belatedly recalled why she'd rushed home. "Oh, dear God, Susanna's in danger!"

He blinked and his grip on her arm eased.

"We must find them before it's too late," she cried, pulling away from him and hurrying toward the kitchen. "Did they take the wagon?"

"Danger? What danger? Another of your tricks?"

He followed so closely behind her he was practically breathing down her neck. Even in her agitation, she felt an unwelcome frisson at his nearness.

"We don't have time to argue," she said as she pushed through the back door. "The Dakota are on the warpath. With Susanna and Ronald out there somewhere, unprotected and unsuspecting."

"Dakota? You mean the Sioux Indians? I don't believe you."

Jennara ignored him, striding into the barn. The wagon

was in its usual place, but she saw the extra saddles were gone. They were riding Soot, the black mare, and old Ben, the wagon horse. She turned to leave and found Bramwell looming in the door, blocking her exit.

"Will you get out of the way?" she demanded. "How often must I tell you we have no time to lose?"

"I heard nothing about any Indian uprising when I asked the way to your house," Bramwell said, leaning against the doorframe. "Strange your nearest neighbors weren't aware of it."

What was wrong with this man? She couldn't expect him to worry about Susanna, but deadly danger stalked his step-brother as well. Didn't he care? Jennara took a deep breath and let it out slowly. She was tired of listening to his wild accusations, she was through trying to make him listen to reason.

"Let me pass." The words hissed through her teeth.

"When you admit the truth."

She had to ride after her sister, before it was too late, but she couldn't push past him—he was too big and too strong. She could think of only one thing to do. Jennara clenched her fists, lowered her head, and charged toward the doorway.

She took him unawares, her head ramming him in his midsection, sending him staggering back. Bramwell grunted, clutching for support, and his fingers caught Jennara's braid, pulling her with him. They slammed onto the dirt floor of the barn, Bramwell's body cushioning her fall. For a moment neither moved.

Bramwell's deep brown eyes stared up into Jennara's from a scant two inches away. Alarmed, she shifted position, but before she could slide away, his arms tightened around her, pinning her to him.

"If you're trying to distract me," he murmured, "I have to admit you've succeeded."

She'd never been this close to a man, had never met a man she'd wanted to be this close to. It must be panic making her

13

bones feel as mushy as tallow; it must be the heat of August burning inside her.

Bramwell raised his head until his lips brushed against hers, tasting her sweetness. Her enticing woman scent and the softness of her curves against him were almost enough to make him forget the reason he was here.

She jerked her head back, ending the kiss, then twisted and drove an elbow hard into his stomach. Taken by surprise, he grunted with pain, loosening his hold. Jennara sprang to her feet. Without a backward glance she ran from the barn.

He rose slowly and brushed dirt and straw from his brown sack coat and trousers. Damn the woman! There wasn't one a man could trust, and if Jennara Gray thought she'd outmaneuvered him, she'd soon find out how mistaken she was.

He stomped from the barn, up the back steps, and into the house. Jennara was in the kitchen, hastily cramming a quarter wheel of cheese and a half loaf of bread into a cloth sack. She eyed him warily but went on stuffing food into the sack.

He stalked past her, retrieved his broad-brimmed derby from the parlor, and opened the front door, planning to ride in search of the elopers. He damned well didn't intend to let either of the Gray sisters trap Ronald.

The sight of the red paint smeared on the door in some obscure design startled him. How could he have missed seeing that when he entered the house? Shrugging, he dismissed it as unimportant and stepped over the threshold.

The faint pop, pop, pop of rifle fire stopped him short.

Jennara came flying from the kitchen. "Did you hear gunshots?" she cried.

He nodded, taking in her fear-widened eyes. Was it possible she was telling the truth about the Indians? Or was she, as he suspected, a consummate actress?

"Could you tell what direction the shots came from?" she asked.

He shrugged. "They seemed to be a good distance away. I

14

shouldn't think rifle fire would be uncommon in these parts."

Her hands twisted together. She didn't answer as she glanced distractedly from him to his horse tied at the post outside, a perfect picture of a frightened woman.

"I bid you good day." He spoke curtly, angered by his momentary weakening. The woman was a liar in words and actions.

Her attention swung back to him. "You can't be so stupid as to ride off alone after hearing that shooting."

Bramwell glared at her, thinking Jennara could rile him quicker and easier than any other woman he'd ever met.

Her eyes went back to the horse. "You don't even carry a rifle. How about food? Blankets?"

"Since I didn't need them on the way here from St. Paul, why should I need a rifle or blankets on the way back? Ronald will be heading there. I expect to catch up with him before nightfall."

She shook her head. "Neither Ronald nor Susanna has any money."

Bramwell took a moment to digest this. Since steamboat passage down the Mississippi was restricted by the Army because of the war, the quickest way to travel to St. Louis would be by railroad from St. Paul. But if the eloping pair had no money . . .

"They'll be riding south instead of north to St. Paul," he said as much to himself as to her.

"On horseback," she added. "Unarmed. Camping at night. Fair game for Dakota warriors. And even if Ronald and Susanna *were* aiming for St. Paul, they wouldn't be out of danger." She threw him a scathing look. "Do you understand now what I've tried to pound into your thick skull?"

"I've only your word for—"

"What's the use?" she cried. "Go on, take yourself off and be killed for your stubbornness. I intend to do all I can to keep myself alive while I attempt to save your stepbrother and my sister." She turned her back on him and hurried to the stairs.

Bramwell stared after her. Damned if he wasn't halfway convinced. He hesitated, then strode to the foot of the stairs—no harm in going armed, just in case.

"Miss Gray," he called, "do you have a spare rifle?"

Her answer was to toss two blankets down at his feet. "Pack one of these in your saddlebags. Then—"

"The rifle?" he repeated impatiently.

"Stop wasting time and start packing. I've only one rifle, so we'll ride together."

He opened his mouth to refuse, then closed it without a word. The idea had merit. For one thing, she couldn't do much conniving with his eye on her. For another, she knew the area. For a third . . . he pushed that thought aside as inappropriate.

Whatever her other failings, Jennara was the most efficient woman he'd ever met. In less than ten minutes they were riding south from the house, saddlebags bulging, rifle handy in its scabbard on her pinto. He could hardly object, since the rifle belonged to her.

She strode astride in her divided skirt, a fur pouch dangling from her waist and a man's tan wide-brimmed hat on her head. He had to admit the odd combination was practical for this frontier country, though she certainly lacked the grace and charm of a lady riding sidesaddle with cascading skirts and petticoats.

"Your horse is rather small," he observed. "Can he take long hours of travel?"

She swept an appraising glance over his much larger chestnut gelding, the best of the horses for hire he'd seen in St. Paul, and a fine-looking animal.

"Where did you get the idea size has anything to do with performance?" she asked. "Sage'll outlast that chestnut without even working up a sweat. Dakota ponies are tough critters."

Just as he suspected. If the Indians were friendly enough

to sell or trade horses with the settlers, wasn't it unlikely they'd be on the warpath, as she claimed? Besides, there were soldiers at that fort he'd passed on his way to the Gray homestead. The Army would keep the Sioux in line.

"Sage was a gift from a friend of my father's," she said. "A Dakota medicine man."

"Why do you call the Indians Dakota?"

"That's their name for themselves. The whites call them Sioux, but that's a Chippewa word for the Dakota, and the Chippewa are their bitter enemies."

He gazed curiously at her. What a strange woman with her odd scraps of knowledge, peculiar costumes, and complete lack of coquetry. He'd gathered from the not-very-near neighbor who'd given him directions to the Gray house that Jennara had taken her father's place as the local doctor and was doing a good job. She had no formal medical training, but apparently the new state of Minnesota lacked physicians in the outlying areas.

"Dr. Gregory Gray was a fine man," the woman had said, "but we think the world and all of Miss Jennara. She's the equal of her pa and more."

He found himself remembering how soft Jennara had felt in his arms there in the barn and how sweet her lips had tasted. He shook his head. . . . Jennara and he were as much enemies as the Sioux and the Chippewa.

Jennara turned away from Bramwell's speculative dark eyes, wishing she were alone. How odd she must look compared to city women. He probably thought she didn't even own a gown. Not that she had one with crinolines or hoops, like Susanna told her fashionable St. Louis women were wearing. She smiled to herself at the idea of attempting to deliver a baby while wearing a hoop skirt.

She had no time to care what Bramwell thought of her appearance anyway. Given the chance of confronting angry warriors at any moment, they'd be lucky to stay alive. With his lack of knowledge of the territory and his stubborn disbelief in anything she tried to tell him, he was a liability she could ill afford.

Still, how could she have let him ride off alone, unarmed? He might not know what could be lurking behind every bush and tree—but she did. She'd do the same for any stranger.

It had nothing to do with the way he'd held her in the barn, not a thing to do with the way his lips found hers in a swift and strangely gentle kiss that left her breathless and yearning.

Sage shook his head and snorted. Jennara nodded ruefully. The horse was right . . . forget the barn and what happened there.

She was well aware of what went on between men and women, even though by choice she'd never had a man of her own. She was a female, Bramwell was a male. He'd taken her by surprise and she wasn't accustomed to being held by a man. Likely it was quite normal for a woman to feel wild and unusual inner disturbances when embraced by an attractive man.

But she intended to make very sure nothing like that occurred again. Not with this man she disliked and mistrusted, not with Bramwell Sumner, who'd clearly announced he was her enemy.

They'd been riding in silence for almost a half hour when the pinto's ears pricked forward and Jennara came alert. Her gaze searched among the bushes along the creek bank, then swept the open valley to the left while she listened, her breath held, for any unfamiliar sound.

A piercing shriek split the morning's quiet, forcing Jennara's breath out as the hair rose on her nape. The sound came from up ahead.

"Good God, what was that?" Bramwell demanded.

She reined in Sage, whirled, her finger to her lips, and jerked her head toward the tangled brush next to Porcupine Creek. He obeyed without comment, sliding off his horse when she dismounted, and led her pinto into cover. He followed with his chestnut.

When Jennara was satisfied they were as well concealed as possible, she leaned toward Bramwell. Precarious as their position was, she felt a perverse satisfaction as she whispered, close to his ear, "That, Mr. Sumner, was a Dakota war cry."

Chapter 2

Jennara pressed closer to her pinto, struggling to contain her fear while the warriors' shrieks and whoops grew louder, the yells echoing from the river bluffs as hooves pounded nearer and nearer. The brush hiding her and Bramwell was too thick to see the warriors passing, but she knew that to any Dakota eye they'd left an obvious trail of their hasty retreat into cover. Their only chance to avoid discovery was for the Indians galloping past not to be checking the trail for previous riders—reading sign, the Dakotas called it.

She held her breath, waiting, the rifle clutched in her hands, expecting at any moment to see painted warriors crash through the brush into their hiding place.

It seemed hours before the noise lessened, finally fading away. She eased her breath out carefully, hardly able to believe their luck. The Dakotas hadn't read the sign!

"They're heading north," Bramwell whispered.

Toward her house, she thought, frowning as she smelled burning wood. Would hers be the next to go up in flames, despite No Cloud's medicine marks painted on the doors? After listening to the frenzied cries of the warriors who'd just passed, she was convinced no whites or their belongings were safe from attack.

As soon as Jennara was positive the Dakotas were truly gone, she led Sage cautiously from cover, Bramwell following with his chestnut.

"Heiden's farm is less than a mile ahead," she told him. "I was planning to stop there and ask if they'd seen Susanna."

"Well?"

She met his gaze levelly. "The warriors came from that direction."

He grimaced in comprehension.

"We'll still stop to make certain there's no one left—" she swallowed "—for us to help."

They found forty-year-old Kurt Heiden shot in the chest, dead between the burning barn and the flaming house.

"He lived alone?" Bramwell asked, his eyes flicking from the sprawled body to search the barnyard and field.

"He had a wife, a son, and a pregnant daughter-in-law." Jennara forced the words past a throat raw with held-back tears and the harsh stench of smoke. "They must have taken shelter in the house."

Both stared at the flames without speaking. No one in the house could possibly be alive.

Jennara knelt to close the dead man's eyes and fold his hands on his chest. Nodding toward a tipped-over wagon, she directed, "See if you can find something to cover him."

Bramwell returned with a tattered piece of canvas and laid it over the body.

"We'd best get on," Jennara said after they'd weighed down the edges of the canvas with stones. "Susuanna and Ronald are well past here if they left before midnight."

"So you *do* know when they left." The chill returned to Bramwell's voice.

She didn't bother to answer. Let him think what he wanted, she no longer cared. The massacre of the Heidens forced her to realize the horror of being a victim of Dakota warriors on a rampage. Unable to bear thinking of such a grisly fate for her sister or Ronald, she prayed Susanna and Ronald *had* left by midnight, because then they'd have traveled far enough so they might well be safe from all marauding Indians. But since she'd left the house about eleven last night and hadn't returned until dawn, she had no way of knowing if they'd decamped on her heels, just before Bramwell's arrival, or at some hour in between.

"Let's go," she said sharply. "We'll ride west to Gooden's farm."

Bramwell didn't argue, and she noticed with grudging approval that he rode with eyes and ears alert for danger.

They met the Goodens near noon, the mother and father riding with a small child hanging on behind each of them.

"Turn back, Miss Gray," Jack Gooden called, slowing as he neared. "The Sioux—"

"We know," she told him, halting Sage. "They burned Heiden's place."

Gooden shook his head. "Best join us. We're making for Fort Ridgely. I reckon the soldiers'll keep us safe."

If you get there, Jennara thought unhappily, but said instead, "God grant you safe passage. We can't turn back because we're looking for my sister Susanna and Ronald Claridge. Did you see them pass earlier?"

Gooden checked his horse. "Reckon I did. Going on three this morning, I was in the barn helping my old mare to foal. Heard a horse nicker and a woman laugh, so I called to see who 'twas. Heading south, they was."

"Jack, please," Molly Gooden begged fearfully from up ahead of him. "We got to hurry."

"Good luck to you." Gooden dug his heels into his horse and rode on.

"Three this morning," Bramwell repeated. "Your sister and Ronald have a good start on us."

"Thank heaven!" When he glared at her, she ignored his hostility. "That start may keep them ahead of the Dakota until they get well into Iowa, where they'll be safe."

"From Indians, maybe . . . not from me. I have no intention of allowing Ronald to marry your sister. Or you, for that matter."

Jennara pressed her lips together to keep from answering as she urged Sage back onto a southerly course. She had no intention of admitting to Bramwell her own doubts about the wisdom of Susanna and Ronald marrying . . . or telling him why she had those doubts. She loved Susanna, but she didn't trust her.

As for herself, she'd never marry Ronald, but it was wasted breath to try to convince Bramwell of it.

"If all the Indians make as much noise as those we've encountered already," Bramwell observed, "we'll have little trouble avoiding their war parties."

She stared at him, biting back a tart rejoinder. He wasn't actually stupid, he was merely an Easterner. What did he know of life on the Minnesota frontier or of Dakota ways?

"Hidden warriors could be stalking us even now," she explained as patiently as she could. "If they are, unless our horses alert us, we won't see or hear anything until the warriors attack."

Bramwell blinked, then cast a quick glance around.

There was nothing to see except the midday sun casting hot August rays on wooded river bluffs, sparse groves of cottonwoods and maples, and the willows lining the creeks. Two hawks circled high to the left, dark silhouettes against the pale blue sky. Thready clouds huddled together in the west.

"Any settlements in this direction?" Bramwell asked after a time.

She shook her head. "Only farms this way, and those few and far between. Hoefferle's is next. We'll ask there if . . ." Her words trailed off.

His glance told her he knew what she hadn't said. *If we arrive ahead of the warriors.*

Fatigue blurred her vision as the unrelenting heat boiled away what little energy she had after being up most of the night. She mopped her sweaty face with a man's handkerchief, but could do nothing about the perspiration trickling unpleasantly between her breasts.

Bramwell removed his sack coat, and tired as Jennara was, she found herself noticing how his white shirt revealed the breadth of his shoulders and contrasted agreeably with his dark complexion. Ronald's fair complexion and slender build made him seem boyish, but Bramwell was very definitely a man . . . a handsome man. A man she wished had never left Philadelphia.

Though she hated to take the time, they must stop soon to water the horses and let them rest. She hoped Susanna and Ronald had enough sense to take proper care of the horses they rode. Old Ben could still pull a wagon, but he wasn't used to being ridden, and because of his age, she doubted he could last all the way to St. Louis. She could only hope Ben would make it as far as Iowa. Traveling on foot could be perilous in this country — it had almost killed Ronald once already. Doubly dangerous now, with the Dakota running amok.

"The horses—" she began, breaking off when Bramwell held up a warning hand. He slowed and placed a hand behind his ear in a gesture of listening.

Jennara straightened in her saddle, focusing her fatigued mind on hearing what he heard. After identifying the distant noise coming from somewhere ahead of them, she half-smiled. "A mule."

He scowled. "You're sure?"

"A mule's bray is unmistakable."

"Who'd be riding it?"

"I've never seen a Dakota riding a mule or a donkey. Most settlers don't either. They use them for pack animals. Like the soldiers do."

Bramwell's face brightened. "Maybe we're in luck."

She shrugged. "I don't think we'll come across any soldiers in these parts. They keep close to the two reservations and those are behind us, near Fort Ridgely."

"The soldiers could be pursuing the warriors who passed

24

us."

Jennara's thoughts moved as sluggishly as Porcupine Creek in a dry summer. If she didn't rest she'd soon fall from the saddle. She pushed her words out with an effort. "I think the Indian raids have just begun. The Army won't discover the Dakota are on the warpath until the surviving settlers start reaching the fort. Or unless the fort is attacked."

"How did *you* find out?"

"My friend No Cloud warned me."

"He's the Indian medicine man, I take it." Distaste flickered across Bramwell's face. "How can you call any Sioux your friend after what we saw at that farm?"

Irritation sharpened her wits. "The same way you call one white man a friend and another a foe. By knowing him. Indians aren't all murdering fiends or ignorant savages, they differ from person to person as much as we do."

His expression told her she hadn't convinced him. He had to be shown everything before he'd believe it, he was as stubborn as a Missouri mule.

And she was too tired to care. "We'll stop and water the horses," she told him. "They need a rest. So do I."

Did she think *he* was indefatigable? Bramwell wondered as he gratefully slid off the chestnut. Only pride had kept him straight in the saddle this last hour. He wasn't used to long trips on horseback and he'd ridden hard from St. Paul to reach her home, taking only a few hours' sleep at travelers' rests on the way.

Damn her interference! If she hadn't set up the elopement to thwart him, Ronald would have been at the Gray house and the two of them would be well on their way to St. Paul at this moment. Instead, he was God knew where in this hot-as-hell Minnesota country with bloodthirsty Indians liable to leap out from behind the next bush. And Ronald was in as much danger somewhere ahead.

25

Yet Jennara Gray could look him in the eye and announce that one of those savages was her friend. He snorted and saw her glance his way as she led her pinto to the creek.

After watering the horses, they tied both animals among the willows for concealment. A few quick swallows of water and bite of cheese later, Jennara sat on the ground, her back propped against a gnarled bole, a low branch drooping slender pale green leaves to half-hide her face. The sweet smell of drying grass came to Bramwell as he stretched out at her feet, propping his head up with his arm.

She took off her hat and eased the thick braid of her brown hair over one shoulder, where it hung over her breasts. Perspiration dampened the thin cotton of her loose shirt so the material molded itself against her upper body. Whatever undergarment she wore didn't hide the shape of her firm, round breasts and Bramwell felt an unwelcome stir of desire.

He looked away. This certainly wasn't the time or the place . . . or the woman. Bramwell grimaced when he found himself envying Ronald for being alone in that house with her for at least six weeks before the sister came home. He did *not* want any entanglement with Jennara Gray.

"When exactly did Susanna return from St. Louis?" he asked abruptly.

Jennara jumped at the sound of his voice, her eyes flying open. "St. Louis?" She sounded dazed. "How did you know that's where she was?"

"Ronald wrote me — you must have told him."

Jennara rubbed her eyes. "Evidently I did. She's been back home two weeks."

Long enough to convince Ronald to switch his affections, apparently. Not that Ronald could be described as constant, with a new girl catching his eye on the average of once a month. It hadn't been the girls who bothered Bramwell, it was the calculating women, older than his stepbrother, who sought to trap Ronald into marriage because they knew he was a rich man.

Women like Jennara Gray.

"We must push on," she said, reaching for her hat.

Bramwell ignored the protest of aching muscles as he rose to his feet. Time was of the essence. God and the Sioux willing, they'd soon make up the start Ronald and Susanna had on them. He'd put an end to the Gray sisters' scheming and get back to Pennsylvania, where he had far more important business to attend to.

His chestnut showed an inclination to walk rather than trot and had to be prodded to the faster pace of the pinto.

"Ronald's like the chestnut," Bramwell observed. "I doubt he'll be traveling fast unless your sister, having her own good reasons, forces him to."

"I know Ronald." Jennara's voice was tart. "But despite what you think, Susanna's unlikely to be hurrying him along. She doesn't care for riding, and neither of their horses is as sound as the pinto. I'm surprised they didn't take the wagon."

He scowled at her slim figure. Her braid hung down her back like a little girl's, but she was far from the innocent she pretended to be. Why was she so determined to keep up the farce of not having known Ronald and her sister had eloped until she'd read the note? Quite likely she'd stood over Susanna while she wrote it and he'd made it obvious that he realized this. Anger tightened his jaw. Did she think because he allowed her the lead in unfamiliar country, he meant to yield to her in every way?

And why should she lead? Ruts in the grass and soil marked the road clearly enough. He urged the chestnut past the pinto. "I'll scout ahead," he announced bluntly as he passed, kicking his horse into a gallop.

The chestnut raced along the trail through a grove of large oaks and maples which thinned rapidly to saplings on cut-over land. Then he left the woods and was on the rolling prairie. Under other circumstances he might find the country attractive.

His mount labored up a steep hill. As he reached the

27

summit, Bramwell saw a peaceful scene below—a field of tassled corn, cows in the shade of cottonwood trees chewing their cud, two horses and a mule standing apart from the cattle, a one-story log house, a barn. No doubt the people living here could tell them how long ago the elopers had passed. He started down.

Suddenly, from nowhere it seemed, ten mounted warriors sprang into a circle around the house and barn. A rifle cracked and he heard again the eerie hair-raising Sioux war cries. Desperately Bramwell yanked on the reins, but the horse couldn't stop his downhill plunge.

Jennara's pinto swept past him. "This way," she hissed, angling toward the cottonwoods between the hill and the farm buildings.

Feeling certain they'd be spotted before reaching the dubious cover of the trees, Bramwell hunched his shoulders against the expected bullet. Once among the cottonwoods, he saw a stream beyond. Jennara urged the pinto through the water, slid off, led the horse into thick willow brush, and stopped. Bramwell wondered if it was wise to go even closer to the house, as she was doing, but he had no better solution than to follow her. Rifle fire spooked the chestnut, and Bramwell calmed him as best he could.

"I hope we can save the horses," she said in a tone so low he scarely heard her. He watched uncomprehendingly as she undid the pinto's saddle. "Take your saddle off," she ordered.

"Why?" He took care to keep his voice down.

"I'm going to hide them. We can't ride the horses out of here without being seen—if we haven't been already—and we can't risk losing all our supplies. Hurry."

She was right, they were trapped in this willow thicket. Bramwell knew they couldn't outride the Sioux—not with tired horses. He unbuckled his saddle and helped her find a depression that, with brush pulled into place over it, made a natural concealment for their gear.

"We need the rifle," he protested.

To his surprise she handed it to him, along with the ammunition. "You *can* shoot?" she asked.

He damped down his annoyance at her implication of his ineptness and merely nodded as he checked the rifle, noting with some amazement that it was one of the new Spencer repeaters. He was damned if he'd tell her he'd been target shooting for months . . . or why. He didn't need to justify himself or his skills to her.

The pop of rifles, blast of shotguns, and yells frightened the chestnut into frantic thrashing, loosening the reins tethering him to a willow branch. He rolled his eyes and the whites showed, bloody froth oozing from his nostrils. The pinto shifted uneasily, catching the chestnut's panic.

Bramwell struggled to retie the terrified horse, the stifling heat and a gamy stench from somewhere nearby combining to make his stomach roil uneasily. "What's that stink?" he asked once he had the horse under control.

"Green hide." Jennara waved a hand, and peering through the leaves, he made out an animal skin, head still attached, stretched onto a drying rack.

"I feel as blind as a bird in a covered cage," she went on. "I've got to see what's happening."

Bramwell agreed wholeheartedly. Outnumbered and outarmed as they were, they could hardly take the initiative, but at least they could watch for warriors stalking them.

"How many Hoefferles?" he asked as they left the horses to push cautiously through the brush, careful to stay under cover.

She looked at him. "Six. Three small children and an old grandmother, leaving two adults to stand off the Dakotas. I counted ten warriors. And we have only the one rifle." Tears brightened her eyes and she brushed them hastily away. "Likely it's too late to try and help the family — we'd doom ourselves without saving them."

He clenched his teeth at the thought of helpless children at the mercy of the shrieking, naked warriors as he watched the crouching Jennara peer through the thinning brush ahead of him.

She drew back quickly. "I see just seven warriors. The others may be stalking us. You take a look."

As he eased into the spot she'd left, he realized with dismay that the yelling and shooting had stopped. Thirty feet ahead was the house, its roof in flames. A warrior carrying a cloth bundle ran from an open door. Others rounded up cows. He counted eight Sioux, with no sign of the other two. He heard nothing but the crackle of flames and a bee buzzing somewhere above him.

"I see eight," he reported, turning back to Jennara. To his amazement, she'd taken the not-yet-cured hide from the rack. A wildcat's head, teeth bared in a death snarl, flopped over her arm. What the hell did she want with that stinking thing?

While he watched in disbelief, she yanked her hat off and draped the fur over her shoulders, positioning the cat head until it snarled atop her hair like a grotesque bonnet. Evidently noticing his expression, she smiled one-sidedly.

"No Cloud named me Medicine Cat. I hope he's right."

Her words made no more sense to him than her donning the wildcat skin.

Jennara opened the fur pouch dangling from her waist and carefully removed a small leather container. He was beyond surprise when she loosened a thong and spit into it. Reaching in with her forefinger, she stirred, then lifted out a lump of red paint. Carefully, she dabbed some onto the forefinger of her other hand and ran it down from forehead to nose to chin, bisecting her face with a red stripe.

"You'll have to help with the rest," she told him. "Jagged marks on both my cheeks—" she demonstrated with a zigzag motion in the air—"and a rayed circle on my chin. Put the rest of the paint into the cat's empty eye sockets."

Refraining from comment, Bramwell painted her face to order and gingerly dabbed red onto the cat head.

"Don't let any warriors see you," she cautioned. "No matter what I do, you keep out of sight. And don't shoot unless I tell you to."

He opened his mouth in protest.

"Don't argue." She scowled at him.

With her face painted and the wildcat's red eye sockets staring from the top of her head, she looked as savage as he imagined her medicine-man friend must. Replacing the container, she took a small white object from the pouch, dropped to a crouch, and eased into the thinning brush. After hesitating momentarily, he followed.

A wildcat's scream shattered the silence. Bramwell jumped, jerking the rifle up. Jennara sprang from the bush into the open. Two painted warriors, naked except for breechclouts, erupted from cover within five feet of Jennara, who was crouched between him and the Sioux. Had that eerie scream actually come from her?

One warrior carried a bow, his arrows in a quiver on his shoulder; the other dangled a club. Carefully Bramwell aimed the rifle at the Indian with the bow.

Jennara began a high-pitched chant in a language he assumed must be Sioux, alternating growls with words, while she pointed what looked like a white seashell at the two warriors.

With luck I can pick off two before the others get here, Bramwell told himself, starting to tighten his finger on the trigger. Before he completed the movement, one of the warriors began to edge backward. The other stood his ground. At that moment the chestnut burst free from the tangle of brush, its eyes rolling wildly. It shied away from Jennara and galloped directly toward the two Sioux. They broke and ran toward the burning house, shouting.

"For God's sake, don't shoot either of them," Jennara said over her shoulder to Bramwell, keeping her voice low.

He eased his finger off the trigger.

She backed toward him, her eyes on the warriors. The two

who'd challenged Jennara gesticulated frenziedly as they conferred with the others.

"Preparing to attack us," Bramwell muttered. "I should have killed the two while I had the chance."

"They won't attack." She spoke without turning. "They think I stole the horse's spirit and they're afraid I can steal theirs, too. They won't come near me because they know bullets, arrows, and clubs are of no use against a Sky Being. Whether or not they saw you when we came down the hill, they won't stay around to investigate."

Bramwell stared incredulously at her. Did she really believe she could rout ten bloodthirsty warriors with her wildcat mumbo jumbo? Her appearance was certainly outlandish, but underneath the paint and fur, even a superstitious Sioux ought to be able to see she was a white woman, not some kind of Indian spirit. He gripped the rifle, keeping it aimed toward the warriors, meaning to take as many as possible with him if he had to die.

He couldn't believe his eyes when the Sioux hastily gathered bundles of loot, mounted, and driving captured livestock ahead of them, rode southward from the farm.

"They're taking one of the Hoefferle children," Jennara said, and Bramwell realized what he'd thought was a bundle of clothes was actually a living child. He also knew there was nothing he could do about it.

"They adopt young captives and treat them well," she added.

She'd said there were three Hoefferle children. No doubt the Sioux had murdered the other two, along with their parents and grandmother. Why did she keep defending these rapacious savages?

When the warriors were out of sight, Jennara yanked off the wildcat skin and, carrying it, pushed her way into the brush where Bramwell waited. The effort of convincing the warriors that she was a wildcat spirit had exhausted what strength she had left. They didn't dare camp here, so she had to summon enough energy to move on, but she wouldn't be able to travel far.

Retrieving her hat, she returned to where they'd hidden their gear. She disposed of the skin in the gully, covering it well. Without speaking, Bramwell helped her saddle the pinto, then carried his saddle and gear to the farmyard.

The house had burned almost to the ground. Edging as close as she could to the heat, she counted five charred bodies inside before tears she was too tired to hold back blurred her vision. The senseless killing appalled and sickened her. She could understand the Dakota having a grudge against the Indian Agency, but these people, like the Heidens, were innocent.

When Bramwell told her the warriors had taken every animal, even the mule, she gathered herself together, ignoring the tears streaming down her cheeks, and helped him fashion a makeshift travois which they attached to the pinto.

With Bramwell's gear lashed onto the travois, Jennara mounted Sage, knowing neither she nor the horse could go on much longer. Bramwell strode along beside the pinto.

"We're heading north," he noted, a question in his voice.

"You saw the warriors ride south," she said slowly. "I suspect they're not reservation Indians like the others we met. There's a Dakota encampment beside Lake Pepin, near the Iowa border. At first I thought only No Cloud's lower agency Dakotas were involved, but it looks like every Dakota village in the region is on the warpath. We're asking for trouble if we continue traveling south — especially with only one horse."

She braced herself for an argument about overtaking Ronald and Susanna, but all Bramwell said was, "With me on foot, what are our chances of getting to Fort Ridgely?"

So he'd come to the same conclusion she had. The fort was the only safe refuge until the soldiers put down the uprising.

"I don't know. At this moment all I can think of is finding the right place to camp for the night."

"We ought to be able to find a site we can defend in the

33

woods I rode through."

Jennara nodded. The woods were as safe as anyplace else.

After she'd picked a spot by a stream, not too near the trail, she slid off the horse and pulled a clean shirt and camisole from her saddlebag. "I'm going to wash off the wildcat," she told him, "then rest."

"I'll stand guard," he assured her.

"Once it's dark we can both sleep," she said. "The Dakotas prefer daylight raids."

The evening passed in a blur of drowsiness for Jennara. Before the moon rose she'd fallen into a deep sleep. She woke in darkness to find Bramwell had covered her with one of the blankets. Careful to make no noise, she sat up. By the faint starlight filtering through the canopy of leaves, she saw him slumped against a tree, asleep. Leaning closer to him, she noticed he held the rifle across his lap, and she smiled slightly.

Obviously he'd meant to stay awake despite what she'd told him. Dakotas believed evil spirits roamed the dark, and so stayed close to their encampments at night. In a moment she'd wake him and they'd travel toward the fort until dawn, then hide during the daylight hours. They'd have to be unusually lucky to find another horse for Bramwell—otherwise it would take two more nights to reach Fort Ridgely.

Bramwell wasn't the ideal trail companion, his reckless ignorance yesterday had resulted in depriving them of his horse and came close to costing their lives. The lack of that horse might yet prove fatal. Ronald had told her his stepbrother Bramwell was a lawyer, and Bramwell had certainly played the lawyer with her, treating her as though in caring for the desperately ill Ronald she'd committed a crime. He examined every word she said with suspicion, suspecting a lie. She could hardly wait to be rid of this educated eastern male who was so positive he was superior.

Edging nearer, she inspected his face, shorn of its harsh lines by sleep. A strand of dark hair strayed over his forehead, giving him a boyish, innocent look that tugged at her heart. Is this what he was like underneath all that arrogance? She shook her head. Possibly at one time, long ago—but there was no trace of the boy in his present behavior.

It had been no boy who'd kissed her in the barn—she'd been pressed close to a man's body. God knew she wanted to forget how he'd made her feel at that moment. Why couldn't she?

Bramwell awoke with a start, convulsively clutching the rifle as he stared at her. "Jennara!" he exclaimed, reaching to touch her face.

The sound of her name on his lips, the brush of his fingers on her cheek sent a warming quiver through her. For a moment she forgot she disliked him, forgot danger surrounded them, forgot everything except Bramwell.

He sat up, his hands settling on her shoulders, drawing her closer. "I dreamed you were a prisoner of the Sioux," he murmured.

A small voice in her head whispered to Jennara of how Bramwell Sumner could prove as dangerous to her as any Dakota warrior, but the warning fought against her increasing need to melt against him and experience that danger as soon as possible.

She swayed toward him.

Chapter 3

Jennara drew back abruptly and Bramwell's hands fell away from her shoulders. What was the matter with her? she wondered. Another moment and she'd have been in his arms . . . in the arms of a man she didn't even like.

He cleared his throat and settled against the tree again. "It must be near dawn." He spoke calmly, evenly.

"Over an hour away," she told him, hoping her voice didn't reveal how unnerved she was by her inexplicable behavior of a few moments ago. She felt on edge, without the slightest inclination for more sleep. "We can't go on until it's light enough to see possible danger ahead."

"You're still thinking of Fort Ridgely?"

"We don't have a choice."

"Since I'm unfamiliar with the territory, I can't argue. In St. Paul I bought a map of the state of Minnesota. Before we start, why don't you point out on this map where we are in relation to the fort, so I have some idea how we're going to get there."

Jennara thought she, too, would like to know how they were going to get to Fort Ridgely. She wished it were as simple as looking at a map and following the most direct route. Their arriving at the fort depended on whether they'd be lucky enough to avoid being killed by rampaging Dakota warriors on the way. She wished she was sure she was right in

36

choosing to head for the fort, and she prayed Susanna and Ronald were still alive and safe, wherever they were.

"You *are* familiar with maps and how to read them?" Bramwell asked.

Jennara stiffened. His attitude was insufferable. Did he doubt her ability because she was a Minnesotan or because she was a woman? Or both? How she longed to be rid of his company! She'd certainly stand a better chance of arriving at the fort if she didn't have Bramwell to shepherd through hostile territory on the way.

"I'll point out anything you like on your map," she said tartly, "but no map ever drawn will help us in the present circumstances."

"The soldiers ought to have the rebellion well in hand by now." He rose and stretched. "From what I've heard, these uprisings don't amount to much."

Jennara was speechless with anger. Getting to her feet, she turned toward him. Already the morning had grown lighter. She could see his dark stubbled face quite clearly in the grayness. Taking a deep breath, she let it out slowly to regain control. "You haven't the least notion of how Indians behave. How dare you say such a thing? Not amount to much? Does that include the massacre of the Heidens and the Hoefferles?"

"I didn't mean to trivialize the deaths of those farm families. But armed soldiers aren't helpless civilians. I'm sure we'll find the Army has everything under control."

"Do you know nothing of history?" she demanded. "When have Indian warriors ever fought battles as soldiers do? If you mean that the US Army has better weapons, you're no doubt correct. And I agree the Army must succeed in the end. But the Dakota, like all other Indians, fight as individuals, individuals who from time to time temporarily band into groups. It's both their strength and their weakness. The Army will need weeks, perhaps months, to chase down each separate marauding band of warriors."

Noticing the stubborn set to his jaw, she was certain he

didn't accept what she was telling him.

"I didn't take you for a fool," she snapped, "but I see I was wrong. You may believe whatever you wish, that's your privilege. If you plan to travel with me, though, you'll either go along with what I say or you'll go alone. Have I made myself clear?"

"Eminently." His amused tone set her teeth on edge.

"Where's your map?" Her words were sharp.

In the gray predawn light, Jennara unfolded the map he handed her and laid it on the ground. When a vagrant morning breeze lifted the paper, Bramwell pulled a clasp knife from his pocket, opened it, and to her surprise, flipped the knife in an arc. The blade stabbed through the map in the exact center, pinning the paper to the ground. She raised her eyebrows.

"Mumblety-peg," he muttered.

She could hardly believe this stubborn, difficult man had ever been a boy playing childhood games. No doubt he'd been intent on winning even then.

They both crouched over the map as she put her finger on a spot less than fifty miles from the Iowa border and an equal distance from the eastern border of Minnesota. The western border of Minnesota was where the Dakota Territory began.

"We're about here. This is Fort Ridgely, maybe twenty miles north. Between us and the fort is the beginning of the Indian reservation. The only way to avoid it is to circle east through New Ulm."

Jennara's finger slid up diagonally from the fort to the Dakota border. "The reservation runs like this for one hundred and fifty miles on into Dakota. No Cloud once told me fifteen chiefs had villages along the rivers cutting through the land. Who knows the population of each village? Fifty? A hundred? This doesn't count the Dakota who prefer to live off the reservation or those who live in the Dakota Territory."

As Bramwell studied the map, Jennara became more and more aware of how close he was to her, so close she could feel the heat of his body. Deciding he'd be amused all over again if she edged away, Jennara remained where she was.

"So it's possible there could be as many as several hundred Sioux on the warpath?" he asked.

She nodded. "Depending on how many followed the war leaders."

"But why? Our government pays them annuities, it clothes them, feeds them—"

"The government is *supposed* to, you mean. No money has come for them yet this year. The agency food's run out, no more has arrived, and the buffalo herds now travel so far to the west that the hunters can't find them. No Cloud said the children in his village were crying with hunger." Jennara sighed. "The Dakota have a right to be angry, but I never thought it would come to such horror."

Bramwell pulled the knife from the map and slid it into his pocket. As he refolded the map he said, "I may have been hasty in assuming the uprising had been quelled. I assure you I'll abide by your rules on the trip to Fort Ridgely."

He spoke so stiffly that she saw he resented having to retreat from his stand and offer the halfhearted apology.

"For safety we'll have to stay off the road and the trails," she said. "It's best if we both walk. I'll scout ahead and you lead Sage. Watch the horse. He'll sense danger before either of us will."

Bramwell opened his mouth—to protest, she was sure—but closed it without speaking.

"We'll also need food, so when we pass a farm—" She didn't finish, remembering the terrible scene at the two farms they'd come to. Would they find any farms left unmolested?

Bramwell nodded. "Live off the land."

Sage, who'd found a patch of grass between the trees, had a better breakfast than they did. Walking ahead of Bramwell and the horse, Jennara moved cautiously through the woods. Her divided skirt felt stiff with dust and dirt, and she wished she'd thought to bring more than one clean shirt, although it was ridiculous to worry about clean clothes when her life was in danger. What did it matter how she looked?

In Philadelphia, women must wear the very latest styles, like those Susanna had told her about—hoopskirts, crinolines, ruffles and bows. Even if she donned her best, Bramwell would find Jennara Gray sadly lacking when it came to fashionable gowns, so why should she care what he might think of what she wore at the moment? Why should she care about him at all?

Never mind what Bramwell does or doesn't think, she admonished herself. Keep your attention on what's ahead, keep alert to the perils lying in wait. If you don't, you won't live long.

She'd told him to lead the horse, Bramwell thought darkly. She'd told him to pay attention to the animal because Sage knew more than he did. Jennara hadn't added that the horse was also more useful, but she'd certainly implied it. From the beginning she'd considered him a liability. He shook his head. To think he'd been reduced to showing off his prowess with mumblety-peg, of all things. How the mighty had fallen! Ronald would be amused.

He'd known damn well she could read a map. It wouldn't surprise him to discover drawing them to scale was among her many frontier talents. He'd questioned her ability in retaliation for her asking if he knew how to use a rifle. That had stung. What kind of man did she take him for? It puzzled him that he should care so much what this country spinster thought of him.

The trip to Minnesota, bringing Ronald to terms, and returning east with him had seemed so simple in Philadelphia. True, Jennara had proved more formidable than he'd expected, but he'd have triumphed over her and caught up with Ronald if it hadn't been for the blasted Indians—Sioux, Dakota, whatever the hell they were.

He hoped Jennara was wrong about the seriousness of the uprising, but if she wasn't, they'd be lucky to survive long

enough to reach the fort. On foot it was all the more dangerous, and admittedly it was his fault they were short a horse.
No wonder she found him inept. But damn it, he wasn't.
Once he knew the terrain and mastered the art of frontier
behavior, he'd be as good or better at survival than the next
Minnesotan. Unfortunately that took time, and he had precious little of it at his disposal.

Bramwell glanced back at Sage. The horse, loaded with
their gear, flicked his tail to discourage flies, but otherwise
seemed calm enough. From a branch overhead a jay
squawked, startling him but not Sage. The horse didn't so
much as twitch an ear.

The early breeze had disappeared, it was stifling in the
woods, another hot day was in the making. Ahead of him
Jennara's braid flipped from side to side as she peered between the trees, searching for Sioux. He shifted his grip on
the rifle. Maybe she was wrong and the Indians, their blood-
thirst satisfied, had crept quietly back to their tepees. Even if
this proved to be true, he knew he and Jennara didn't dare
take a chance.

With no warning at all, two naked and painted savages
sprang up ahead and to either side of her. Bramwell dropped
the lead rope, brought up the rifle, and fired at the one on
the right. The Indian dropped. Bramwell swung the rifle to
the left, thanking God it was a Spencer repeater. As he fired,
the second Sioux ducked, diving into the undergrowth. Jennara raced back to Bramwell and grabbed Sage's lead.

"Two down," she said. "Good shooting."

For a moment he didn't understand and his expression
must have given him away.

"You got them both," she explained, hurrying Sage off to
the left, deeper into the woods, away from the road. "Let's
hope they weren't scouts but were on their own."

Bramwell, who'd thought his second shot had missed,
frowned as he followed her. "The one on the left—are you
sure about him? Maybe we should check."

"He didn't move once he hit the ground."

The bullet must have caught the Sioux in the head when he ducked, Bramwell decided. He stared at the rifle and grimaced. He'd killed his first man . . . two men. Taking a deep breath, he released the air in a sigh.

"You saved my life," Jennara said as he drew up even with her.

"And my own," he added quickly. From dolt to hero was too rapid a promotion. It made him uneasy.

"I owe you an apology for doubting your ability with guns."

He ought to be a good shot. He'd been practicing six days a week for the past three months on the theory that if a man meant to take on a job, he must be prepared to do it well. God knew he never dreamed he'd wind up killing Indians. His second shot finding its target had been pure luck, but if he said so it might sound like false modesty.

Jennara touched his arm briefly. "Thank you."

"I didn't see their rifles," he said, embarrassed by her thanks.

"Not all warriors carry guns. Especially the very young— they have to earn them."

Bramwell stared at her. Did she mean he'd shot unarmed striplings?

"But these had knives and clubs," she added. "They were painted for war and primed to kill."

Giving him no choice . . . but it left a bad taste in his mouth.

"If they weren't alone, others will be on our trail by now." Her tone was so matter-of-fact he could hardly credit her words. "They'll have horses, so we won't stand much of a chance of getting away."

"*You* could." He nodded toward Sage. "Dump the gear and ride him."

She shook her head. "We'll make a stand together, if it comes to that. It may not. Because they were so young, there's a good chance those two were out to prove themselves

42

before being allowed to join the warriors. I wish we'd had the time to look for their ponies."

He stopped. "We need another horse. Why not go back if you think they were alone?"

"Too risky. Besides, the ponies are probably halfway back to one of the reservation herds by now."

Her knowledge of the Sioux had helped keep them alive. She was the most unusual woman he'd ever met. It surprised him how attractive he found her in her absurd clothing. No wonder Ronald had lost his head over her. Why had he run off with the sister?

"Does your sister look like you?" he asked as they circled north through the woods.

Jennara's eyebrows rose. "No. Susanna is very pretty, with fair hair and blue eyes. She resembles our mother, I favor our father. Actually, we look so little alike we might as well be no blood relation at all, like you and Ronald." She turned away from him to scan their surroundings. "The trees are thinning."

He recalled from yesterday how scant the cover had been before they'd come to the woods—low hills with trees and brush only along the rivers and streams. "We'll soon be in the open," he said.

She nodded and halted, raising her head to sniff the air. "Smoke."

He smelled the acrid scent as soon as she said the word. Did he imagine it, or could he also hear faint yells?

"Do we take the chance and go on?" he asked.

"We both know what the smoke means. Yet we can't hide in the woods forever. We need food, for one thing. Maybe we ought to camp here for the rest of the day and travel by night. As I told you, the Dakota don't care to fight in darkness."

"Since the reservation's between us and the fort, will we ever reach Ridgely? Is there any other safe place nearby? Your house can't be too far away."

"You're right to wonder about reaching the fort. Running

into those two warriors here makes me afraid there are so many more roaming around that we can't possibly get through to Ridgely alive. As for my house, even if we could get there I fear we'd be worse off. All houses are Dakota targets right now, and I doubt if No Cloud's medicine sign would save us. To tell you the truth, I'm not sure what we should do. There are Dakota villages off the reservation both to the east and west of us. Our chances of finding any safe place are poor."

"South," he said. "You didn't mention south."

"There's a Dakota village by the Iowa border. I know they had Indian trouble last year at Spirit Lake, just across the border."

"Are you telling me it's hopeless?"

"Never! But staying under cover until things settle down seems wise. We can forage for food at night."

Bramwell had no reason to oppose her. In fact, despite the two Sioux who'd tried to ambush them in the woods, he felt reluctant to venture out from under the trees.

They turned the horse and retreated deeper into the woods, keeping away from the road. At last Jennara chose a rocky rise thick with trees for their camp. A creek ran at the foot of the hill, and grass growing along the far bank provided graze for Sage.

Tonight, he told himself, mopping his sweaty forehead with a distinctly grimy handkerchief, when it's good and dark, I'm going to strip and plunge into that stream.

Even if they weren't safe, he was almost lulled into feeling safe by soft gurgle of the stream, an occasional birdcall, the stir of a lazy breeze through the maple leaves. Despite the dense shade, the day's heat seeped through, sapping his vigor until he wondered if he'd be able to raise the rifle from his lap if the need arose.

"Doesn't it ever rain here in August?" he asked.

"We have thunderstorms, yes. I love the storms."

He glanced toward her. They had their backs against tree

44

trunks, but they sat angled away from one another so that each watched a different section of the woods. Thunder and lightning frightened most women Bramwell knew . . . or at least, they pretended it did. A sliver of sunlight slanted through the canopy of leaves and touched her braided hair, infusing its walnut brown with a glint of gold.

"Why did Ronald run off with your sister?" he asked.

She turned to look at him. "They thought I wouldn't approve of them getting married."

"Do you?"

"Yesterday you were accusing me of engineering their elopement to foil you."

"I may have been wrong." Seeing her eyes flash with anger he said hastily, "I no longer believe you persuaded them to elope."

"Persuaded them! I wasn't even aware they had any such harebrained scheme in mind. Neither of them has the sense of a goose. I only pray they started early enough to be well into Iowa by the time the Dakota began their raids."

"I take it you don't approve."

"How can I? Susanna is—" She stopped abruptly. "Marriage isn't something to be rushed into. They hardly know one another."

"You, on the other hand, had months to become acquainted with Ronald." There was an edge to his words.

"It took months for Ronald to recover. Naturally we became acquainted." She spoke as sharply as he had.

Months alone with her . . . Bramwell found himself envying his stepbrother. Of course they'd been lovers, that was how she'd trapped Ronald. Was she jealous of her sister? Or had she cared so little for Ronald that it made no difference to her which of the sisters married him? She claimed she didn't approve of the marriage, but he didn't believe her for a minute.

That Ronald didn't have the sense of a goose, on the other hand, was the absolute truth.

"Your sister—will she be able to outguess the Sioux, as you've done?" he asked.

Jennara shook her head. "Susanna never cared about Dakota customs. Music is her only real interest." Also fashionable clothes and the doings of fashionable people. Not that she meant to tell Bramwell. What did it matter that Susanna rushed into things without thinking? She was sweet and kind and pretty, and Jennara loved her dearly.

"What was your sister doing in St. Louis?" Bramwell asked. "Do you have relatives there?"

"I fail to see that it's any of your business." Annoyed at his probing, she said tartly, "May I remind you that we must stay alert?" She turned away from him, once more scanning the dim and shady spaces between the trees for any sign of movement.

She had no intention of admitting to Bramwell that Susanna had run off with a troupe of traveling actors shortly after their father died and that she'd been away ever since . . . until last month, when Susanna had arrived home penniless and afraid.

"If he finds out where I am, he'll kill me," Susanna had whispered that first night. After that, she'd refused to say any more. Who "he" was, Jennara had no idea. She had her suspicions as to what was wrong but didn't push her sister. In time, she'd been sure, Susanna would tell her everything.

Instead, she'd eloped with Ronald.

"Your sister has never outgrown a childhood belief in magic," their father had once confided in Jennara after chiding Susanna for lying to him. "She seems to think if she wishes a thing to be true, it will somehow come to be. A dangerous philosophy for anyone, especially a young woman."

Apparently Susanna still thought that way. Marriage to Ronald was no solution to her problems, since he was as penniless as she—and impractical as well . . . a young man with his head in the clouds, talented in drawing and painting

46

and interested in little else.

Why had Bramwell told her Ronald was wealthy? Could it possibly be true? She glanced over her shoulder at him and found him watching her.

"Not a Sioux in sight," he said, smothering a yawn.

"You stood watch last night. Why not get some rest while you can? I'll take my turn later."

Without a word he passed her the rifle and the ammunition pouch. He'd long ago crammed his jacket into a saddlebag, and now he retrieved it and stretched out on the ground, using the folded jacket as a pillow.

When Jennara glanced at him a few minutes later he was sound asleep. His whiskers had grown during the day, darkening his face. He'd look quite distinguished with a beard and mustache, she decided. It might even hide the sardonic twist of his lips, a twist that sleep removed, leaving his lips softly curved, in their natural state. She knew from experience how warm and sweet those lips could be. . . .

Keep your mind on the Dakota, she warned herself, wondering where her friend No Cloud was. Not out marauding, she was certain of that. He was a healer and believed it would destroy his medicine to become a warrior.

No Cloud's knowledge of both medicinal and deadly plants was extensive. He'd once shown her several that could be mixed together to produce what he called "love medicine."

"The maiden sprinkles the mixture into the food or drink of the brave she longs for," No Cloud told her. "He eats. He cannot resist her. They marry. It is more difficult for a brave to persuade a maiden to eat or drink what he's prepared. If she isn't suspicious, she eats. She cannot resist him."

"You left out 'They marry,' " Jennara observed.

"The way of men is not that of women. It is wise for maidens to be suspicious."

Evidently the Dakota were not so very different from anyone else when it came to love and what happened between men and women.

Bramwell's brow furrowed in his sleep. Was he dreaming of the danger surrounding them? She checked her impulse to place a hand on his forehead and smooth away the lines. She wanted to comfort him, she assured herself, only because she too was a healer.

He'd proven to be a crack shot, something to be thankful for. And he seemed to know a bit about camping. If he'd just not argue with her every step of the way and pay attention to what she told him, they might have a chance of surviving.

Hiding was against her nature. She chafed at inactivity. How long she'd be able to tolerate huddling in the woods she didn't know. At the moment, staying under cover was not a choice but a necessity. And Bramwell's company, if not an outright irritant, was unsettling. Though after that shameful episode in the barn, he'd behaved more or less like a gentleman. She apparently could trust him in that way, however unsure she might be of him in other ways.

It's myself I have to worry about, she thought wryly, smothering another urge to soothe him as she watched his restless sleep. If he woke he might not realize why she'd touched him, might mistake her meaning. Heaven only knew what might happen then.

The day dragged on, with Jennara dividing her attention between watching for Dakota and glancing at Bramwell. Occasionally she got up and stretched to avoid falling asleep. Since there was no more food, she took frequent sips of water to try to assuage her hunger pangs. In the early afternoon, finding her flask of water empty, she decided to refill it at the stream below.

She descended the hill, alert for danger, rifle in hand. As she bent to the water, she noticed Sage's ears flick and immediately straightened, glancing all around. What had the pinto heard? A jay called from a tree halfway up the rise. Jennara could see or hear nothing unusual, but the hair on her nape prickled. From where she stood, Bramwell's supine figure wasn't visible.

Abandoning all thought of filling the flask, she eased back up the rise, her heart hammering, straining for a glimpse of Bramwell. To her horror, a painted and bloodstained warrior bent over him, knife raised. If she shot she risked hitting Bramwell.

Jennara gripped the rifle by the barrel and, swinging it, ran screaming across the space separating her from Bramwell. The warrior flung himself around to face her and the rifle stock struck the side of his head with a horrible smashing sound. He staggered and dropped as Bramwell leaped up.

Bramwell, on his feet, leaned down and grabbed the knife from the warrior's limp fingers. Jennara, standing back, leveled the rifle at the fallen warrior. The brave lay unmoving.

"He's dead," Bramwell said.

Jennara knew he was right. She, who wanted only to ease suffering, had killed a man. Turning from the dreadful sight, she scanned the woods, waiting apprehensively. Where were the other warriors?

"Damned if he doesn't have a bullet hole in his temple," Bramwell said from behind her. She glanced back to see him on his knees beside the Dakota. "I think he's the one who ambushed us earlier, the one I wasn't sure I'd shot. My God, do you suppose he trailed us here with a bullet in his brain?"

Jennara whirled around and stared at the dead man, noticing for the first time how young he was. If he was able to, a wounded Dakota warrior would certainly trail and kill the man who shot him. She nodded to Bramwell. This was the same man. He'd come here alone. They were safe for the time being.

But she'd had to kill him, to save Bramwell. The rifle fell to the ground as she covered her face with her hands and burst into tears.

Chapter 4

Bramwell, his arms around Jennara, patted her back as she sobbed against his shoulder. "It's all right," he murmured, "all right, all right."

He scanned the woods as he tried to soothe her. Had the dead Sioux come alone or had he found and brought reinforcements? Though alert for danger, Bramwell was conscious of the feel of her body against his. The soft press of her breasts urged him to hold her closer, but this was neither the time nor the place.

Jennara pulled away from him, and he loosened his hold reluctantly. Plucking a handkerchief from the pocket of her skirt, she wiped her wet face. He picked up the rifle, keeping his eyes on the trees below.

"I never expected to be forced to kill a man," she said haltingly.

He glanced at her and saw she was looking at the dead Sioux.

"If you hadn't, I'd be the one lying there," he said.

She nodded. "I had no choice. I pray it never comes to that again." She turned to him. "We can't stay here. Not with—" She bit her lip.

She didn't have to finish. He, too, found the sight of the dead man unnerving.

"Besides," she added, "when he and the other warrior don't return, men from their village will search for them. They try to retrieve their dead if they can. How a Dakota is treated after death is important to them."

As they packed the gear onto Sage, Jennara rattled on, words pouring out as her tears had earlier. "The Dakota build scaffolds in trees for their dead. They never bury them in the ground. It's important the dead person's favorite belongings are with him. They paint the face and dress the body in his best clothing, wrap a robe or a blanket around it, and place the body into a rawhide bundle. After the bundle's put onto the scaffold, the relatives, hair cut short in mourning, wail for hours, sometimes for days.

"The Dakota believe in a heaven — *Wanagiyata* — somewhere to the south. Green fields, clear streams, good hunting, warm weather, no war. The spirit is carried by an eagle along the Milky Way to this everlasting Eden. My father always said *Wanagiyata* sounded better than the pearly gates to him. I'd like to think the warrior I killed will be happy there."

"He'd have killed both of us with no remorse," Bramwell said. "And with no good wishes for an afterlife either, I suspect."

"He wanted to be a warrior. I don't. I've dedicated my life to healing. I fight death, not cause it. I honor life, not take it." She glanced toward the hill where the Sioux's body lay out of sight. "May *Wakan Tanka* be with you," she said softly.

The Sioux equivalent of God, he decided. He hoped the prayer would ease her mind. While he hadn't enjoyed shooting a man, he didn't feel Jennara's intense remorse. It was just as well. He'd devoted his life to upholding the law and had never wanted to be a warrior or kill men, but if he was fortunate enough to survive Minnesota, he'd soon be doing just that: kill or be killed.

Ronald mustn't come to such a choice, he wouldn't survive.

"I can't let him reach St. Louis," he muttered.

Jennara paused in her buckling of a saddlebag to stare at him. "If you mean your stepbrother, I hope he *has* the chance to get there."

"The Sioux won't catch him. Lady Luck always favors Ronald."

"He was more than half dead when No Cloud brought him to me."

"But he didn't die. A Sioux medicine man and a Minnesota healer saved him. Someone always comes along to save Ronald."

She finished with the saddlebag and faced him. "And now you're here to save him from himself?"

"Something like that, yes."

"Why not allow him to live his own life? You're so sure he's making a mistake, but maybe he's not. If it does turn out wrong, he'll learn from the mistake."

"You said yourself that he has no sense. A wealthy man as naive as Ronald needs protection."

"He never once mentioned money to me."

His smile expressed his disbelief.

She shrugged and turned to untie Sage. Without a word she led the horse from the stream, leaving Bramwell behind.

His stomach growled as he followed her, matching his state of mind perfectly. Along with everything else that had gone wrong since he'd met Jennara Gray, he was hungrier than he'd ever been in his life. And it was hours yet until dark. What he wouldn't give for a large serving of roast beef with plenty of gravy! His chances for anything so tasty were nil. He'd bet they'd find no more than a few vegetables tonight. He hated raw vegetables, but a starving man couldn't be choosy.

He should be grateful he was alive . . . grateful to Jennara. If not for her, he'd be dead. Damn, but those Sioux were tricky. He'd had no warning, none at all. One moment nothing was there, the next the Sioux was beside him, knife poised to kill. Bramwell grimaced and shifted his shoulders uneasily, reliving the experience. He glanced behind him, sweeping his gaze along the trees, probing the spaces between.

Strange, he reflected, how a man could worry about being hungry when it was a moot point whether he'd survive long enough to eat. And this heat! Bramwell wiped the sweat from his forehead, ignoring the dirty handkerchief. Despite the opened buttons on his shirt, he was sweltering. He'd done his best to observe the amenities up until now, but enough was enough. Jennara wasn't the type to swoon at the sight of a man's bare chest anyway. Pausing to set down the rifle, he yanked off the shirt. Rifle in hand again, he trotted to catch up with Sage and thrust the shirt under the strap of a saddle-bag.

What would it take to make her swoon? he wondered. Most of the women he knew would have fainted a dozen times over at what he and Jennara had seen and endured. He couldn't help but admire her courage. Still, it didn't excuse how she'd manipulated Ronald into offering to marry her.

By the time they halted at a tiny trickling creek, the August afternoon had grown so stifling that Bramwell threw all caution to the winds. Tossing the rifle to Jennara, he leaped into the water and stretched out full length in the shallow stream, splashing himself with the water's welcome coolness.

"Ah," he said, "bliss."

Jennara, on the bank, alternately watching him and keeping an eye on the woods around them, devoutly wished she dared follow his lead. She was surprised at Bramwell, though. She could easily imagine Ronald behaving so boyishly, but not his stepbrother, the disapproving eastern lawyer.

He'd even removed his shirt. The dark curls of his chest hair glistened with crystal droplets as he scooped water over himself. Jennara had found comfort earlier leaning against that broad and muscular chest, and now her heart beat faster at the sight of his bare torso. In her doctoring she'd seen many a bare chest, but no man's had ever affected her like this. She looked away.

Stray drops sprinkled her face as he continued to splash,

teasing her. How sultry the day was, and how marvelous it would feel to toss propriety and caution to the winds and jump into the creek, too—where they'd both be easy pickings for Dakota warriors. Even without that danger, she wouldn't dream of behaving so irresponsibly—especially with this man.

When he rose, dripping, and stepped onto the bank, she handed him the rifle. Kneeling by the stream, she cupped her hands to scoop water, laving her face over and over. She rinsed out her handkerchief and lifted her braid to lay the cloth, sopping, on her nape so trickles ran down her back under her shirt, moistening her chemise.

"A plate of roast beef, rare, and I'd be content," he said.

"With horseradish?" she asked.

"Why not? And new potatoes and peas, boiled together, served with fresh churned butter."

"If we're lucky we'll dig up a few potatoes," she said. "And maybe carrots. It's too late for peas."

He ignored her. "For dessert, I'll take a large slice of butterscotch pie with a possible encore if the filling's up to my standards. How's your butterscotch pie?"

She shook her head. "Susanna's the one who enjoys baking."

"You disillusion me. I supposed you capable of anything."

Was he mocking her again? Jennara's voice acquired a slight edge. "I'm hardly the ideal cook. I don't have the time or the inclination. In any case, what vegetables we find tonight we're likely to have to eat raw."

"Man was not born to be a rabbit."

"Not every man was born with a silver spoon in his mouth, either. You eat what's available."

His eyebrows raised. "You've read *Don Quixote?*"

"As it happens, yes." She shouldn't have been surprised he'd recognize the silver spoon quote, but she was. Nobody she knew except her father had ever read Cervantes' book.

"Shall we hope with the good Señor Cervantes that the

worst is behind us?" he asked.

"I'd like to believe it," she admitted, "but I can't." As she spoke the day darkened and she peered up at what sky was visible between the green of the leaves. Bramwell looked up, too.

"Black clouds," he observed. "A storm'll cool the air."

"If it rains. Clouds often pass on to the east."

"We never seem to quite agree."

What did he expect? she wondered. Why should they think alike? The two of them had absolutely nothing in common except their worry over Susanna and Ronald and their shared danger from Dakota warriors.

Not only his attitude bothered her. The way he looked at the moment did, too. He might as well be standing naked before her the way his wet trousers were plastered to his body. She had to keep her eyes averted. Had he no shame? While it was true she'd more than once seen Ronald in the nude when she was nursing him back to health, that was different. He was her patient and very ill, and he wasn't Bramwell.

"If we camped here," he said, "you could get some rest before dark."

Jennara roused herself from her uneasy musing to examine the site. She *was* tired and this spot looked as good as any other. They weren't really safe from the Dakota anywhere.

She found a place under a tall maple and curled onto her side away from Bramwell, who propped his back against the trunk, the rifle in his arms. It was a relief to lie down, but she couldn't sleep. She tried to focus her thoughts, to ascertain as best she could whose farm they might be closest to when they crept from the woods tonight, but her mind skittered this way and that.

Were Susanna and Ronald safe?

What did Bramwell think of her?

Was her own house still standing, or had warriors looted and burned it?

Did he see her as a drab from the country?

Were the soldiers from Fort Ridgely subduing the Dakota, or were there too many warriors and too few soldiers?

Was he as aware of her as she was of him?

Were there any warriors lurking in the woods?

Did he remember kissing her in the barn?

Stop it! she ordered herself. It makes no difference what Bramwell thinks about you . . . no difference at all. You've been thrown into each other's company, but sooner or later that'll end and he'll return to Pennsylvania without any regrets. Without a backward look. And certainly without a thought for you.

You really don't care about him, anyway. It's just that you've never lived with a man you weren't related to. Ronald doesn't count, he's a boy, really. Bramwell's a man. These unsettled emotions of yours come from that. You're isolated with an attractive man and you can't help feeling drawn to him. That's all it amounts to. A normal instinct, Father would say. Normal, maybe — but not something to give in to.

After a long time she drifted into a troubled sleep. A low rumble roused her from a disturbing dream in which No Cloud changed into a spotted eagle and flew away from her. She sat up, blinking. No sun slanted through the leafy branches overhead. Was it evening already? She turned toward Bramwell, who was standing a few feet away.

"Thunder," he said. "Not close, not yet."

"You sound disappointed. I believe you're looking forward to getting drenched." She stretched and got to her feet.

"The only thing I'm looking forward to is relief from this heat — plus a good meal. And cessation of Sioux hostilities."

She smiled. "For once we're in complete agreement."

Though the thunder never sounded close by, it continued to rumble in the distance. Rain began near dark, a steady patter through the leaves.

"It's safe to risk leaving the woods," Jennara said. "Warriors don't like to get wet any better than we do."

"Speak for yourself," he said, lifting his face to the rain.

The rain did feel good, cooling her pleasantly as they led Sage through thinning trees to the edge of the woods. Peering into the gathering darkness, her vision limited by the downpour, Jennara caught sight of three oaks and a barn beyond. "LeMonde's farm," she muttered, recalling how Pierre LeMonde had left the trees uncut to shade the barnyard.

LeMonde was a French Canadian married to a woman who was a part Indian . . . not Dakota, but Chippewa. They had five children ranging from the baby Jennara had helped birth to a boy in his teens. Because the wife was from an enemy tribe, the LeMondes wouldn't be safe from Dakota warriors. Jennara bit her lip. She couldn't bear to come upon another slain family.

"What's the matter?" Bramwell asked. He was watching her, she saw.

No matter how she felt, with the LeMonde farm so close it would be foolish not to try for food there first. Standing up straighter, she said, "Let's go."

Though no livestock huddled against the rain in the fields as Jennara and Bramwell cautiously approached, the farm buildings were intact. Was it possible the warriors had contented themselves with running off the cattle and that the LeMondes were safe? Then she noticed the back door of the house was open, blowing back and forth in the wind, and shook her head . . . a bad sign.

Bramwell insisted on striding ahead of her to enter the house first, rifle at the ready. She followed him, pulling Sage in after her and tethering him to a hook on the wall of the back room, a kitchen. The floor was white with spilled flour, and in the gloomy storm dusk she saw smashed jars of fruit on a table—signs that warriors had looted the place. The cookstove was stone-cold. Whatever had happened to the LeMondes, they hadn't used the stove for at least a day.

Trailing after Bramwell, she found clothes and family belongings strewn around the three downstairs rooms. No one, dead or alive, was in this part of the house. She stared apprehensively at the ladder leading to the dark sleeping loft.

Again Bramwell forestalled her by climbing the ladder. "Nothing up here either," he called down.

Maybe the LeMondes had been lucky enough to get away in time, to reach the fort. She'd hold to that and pray she was right.

"Wait, I'm wrong," Bramwell cried. She tensed. A moment later a frantic squawking interspersed with his curses told her what he'd found. A white chicken flapped wildly down the loft. Jennara, lunging, captured the hen and tucked it under her arm.

Bramwell appeared on the ladder and descended quickly. He gazed from the chicken to Jennara and smiled. "Next to roast beef, roast chicken's my favorite."

"Stewed," she amended. "This hen's too old for roasting, even if we did have time to wait for the oven to heat."

"I'm agreeable, so long as it's not raw."

Deciding it was safe enough to risk a fire—the rain and coming darkness should keep the Dakota under shelter—she said, "If you'll take the hen into the yard and kill her, I'll get the stove started."

He took the chicken from her, holding it awkwardly by the legs. He stared at the flapping hen uneasily. Jennara raised her eyebrows. What was the matter now?

"I've, uh, never had occasion to kill a chicken," he said at last. "How—?"

She sighed. "You *can* start a fire? In a cookstove?"

His nod seemed uncertain, but she decided to trust him with the stove while she took care of the chicken. When she came back in with the decapitated, still twitching hen, the back room was filling with smoke.

"The damper!" she cried, rushing to the stove and reaching to the metal chimney to twist the damper handle fully open.

Once the fire had taken hold, she raised a stove lid and seared the feathers over the open flame before showing Bramwell how to pluck the chicken. Locating a large pot, she pumped water into it, set the pot on the stove, then went outside again to grub what vegetables she could from the garden patch.

"She's ready to be cooked," Bramwell told her when Jennara returned with seven carrots and five potatoes.

"You've cleaned the chicken?"

"Plucked every last feather. I never knew there was so much work to cooking."

"I mean have you cleaned out the insides?"

"What for?"

She dropped the vegetables onto the floor and took the chicken from him. When she finally had the chicken simmering in the pot with the carrots and potatoes and a stray onion she'd found on a pantry shelf, she cleaned the broken glass and sticky fruit from the table. Bramwell, broom in hand, did a creditable job of sweeping the floor.

Now, while the chicken stewed, she had the chance to tend to herself. Wherever Antoinette LeMonde was, she surely wouldn't mind if Jennara borrowed a gown to wear while she washed and dried her filthy skirt and shirt. First she'd have to draw more water from the pump. She picked up the bucket.

"Where are you going?" Bramwell asked as she headed for the rear door.

She told him.

"I'll get the water," he said, all but snatching the bucket away from her and stomping out.

After the fiasco with the stove, and knowing of his ignorance in the matter of preparing a chicken, Jennara couldn't be entirely certain Bramwell actually knew how to work a pump. She'd primed it earlier, so he shouldn't have much trouble even if he'd never lifted a pump handle in his life — and that was hard to believe.

Bramwell had insisted Ronald was wealthy. Wouldn't that mean he must be, too? He certainly acted like a man who'd never had to lift a finger around a house or a barnyard. A rich man, with paid help to do things for him. So maybe what he'd said about Ronald was true. It made no difference to Jennara whether Ronald was rich or poor, but she knew her sister had always dreamed of marrying wealth. Had Susanna somehow learned that Ronald was a rich man?

Bramwell sat in a chair by the table in the back room, his eyes on the door Jennara had closed behind her after taking the only candle. The clothes she had on were as wet and dirty as his own. He'd set the bucket of water for her to bathe with on the floor of the front room only minutes ago, and he couldn't help picturing her discarding her skirt, her shirt, and whatever underthings she wore, imagining her standing naked while she washed her face, her neck, her breasts . . .

Her breasts would be round and full in his hands, he knew. Her nipples would be the color of honey and taste as sweet. Her hair would be loosened from the braid, a dark and silken fall around them as he stroked her soft skin . . .

Bramwell groaned. Why tantalize himself? He might lust after her, but even if she'd allow it, he didn't mean to touch her. He was no Ronald about to be trapped by the enticing flesh of this woman.

Contemplate the damn chicken instead, he advised himself, inhaling the mouth-watering aroma that came from the bubbling pot on the stove. At first he'd wondered if the final result would be worth the trouble and stench, but the burnt feather stink had finally dissipated, thank God.

Jennara hadn't said a word about the smoky fire or his ineptness when it came to killing chickens, but she must think him inadequate. No doubt every yokel she knew could start up a stove with one hand while dispatching chickens with the other. He slid lower in his chair. At the moment, what skills he had were of little use, except sharpshooting. She did trust him with the rifle. When she came back with the candle, he meant to clean the gun as best he could without proper equipment.

Her sister was the pretty one, Jennara had said. Bramwell, picturing Susanna from the description, saw a vapid-faced blonde who masked her calculating blue gaze with little-girl coyness. Why would Ronald prefer such a simpering ninny when he could have Jennara's more subtle beauty? Not to mention her quickness of mind and her originality.

You forget, he warned himself, she's as calculating as Susanna . . . and stubborn — not one to give up easily. He'd best remember to keep a tight lid on his increasing desire for her. "Those who play with cats must expect to be scratched," he muttered, quoting Cervantes.

Who'd have expected Jennara to know *Don Quixote?* No woman of his acquaintance did. She continually surprised him.

The door opened and he sat up straight, staring. She walked toward him wearing a simple white short-sleeved gown tied around the waist with a red ribbon. Her bare feet peeked from under the hem of the dress. The neckline was modest, but lower than the shirts she usually wore, and because the bodice was loose, he caught a teasing glimpse of shadowy roundness when she leaned to place the candle holder on the table.

"Antoinette LeMonde is somewhat larger than I am. I had to tie a piece of yarn around my waist to make the dress fit." Her voice was uncertain, tinged with self-consciousness.

He rose and bowed. "You look charming." It was only the truth. She also looked so unexpectedly vulnerable that something twisted in his chest, and he fought an urge to take her protectively into his arms.

Jennara failed to repress a pleased smile at his words. Hastily she said, "It's your turn to bathe. You have time before the chicken's done." Before he could say or do anything further, she hurried to the stove and peered into the stew pot.

She insisted he take the candle, but because he didn't want to leave her in the dark, he wouldn't, but compromised by leaving the front-room door ajar while he washed. There

61

were no clean clothes for him to put on, so he wore his still damp trousers when he padded barefoot back to Jennara.

He found she'd washed his two shirts along with her own clothes and spread them to dry near the stove. She flushed when he thanked her.

"If you'll sit down, I'll put the pot on the table," she said. "I couldn't find any forks or spoons so we'll have to use our fingers."

With the tin cup she handed him, he ladled stew onto a wooden plate, finding himself so hungry he risked burning his hand in his rush to begin eating.

The chicken was a bit tough, but it tasted so good to him, he didn't care. "Compliments to the cook," he said as he ladled another cupful of stew onto the plate. "I'd never have guessed you don't like to cook."

"Anyone can stew a chicken. I daresay you could after tonight."

He grinned at her. "Not unless someone killed it first."

She laughed. "No doubt you're a very good lawyer."

"I'm beginning to realize that's not much use in our present circumstances. My only assets seem to be shooting the rifle and pumping water from a well."

"You're a stimulating companion."

"I'm sure that's a compliment."

She smiled slightly, neither admitting it was or wasn't.

"I can't help looking over my shoulder from time to time," he said, "wondering if the Sioux have surrounded the house and will suddenly burst in shrieking their war cries. It even seems strange to *be* in a house. I hope the family who lives here is safe at the fort."

"We're in no danger at the moment. But we must leave soon so we can travel in darkness."

"The Sioux have looted the house already. Will they return?"

"The same warriors won't, but others may come to see what's left for them. We can't take the chance."

"Where to, then? Back to the woods?"

She shook her head. "If they find the dead warriors, the Dakota will comb the woods from one end to the other. We'll find another hiding place and go to ground before dawn."

"Strange how comfortable being in a house is. This one's no palace, but I hate to leave it. Here we are, sitting at a table like civilized people."

"Eating with our fingers," she reminded him. "With a horse in the same room."

He shrugged and picked up a drumstick.

They packed up Sage as soon as they finished the stew. There was none left to take along, but Jennara scavenged a few more potatoes and carrots. The rain had stopped and they traveled by the faint light of starglow . . . westward, he thought.

"Couldn't we try to get on the road to St. Paul?" he asked.

"There's so little cover between where we are and the road that I'm afraid to take the risk. Besides, the Dakota aren't fools, and that's one of the roads they'll be watching."

Bramwell subsided. Map or no, he didn't know the territory.

Well before dawn, they found a thick clump of trees and brush along a good-sized stream and eased into the copse with the horse. Bramwell, who knew Jennara had slept but little that afternoon, announced he'd take first watch.

She fell asleep almost immediately, a white wraith curled by his side, still wearing the borrowed gown. He touched her hair lightly but quickly drew his fingers back, not wanting to rouse her. So strong a woman and yet so vulnerable. A feeling rose in him, strong and intense. Not lust this time but tenderness, the urge to protect, to take care of, to keep her from harm.

Some chance you have of doing that, he mocked himself, against bloodthirsty Sioux warriors. Jennara's more likely to wind up protecting you.

Chapter 5

Jennara woke at dawn to the chirping of birds. Warblers, she thought, yawning. For a few moments between rousing and becoming fully aware, she drifted, listening to the cheery twitterings. The little yellow birds liked to be close to open fields and also near a stream. With their fondness for caterpillars, warblers were the farmer's friend.

"Jennara?" Bramwell said softly.

She sat up, suddenly very much awake, and turned to look at him. He sat to her left, arms over his knees, wearing a shirt draped over his shoulders. Otherwise his chest was bare, an acknowledgment of the already warm day. Last night's rain hadn't brought cooler weather in its wake. Her gown, damp from the ground, felt comfortable.

"Nothing stirring but the birds," Bramwell said. "Sage is getting restless, though."

Jennera rose and walked to the horse. As he watched her approach, his ears kept twitching. What did he hear that she didn't? His nostrils flared and he tossed his head.

"No you don't, boy," she told him. Reaching for Bramwell's folded coat atop the saddlebags on the ground, she deftly wrapped Sage's head in the coat, speaking soothingly to him as she did.

Bramwell was on his feet, rifle in hand, before she finished, frowning as he cocked his head to listen.

"Sage was on the verge of nickering," she whispered. "Another horse must be headed this way."

"A warrior tracking us?"

"Maybe, maybe not." She looked quickly around. They were as well hidden as possible in the thick brush. Which would do them little good if they *were* being tracked.

Faint at first, the drum of hooves grew louder, the rhythm gradually slowing. "Coming fast." Bramwell's voice was grim. "And more than one horse."

It seemed an eon before Jennara, through a miniscule gap in the branches, caught sight of the first mounted warrior. Her impulse was to duck further into cover but she resisted, keeping her hold on Sage's head. It was best to stay still — motion attracted attention.

She also saw what she hadn't noticed in last night's darkness. The spot they'd chosen was uncomfortably close to a narrow trail leading to the stream, the trail the warriors were following.

The first Dakota passed, so close to them that she could see the color of the hair on the scalps dangling from his waist thong: two black, one blond. Her stomach lurched.

Six riders went by. Their horses paused at the stream to drink. Sage, sensing them, shifted his feet and Jennara held her breath. Would a warrior notice the slight movement? It was pure bad luck to have gone to cover so close to what must be a favorite watering place for the Dakota.

Unlike the youthful braves who'd stalked them in the woods, these were mature men, full-fledged warriors . . . with rifles. Bramwell might pick off one or maybe two before the others dived for cover if the Spencer didn't jam, which it had done once for her.

As she watched the warriors and their horses, she thought back to the day the rifle had come, delivered last year by a lieutenant from the East, newly posted to Fort Ridgely.

"For a Dr. Gregory Gray," the officer had told her.

"My father's been dead for two years," she said. "I'm his daughter."

After a moment or two of indecision, the lieutenant handed her the gun and a letter. "Nothing else but for you to take these, Miss," he said before nodding and remounting his horse, eager to be off.

The letter was from an old friend of her father's who'd only recently returned from abroad and so hadn't heard of his death. "Knowing your fondness for complicated gadgetry," he wrote, "I'm sending you Spencer's new invention, a repeating carbine breechloader. Don't blow yourself up using it."

The Spencer repeater had saved her and Bramwell yesterday, but those young braves had been inexperienced and on foot. These warriors would take shelter behind their horses the moment they heard the first shot. What good was a rifle that fired seven cartridges without reloading if there were no targets to hit?

One of the warriors swung his horse around and, in doing so, stared for an instant straight at her. Jennara, afraid to breathe, tried not to so much as blink. When he urged the horse into motion and rode slowly past her, she couldn't believe he hadn't seen her. Only when all six of the Dakotas had filed by did she dare release her pent-up breath. Even then she waited until the sound of the horses' hooves faded completely before she moved a muscle.

"Close call," Bramwell muttered.

"We can't stay here, we're almost on top of that trail," she said.

Difficult as it was to make their way through the heavy undergrowth near the stream, she feared to go into the open. They struggled upstream with much snapping of twigs as they forced a passage for the reluctant Sage.

"If anyone's listening, they'll certainly hear us coming," he said.

"Have you got a better idea?" she snapped, inadvertently letting go of a branch too soon so that it swung back, lashing him across the head. His scowl told her he suspected she'd done it intentionally.

Did he think she was having a good time? That she enjoyed being hungry and tired and afraid? She might not be an expert on running from the Dakota, but in case he cared to remember, the worst mistake so far had been his, not hers. Last night when they'd shared the stew, she'd thought of them as comrades facing adversity, but it was plain to see that the truce had been temporary as far as he was concerned.

Her anger was still simmering when she decided they'd traveled far enough from the trail to be safe. As soon as Sage was unloaded she reached for the Spencer. "I'll stand guard," she announced crisply.

He took his time choosing a spot to stretch out, laying his shirt on the ground to protect his bare skin. Why didn't he simply pull on the shirt and be done with it? She wouldn't put it past him to be keeping the shirt off deliberately, hoping to provoke her by going around half-dressed. He couldn't imagine she relished the sight!

He fell asleep immediately. Jennara sat beside him, glancing from time to time at Sage to see if the horse was restless. From the stream, she heard a duck quack and others answer. She smelled the dampness of the earth mixed with a faint tinge of smoke. Another farmhouse burning?

The way the brush closed around them made her feel she and Bramwell were encased in a safe cocoon. As the hours slid by, the warmth of the day, combined with the comfortingly normal sounds of nearby birds and animals, made her drowsy and she tried to devise mental exercises to stay alert. Hunger pangs led her to plan her ideal meal.

Roast pork and applesauce, honey-glazed baked squash, chopped spinach, sweet gherkins, soft rolls and butter. Fresh-brewed coffee with cream. For dessert — anything but butterscotch pie!

Hunger was the reminder that people must eat to live. Most raw food wasn't appetizing, so cooking was a fact of life. Most women were tenders of the household, so women cooked — unless they could afford to hire someone to do it for

67

them. Her mother had died when Jennara was fourteen and Susanna seven, and though there'd been hired girls from time to time, Jennara had been responsible for the house since then . . . for the cooking. If she put her mind to it she was certain she could make a creditable butterscotch pie, but the pie would be no match for the one Susanna would throw together without any effort whatsoever.

Father had always said each person was born with some special talent and the fortunate ones discovered early what that talent was. Hers, like his, was healing. Her mother had played the piano beautifully. Susanna loved music and had a fair voice, but her true talent was cooking. Ronald's was drawing and painting. He was an artist.

And Bramwell? If a man had a talent for medicine, then a man could have a talent for law, she supposed. Was that his? Whatever it was, she really didn't care. Furthermore, he'd wait a long time for a butterscotch pie if it was up to her to bake him one.

The distant pop-pop of rifle fire brought her to her feet. At the same time Bramwell woke and sprang up. From the shelter of their cocoon it was impossible to judge accurately but she thought the gun shots came from the northeast.

After a few moments of listening, Bramwell muttered, "Miles away. I'm going down to the stream for a wash."

"Be careful."

He scowled. "I'm not Ronald."

As she watched him push through the branches, tart rejoinders rose to her tongue, but she remained silent. He was no frontiersman, but living in constant peril for two days must have taught him *something*. At least she hoped so.

Two days. It seemed as though she'd been unwillingly yoked to Bramwell forever. His behavior left no doubt that he felt the same about her. This was one of the reasons she'd never wed. How terrible to discover after a few months of marriage that you couldn't bear the sight of your husband, yet were tied to him until death claimed one of you!

She'd never met a man she was tempted to marry. And, being set in her ways and unwilling to change, she was unlikely to meet one who wanted to marry *her.* She didn't care . . . her life was busy and complete without a man. And helping children into the world made up, at least in part, for not having a child of her own.

She thought of the premature baby she'd so recently delivered, the surviving Lawson twin, and bit her lip. The Lawsons were so close to the reservation. Were any of them still alive?

A crackling of branches announced Bramwell's return. Until she was sure, though, she trained the rifle toward the sound.

Droplets of water sparkled on his hair and his skin as he came toward her and she stared at him longer than she meant to.

"Your turn," he said, reaching for the Spencer.

The gown she wore was cooler than her own clothes, but impractical for traveling. Jennara gathered her divided skirt and a shirt before heading for the stream. As she passed Bramwell it seemed he meant to say something and she hesitated.

He shook his head. "Nothing."

On the bank of the stream, while she splashed the delicious, cool water over her head and arms, Jennara wondered what he'd changed his mind about saying, annoyed at herself for caring. She walked upstream and drank, hoping to diminish her hunger with the water. Then, in the cover of a thicket of willow saplings on the bank, she slipped from the gown.

Nearby a jay called and she froze. Bluejays warned of intruders — who was coming? When a muskrat plopped into the water directly in front of her screen of willows, she smiled in relief and reached to pull on her black skirt. She'd momentarily forgotten a jay's warning didn't necessarily mean a human intruder. On the other hand, the bluejay could have been alerting the muskrat to her presence.

Back at their camp, Jennara divided the carrots. Two for Bramwell, two for herself, and the odd one a treat for Sage. She was saving the potatoes.

"If anyone had told me I'd come to view raw carrots as food—" Bramwell stopped and shrugged. He lifted a carrot and bit off the end, chewing thoughtfully. "At least it'll take a while to finish these," he said after he'd swallowed. "A man does like to savor his meal." His words were tinged with sarcasm.

"Sage enjoyed his."

"Why not? Horses were designed to eat their food raw." He waved toward the stream with his half-eaten carrot. "I heard some ducks earlier. If we could locate them, I might shoot a couple."

Jennara shook her head. "We can't take the risk. The gunshots might pinpoint us for roving Dakotas. Anyway, ducks are hard to get close to and difficult to bag on the wing."

Bramwell looked unconvinced.

"And, unless it rains again, we can't start a fire without the smoke giving us away," she reminded him. "Do you prefer raw meat over raw vegetables?"

"A man will go to great lengths to satisfy his stomach, but I admit I draw the line at uncooked duck." He took another bite of the carrot and chewed resignedly.

"The shots we heard came from north of here," he said after they'd finished the carrots and Jennara had picked up the rifle once again. "I take it we'll be traveling south again tonight?"

She nodded. "The Dakota don't leave us much choice. At least it's the way we want to go."

"Damn these savages! What does murdering defenseless women and children solve?"

"A week ago No Cloud said to me, 'When bellies rumble with hunger, who follows reason?' The Dakota elders have trouble controlling some of their young hotheads under the best of conditions. This summer has not been good—no buffalo to hunt, and government food supplies not delivered when promised."

"Why didn't the chiefs send a delegation to Washington to ask the President for help? It's well known that Lincoln sees everyone."

"Indians don't think like you . . . or me. Not that we two agree much—more often than not, we're on opposite sides."

"It's true women have devious ways of thinking. Men tend to be more straightforward."

Jennara stared at him. "Devious? You're calling me devious?"

He shrugged. "If the shoe fits—"

"I don't have a devious bone in my body!"

"Enticing Ronald into offering marriage wasn't devious?"

She glared at him. "I'm not to blame if a callow youth confuses his feelings of gratitude for love. I certainly knew the difference if he didn't, and would never have married him. I have enough to take care of without adding Ronald. And don't yammer on about money. For all I know, your stepbrother may be the richest man in Pennsylvania, but when he was in my house, under my care, I didn't realize he had a cent to his name. Or care, for that matter. And I don't care now." Her voice shook with rage, she trembled with the intensity of her anger. How she loathed Bramwell!

He raised an eyebrow. "That's hard to believe."

To her shock, Jennara found herself shifting the muzzle of the rifle until it pointed at Bramwell. Hastily, she turned the gun and herself away from him.

I didn't mean to shoot him, of course I didn't, she assured herself. I'd never do anything so horrible. You don't kill a man just because you despise him. Or for any other reason except to save your own life.

But the irony of it was that she *had* killed a man. And not to save herself. To save Bramwell . . . the man she hated.

Jennara glanced at him but didn't resist when Bramwell eased the Spencer from her grip. He breathed a bit easier. For a split second there, looking into the round end of that muzzle, he'd been frozen in place. What had she intended? To intimidate him? To shoot him? If looks could kill he'd certainly be dead by now.

He didn't believe a woman existed who didn't care about money, but was it possible she really hadn't known about Ronald's wealth until now? He found that hard to swallow. But perhaps the subject was best left alone until they were out of danger. He was on edge; she must be, too. No more arguments. This was a time to remain united against a common foe.

If only she wasn't so damned attractive. Earlier, when he saw she meant to change from her white gown, he'd almost told her not to, told her he enjoyed how the light and gauzy material flowed against the curves of her body. She moved with an unconscious grace, no matter what she wore, and in the gown her movements were all the more enticing. He tried to imagine her in a hoop skirt and could not. He found it much easier to picture her with no clothes on at all.

She must realize how she affected him. Women always knew. Most took pleasure in flirtatious remarks and gestures, in promising and then coyly refusing. Jennara wasn't a flirt or a tease — her method of beguilement was far more subtle. So subtle he couldn't be sure she wasn't merely behaving naturally, with no thought of ensnarement in mind.

He watched her as she groomed Sage, her face turned from him. He'd learned about women the hard way and he prided himself on understanding them, but here was one he couldn't quite fathom. If they'd met under other circumstances — but then, under other circumstances he wouldn't have come to the outlands of Minnesota and he couldn't imagine her visiting Philadelphia.

If not for Ronald and his feckless nature, I'd never have met Jennara, Bramwell thought.

"What the hell was he doing in Minnesota, anyway?" he muttered.

Jennara glanced at him. "If you mean Ronald, surely he told you."

Bramwell shook his head. "Ronald tends to grow lyrical about the beauties of nature and his drawings take up the other half of his letters. Did he tell you?"

"Not exactly. When he'd recovered enough to be coherent, he tried to pass himself off as a businessman from St. Louis, but Ronald has to be the world's most transparent liar. I didn't let on I knew better. Eventually he told me the truth, about being in sympathy with the Rebel cause. You, he said, were a staunch Unionist and wouldn't hear of him joining the Confederate Army."

"His romantic ideals won't do him much good as a soldier. He wouldn't last two days. But why come to Minnesota? This state doesn't favor the South."

"He was traveling to St. Louis, where he planned to join Quantrill's Raiders. It seems he met two men in Chicago and went to dinner with them. He didn't seem quite sure what happened after that, but somehow he found himself on a train to St. Paul instead of to St. Louis, without a cent in his pockets."

"He'll trust anyone. Anyone at all. He never seems to learn." Bramwell sighed. "What happened in St. Paul?"

"Ronald traded his watch for a horse and supplies there and set off for St. Louis again. Bandits robbed him somewhere near the Indian reservation and left him for dead. If No Cloud hadn't obeyed a vision dream and found Ronald, he would have died."

"Indian bandits, no doubt."

"No, Ronald said they were white men. Before this uprising two days ago, the Dakota didn't give us any problems."

"They're making up for lost time with a vengeance. About Ronald, now—do you think he's still committed to this hare-brained scheme of joining Quantrill?"

"I don't know. Susanna's with him, after all."

"So she is. But even if they manage to marry before we catch up to them, I don't put it past Ronald to ride blithely off with Quantrill, leaving his new bride to survive as best she can."

"Susanna won't let that happen."

"Ronald's easily led, I'll admit, but he has a stubborn streak. If he's determined to join the Rebs, no woman will stop him."

"You don't know Susanna."

"Maybe not, but I mean to halt the marriage if I can break free of these damn Sioux. And bring Ronald back to Philadelphia to face his responsibilities there."

He watched one expression after another flit across her face—anger, distress, indecision, and finally, determination.

"Don't you think it's high time Ronald made his own choices?" she asked.

"I can't permit it." He spoke with finality. "And I think you know why. Answer me honestly . . . do you believe your sister agreed to marry Ronald because of love alone?"

She didn't respond immediately, but looked away from him. When her eyes met his again, she said, so low he hardly heard the words, "I hope so. Dear God, I hope so."

When dusk deepened into full darkness, they emerged cautiously from the thickets by the stream and headed south, following a trail Jennara admitted she'd never been on, though she'd ridden as far south as Rice Lake, across the Iowa border, several times with her father.

Once Bramwell thought he heard a dog bark, but she thought it more likely a fox. They walked for the better part of an hour before coming to cultivated fields, a small stand of corn that hadn't been harvested and a burned farmhouse and barn. There was no sign of the farm family.

"Roast corn," he murmured longingly.

"We'll risk a pit fire at the edge of the field," Jennara said. "See if you can find something to dig with."

Bramwell searched near the ruins of the barn as best he could in the dark and found a spade whose handle had been burned away. Jennara lined the pit he dug with fallen bricks she'd gathered from a ruined chimney and kindled a fire. After it had burned down to coals, she put brick chips over the embers.

Leaving the corn inside the husks, she wet them and laid them atop the chips, added the six potatoes with a layer of brick chips over them, then had Bramwell shovel the dirt back into the pit.

While the corn and potatoes baked in this earth oven, they scouted for more edibles.

"Carrots," Bramwell muttered as he grubbed two from a garden patch. "Nothing but carrots."

When they moved on again, what they hadn't eaten of the roast corn and potatoes were packed in Sage's saddlebags, along with ten raw carrots.

"How far are we from the Iowa border?" he asked after they'd been traveling for some time.

"By my reckoning, about thirty-five miles."

"At this pace it'll be three nights more before we're across. Unless we find a farm the Sioux haven't devastated and I can buy a horse."

He waited for her to reply, but she didn't. Any other woman, he felt, couldn't have resisted reminding him how he'd lost the chestnut gelding. Perversely, he was annoyed because she said nothing.

Jennara called a halt as soon as the sky began to gray. "We'll go to ground here," she said, leading Sage off the trail toward a green thicket beside a stream.

Bramwell had noticed there were fewer trees the farther south they traveled. Here, except for those along the streams and rivers, there were no trees at all. The land also sloped more gently.

It was her turn to sleep. Bramwell slumped against a tree trunk, trying to keep his eyes open. When he found himself drowsing, he got up and circled the tree several times, but his feet hurt from the long hike and he soon sat down again. He set himself the exercise of translating his thoughts into Latin as a method of staying awake, but he failed.

Bramwell woke to broad daylight and the thunder of hooves. He sprang to his feet, glancing quickly at Sage. The pinto's ears were pricked, but he showed no inclination to whinny. Bramwell looked at Jennara and found her on her knees, prying branches apart to see the trail, some twenty feet away.

Before he could join her she turned to him, smiling. "Soldiers!"

The nightmare was over, thank God. He began to thrust himself through the brush, she caught at his arm.

"Wait."

"They'll be past and gone!" he protested.

She clung to his arm. "Wait," she repeated.

About to pull free, he froze as a rifle cracked—then another, and another. A fusillade. Over the gunshots he heard a high ululation and the hair on his nape rose. War cries. The Sioux!

Bramwell drew back into the dubious safety of their shelter and, crouched beside Jennara, peered at the melee beyond the trees while the stink of gunpowder stung his nostrils.

Horses plunged off the trail and into the grass and weeds, rifles cracked, men fell. Painted and shrieking warriors on ponies intermingled with the mounted men in blue. Though he knew bullets might well penetrate their cover, he couldn't move, but stared in fascination at the fighting. Knives, bayonets, rifles, bloodstained uniforms.

Suddenly, although there was no signal Bramwell could hear or see, warriors withdrew from the battle, urging their ponies southward. The soldiers regrouped and galloped in pursuit, guns popping as they fired after the retreating Indians.

Jennara rose to her feet and pushed through the brush.

"Where are you going?" he hissed.

"To see if I can help."

Only then did he become fully aware that four bodies lay on the ground to the other side of the trail. He followed her.

She glanced briefly at two fallen soldiers and went on. As Bramwell passed them, he saw both were dead. He drew in his breath, shocked, when he looked at the next body. A child! Beyond was a still smaller figure. Both were Indian children.

Jennara knelt beside them. After a moment she lifted the limp arms of the larger child, a girl, and crossed her hands on her breast. She turned to the other.

"He's alive," she said when Bramwell approached. "His left leg's broken — the tibia — from the horse stepping on him, I think. The girl was shot, but I can't find a bullet wound on him."

The Indian boy, about seven or eight, stared from Jennara to Bramwell with eyes so dark they looked black. Jennara spoke soothingly to him in what Bramwell knew must be Sioux.

The boy's attention fixed on her, and haltingly he asked her something.

Whatever she answered made tears well in the boy's eyes.

"I told him his sister was dead," Jennara told Bramwell.

He glanced along the trail south, then north. There was no sign of soldiers or Sioux.

"I'll have to splint the boy's leg," she announced. "Would you carry him into our shelter?"

Being in the open was unnerving. At any minute Bramwell expected to see warriors riding toward them. Hadn't Jennara told him they usually returned for their dead? If she was determined to help the boy, it was better done under cover. As soon as Bramwell bent and lifted the child, the boy began to struggle and gabble in Sioux.

"He says he won't leave his sister," Jennara translated. She spoke sternly to the boy, who quieted as he listened and made no more attempt to fight when Bramwell picked him up, careful to support the left leg.

"What did you say to him?" Bramwell asked as he eased himself and the boy through the branches Jennara held aside.

"I said we'd make a scaffold for his sister and put her body into a tree."

Bramwell was speechless. Was Jennara out of her mind? He was about to protest when it occurred to him that perhaps she'd said what she had to keep the boy quiet while she took care of his leg.

"We'll have to move on when you finish with the boy," he said, thinking of the possible return of the Sioux. If they left the boy beside the trail, he'd soon be found.

"You can build a scaffold of branches while I splint his leg," she told him.

"Why bother? You told me the Sioux always come back for the dead and wounded."

She gave him a level look. "Who knows how long that may be, with the soldiers pursuing them? The poor little boy is in pain with his broken leg. Even if he wasn't hurt, I'd never leave him here alone. We're taking him with us."

Chapter 6

Perspiration beaded Jennara's forehead and trickled between her breasts as she helped Bramwell with the body-laden scaffold. They were in the thicket now. Perched in the crotch of a young sycamore, the largest tree near them, Bramwell carefully pulled the scaffold up to him with ropes. The Indian boy, lying on the ground a few feet away, a crude splint tied to his left leg, watched as his sister's body, wrapped in one of Jennara's shirts, rose into the air.

Jennara knew it must have hurt when the splint was applied, but the boy had made no sound. He remained silent at the sight of his sister being lifted to her final resting place.

"Got it," Bramwell muttered, grasping the scaffold he'd fashioned of interlaced boughs. He wedged it into place in the crotch, untied the rope and, hanging from a branch, dropped to the ground. He gazed up at his handiwork and nodded with satisfaction.

"Spotted Eagle will fly with her spirit," the boy said, as though to himself.

"Is the cub hungry?" Bramwell asked Jennara.

She glanced away from the pitiful bundle in the sycamore and looked at the boy, who was gazing warily at Bramwell. She hurried to take an ear of roasted corn from their meager food stock and the boy reached for it while she was peeling the husk away. He finished tearing the husk off himself and immediately began to gnaw the kernels from the cob.

"When I was a boy," Bramwell said, "there was a farmer on

the edge of town who'd rescued a bear cub after killing its mother. That little bear fascinated me and every other boy for miles around. Despite the farmer's warnings to keep away, we'd sneak into the yard where the cub was and play with him. One day the cub swiped a friend of mine across the face. His claws tore out the boy's eye."

Bramwell nodded at the Indian boy. "He reminds me of that little bear . . . engaging, but not to be trusted. What happens when we try to hide from roving warriors and he calls to them?"

The boy stopped eating. To Jennara's amazement, he asked in Dakota if the man's heart was bad against him. How had he known? And what was she to tell the child? Bramwell didn't really dislike him. He simply mistrusted him, but that would be difficult to explain to a child. Inspiration struck: a Dakota took more than one name in a lifetime, she'd use that.

"He's given you a new name," she said. "We'll call you Little Bear. In our tongue the word is 'Cub.' "

To Bramwell she said, "I'll explain to Cub why he must be quiet."

"Do you really think he'll believe you and abide by what you say? The boy's a Sioux, after all . . . a budding warrior himself."

Jennara bit her lip. The truth was that she had no idea what the boy might do. "If I say we're hiding from soldiers as well as warriors to avoid being caught in a battle, he should be convinced it's best to stay quiet." At least she hoped so.

Bramwell grunted.

"He makes sounds like a bear," Cub said, his eyes on Bramwell.

"Sometimes, yes," she admitted. She'd already learned that Bramwell could be as cross as a bear roused from hibernation.

To her surprise, Cub smiled at Bramwell, whose scowl faded as he noticed the boy's expression.

"I don't trust you an inch," Bramwell told him, "but your only a poor hurt young cub. You're not to blame for anything that's happened." Cub didn't understand a word of it, but responding to the sympathetic tone of Bramwell's voice, continued to smile shyly.

That night Cub came along with them willingly, apparently resigned to leaving his dead sister behind in her tree scaffold. They'd discussed fashioning another travois for Sage to drag and Cub to ride on, but Bramwell had decided against it.

"Every bump would jar his leg," he said. "Cub's had enough pain. I'll carry him."

For all his doubts, Jennara thought, secretly pleased, Bramwell's as concerned about Cub as I am.

The boy seemed almost a lucky charm. At an abandoned farm, they found a cow the Dakota raiders had missed and also two chickens, a nest of eggs, and in the house, an intact jar of peach preserves.

Jennara killed and cooked the chickens. She milked the cow and beat the eggs into the milk to serve with the peach preserves. She'd have liked to take the cow with them, but knew they couldn't encumber themselves further.

After they'd eaten, packed the extra food, and started on their way again, helped by the light of a crescent moon, Bramwell told her he'd found a dead man behind the barn.

"Scalped," he added. "No sign of anyone else."

Jennara grimaced. She didn't know whose farm it was, but there must have been a wife and children. Were they captives?

Their own good luck was continuing, Jennara told herself when, near dawn, they came across a small valley running east and west, no more than a mile long and less than that across, thickly wooded, with a creek at the bottom — a perfect hiding place. She said so.

"A perfect trap, you mean," Bramwell argued in a low tone, glancing at the boy asleep in his arms. "Once we're down there, one squeak from Cub and we have no way to escape."

"If warriors find us, we won't manage to run far, no matter where we hide—so it makes sense to find the best cover. As for Cub—he knows we're his friends and he understands why it's dangerous to call to his people. He remembers how his sister died."

"Even if you're right about Cub, I still don't like making camp in a hole in the ground."

Jennara drew herself up and stared at him. "Perhaps you haven't noticed, but it's getting light. Do you have a better suggestion?"

He shrugged. "I suppose there's no choice. But I'll be looking forward to dark so we can move on and get away from this spot."

When they reached the bottom of the gully, surrounded by towering maples and sycamores, Jennara reached to take Cub from Bramwell. The moment she touched the boy, she drew in her breath in alarm.

"He's burning with fever!"

Leaving Bramwell to scout the area, tend to Sage, and set up the camp, Jennara laid the boy on the ground and hurried to the creek, where she filled the pan she'd brought from the farmhouse. Using her last clean handkerchief, she bathed Cub in cool water. Leaving the damp linen cloth on his forehead, she opened the medicine pouch and removed one of the tiny leather sacks. This one, she knew by the blue color of the thong drawing it closed, contained ground bark of white poplar, effective for reducing fever.

She also had quinine and opium in a metal case that had belonged to her father, but she thought Cub might be more willing to swallow medicines he knew were used by the Dakota.

Most dry medicines dissolved better in alcohol than in water, so she poured a dram of brandy from a metal flask into its cover and mixed in some of the ground poplar bark.

82

"Little Bear," she said softly in Dakota. "Wake, Little Bear." His eyes half opened.

"I have medicine for your sickness," she said. "Dakota medicine. You must swallow this to rid yourself of the bad spirit inside. Do you hear me?"

His eyes opened wider and she took this to mean he agreed. Lifting his head with one hand, she held the cap of the flask to his lips, saying, "Swallow."

He obeyed, screwing up his face as the bitter taste of the bark penetrated through the mask of the brandy.

"I'll bring you water to drink," she assured him and did so. Afterward, she ran her fingers gently along his injured leg. The skin, though bruised, was intact, so it was unlikely that the broken bone had caused the fever. She put her ear to his chest and listened. Though he breathed rapidly, air passed in and out of his lungs normally.

Cub's eye closed again and she crouched by his side, watching him. He didn't have pneumonia or a wound inflammation, two of the obvious causes of fever. Nor did he have any skin rash. She had no idea what was making him sick. No Cloud would say that an evil spirit had entered Cub and must be driven out. It wasn't her father's explanation, but it was one Cub could understand.

"Belief in the physician's remedy is always an aid to healing," her father had often said. "In the end it's up to the patient and to God whether or not he recovers."

One thing that would help Cub recover was proper nourishment—he was far too thin. She knew he wouldn't feel like eating until his fever abated and she wished more than ever that they'd been able to bring the cow. Milk was just what he needed.

When Bramwell came to see how Cub was faring, she told him how and why she regretted leaving the cow behind.

"With Cub sick, will we be able to go on tonight?" he asked.

"I'd rather not. He should rest quietly."

Bramwell shook his head as he glanced down at Cub, who slept restlessly. "He's a plucky little guy. I couldn't help stumbling last night—you know how it is, walking in the dark. It must've hurt his leg, because each time I stumbled he stiffened. But he never once so much as moaned. I don't want him to suffer through another night's travel while he's sick—much as I hate staying here any longer than a day."

Jennara glanced around at the tall trees surrounding them, their leaves blocking the heat and glare of the rising sun. Birds called and the air had a faint sweetness from some unseen late summer bloom. "We've been in worse places these past few days."

"I'll admit, it's pleasant enough." He reached to tuck a stray wisp of her hair behind her ear, his fingers lingering so long that she felt a tingling along her spine. Before she could bring herself to pull away, his hand dropped. "You look tired," he said. "I'll take first watch."

About to refuse, she paused. There was little more she could do for Cub at the moment. Later, if his fever still held, she'd dose him with the poplar bark again. It might be best for her to sleep now, the better to care for Cub later.

"Wake me if he seems worse," she said, "and give him water if he rouses."

"Children shouldn't have to suffer," he said, his eyes on Cub. "And certainly not from war."

War. The word echoed in Jennara's head as she settled herself to rest. She hadn't thought of it in those terms, but this *was* a war they were caught in, the settlers and soldiers on one side, the Dakota on the other. And they, on the side of the soldiers, nursed an enemy child.

If a child could be an enemy. Not to her, never to her. Or to Bramwell, either, it seemed. His attitude toward Cub showed her that Bramwell was far more tender-hearted than she'd ever suspected or thought possible.

She woke near noon. While Bramwell slept, she dosed Cub again and bathed him with the cool stream water. She tried to coax him to eat, but he'd take only water. In the drowsy peacefulness of the wooded gully, it was difficult to remember that danger lurked all around, but she kept the Spencer close at hand.

If only she knew more about illness — what caused fevers such as Cub had and how to cure them.

"You know as much as I do about healing, Jennara," her father had assured her only months before he died. "You're a fine doctor."

He'd taught her all he knew and she'd learned from No Cloud, too, who'd shown her that illness can sometimes be of the spirit rather than the body. His methods of dealing with spirit sickness were bizarre by her standards and would never be effective with white people, but they often worked for the Dakota.

She was jerked to alertness by rifle fire, too faint and far-off to be an immediate threat, but a sign the war was not only far from over, but far too close.

The other war was farther away, too far to affect Minnesota. She doubted if there was a Rebel sympathizer in the state. The settlers were either neutral or pro-Union. She knew no Confederate sympathizers except for Ronald, and she didn't truly believe he wanted to fight for slavery as opposed to fighting against it or against union. His impractical and artistic nature swayed him toward what he saw as a romantic cause.

Much as she mistrusted agreeing with Bramwell in any way, he was correct in believing that Ronald wouldn't last long as a soldier. He wasn't someone who could endure the horror of battle. She tried to picture men shooting and bayoneting each other while cannon boomed, but failed. Seeing instead the bloody aftermath of wounded and dead, she shuddered.

Bramwell woke before dusk and they ate cold chicken and the last of the potatoes. Again she tried to feed Cub, but he turned his face away, refusing. His skin burned with the heat of his fever.

"Worrying won't help him," Bramwell told her.

"I know. I just wish I could do more for him. And that he'd eat. I couldn't bear it if he—" She stopped abruptly, recalling the scaffold they'd left behind them, the scaffold with Cub's sister's remains. She didn't want to think Cub might die, she wouldn't think it. Yet in her heart she knew he could.

After twilight was routed by the true darkness of night, Bramwell rose from where he sat on the other side of Cub. "I think I'll scout around a bit," he said, his voice casual. "No need to worry if I don't return immediately."

When he disappeared into the night, she was unprepared for her feelings of desertion and she chided herself. They'd been forced to live practically in one another's pockets since the moment they'd met. It was difficult enough for friends, or even a husband and wife. For strangers, as they were, strangers not suited to be friends, it was a wonder they hadn't been at each other's throats constantly.

Not that they'd gotten along well. At least once Jennara had momentarily wished him dead and often devoutly wished him anywhere but with her. No doubt he'd felt the same about her, did feel the same, or else he wouldn't have gone off and left her alone.

Not alone, you goose, she admonished herself . . . Cub's with you. Shame on you for feeling neglected instead of concentrating on nursing him!

She offered the boy another drink of water and was pleased when he took a few sips. He'd perspired a little in the late afternoon and she'd hoped the fever would break, but now his skin was fiery under her fingers again. He turned restlessly, moaning a little. Taking his head into her lap, she stroked his hair and crooned a lullaby she remembered her mother singing to Susanna when her sister was a baby. As Jennara sang softly, she substituted boy for girl:

Bye low, my baby

Bye low, my bouncing baby boy
Bye low, my baby
Bye low, my bouncing baby boy.

Realizing the words would make no sense to Cub, she tried to translate them into Dakota only to discover she couldn't, so she continued the song in English. He quieted at last. Lulled by her own voice and the somehow comforting weight of the boy's head in her lap, Jennara half-drowsed herself.

Jennara had no idea how much time had passed when the hooting of an owl startled her into awareness. *Hoo, hoo-hoo.* The call was repeated twice. Despite her belief that the Dakota preferred not to venture far from their camps at night, she wondered if she'd really heard an owl — or merely a clever imitation of one. The Dakota were masters at bird and animal calls. Apprehensive, she looked around for Bramwell but couldn't see him.

Carefully, she eased Cub's head from her lap and rose to her feet, rifle in hand. Taking a few steps away from Cub, she peered into the darkness. Where was Bramwell? Tensely she waited for the owl to hoot again but all she heard were frogs shrilling.

"Bramwell?" she said in a low tone.

No answer.

She called his name again, louder.

Still no response.

Quelling her impulse to shout, she retreated to the base of the maple where Cub lay and stood with her back braced against the trunk, staring into the unknown menace of the night.

Where was Bramwell? What had happened to him? Surely he wouldn't deliberately desert her and Cub. On the other hand, she scarcely knew the man. He might be capable of anything.

But she did know him — at least she thought she did. The Bramwell she'd traveled with these past days would never abandon her, never leave her alone with a sick child, not willingly.

Had the hoots been from Dakota warriors signaling to one another as they crept through the woods toward her? They could have tracked Cub. They could have captured Bramwell already.

The minutes crept by. She held her breath until she had to give up and gasp for air. The muscles in her arms began to ache from keeping the muzzle of the rifle up and pointed into the darkness. The frogs, she noticed, still sang their high-pitched songs. Wouldn't human intruders silence the frogs?

Slowly, cautiously, Jennara lowered the rifle. If warriors had tracked Cub here, they certainly knew where she was and would have finished her off by now. Likely it *had* been an owl calling, likely the Dakota remained in their camps and villages and weren't skulking in these night woods at all. She'd frightened herself for naught.

But where was Bramwell?

Finally she eased down the trunk of the tree until she sat against it. She reached to touch Cub's shoulder for her own reassurance. How hot he was! If only No Cloud were here to treat the boy. Jennara shook her head. The medicine man could do no more for Cub than she was doing. Fevers weren't diseases of the spirit but of the body and she had, in her medicine pouch, the same powders and herbs No Cloud would use.

What had happened to Bramwell? Damn him! Jennara clenched the hand that wasn't holding the Spencer and beat her fist against the ground. Why was he scaring her like this? She didn't know how long he'd been gone, but hours had passed, she was certain. Never had darkness seemed so menacing. She couldn't search for Bramwell, there was nothing she could do until dawn except wait . . . watch and wait.

The dankness of night rose to her nostrils and the shrill cadence of the frogs echoed in her head until she imagined they told her over and over, *He's gone, he's gone, he's gone.*

An eternity later, a crackling in the woods brought her to her feet. Someone, something came toward her with no attempt at silence. The frogs abruptly ceased shrilling. A low, deep moaning call set the hair on her nape prickling. She swallowed.

The sound came again. This time she recognized it and could hardly believe her ears. "Moooo."

A cow.

She lowered the rifle and waited, almost certain now where Bramwell had gone.

"Jennara?" Bramwell's voice.

"Here." As he appeared out of the night, the cow in tow, she felt like crying with relief and at the same time clouting him over the head with the gun barrel for causing her such anxiety.

"Why didn't you tell me what you meant to do?" she demanded as he tied the cow to a nearby tree.

"You'd have wasted time by arguing against my going."

"Didn't it occur to you how upset I'd be when you stayed away so long?"

"I thought you'd be glad to get rid of me for a while."

"Don't mock me." To her distress, her voice broke and tears flooded her eyes.

His arms closed around her, the comforting length of his body pressed warmly against hers. She dropped the rifle and clung to him, she couldn't help herself. His lips brushed her hair, her cheek and, as she raised her face, settled gently against her mouth.

There was nothing of demand or challenge in his kiss, and its sweetness disarmed her and took away her breath. The kiss lasted for an earthshaking eternity, yet seemed to be over far too soon.

"You said Cub needed milk, so I went back and brought the cow here," he said, releasing her. "What else could I do?"

She sighed. He was right, she'd have absolutely forbidden him to risk the trip. For one thing, she'd have been convinced he'd never find his way there and back. Evidently she'd underestimated Bramwell.

"At one point I decided warriors had captured you," she told him, ashamed to admit she'd also been afraid they were surrounding her while hooting like owls.

"Nary a trace of any Indians. How's Cub?"

"No better."

In the gray predawn, Jennara milked the cow with Bramwell watching how she did it. "I'll admit it looks easy," he said, "but I have the feeling it's more difficult than I think."

"The secret is squeezing and pulling at the same time."

She dosed Cub with more poplar bark and coaxed him to swallow an almost-full tin cup of milk. As he drank, the boy's gaze clung to Bramwell's face.

"It'll make you better," Bramwell assured Cub, kneeling beside him.

"He says milk fights the bad spirit," Jennara translated. "That's why he brought the cow to us."

Cub's eyes drooped closed again.

"You sleep, too," Jennara told Bramwell. "I'm not tired yet."

It wasn't quite a lie. Though she *was* tired she knew she wouldn't sleep. She was still taut as a bowstring from the night's alarms, coupled with her worry over Cub.

Sitting with the rifle across her lap, she glanced toward the brown cow and shook her head. The last thing in the world she'd have expected Bramwell to do was go after the cow. Thank God nothing had happened to him! Whether she wanted to admit it or not, she preferred having Bramwell with her to being alone with Cub.

He was another adult, someone to share the chores and some of the responsibility, someone to talk things over with, someone to depend on. He might be a city man unaccustomed to the frontier, but he learned fast.

Why had he kissed her? To soothe her? It was true that a kiss could be comforting. Yet his lips had offered more than comfort. . . .

The sun was well up in the sky when Cub opened his eyes and spoke to her.

"It's leaving," he whispered.

Jennara blinked, uncertain of what he meant.

"The medicine song shot arrows into it. Now the milk burns in the arrow holes."

She realized then he was talking about the evil spirit she'd told him was the cause of his fever.

"I understand about the milk," she said. "What about the medicine song?"

"The song you sang in the dark."

The lullaby. Jennara put her hand to his forehead. Warm, but not burning hot. The fever was ebbing. "I can tell the bad spirit's weaker," she told Cub. "Soon you'll be free of it."

"It came inside me because this is a sacred place." Cub's dark eyes were wide and frightened. "The People don't camp here."

What now? Jennara wondered. Evidently Cub recognized where they were as taboo to the Dakota. To make certain he recovered, she had to convince him the spirits of the sacred site wanted them to stay.

"My medicine song asked permission of the sacred spirits," she said carefully, "and they granted it. Did you hear the owl hoot last night to tell me we may remain here as long as we choose?"

"I dreamed of Owl," he said solemnly.

"So you know the truth and soon you will be well again."

When Bramwell woke, she told him what had happened. "If he's improving, maybe you should ask Cub where his people camp," he said.

In the afternoon, after Cub drank another cup of milk, she did.

The boy, who was sitting propped against her, looked toward the stream, then pointed south. "A village is there."

"How many sleeps away?" she asked.

"No sleeps. Close. He looked to the east. "A village is there. Close." His gaze shifted north. "Almost one sleep away is a village."

She told Bramwell.

"I said this was a trap," he muttered. "No way to go but west, unless he hasn't finished relating the bad news."

Jennara pointed to the west. "No villages?" she asked Cub.

Tears swam in his eyes. "My village," he said sadly.

"Wonderful," Bramwell said when she translated. "We're surrounded by hostile Sioux. Maybe they won't violate a sacred site by attacking us in the gully, but what's to prevent them from posting scouts to notify the warriors if we try to leave?"

"Don't forget that *you* managed to leave here last night and return — with a cow. I don't think they're aware of us, I think we're safe enough. And with Cub to warn us if we're too close to a village, we can go on from here as soon as he's entirely well — perhaps tomorrow night."

"Won't Cub want to return to his village?"

Jennara asked the boy.

He began to cry in earnest. After she'd hugged and comforted him, he told her why he and his sister had been on the trail with the warriors.

"It's so sad," she said to Bramwell. "Cub's mother died and his father was taking him and his sister to their grandparents in a village by Lake Shetek. Since his father's a warrior, he rode with a war party planning to raid the settlers' farms near the lake. When their scouts reported soldiers riding behind them, they stopped and ambushed the bluecoats. Cub's father was wounded almost immediately and fell off his horse. The girl sprang from her hiding place to help him, got caught in the crossfire, and died. Cub, who followed her, was trampled by a horse. Presumably his father was rescued by a fellow warrior. Cub says he'll stay with us until he finds his father."

Chapter 7

Though he ran a fever through the night, Cub improved so rapidly that he began trying to hobble around, splint and all, late the next morning. Since it proved impossible to keep the boy off his feet, Bramwell fashioned a rude crutch from a fallen branch and showed Cub how to use it.

"He gets around amazingly well for a boy with a broken leg," Bramwell commented.

"I think he has what my father called a greenstick fracture," Jennara said. "The bone splinters like green wood, but doesn't break in two. That's common in the young because their bones haven't grown brittle yet."

Apparently Cub had never been close to a cow before, because he was fascinated by her. Luckily, she was a tame barn cow and chewed her cud placidly while he touched her horns, stroked her nose, and pulled her tail.

Bramwell smiled as he watched the boy. How accepting and adaptable children were! Cub seemed at home with the two of them — two white people. He even trusted them to reunite him with his father.

Cub was their responsibility, his and Jennara's, but even if the warrior-father had survived his wounds, the task of finding him was impossible at the moment. They wouldn't keep the boy with them forever, though. Once the army quelled this bloodthirsty Sioux uprising, Cub would be returned to his people, to his grandparents, if not to his father.

Now that Cub's fever was gone, the boy's appetite returned with a vengeance. He ate more than Jennara at noon, all but cleaning out their food supply. Only a few raw carrots were left, plus whatever milk the cow provided.

Jennara hardly ate anything. Bramwell was about to ask her why when Cub hobbled over to him. Looking expectantly up into Bramwell's face, he made a series of gestures that Bramwell took to be pulling an arrow from a quiver and fitting it to a bow.

"You want your bow and arrows, don't you? I brought them along." Bramwell glanced toward Jennara in the expectation she'd translate.

She didn't appear to have heard. He looked closer at her, noting with alarm the paleness of her face.

"Are you all right?" he asked her.

She turned toward him, blinking. "I—my head aches. It's nothing serious."

Not only was she pale, but the whites of her eyes were bloodshot. Without thinking what he meant to do, he laid the back of his hand gently against her cheek. She pulled away, but not before he'd felt the heat of her skin.

Startled, he stared at her. "No wonder you didn't eat. You're feverish."

"With rest, I'm sure I'll recover quickly." Her voice quivered.

He insisted she lie down immediately and when she did, he stood frowning at her. She looked so small and frail curled in the shade of the maple, so vulnerable. Somehow he'd never imagined strong and self-confident Jennara would be taken ill.

"There's quinine in a tin box in my saddle pack," she said. "I should take a few grains."

He brought her the tin box, Cub trailing anxiously after him. The boy crouched by Jennara, gazing worriedly into her face. He said something to her that made her smile

94

slightly, and she answered in Sioux. Whatever she said seemed to reassure Cub a little.

Bramwell fetched water for Jennara and she swallowed the quinine. When he replaced the box, he recalled Cub's child's bow and quiver of arrows and retrieved them from among his belongings. He presented them to the boy with a flourish, hoping to distract him. Jennara would rest better without Cub hanging over her.

Cub gestured to Bramwell—in thanks, he decided. Further gesturing indicated the boy meant to hunt with the bow. Even assuming he was skillful enough, what he expected to bring down with the child-sized arrows, handicapped with the splint and the crutch besides, Bramwell couldn't imagine. But he nodded solemnly to preserve the boy's dignity. After all, Cub couldn't possibly get lost or come to harm within the limits of the little valley. His leg would keep him from going far. Let him play his hunting game.

Cub wasn't the only one worried about Jennara, but knowing he shouldn't hover over her, Bramwell chose another tree to prop his back against, sitting with the rifle across his lap. She'd said her fever would soon break. Since she was used to doctoring, she ought to know. On the other hand, it might be wishful thinking on her part or an effort to reassure him.

He felt lost without her trying to boss him, without her arguing with him, without her expert advice and practical knowledge. Hell, he wasn't even sure he could milk the damn cow.

Would they be able to travel tonight as planned? He shook his head. When they left this place, Jennara must be completely well and alert. He didn't like remaining here, but he couldn't deny they'd been safe in the valley so far. It was riskier to travel with her sick than it was to stay and give her a chance to recover.

If they stayed, what were they going to do for food? He hadn't seen a deer, but there were deer tracks aplenty in the soft earth by the stream. He wasn't a hunter, but he had no doubt he could bring down a buck with one bullet. Staring at the rifle, he wondered if he dared chance a shot. Would it bring Sioux warriors down upon them in full cry, determined to oust the intruders from their sacred site? If he did get away with killing a deer, the meat would need to be cooked. Was a fire safe, or would the smoke pinpoint their location too well?

Bramwell pondered the problem, occasionally glancing toward Jennara, who slept, her face now flushed with her fever. Finally he decided he couldn't risk trying for a deer. Could he set snares for rabbits? He'd never done such a thing in his life or even seen it done. Probably there were fish in the stream, but he wasn't a fisherman and hadn't the slightest idea how to catch a fish without a line and a hook. And fish, like meat, had to be cooked.

He began to wonder where Cub had gotten to. It was high time he returned. Had he fallen and hurt his leg so he couldn't get back to camp? If Bramwell went to look for him, he'd have to leave Jennara by herself and he disliked the idea. Damn it, he shouldn't have allowed the boy to go off alone in the first place.

A rifle cracked, driving him to his feet. The shot sounded uncomfortably close, coming from above the rim of the valley and to the south, possibly less than a mile away. Other guns fired, sporadically at first, then in a barrage of shooting. Jennara moaned, her eyes fluttering open.

"No one's shooting at us," he assured her. "No need to get up."

She struggled to stay awake but when her eyes kept drooping shut he realized with dismay that she must be sicker than he'd thought. He eased over, bent to touch her forehead, and grimaced. It was burning hot.

His father had died of typhoid fever when he was nine. Bramwell recalled the terrible despair of his mother when the doctor had told her what it was.

"There's no hope, then," she sobbed and nothing anyone said convinced her differently. She'd been right.

96

There were dozens of other fevers. Jennara didn't have typhoid—he wouldn't let himself believe it.

His mother's words echoed in his head. "No hope."

Above the rim, the unseen battle waxed and waned with a flurry of shots followed by a lull, then more firing. Bramwell longed to find out exactly what was happening, but feared climbing to the rim might expose him to the Sioux.

He worried about Cub—where was he? Had the boy deceived both of them? Had he waited for his chance to bolt for his village?

Uneasy about the battle and about Cub, and frustrated by his inability to help Jennara, Bramwell stomped down to the stream, soaked his cleanest handkerchief in the water, and carried it dripping back to Jennara. He knelt and bathed her face. Without opening her eyes, she put up a fumbling hand and moved the cloth to her forehead. He left the wet handkerchief there, hoping that was what she wanted. He'd never before taken care of a sick person.

How well-rounded he'd thought himself in Philadelphia— an expert in law, a connoisseur of food and wine, a man-about-town, popular with the ladies but cagy enough not to be snared by one. He played a shrewd game of cards, rode well, and had recently become a sharpshooter. He might not be a true connoisseur of the arts, but he fancied he could tell good from bad, and he truly enjoyed music. As for business, he'd not only halted the decline of Claridge Mercantile, he'd increased profits to the point where Ronald was close to being the wealthiest man in the city.

None of his accomplishments had prepared him for the Minnesota frontier, the Sioux, or Jennara Gray.

She had to get well!

As he stood beside her, worrying, his gaze swept the woods around them, rising to the south rim as the popping of rifles continued. Between soldiers and Sioux, who would win?

Some movement by the creek caught his eye and he brought up the rifle, hardly believing his eyes when a spikehorn buck stepped from between two trees, head raised, wary, no more than fifteen feet away. Without stopping to think, Bramwell aimed just behind one of the ears and pulled the trigger of the Spencer. The rifle cracked, the buck staggered a few feet, the front legs buckled, and the buck toppled over into the stream.

Jennara sat up, crying his name. He turned and crouched beside her, smoothing tangled strands of hair from her face. "Nothing's wrong. I shot a deer, that's all." He tipped his head toward the south rim. "I figure they're too busy up there to notice one extra shot." At least he fervently hoped so. He eased Jennara down again.

As Bramwell strode toward the deer, Cub hobbled into view, blood running down his side from a squirrel and a rabbit he held tucked under the arm not encumbered by the crutch. "Oo-koo-hoo!" Cub called to Bramwell.

Bramwell greeted him as one successful hunter to another, making much of the boy's game. How he'd managed to kill animals as fleet of foot as a rabbit and a squirrel was beyond Bramwell, and with the child's bow and arrows besides!

Cub was definitely impressed with the buck, gravely examining the bullet hole in the deer's head and then gesturing to Bramwell.

"You're saying I'm a great shot?" Bramwell said. "Thank you. You're not so bad yourself." Actually, he didn't have the slightest notion what the boy meant, but it seemed like approval.

Nor did he know what to do with the deer, now that he'd killed it. Whatever had to be done would take a knife, so he slid the clasp knife from his pocket and flipped it open. He saw no point in dragging the kill from the stream, so he removed his boots and socks. Cub sat down and watched him expectantly. When Bramwell continued to stare uncertainly at the deer, Cub drew a finger across his throat and then pointed to the buck.

Deciding Cub knew more about this than he did,

Bramwell slit the throat. Bleeding the deer apparently was necessary. Cub's next gesture was also clear and logical, so Bramwell gutted the animal, as instructed. He intended to let everything inside wash downstream, but Cub scuttled into the water and retrieved the heart and liver.

Now what?

Cub held out his hand for the knife. Bramwell hesitated a moment, then gave it to him. Slitting the hide along the deer's spine, Cub peeled it down and hacked off a sizable chunk of loin meat before carefully laying the hide back in place. With a quick motion of his head, he indicated that Bramwell should drag the carcass into the deepest part of the stream.

Of course—the cool water would keep it from spoiling.

Now the meat must be cooked. Though the shooting from above the rim had grown more desultory, there was still quite a fight going on. The warriors should be too distracted to track down where the smoke was coming from. Bramwell gathered dry twigs and wood from fallen trees only to find his idea of a fire was far more grandiose than Cub's.

Cub laid a fire so small that Bramwell couldn't believe it would cook anything, but he didn't argue. The smaller the fire, the less smoke there would be.

Leaving Cub to watch the fire, Bramwell hurried to Jennara's side. She dozed restlessly, still flushed with fever. He lifted her into his arms and she roused, but made no protest as he carried her to where the tiny fire blazed. He laid her gently on the ground nearby.

Cub hunched himself over next to her and spoke in Sioux.

"He says you should put some of the meat into the pan with a little water and cook it." Her voice was weak and her eyes drooped shut as she finished.

Bramwell, under Cub's watchful eye, did as he'd been told. Cub also supervised cutting the liver into thin strips and carefully fitted the strips onto two green sticks. Once this was done, he took Bramwell's knife and gutted the squirrel and the rabbit, then plastered them with mud he'd carried from the stream bank.

As the firewood began to turn to coals, Bramwell set the pot onto them. Then he and Cub roasted the liver strips over the coals. The ends cooked first, Bramwell discovered, and had to be eaten or they'd burn. He learned to bite off the ends and, while chewing them, roast the remaining meat longer. Charred or half-done, it tasted delicious.

Jennara turned her face away when he tried to coax her to nibble on a strip of cooked liver. Cub pointed to the pot and made motions of drinking. Of course! After the meat released its juices into the simmering water, there'd be broth for Jennara.

The loin meat he hadn't put into the pot had to be sliced thin and cooked, too, or else it wouldn't keep. By this time Cub had buried the mud-covered squirrel and rabbit under the coals. Cub himself was a sorry mess, with dried animal blood and mud streaking his skin. Bramwell, glancing down at himself, saw he needed a wash almost as badly as Cub.

Pantomiming what he meant to do, he hefted the boy under one arm and splashed into the creek upstream from the deer carcass, which was now attracting flies. When they were as clean as they could get without soap, Bramwell brought Cub back to where Jennara lay. As he passed the cow, it turned her head to look at him and mooed plaintively.

"She needs milking," Jennara mumbled.

Cub couldn't help him there, Bramwell knew.

"Sing to her," Jennara half whispered.

She's delirious, he thought worriedly, hurrying to fetch a cup of water. She took only a few sips before pushing the cup away. Should he give her some more quinine? He shook his head. Best not to, unless she specifically asked for it.

The cow made no objection when he knelt beside her as he'd seen Jennara do. He positioned their only other pan under her udders and grasped a teat in each hand. Squeeze and pull at the same time, Jennara had said. He tried and found it easier said than done. No milk came. The cow turned her head to see what was going on.

After a frustrating few minutes, with the cow growing progressively more restive, Bramwell decided to take the rest of Jennara's advice, given in delirium or not. He had nothing to lose.

Leaning his head against the cow's flank he began softly to sing the first song that came to him, an old favorite of his mother's:

By yon bonnie banks and by yon bonnie braes
Where the sun shines bright on Loch Lomond . . .

When he reached "You take the high road," a trickle of milk hit the bottom of the pan. Though the milk didn't flow as rapidly as it had for Jennara, the pan eventually filled to the brim and he stopped.

He persuaded Jennara to drink a half-cup of the warm milk, and later she asked for more quinine. By sundown she was ready to try the venison broth. Cub's game was roasted by then, and Bramwell watched with interest while Cub cracked open the hot and hardened mud shells. The fur peeled away with the shell, leaving the tender meat ready to eat.

Cub stretched out after the meal and was asleep before dark. Bramwell sat beside Jennara in the blue evening light. Was she better? He couldn't be certain, but at least she was keeping her eyes open.

"I heard you singing," she murmured. "Are you Scottish, then?"

"My mother was. She came to Pennsylvania from Scotland when she was ten years old. Bramwell was her maiden name."

Jennara raised her head a little, listening. "The shooting's stopped."

Bramwell nodded. "It began to sound more like a siege than a pitched battle near the end. If so, I expect we'll hear

101

rifles again in the morning."

"I'll be better then—I know I will."

I hope you're right, he thought. The sooner she was back on her feet, the quicker he'd have peace of mind—not only because of their precarious situation. He wanted her better, wanted her well, healthy. He didn't want anything bad to happen to Jennara or to Cub. Shared danger and illness had drawn them close, and the three of them were almost like a family. He smiled at the thought of Jennara's outrage if he should try to tell her that he was the papa and she the mama.

They'd have to move on as soon as possible. Maybe she'd be well enough by tomorrow night, maybe not. They couldn't go until she could travel unaided. West would be the best direction. Cub would be familiar with the territory and could guide them past his former village safely, if they could trust him.

"My hair feels so awful," she said, trying to smooth stray strands with her fingers. "All snarled."

"I'll fetch your brush." He knew she'd brought one along because he'd seen her using it.

When he returned with the brush, Jennara had propped herself against a tree and sat unbraiding her hair. She sighed when she finished. "I'm so weak."

Her hair rippled over her shoulders, dark around her pale face in the twilight. He reached to touch its softness. "Let me brush your hair," he said.

Though as a child he'd watched his mother at her toilette, he'd never before brushed a woman's hair. At first he was afraid of hurting her, but he soon plied the brush with confidence, savoring the touch of the silken strands of hair.

"That feels so good," she murmured.

Yes, he agreed silently, very good . . . too good to stop. Everything else faded from his ken—the danger waiting outside the valley, the worry over Ronald, what to do with Cub. There was nothing but the two of them, him and Jennara in the deepening darkness. The promise of something more than the erotic feel of her hair under his hands beckoned teasingly and the rhythm of his strokes slowed, grew languid.

As if she sensed what was happening and feared it, she turned to look at him. "I think it's time to rebraid my hair," she whispered.

Braiding was beyond him, so he had to give up the brush to her and leave any beckoning promises unrealized.

In the middle of the night, Jennara woke. She rose and went to where he sat against a tree with the rifle. "My fever's gone and I'm wide awake," she said. "Why don't you get some rest?"

Since he'd been dozing off and jerking awake for hours, Bramwell hesitated to refuse. He needed sleep. Touching her forehead, he found her skin cool.

"If you promise you'll call me in an hour—or sooner if you start to feel weak," he said at last.

She agreed. "Cub's all right?" she asked.

"Eating enough for two boys. He wore himself out hunting and hasn't stirred since he fell asleep." Bramwell handed her the rifle, yawned and stretched. "I've heard nothing but frogs."

He woke to a grayness that hinted at dawn and immediately sat up. Jennara, by the tree, smiled at him. "That was a long hour," he chided her, rising to his feet.

"I'm fine now and you needed the rest."

He made his way to the creek to wash. When he returned, he urged her to lie down again, but she refused.

"I caught up on a week's sleep yesterday," she said.

"No alarms?"

She shook her head. "This is truly a *waka* place. I half expect to see the sacred blue lightning of the Dakotas playing over the valley. The night was peaceful, frogs and owls kept me company, and I—"

The crack of a rifle interrupted her. Bramwell whirled to gaze toward the south rim. "Same place." A second gun popped, then another and another. "Taking up where they

103

left off last night."

Cub roused and, using the crutch, hobbled over to them. His eyes brightened when he looked at Jennara and he began talking rapidly, as if making up for lost time.

"He says he's happy I've lost my evil spirit and mentions that you're a very good hunter, a very good shot, but he seems to have a few doubts about some of your other abilities," she told Bramwell.

He grinned at Cub. "He's a good teacher. Though I did manage to milk the cow without his help." He raised an eyebrow at Jennara. "What's this about evil spirits?"

"The Dakota believe evil spirits cause illness."

Cub spoke again, urgently.

"He says if you don't turn the deer carcass in the stream over and cut the meat from the other side soon, all of it will go bad with blowfly maggots."

"Do we dare risk another fire?"

"If we keep it small. Not much smoke rose from the one you kindled yesterday."

Thanks to Cub, he thought. Getting out his knife, he headed for the carcass. When he passed the cow she mooed. "Wait your turn," he muttered. "Besides, it's too early for me to sing."

Returning with the venison, he found Jennara milking the cow. Cub had begun to gather sticks and wood for the fire. By the time the fire was burning well, Jennara was finished and they began breakfast with the warm milk.

She had him cut some of the meat into pieces for the pot. "I'll put the carrots in, and the stew can cook while we're roasting the rest of the meat."

"This is the last of it. Cub was right—only the part immersed in the water was fit to eat. I dragged it clear of the stream so the water won't be fouled." He grimaced. "It's beginning to stink."

"I noticed. We'll have to move the camp to another part of this valley today anyway. There's no more graze here for Sage and the cow."

"Near the west rim, maybe? I was thinking that's the direction we'll have to take when we travel on."

"We'll try camping there. About the direction — I just don't know."

"I hate to leave the cow behind when we quit this valley," he said, "I'm getting downright fond of her."

As the day brightened, the rifle fire picked up. After they had the meat all roasted and had eaten enough to satisfy their hunger, Bramwell loaded Sage, perched Cub on the horse's back, and led the pinto west along the valley while Jennara followed with the cow.

Once the new camp was set up, Bramwell grew restless. With Jennara so improved, there was no reason to watch over her. As for Cub, Bramwell had acquired considerable respect for the boy's ability to look after himself.

"I'd like to find out what's going on up there," he told Jennara, nodding toward the south side of the valley.

Her eyes widened. "What if you're seen?"

"I won't be. The shooting makes enough racket to cover any noise I might make, and I have enough sense to stay under cover." He smiled one-sidedly. "Believe me, the man you see before you is not the same Bramwell Sumner you met a few days ago."

"I still don't like the idea."

Bramwell, whose mind was made up to go whether or not she approved, shrugged. "I think we should know who's battling who and which side is winning. If soldiers are fighting and winning, our troubles could be just about over."

She signed. "You'll go no matter what I say, no matter how foolhardy an idea I think it is." Turning away, she gathered the soiled clothes and started for the stream to wash them.

He almost went after her. No, he told himself — you know what you're doing, you're no longer merely a city lawyer out of your depth, you've learned to take care of yourself. Do what you think should be done. Nowhere is it written that

Jennara Gray is always right.

When he started south, Cub tagged after him, and Bramwell stopped to convince the boy he couldn't come along. Once Cub turned back to camp, Bramwell went on. He'd left the Spencer with Jennara. Unencumbered, he made good time striding between the trees, reaching the south edge of the valley in less than a half hour.

There he found the slope far steeper than the one they'd climbed down originally. Determinedly he began to climb, pulling himself up by grasping saplings and bushes while branches and brambles lashed his face and naked torso. The noise of the guns pounded in his ears as he neared the top, and the stench of powder grew overbearing. He smelled death, too — the rotten scent of decay. Men shouted and a horse screamed in agony.

Directly above him the sky was bright blue, with large white clouds drifting lazily across the sun now and again. A hawk soared over the valley, circling before reaching the south rim.

Bramwell, the top of his head level with the rim, slowly raised it high enough to peer out. He found himself staring directly into the painted face of a Sioux warrior.

Chapter 8

For an interminable moment Bramwell froze in place, his eyes fixed on the equally immobile warrior. The Sioux opened his mouth, whether to shout in defiance or as a warning to others, Bramwell didn't wait to find out. Holding on with one hand to the rocky outcropping at the rim, he gripped the brave's braided hair with the other, let go of the rock, and flung himself backward, dragging the warrior with him.

Both fell down the embankment, bouncing off shrubs and slamming into saplings on the way to the bottom. Halfway Bramwell hit up against a fallen tree. The blow knocked him breathless, making him lose his hold on the warrior's braids. The Sioux tumbled on down the steep incline. By the time Bramwell regained his breath, the warrior was on his hands and knees, reaching for his dropped rifle.

Bramwell scrambled rapidly to the bottom, reaching the Sioux as he swung up the gun barrel. Bramwell kicked the rifle from his hands. The warrior sprang to his feet and lunged at Bramwell. Though not much taller than Bramwell, he was broader and heavier. Bramwell sidestepped, dropping into a sparring stance, fists ready. For sport he'd often boxed with a trainer and with friends, but never before had his life hung in the balance.

If that brute gets his hands on me, I don't stand much of a

chance, Bramwell thought, watching the Sioux warily and wondering if it were possible to keep out of his reach and at the same time manage to fell him. He knew he couldn't get to the rifle before the warrior grabbed him and he also knew he had to keep the brave too busy to dive for the gun.

He feinted with his right fist and, as the man ducked away, jabbed with his left. The blow landed on the warrior's chin between zigzagging white and red lines. The Sioux staggered back, but quickly regained his footing. He glared at Bramwell, a terrifying apparition, one half of his face painted white, the other red. He wore nothing but moccasins and a buckskin breechclout and his naked torso was streaked with dirt. Blood trickled from a cut on his shoulder.

Except for the painted face, I don't suppose I look much different, Bramwell thought fleetingly as he danced back and forth in front of the warrior, fists up and ready.

"Come on, you bastard," he muttered, "give me an opening."

He wasn't prepared when the Sioux threw himself forward and down, grabbing Bramwell's legs and toppling him backward. As he fell, Bramwell twisted to the side, wrenching one leg free. He kicked, ramming the Sioux in the chest. The man grunted and let go. Bramwell rolled away and sprang up.

The Sioux was on his feet just as quickly, his dark eyes malevolent in his painted face. He muttered in his own tongue, nothing favorable, Bramwell was sure. Bramwell feinted again, this time with his left, then danced backward. The warrior came after him, forcing Bramwell sideways to avoid a tree trunk.

"Wear 'em out by keeping 'em guessing." The trainer's advice echoed in Bramwell's head. Not good advice in this case. The damned warrior could probably outlast him. He'd rocked him once with a left, though. His best bet was to get close enough to let loose his bottom-of-the-boots left hook.

He soon discovered getting close without getting caught

was a major problem. The Sioux had a long reach and he lunged every time Bramwell tried to edge in, forcing Bramwell to dodge before he had a chance to unwind the killing hook. Again and again he tried to work closer and failed because of the warrior's strength and agility. The tall trees of the valley bottom hemmed them in, obstacles hard for Bramwell to avoid.

"*Tahaci!*" The call, in Cub's clear, carrying voice came from behind the Sioux, startling him. He started to turn, then held, eyeing Bramwell uncertainly.

"*Tahaci!*" Cub called again. Bramwell tried to spot the boy but failed. The warrior's agitation increased, but he still watched Bramwell.

Laughter shrilled from overhead, a strange high-pitched trilling sound that set Bramwell's teeth on edge. Fear distorted the Sioux's features as he gazed frantically all around, only a fraction of his attention on Bramwell. As the awful laughter continued, Bramwell ducked behind the thick trunk of a maple, planning to dash back and recover the warrior's rifle while he was distracted.

To his horror, Jennara, her hair unbound, wearing the white gown unbelted so it floated about her, walked along a large tree limb until she stood directly above the Sioux.

"*Itceci,*" she called, trilling her voice.

The warrior whirled, staring upward. Bramwell tensed, ready to spring. To his surprise, the Sioux, obviously terror-stricken, backed away from the tree. A moment later he was running desperately toward the southern rise of the valley, rifle forgotten. Bramwell, trailing him, the warrior's gun in hand, watched the man climb toward the top twice as fast as he'd been able to pull himself up.

"Don't shoot him," Jennara advised quietly from behind him.

"He'll warn the others," Bramwell protested without turning.

"If he says anything, it'll only be a warning to stay away

from the *waka* valley where *Wianubapka*, Double-Woman, lives."

Keeping part of his attention on the Sioux, Bramwell glanced at her. "You can't be certain of that."

"Oh, but I am." She spoke so softly he strained to hear her. "You disappeared at just the right moment. He thought you'd turned into a woman and leaped into the tree, making him sure you and I were the evil and powerful Double-Woman. She's especially vengeful if disturbed. Since this is a known sacred place, he must have been uneasy down here to begin with. Cub and I just added a few embellishments."

"I could have handled him," Bramwell grumbled, annoyed that he was cheated out of the chance.

"If you'd knocked him out, what then? Would you shoot him as he lay dazed and helpless?"

Startled, Bramwell realized he hadn't gotten around to thinking about the aftermath of the fight. What *would* he have done? He doubted he could have brought himself to kill the warrior in cold blood.

He saw the Sioux had gained the rim and was heaving himself to his feet. Slowly, reluctantly, Bramwell lowered the rifle. Without looking back, the warrior began to run and was soon lost to sight.

Cub hobbled into view, speaking excitedly in his own tongue. Jennara answered him.

"Cub and I followed you," she told Bramwell, "just in case. Cub played his part to perfection by hiding and calling the warrior his cousin. When I did the same — the word is different, depending on whether a man or a woman says it — the man was convinced he heard Double-Woman speak to him."

Bramwell stared from her to the boy and back. "But for Cub, that meant going against his people."

"I explained how he and I must try to stop the two of you from killing one another. I turned it into a game, knowing if I mentioned Double-Woman that Cub would be as frightened as the warrior. To any Dakota she's a very menacing spirit."

Bramwell knelt beside the boy. "You really didn't want me dead?" he asked.

Cub, not understanding a word, smiled shyly.

"You named him," she said. "A name-giver is a friend to be valued."

Bramwell tousled the boy's hair and got to his feet. "I still can't believe the Sioux won't be back in force. If that warrior thinks it's over, how long will he stay fooled? You and I are both white, after all. His enemies."

"Have you seen yourself?"

"What's that got to do with it?"

She grinned. "Your face is a mass of scratches, with an interesting design of dried blood connecting them. There are bloodstains and dirt smeared over your back and chest. You certainly don't look like an ordinary white man. I'm not sure your Philadelphia friends would recognize you."

Bramwell resisted the urge to run his hand over his bearded cheeks. "Even if they don't come after us, it'd be wise to leave this valley tonight," he said. "Something down here attracted that warrior's attention. The smoke of our fire, maybe."

"Or the noise of your climb."

He couldn't deny the possibility. "Whatever the Sioux smelled or heard or saw, he was lying on his stomach, about to peer over down into the valley when I arrived at the top. How do we know he's the only one who suspects our presence here?"

"I agree it's not safe to remain any longer," she said. "I'll talk to Cub about his village near the west rim and we'll break camp tonight."

Back where Sage and the cow were tethered, Bramwell's wash in the stream inspired Cub to imitate him and they were both still dripping when they joined Jennara.

"How convenient to be a male in August," she said, wiping her perspiring face with her handkerchief.

"Personally, I envy Cub," Bramwell said. "He wears the perfect late-summer costume."

Jennara glanced at the boy in his moccasins and brief breechclout. When an image flashed into her head of Bramwell stripped to nothing but a breechclout, she stood pleasurably bemused for an instant. Then, realizing what she was doing, she flushed and turned away from Bramwell's all-too-perceptive gaze.

"Cub," she said, focusing on the Indian boy, "we must talk."

Later she translated for Bramwell. "Cub insists he has no family in the village now and he doesn't want to return there. He wishes to find his father, who he believes is heading west."

"It's possible his father's too badly wounded to travel. He may even be dead."

"Cub won't—or can't—face the possibility. Anyway, he offers to guide us safely past the village."

"Intending to come along with us, I take it."

"Not only that, he wants to bring the cow. I explained why it wasn't safe for us to travel with her, so he asked if we couldn't leave her near the village for his people to find. They're hungry, he says."

Bramwell sighed. "So the cow's to be delivered to the village instead of Cub."

"If you want his wholehearted cooperation."

"I hate to think our lives depend on a seven-year-old Indian boy."

"Almost eight. He was born in the Moon of Rice-Gathering, and that's late August. He's a remarkable child, don't you think? Already he's adapted to us—enemies, as you said—and even hunts for us, with a broken leg in a splint."

"Cub's all right." Bramwell's voice was gruff. He knew he was becoming attached to the boy, and he also knew he must limit that attachment. Cub was a Sioux. Even if he never found his father, sooner or later he'd return to his people. Because of her long acquaintance with the Indians, surely Jennara understood this.

"If we're to travel tonight, shouldn't you sleep?" she asked.

He shook his head. "You're the one who's been sick."

"Very well, we'll take turns."

Cub curled up alongside Jennara in the deepest shade of a huge maple while Bramwell watched over them. Despite Jennara's assurance that the warrior wouldn't alert his comrades to enemies in the valley, Bramwell remained alert. The gunfire to the south diminished as the afternoon wore on, finally ending altogether.

A truce? he wondered. Not likely. One side had won, the other side had retreated or were dead or captive. If the Sioux were the victors, would they now turn their attention to the valley?

Waka, Jennara had called this place . . . meaning powerful, a spirit home. He recalled how Cub had touched the head of the deer he'd shot and then spoken words that had seemed to be thanks mixed with apology. Bramwell had then felt that violence had no place in this peaceful valley. They didn't belong here either.

If the Sioux did decide the valley was too *waka* to invade, what was to prevent them from camping near the rim, waiting for the intruders to emerge? On the other hand, with lucrative raiding to be found all over the countryside, why bother?

Jennara was probably right about the Sioux, she usually was. He glanced at her, sleeping on her back, hands crossed below her breasts, her braid wound around her head. In spite of her man's shirt and divided skirt, she looked positively demure. No more than a few hours ago he'd seen her standing like a dryad on the tree limb in the white gown, her hair loose, a wild and beautiful vision he knew he'd never forget.

He'd brought them all close to disaster by climbing to the rim, and she'd averted that disaster. She must think him an incompetent bungler. But, damn it, he'd have subdued the warrior himself if she'd given him the chance. Never mind the problem of what to do with the man afterward. He resented not having had the chance.

I'll show her what I'm made of yet, he vowed, prove to her a city man can be as capable as any Minnesota yokel. To tell the truth, he no longer felt like a city man. Philadelphia seemed as far away as the moon and his life there like something he'd only dreamed.

Cub woke before she did, coming awake instantly, his bright gaze sweeping all around them. Bramwell, unused to children, wondered if this was a characteristic of childhood, or something Cub did solely because he was an Indian.

Cub's eyes settled on Bramwell and he smiled, hunching over to sit beside him. Pointing toward the cow, he made the unmistakable sign of milking, then pointed to himself.

Bramwell grinned. Cub would soon discover it wasn't that easy. Bramwell urged him to go ahead. Cub picked up the pan, then went to the cow. Bramwell stood to watch. When he glanced sideways at Jennara, he found she was awake and on her feet.

"Cub has a surprise coming," he told her, nodding his head toward the cow.

She looked, then shook her head. "He'll manage. Children are natural imitators. Haven't you noticed how Cub trails you, doing his best to become a miniature Bramwell Sumner?"

He was taken aback, gazing at her in astonishment. "We don't even speak the same language," he protested. "The boy's much fonder of you."

"I'm a woman. He knows he can't behave like me."

"But I'm not a warrior. I'm—well, I'm a lawyer. God help the boy!"

Jennara laughed. "You're a man, and that's what counts. Besides, you've already proved yourself in his eyes by killing a deer with one shot and facing a warrior unafraid."

He wanted to ask what it would take to prove himself in her eyes, but instead he said, "The deer was a lucky shot. As for the warrior, I had no choice."

"You did bring that on yourself."

Like losing the horse, he thought grimly.

"Anyway, after he saw you milk the cow," she continued, "Cub decided milking's not just woman's work, so it's safe for him to try it."

"Twice now you've routed Sioux warriors by playing on their fear of the supernatural. Where did you learn about their superstitions? From the medicine man?"

"Not entirely. When I was a girl I used to listen when the old Dakota women and the old Dakota men told stories to the children in the winter. That's where I heard about Double-Woman. Susanna never liked to go to the tepees, but wild horses couldn't have kept me away."

"Your parents didn't object?"

"Not my father. And he convinced my reluctant mother that I'd come to no harm."

"An unusual man."

"He was. And so is his friend No Cloud. I hope he's safe."

Bramwell raised his eyebrows. "Why shouldn't he be? After all, the Sioux are the aggressors."

"When there's an Indian uprising, after things settle down the soldiers and the settlers are inclined to shoot any Indian they see, whether or not he was a part of the raids. That's what happened five and a half years ago when Inkpaduta's band killed settlers near Spirit Lake in Iowa. For at least a year after that, harmless Indians on hunting and fishing trips were shot and killed without a chance to defend themselves. The settlers and the Dakota have never really trusted each other since. I knew the Dakota were resentful, but I never thought —" she paused and waved a hand upward "— anything so terrible as this would happen. When the soldiers finally put down the uprising, I'm afraid no Indian will be safe ever again, women and children included."

"After the massacres we've seen, you can't blame the settlers for hating and fearing Indians."

"No." She sighed. "I only wish there could be a more

115

peaceful way to solve differences."

"There is, by law. Unfortunately, people don't always abide by the law. Laws didn't stop the South from seceding from the Union."

"No Cloud believes that your law and mine is for the advantage of the white man only and the white man refuses to recognize unwritten Indian laws." Jennara glanced toward Cub, who was chanting to the cow as he pulled on her teats. "What he's singing to her is a simple child's song, but it's meant to teach a Dakota boy or girl to put what's best for the village ahead of what he or she wants. An unwritten Dakota law the warriors conveniently forgot when they began the uprising. Written or unwritten, laws aren't the solution."

"Maybe not, but we'd have chaos without them." Bramwell belatedly covered a yawn.

Jennara reached for the Spencer. "I shouldn't waste time arguing with you when you need rest." Taking the rifle, she added, "I suppose it's futile to argue with a lawyer, anyway."

"That hasn't stopped you up until now."

She smiled. "And it probably won't in the future."

He stretched out under the tree and closed his eyes. "Unlike most other women," he murmured drowsily, "you have the makings of a good lawyer yourself."

Jennara turned Bramwell's comment over in her mind as she watched his breathing slow and deepen. Was it the compliment it appeared to be on the surface? Surely it meant that he appreciated her clear thinking and her logic, qualities on which she prided herself.

It was possible Bramwell felt those qualities were the only ones he could admire in her, unwomanly though he found them. He couldn't think her very womanly. After all, she'd admitted cooking didn't appeal to her and it was evident she didn't dress fashionably. Flirting, a skill Susanna seemed to have been born with, had always been completely beyond Jennara. And when she knew what should be done, she took charge, never considering that she might defer to a man.

116

Why should she?

She'd had several suitors, but they had quickly lost interest when they came to realize she wouldn't change her ways for any man. Who wanted a wife who put healing others before her own household chores? Who'd leave a husband supperless to take care of a sick Indian child? Who called a heathen Indian medicine man friend?

Jennara hadn't cared about any of them, it didn't matter what they thought of her. It shouldn't matter what Bramwell thought of her, either.

Unlike most other women. She had to admit she was different. Since the words were true, why did she mind hearing them from him? Was it because it implied he didn't view her as a woman, but as he would another man?

I may be unlike most of them, but I *am* a woman, she told herself fiercely. I may have learned to think like a man, but I have a woman's body and a woman's feelings . . . a woman's heart.

Bramwell hadn't tried to kiss her since he'd held her in his arms after she'd had to kill the young warrior, and that had been no more than a comforting kiss, unlike the one in the barn. That first kiss had made it clear he desired her. Lust, obviously, but at least he'd thought of her then as someone desirable.

Now he appreciated her clear thinking and logic, but he no longer saw her as someone to bed. Jennara took a deep breath as the truth seeped into her mind. She didn't want the one or the other. If she didn't wish Bramwell to view her as a man, she hadn't liked being nothing but the focus of his lust, either. What she wanted from him was a little of both. Would it be so difficult for him to desire her, yet still enjoy her logical thinking?

Apparently it was impossible. And just as well, because she had no intention of being bedded by him under any circumstances.

Cub called softly to her. She saw he'd been successful and

needed someone to help carry the pan of milk. Smiling, she hurried to help him. What a clever boy he was! She had no doubt he'd soon learn English and could be taught to read and write as well. She'd already decided that he'd live with her until he was old enough to be sent to a boarding school, then to the university. He'd have to be sent to school because if he stayed on with her as he matured, he might not be sure whether he wanted to live like a Dakota or like she did, and might never be happy as either one.

If he went to a university, he'd gain the knowledge to make a wise choice, and if he did return to the Dakota, he'd have skills to help his people. She hoped he'd decide to become a doctor.

She'd rescued Cub and she didn't mean to give him up. His father must be dead. Hadn't his sister seen him fall, mortally wounded? Cub had no other close kin, she'd take the place of the mother he'd lost. She'd teach him another way of life, have others teach him arts and skills so he wouldn't grow up to die from a soldier's bullet.

He chattered to her as she took the clothes she'd washed from the lower limbs of the trees and folded them into a saddlebag. Now that they had two guns, he could learn to shoot one of them, he insisted. The man would teach him to shoot straight and true, so *he* could kill a deer with one shot, too. He'd become a great hunter and a great warrior.

Cub was all Dakota yet, she told herself, but he'd learn there were other honorable paths to follow besides those of a hunter or a warrior. She'd teach him gradually, not forcing him.

"We travel west," he said. "Lakota live in buffalo country to the west. Lakota are friends, speak our tongue."

"Not so far as Lakota country," she told him. "Just to the big river. If the fighting doesn't end, we may float down the river in a boat."

Cub's eyes widened when she mentioned the boat. Excited, he plied her with questions she couldn't answer because she didn't know what kind of boat, or even if they'd need to go down the Missouri River at all.

"I hope the fighting will end and we can go home," she said. "Then you can live in my house with me."

He eyed her solemnly. "My father, too?"

"We'll ask him," she temporized, unable to bring herself to say she was certain his father was dead.

Cub thought this over. He looked toward Bramwell, then back at her. "The man lives in your house?"

"No. He lives far to the east in a place of many houses."

"When he goes home, he'll leave one of the guns," Cub said, his tone as certain as if Bramwell had promised that very thing.

Jennara realized she had a long way to go before Cub learned to stop reasoning like a Dakota.

When Bramwell woke, they ate the rest of the stew and drank the milk. Sage was packed and ready to go by dusk, with Cub perched on his back as nonchalantly as if one leg weren't splinted after all. Jennara reminded herself that Dakota boys learned to ride ponies as soon as they could walk, so it was unlikely Cub would fall off.

With her leading Sage and Bramwell leading the cow, they made their way west along the valley to where it narrowed. As soon as it grew truly dark, they began to climb at a slant up the rise. When they were almost at the top, an owl hooted below them and Jennara saw Cub's head turn to look back.

"Owl's calling farewell to us," she wanted to say, but remained silent. As she'd warned Cub, it wasn't safe to speak or make any more noise than they had to.

Cautiously, her muscles tense with apprehension, Jennara pulled herself onto level ground. Her impulse was to pause and take stock of the surroundings, but since the waxing moon was behind clouds, she couldn't see much anyway, so she continued on, Sage following, then Bramwell and the cow. When all were out of the valley, she handed the reins to Cub and held onto one of the saddlebags so as not to get lost in the dark.

Cub looked up at the stars, then turned the pinto slightly to the north. They walked in darkness, with starshine the only illumination, but neither boy nor pony seemed to need more light. Jennara hadn't yet tired when Cub halted Sage. He leaned toward her and whispered, "Leave the cow here."

Jennara stepped back and told Bramwell. As short search located a sapling and, after tying the cow, Bramwell walked on the other side of the pinto from Jennara, with Cub directing the pony's path.

Before, Jennara had been the leader. She'd taken them over more or less familiar territory, certain she'd come to shelter before the sun rose. But she didn't know the land to the west. Because of this and because Cub was now leading them, she found the night's journey dreamlike, the three of them traveling over an unknown landscape with the pony, unsure where they were headed or what awaited them when they got there.

Jennara, troubled by uncertainty, grew more and more apprehensive. She who tried always to be in control now had none. If she *had* been dreaming, this would be more like a nightmare.

Chapter 9

To Jennara's relief, the first pale glimmers of dawn revealed less than a hundred yards ahead a stand of willows and sycamores that she knew must border a stream.

Bramwell, who'd more than once saved Cub from sliding off the pony in his sleep, took the reins from the boy's lax hands and guided Sage toward the wooded refuge.

Once among the trees, Bramwell eased Cub from the pinto, laid him on the ground, then tended to Sage. Jennara's uneasiness of the night faded as she fell into the now familiar routine of setting up their camp. Afterward she settled down next to Cub and slept. It wasn't until she roused near noon that she discovered what Cub and Bramwell, both awake, already knew.

Across the stream, perhaps a quarter of a mile away, was a Dakota camp.

"Warriors' tepees," Cub told her, which explained the tattered look of the wickiups. These were not permanent dwellings, to be travoised from one location to another when a band moved, but shelters as temporary as their own camp.

"If they're warriors, they'll be moving on soon," Bramwell said after she translated Cub's words.

Jennara thought so, too, and Cub agreed.

But they were all wrong. For whatever reason — care of the wounded, indecision, deliberate planning — the warriors and their camp remained there for two days, days filled with apprehension because Dakota scouts—wolves, Cub called them—might spot their camp, and they didn't dare risk attracting attention by moving on.

By noon of the third day, they'd finished their meager store of food, and Sage had no more graze in the immediate vicinity. Cub, who'd announced the warriors didn't belong to his father's band, had dismissed them as being of any interest and occupied himself by learning mumblety-peg from Bramwell. Now, hungry, he concocted rabbit snares from a short piece of rope he'd wheedled from Bramwell. Cub carefully unraveled the rope into separate lengths of cord and tied them into nooses.

"Even if you catch a rabbit," Jennara pointed out, "we can't build a fire or the warriors will find us."

"We eat raw rabbit," Cub insisted. But neither Jennara nor Bramwell was that hungry. Yet.

Cub set his snares and sulked when he found them empty. Bramwell grew more and more taciturn. Jennara was relieved when they both fell asleep. In the late afternoon she sat with the Spencer, staring at the bedraggled tepees of the warriors and willing them gone. She blinked, unable to believe her eyes when the first tepee flattened to the ground. Only when she saw a warrior strike the second tepee did she decide the Dakotas must be getting ready to leave.

Her relief was tempered by worry. What if the warriors decided to ford the creek and chose a spot directly opposite this camp? Quickly she roused the other two and set Cub to keeping Sage quiet in case the Indian ponies came close. Bramwell checked the Springfield breechloader he'd taken from the warrior in the valley and carried it with him as he came to stand beside Jennara, watching the Dakotas as they mounted their ponies.

Outside of an occasional shout or whinny, the breakup of the camp was remarkably quiet, though everything seemed disorganized until one warrior broke away from the others, wheeled his horse, and headed south. The others streamed along behind him.

"—fifteen, sixteen," Bramwell counted. "And six extra horses. I wish we'd had a chance at a couple of those ponies."

"Be grateful the warriors are riding south," she said, "and not toward us."

Cub hobbled over to them. "I caught a rabbit in my snare," he announced proudly. "Now we cook him."

One rabbit couldn't satisfy three hungry people, but it helped. By evening they were eager to get started. At Bramwell's request, Cub drew a crude map in the dirt with a stick. It showed, in Cub's words, "A big river, then the place of the pipes." After that, "Buffalo home, Lakota home."

Though she'd never been there, Jennara knew from No Cloud that the place of the pipes was the quarry where all tribes came for the red stone to make their tobacco pipes. It was a place of peace. Even ancient enemies such as the Chippewa and the Dakota refrained from war when they came to gather the sacred pipestone, stained with the *waka* blood of Star Man's wife. Jennara hoped they, even though white, would also be safe at the quarry.

The Big River, she thought, must be the Des Moines, because they were still far from the Missouri—the Big Muddy, it was called. As for buffalo country, that was the Dakota Territory, wild and unsettled. They wouldn't venture far into it. Once past the pipestone quarry, the shortest route to the Missouri would be south, not west. By then they should be far enough beyond the raiding Indian bands to travel south in safety and reach the Missouri River somewhere in Iowa.

She shared her knowledge and speculations with Bramwell, checking his map with him as they planned their escape from Minnesota and the Dakotas.

"With luck, two nights to the quarry, three at the most," he said.

At nightfall they set off to the west, Cub once again on Sage. The sky was clear, and the moon, slightly past the quarter, gave more light than they'd yet had for their travels, but also made Jennara nervous. If they could see better, others might also see them.

Sometime after midnight, Cub leaned down to touch Jennara's arm. "Sage knows ponies are close," he said softly.

"Horses nearby," she translated for Bramwell, halting the pinto.

"Where?"

After a whispered consultation, Cub decided the ponies were directly ahead, so they began a cautious circle to the south.

"Camp," Cub muttered just as the scent of smoke drifted to Jennara. "Dakota."

Bramwell understood the last word and stopped Sage. Now what? Jennara asked herself. Backtrack and circle to the north? Before she came to any decision, Sage tossed his head and whinnied, loud and clear. She froze.

Other horses answered him. Bramwell swore. Jennara grabbed for the Spencer. A call rang challengingly on the soft night air.

"Who comes?" The words were Dakota but, to Jennara's amazement, spoken by a woman.

Quickly making up her mind, she hissed at Cub, "Answer."

"Little Bear, with two friends," he called back.

"Are you crazy?" Bramwell demanded of Jennara.

"A woman challenged us. That means no able-bodied men are in this camp. Women won't kill us."

"After what I've seen, I don't put anything past an Indian, man or woman."

"We have Cub with us, it'll be all right," she assured him, hoping she was right. While it was true Dakota women weren't warriors, with the fighting going on, she couldn't be sure of what might happen.

The challenger invited them to come into the camp, and slowly, reluctantly, Jennara urged Sage on. Four tepees stood in a circle, all the openings facing east, the proper direction.

Three women waited before the first tepee, two young and one older. The two younger women held rifles aimed at the travelers. Inside another tepee an infant wailed and was abruptly hushed.

Jennara lifted her left hand heart high in the universal sign for peace. "We travel west," she said in Dakota.

The women looked from her to Bramwell, then up at Cub, still on the pinto.

"The man and woman are your friends?" the older Dakota asked the boy.

"They cared for me and fed me when I was hurt," he answered. "They seek my father for me."

Silence stretched into an eternity while the woman pondered. Finally she gestured to the younger women and they dropped the barrels of the rifles. "You and the boy and your man are welcome in my tepee," she told Jennara.

There were no explanations that night as the woman assigned them places to sleep inside her tepee. Jennara translated for Bramwell, telling him to stretch out next to Cub on the reed mat provided. Scowling and obviously unhappy at having to leave the Spencer outside, he obeyed.

Though Jennara half dozed from time to time, she too was uneasy. In the morning, pemmican was offered and Jennara ate gratefully.

"Don't refuse," she warned Bramwell, who eyed the pounded and dried meat-and-fruit mixture warily. "That's a deadly insult."

"I'm hungry enough to try anything," he admitted.

Cub chewed happily on the familiar food. "I'll set snares for rabbits, Aunt," he offered, giving the tepee owner the title of respect. "The man will shoot a deer if he finds one. He needs only one shot."

She smiled at him. "We travel on this morning, Little Bear."

"I have my bow and arrows," he told her. "I'll hunt along the way with the man."

Aunt's eyes flicked to Bramwell, then to Jennara. "We travel west."

Jennara had guessed by now that this was a camp of women and small children leaving the reservation for safer territory until the uprising ended, and she decided being with the Dakota women would offer some protection to her and Bramwell. "We'd like to travel with you," she said politely.

Aunt didn't reply immediately. At last she said, "You are a friend of No Cloud's."

Jennara was surprised to be identified, since she'd never seen this woman or the two younger ones before. "He's my good friend. A longtime friend."

"You heal."

"When I can."

Aunt consulted with herself again for long moments before saying, "You and your man and the boy may travel with us for two suns, no more. Then we will see."

Bramwell agreed that joining the Dakota women made sense. Aunt offered Jennara and Cub the use of ponies, so Bramwell rode Sage. On the day's trek, they saw no game. At the night's camp, by a fair-sized river, Cub insisted on showing Bramwell how to night-hunt for deer with a torch.

"Deer comes to drink and sees the light," Cub explained. "Deer watches the light, he can't move. You shoot. Kill him."

Bramwell thought Cub's Dakota method sounded reasonable, but expressed doubts about his own success to Jennara before agreeing to try it. Cub, despite Jennara's worry about his leg, discarded the splint before he and Bramwell set off for the river. To satisfy her, he promised to use the crutch if it hurt too much when he walked.

In the deep blue of late evening, Jennara sat outside the tepee with three of the women, including Aunt, who'd been teaching her how to fashion a pair of moccasins.

"You seek the boy's father," Aunt observed.

Jennara decided to be honest. "Cub saw his father wounded by a soldier's bullet. Comrades carried him away, but the man may be dead."

"How will you know?"

She couldn't answer that question. "If we can't find Cub's father, the boy will go with us," she said at last.

Aunt sucked in her breath, a sound Jennara interpreted as disapproval. The two younger women exchanged glances, but said nothing.

"My heart is warm toward Cub," Jennara told them. "And his toward me."

"Who among us doesn't have a place in her heart for a child?" Aunt asked.

The other women smiled, agreeing.

"The boy is Dakota," Aunt said.

"That's true."

"You speak our tongue, you hold us in your heart, but you are not Dakota. If he goes with you, the boy will be lost to us."

"No!" Jennara protested. "I'll see he never forgets his people." But even as she said the words, she realized she meant him to do just that — forget his people — at least until he was educated, until he knew more of the world, until he was mature enough to make his own choices.

"You and your man will have children of your own. Why take ours?" Aunt asked.

Jennara hesitated. How could she reply to that? It was too complicated to explain to the Dakota women why Bramwell was not her man, would never be her man. She didn't want him, and they certainly wouldn't be having children together.

"If his father is dead, I think Cub would wish to come with us," she said.

"It is true he admires the man as he does his blood father," Aunt agreed. "And he accepts you as a second mother. But he is a child and doesn't yet understand what it means to be Dakota."

"With me, he could learn to be a healer," Jennara pointed out. "A great healer who could help his people."

"If his vision dream is for healing, he will follow that path.

127

If his vision dream is for being a warrior, he will become one." Aunt's voice was calm, her tone firm. "Until he dreams, no one knows what he will do. I can't choose for him, you can't choose for him. If his father lives, he can't choose for him. Only the boy's vision dream can show the way he must go."

Jennara held her tongue with difficulty. She longed to ask what was the use of following a dream if it would only lead to an early death — such as the way of a warrior. But she knew the gap between Aunt's thinking and her own would make her words useless. To the Indians, being a warrior was a noble calling. Warriors had been needed for protection of the Dakota villages in the old days, but on the reservation warriors had nothing to do and their restlessness caused trouble.

Jennara well knew the Dakota had been badly treated by the government and they had a right to be angry, but killing innocent settlers was no solution. Older leaders like Little Crow had more sense. She was sure the younger warriors had begun the uprising, though it seemed, from what she'd learned from Aunt, that most of the bands had now joined in the raiding and killing.

Since she couldn't reason with Aunt about warriors, it was best to keep quiet. No matter what Aunt said, Jennara would never believe it was wrong for her to want to take Cub and raise him in the way she wished him to go — for his own good and for the ultimate good of the Dakota, too — and she was determined to do it.

The crack of a rifle interrupted her musings. Another shot followed. Jennara tensed, waiting. Had Bramwell and Cub found a deer? Or had roving warriors found Bramwell?

Aunt touched Jennara's arm. "Your man used two bullets this time," she said, sounding both amused and positive of what the shots meant. "Come, we'll help you cut up and carry the meat back to camp."

Jennara, recalling the Dakota custom where men did the hunting and women took care of the kill, rose and went to get the knife she'd found at the last abandoned farmhouse. In this case, it would do no harm to follow Dakota ways. She only hoped Aunt was right in her belief that the two shots meant no more than a dead deer.

The four women, leading a pony with a travois attached, headed for the glow of Cub's torch down by the river. All the way there Jennara kept assuring herself that Bramwell was alive and safe, not the victim of a warrior's bullet. By the time they reached the river, Cub's deadwood torch had burned out and she searched apprehensively for Bramwell in the dim moonlight. When she saw him crouched over a dead deer, her heart soared in relief.

She controlled her urge to blurt out, "Thank God you're safe!" and said dryly, "I thought I heard *two* shots."

"I do better in daylight." Despite his efforts to speak levelly, elation tinged his words.

He has a right to be proud, she thought. He's more than proved himself as a hunter, he's provided a camp full of hungry women and children with food.

Jennara, not particularly adept at skinning and butchering animals, let Aunt and the other two women do most of that while she packed the travois with the fresh meat. Back at the camp, other women had fires going with smoking racks in place. Before morning, every scrap of the deer had been cooked, including the head, roasted whole in a pit. During the morning, the two younger women scraped the green hide and began working urine and deer brains into it for softening.

The camp broke up and moved on at noon, every belly full. Yesterday Jennara had counted five young women, two women Aunt's age and two old ones. There were six children, ranging in age from a girl of about ten to a several-month-old baby boy. The oldest woman was from a Lakota band living free in the territory and it was to her people that they were going.

"How does it feel being a mighty hunter?" Jennara asked

Bramwell as she rode beside him on the same buckskin pony she'd used the day before.

He shrugged. "I can't take all the credit. If not for Cub, I wouldn't have seen the deer. He's got eyes like an owl. That boy's going to grow up to be the best hunter the Dakota ever produced."

Jennara wondered if he realized he'd said Dakota for the first time instead of Sioux.

"Cub indicated his father trained him," Bramwell went on. "I almost wish I could meet the man and congratulate him on a job well done."

"His father's dead," Jennara pointed out.

"We can't be sure."

"Don't *you* start lecturing me. I've already heard from Aunt all the reasons why we can't take Cub with us when we leave the women."

"I hope you listened."

Jennara stared at him. "Of course not! I told you I meant to bring Cub with us."

"That was before we met these Dakota women and didn't know what else to do with him. Obviously the boy must go on with them and the other children. Haven't you noticed how he's already made friends with the boys? He belongs with his people."

"I intend to raise Cub as my own child!"

"You're being selfish."

"Selfish?" Anger roiled inside her. "Selfish to want to educate an obviously bright boy, to keep him alive until he's grown and has enough knowledge to choose what he wants to be?"

"Why are you so sure your way's best for Cub?"

"I'm fond of him, I want a better life for him."

His eyebrows raised. "You've told me you admire the Dakota way of life."

"Don't twist my words. They can't live as they used to, not on the reservations. I don't want him to go hungry or have a

130

blighted dream of being a warrior when warriors are no longer needed."

"Have you asked Cub what he wants?"

"How can a child know?"

"Whether he knows or not, he deserves a chance to be heard. Ask him."

Why is everyone so determined to take Cub away from me? she thought rebelliously, urging her pony into a lope and leaving Bramwell behind. She'd do what she thought was right, and to hell with them.

When they camped that evening, near the pipestone quarry, she couldn't help but notice Cub laughing as he and a Dakota boy about his age played with a yellow puppy. Later, he went off to the tepee of his new friend without so much as a glance at her.

It's normal for a boy to play with friends his own age, she told herself. I'll make certain he finds friends when he lives with me. Maybe not Dakota boys, though. That wouldn't be a good idea if Cub wasn't living like a Dakota. She frowned. When the uprising was over, it was unlikely any settlers would allow their children to play with an Indian boy, no matter who was raising him.

I won't let him be lonely, she thought fiercely. He'll go with me, I'll teach him all I know about healing. But she sighed, knowing this would be difficult. It would take years, if ever, before Minnesota settlers would trust any Indian again. She wouldn't be welcome, even as a healer, in a white home as long as Cub was with her.

He'd just have to go to boarding school earlier, he'd make plenty of friends there. Or would he? What would white boys raised in white homes make of a Dakota boy whose home had been a tepee? Who couldn't read or write? Or speak English?

Boarding school would be a disaster until she'd had a chance to prepare Cub—teach him English, how to eat with a fork at a table, how to wear white man's clothes, and the many differences between Dakota ways and white ways.

131

I'll see that he's happy, she told herself—somehow.

Later, when Cub came back to Aunt's tepee to sleep, he was bubbling over with excitement. "Aunt says Black Hand is mine," he told Jennara. She knew he meant the pony he'd been riding, white with black marks like handprints on the withers.

"Aunt's heart is good," she said, wondering if the Dakota woman would let Cub take the pony when he rode off with Jennara and Bramwell instead of his people. She doubted it.

Her annoyance flared. Was Aunt bribing the boy?

"The man and I don't ride west with Aunt and the others," she said, choosing her words carefully. "We can't live with the Lakota."

His eyes widened. "Lakota are friends. Relatives."

"Not of ours. We must ride very far to the south before we can return home."

Cub's face fell. "Buffalo live in the west," he promised. "The man can hunt buffalo."

"We can't live with Lakota. Aunt knows this. No longer must we travel with the women."

"My father will go to the Lakota," Cub said. "I'll find him there." His dark eyes were sad as they looked into hers. "I want you to come with me."

"I can't. But you can come with me and the man."

"My father won't know where I am."

Jennara held out her hand, wishing she didn't have to be truthful because the truth would hurt. "You told me yourself how badly wounded your father was. Think, Cub. He may be dead. I want you to come and live with me."

"My father lives! He'll come and find me."

"If he lives, he can come and find you with me as well as with the Lakota."

Cub blinked and she knew by the telltale brightness of his eyes that he was trying not to cry. Her heart lay heavily in her chest. Not for the world would she hurt the boy.

"My heart will go with you," Cub said, his voice breaking.

Before she could reach for him, he ran from the tepee into the night.

"Ask the boy what he wants," Bramwell had advised. Whether she'd asked or not, Cub had told her. Jennara wrapped her arms around herself and hunched over. Cub had chosen, and whether he was right or wrong, there was nothing she could do. She'd lost him.

Fingers touched her shoulder lightly. "*Wakan Tanka* has shown the boy his path," Aunt said softly.

Wakan Tanka. The Great Spirit of the Dakota. Not wishing to weep in front of Aunt, Jennara rose and fled the tepee much as Cub had done.

As she ran from the camp, strong arms closed around her, halting her. She gazed up at Bramwell. "Cub's fine," he assured her. "He's with the ponies."

She clung to Bramwell and burst into tears.

"It's all right," he soothed, holding her. "I'll miss him, too."

His arm around her, Bramwell led her farther from the tepees, to the bank of the nearby creek where the ghostly trunks of sycamores showed white in the moonlight.

"I can't bear losing Cub," she sobbed.

"You can and you will," he murmured, "for you never had him except in your own mind."

"He's a child," she said brokenly. "He doesn't know what's best for him."

"He knows what's right. And so will you." He stroked her hair. "It's difficult now. I understand. The boy's worked his way into my heart, too. I'm fighting the urge to scoop him up and ride into the night."

He *did* understand. Jennara's sobs lessened as she leaned against Bramwell. His hand was warm on her back, holding her close. Under her ear the steady beat of his heart reassured her.

She wasn't altogether sure when his comforting strokes changed to caresses, perhaps the change was in her mind. But she heard his heartbeat double, pounding demandingly,

133

and warmth rippled within her. Putting his forefinger under her chin, he tipped her face up and his mouth covered hers.

The kiss was anything but comforting. His lips urged, promised, sought. Jennara found herself offering — what, she wasn't certain — as her own lips answered his. She understood dimly that she'd been waiting for him to kiss her like this ever since that moment in the barn. Waiting and yearning . . . wanting . . . needing.

Chapter 10

Jennara clung to Bramwell in the soft summer darkness, his burgeoning beard caressing her face, his lips warm and compelling on hers. Behind them, the camp was quiet, the only night sounds a chorus of frogs from the trees by the stream. Nothing was real to her except his firm back muscles under her fingers, the exciting heat of his body pressed against hers, the urgent pressure of his mouth.

Her lips parted and, as his tongue eased inside, an arrow of fire penetrated deep into her body, spreading flames along its course until she burned with an all-consuming need. She'd never expected to feel an uncontrollable desire for a man, but Bramwell's embrace ignited a passion she didn't know she possessed. She pressed closer to him, desperate for more.

Was this what prompted women to lie with men, this wild, chaotic yearning for fulfillment? Always before she'd supposed that only men were driven by lust, and now her body's increasing demand for assuagement frightened her. Women often claimed they married for love, but what did love have to do with this animal passion? Her need was no different from that of a mare for a stallion, and fully as insistent.

In the wild, stallions fought for the right to mate, only the best ones winning. If he were a stallion, Bramwell would be an unsurpassed leader, king of the stallions—strong and swift, with a heart-stopping dark beauty. . . .

Jennara struggled to think coherently, to regain control, but Bramwell's touch sapped her will as his hands caressed her breasts. She moaned, her nipples aching and tingling, a moist throbbing warmth spreading inside her pelvis.

She must stop, but didn't want to; must free herself from his arms, but couldn't put her mind to it. Jennara wrenched her mouth from his to cry, "No, stop!" but found herself breathing his name instead.

"Bramwell," she murmured, "oh, Bramwell . . ."

In answer he cupped her buttocks with his hands and brought her hard against him. A spinster she might be, but her doctoring had made her well aware of a man's anatomy, and she understood he was showing her how badly he wanted her. The realization added fuel to her own inner fire.

Why should she stop? She'd always listened to reason. Must she go on doing so all her life? Why shouldn't she continue on this exciting journey until she reached the ultimate, unknown, but oh so desirable destination? Why not yield to this insatiable craving, and abandon all control?

Bramwell's ragged breathing rasped in her ear, telling her he too was passing beyond reason into the realm of pure sensation.

Are you naught but a mare then, Jennara? a voice in her head asked. Where is the love and tenderness of your secret dreams? She tried not to listen to the voice, but it persisted. You told your father the only man you'd ever have was the one you loved. Do you call this love?

No, this wasn't love. She didn't love Bramwell any more than he loved her. The realization gave her the strength to pull away from him. Before she could say anything, Cub's voice called to her.

"Jen-nar-a."

Bramwell's dropped and he stepped back from her. The loss of his warmth chilled her, despite the mildness of the night.

"I'm here," she called to Cub. She said nothing to Bramwell. What was there to say?

"It's just as well," he muttered, seemingly as relieved by the interruption as she was.

Cub hurried to them. He gripped Jennara's skirt and buried his head against her. She knelt and put her arms around him, feeling his shoulders heave with sobs, though Dakota boys were taught early not to cry.

"Come with me at the next sun," he begged.

She could not. Nor would it be right, she understood now, for her to urge him to travel south with them. Tears gathered in her own eyes as she said, "Keep me in your heart as I will keep you in mine."

"What's he saying?" Bramwell asked.

"Good-bye." She could hardly force out the word.

"Tell him," Bramwell said huskily, "that he's a boy any father would be proud of, and if I ever have a son, I hope he's as brave and resourceful as Cub."

As she translated, Bramwell lifted Cub into his arms and hugged him.

"I'll keep the name you gave me until I earn another," Cub told him, with Jennara translating. "And you will stay in my heart with Jen-nar-a until Spotted Eagle carries me to the Land Beyond."

They walked slowly back to Aunt's tepee with Cub between them and nothing was said about what had happened before the boy appeared. But it hovered uneasily in Jennara's mind until she finally fell asleep.

The crack of a rifle roused her and she bolted to her feet. She was alone in the tepee and through its open flap she saw dawn heralded by red clouds across the eastern horizon. Hurrying outside, she noticed the children running from the camp, the boys shouting, *"Oo-koo-hoo!"* Peering into the dim light, she made out Bramwell's tall figure standing over something lying on the ground. An animal.

"Your man leaves us a welcome gift," Aunt told her. "He

137

shot an antelope."

When Jennara reached Bramwell's side, he was surrounded by admiring children, including Cub, who was proudly displaying Bramwell's kill to them, saying over and over, "One shot, did you hear? Only one shot."

"I didn't sleep well," Bramwell told her. "I got up before dawn and took a walk with the Spencer. I saw movement, thought it was a deer, swung up the barrel, and shot. He began to run, so I figured I'd missed. I was trying to get another fix on him when he dropped."

With all the women in the camp helping, the antelope was quickly stripped of its hide, and the meat from its bones soon bubbled in kettles or hung in strips on the smoking racks.

"I make a gift to you of the buckskin pony, Swift Runner," Aunt told Jennara when she and Bramwell began packing to leave.

Surprised and pleased, Jennara thanked her.

"You have warmed our hearts by bringing Little Bear," Aunt added, "and your man has filled our stomachs with food from his hunting. May you ride in peace forever."

After Bramwell went to find the buckskin to be loaded, Aunt and Jennara were alone in the tepee. Touching her breast with the fingertips of her left hand, Aunt said, "It is true that advice unasked makes the fire smoke, but I must say what's in my heart. I have seen that you and the man are not husband and wife. I have also seen how it is between you. Marry this man soon and have a fine, strong son with him."

Jennara couldn't think of a reply and was angry when she found herself wondering what marriage to Bramwell would be like. Certainly there was no chance of finding out . . . not that she wanted to! Aunt, unbothered by her silence, laid her hand on Jennara's shoulder for a moment, then left the tepee.

The sun was high and Cub was nowhere in sight when Bramwell and Jennara, their packs loaded, mounted Sage and Swift Runner. Waving to the villagers who were striking their tepees for the journey west, they turned their horses to the south.

"Red sky in the morning, sailor take warning." Bramwell's voice was gruff and she thought he must be feeling sad as she at leaving Cub behind. "That's what the old New England sea captains say when there's a dawn sky like we saw this morning. A storm's coming."

She nodded. The way the clouds were massing in the southwest, a storm was all too likely. Close beside them to the west rose the tall bluffs of Coteau des Prairies and the pipestone quarry. Aunt had assured them that as long as they were near the quarry they'd meet no parties of warriors, so it was safe to ride by day. They'd make time while they could, and if the storm broke, they'd stop and set up camp.

"What makes this pipestone so important to the Dakota?" Bramwell asked.

"They use it for peace pipes. *Inyansha*, they call it, very *wakan*, very powerful and sacred. The story goes that the Thunder Spirit, Wakinyan, who was made from a star, came to earth here when the floor of the sky was split by lightning. The Great Spirit made him a bow from the rainbow and gave him arrows of lightning so Wakinyan could kill animals to eat. He lived on the shore of a lake with beauty and much game all around. But Wakinyan noticed the animals all had mates while he had none, so he grew more and more unhappy until the Great Spirit fashioned for him a woman of sunbeams, Cotanka, the Flute.

"Cotanka and Wakinyan had many children, the Dakota, and were happy together. But the evil water spirit, Witoonti, half-lizard, half-pike, and his turtle wife were jealous of the pair and schemed to destroy their happiness by capturing Cotanka. Witoonti changed to an elk and lured Wakinyan to the northern wilderness, then turned into a swan and outflew the Thunder Spirit's fire arrows.

"Cotanka, bathing in the river, never noticed the evil spirits lurking nearby. When she started to leave the water, Witoonti and his wife sprang on her and sucked the blood from her throat. Some of Cotanka's blood, spouting from the wound, stained the rocks around the river and dappled the pipestone. Too late to save Cotanka, Wakinyan returned and killed Witoonti and his wife with arrows of lightning. Ever since, the rocks stained with her blood must be used only to fashion pipes of peace. And all the tribes agreed no more blood would be shed at the quarry."

Jennara smiled at Bramwell as she finished. "I really shouldn't be telling Dakota tales in the summer. They're for cold weather, when the snakes are asleep."

"Since neither of us is Dakota, I doubt if the snakes will notice."

A pony with a rider clinging to it burst from a copse of cottonwoods to intercept them. Bramwell grabbed for the rifle.

"It's Cub!" Jennara cried joyfully, halting Swift Runner. She hoped against hope Cub had run away to join them.

Cub reined in as he approached. He looked long at Bramwell, then at Jennara, as though memorizing their features. Jennara started to speak, but his solemn face stopped her. He said nothing as he slowly raised both hands, fisted, to his chest, crossing his wrists left over right, above the heart. After a moment he extended his right arm, pointing upward with his index finger. Then he turned his pony and galloped back toward the village.

"Sometimes it's best not to talk," Bramwell said, his eyes sad. "Cub's signs told me more clearly than words what he meant. He loves us. Forever."

Jennara's throat was too choked to do more than nod. For as long as she lived, she'd never forget Cub. She sent a silent prayer to the Great Spirit to watch over the boy.

As they rode south, clouds climbed the sky, white at first, then taking on a darker hue. Jennara began looking for possible shelter, but there were almost no trees. Bramwell pointed out a break in the elongated hill to the west, a wide, two-mile gap cut into the bluffs.

"I've heard of that," she said. "The Indians call it 'Hole in the Mountain.' My father, who journeyed into Dakota Territory when he was younger, thought in ancient times a river must have carved its way through the bluff. He was always going to make the trip again and take me, but it didn't happen."

No matter how many times her father had warned her not to make her work her entire life, he'd not taken his own advice. In his later years he'd all but given up his favorite pastime — fishing. "Too busy," he said in explanation. He'd been too busy to make the trip west with her, too.

The clouds turned an ominous greenish black and lightning flickered in the west.

"Wakinyan's shooting his fire arrows," Bramwell observed. He pointed ahead to a fringe of green. "Trees. Should we try for them, lightning be damned?"

Jennara knew lightning often struck tall trees. On the other hand, the rapidly approaching storm promised to be one of Wakinyan's fiercest and the trees would offer some shelter. It was no joke to be caught in the open while a Minnesota summer storm raged. The first drops of rain struck her face as she dug in her heels to urge Swift Runner into a lope. "Let's go!" she cried.

By the time she and Bramwell plunged into the grove of cottonwoods beside a stream, the rain was a downpour, whipped into their faces by the wind. Lightning slashed across the sky and thunder roared, echoing from the hills. The day had darkened to late evening gloom.

"Don't get under the tallest tree," she called to Bramwell. "Can you tell which it is?"

"Not from here. Your guess is as good as mine."

They chose a tree in the middle of the cottonwood grove whose trunk seemed smaller than some of the others and huddled with the horses against the trunk while the wind tossed the branches overhead and rain slanted through the heart-shaped leaves to soak them. A blinding stroke of lightning zigzagged down. Before the accompanying crack of thunder, they heard a loud sizzle and the ground shook. Jennara found herself clutching Bramwell's shirt sleeve, the unmistakable burnt reek of lightning hit in her nostrils.

"Close one," he muttered, putting an arm around her. "Evidently Wakinyan prefers his own children and means to teach the rest of us a lesson. I only hope he doesn't mistake us for Witoonti and his wife."

"At the moment I wouldn't mind having a turtle shell I could retreat into."

He pulled her closer. When she laid her wet head on his equally wet chest, she heard a rumble inside that she deduced was laughter. "What's so amusing?" she asked.

"I was remembering how, in March, I mentioned to Ronald that life in Philadelphia could be dull. Whatever my complaints about Minnesota, dullness certainly isn't one of them."

Another lightning flash sizzled around them. Thunder rolled over their heads, reverberating in Jennara's bones.

"When this is over, we're likely to find ourselves surrounded by the devil's thumbprints," he said.

"What?"

"That's what my Scottish grandmother called the black marks made by lightning strikes. Grandma Kate considered the devil a real and ever-present antagonist, evil and mischievous. Many of her pithy sayings had to do with how to avoid falling into his clutches. As a child, whenever I tried to alibi my way out of trouble, she'd warn me, 'Tha canna sugar o'er the divil, laddie.' I've often thought some of my clients would've stayed out of trouble with the law if they'd had a grandmother like mine."

We're not the enemies we were when we first met, she thought. He trusts me enough to share with me some of his childhood. "What got you into trouble when you were a boy?" she asked.

"The same thing that leads me into it as an adult. I've always been plagued by curiosity. If something arouses my interest, I have to investigate, whether or not I should. Sooner or later this leads to trouble. Like climbing to the rim of that valley because I had to know who was winning the battle."

Or this damnably urgent need to discover what it's like to make love to you, he added to himself, tightening his grip on her. I know better, but I can't stop myself. Sooner or later I'll find out, and God knows what'll happen then.

"The rain's lessening," she said after a few moments, easing away from him. He let her go, watching as she brushed the water from her face and began wringing her braid.

Any other woman would have been bemoaning her appearance, any other woman would have looked like a drowned rat. Jennara's face, dewy and fresh, shone with beauty. Her drenched clothes clung to her breasts and her hips in a manner calculated to drive whatever scruples he had left completely out of his mind. She caught his intent gaze and flushed, turning from him. He had no doubt she knew exactly what he was thinking, what he wanted, what he was determined to have, sooner or later.

She'd come close to letting him make love to her last night, and she must be aware that, because of what had passed between them, they no longer could be simply comrades-at-arms.

"We can't get any wetter," she said. "Let's move on."

Less than an hour later the sky was blue again and the sun shone brightly, the clouds no more than a dark line to the east. Their clothes dried on their backs as they rode south. The land rolled away from them, mile after mile of yellowing grass, with the high bluffs to the west diminishing, softening as they curved southward. Except for an occasional soaring hawk, it seemed as though the two of them were alone in this all but treeless prairie country.

Eventually they'd have to climb into the hills, but the

upward slope was gradual, so the ascent was easy enough. When they finally reached the summit, the land to the south and west stretched below them. Yellow westward, but green to the south, with the blue of lakes winking in the sun.

"Iowa," Jennara said, pointing south.

They descended into a river valley and found a wagon road to follow. By the time evening shadowed the countryside, they came to a farm. Smoke rose from one of the two chimneys in a white-painted frame house. Remembering the looted farms in Minnesota, they slowed.

"The vegetable garden's on the end of the house with the smoking chimney," Jennara said, "so that's where the kitchen is. It's too warm to need heat so someone has the stove going to cook, and Dakota warriors don't use stoves."

"Shall we take a chance and ride up to the door?"

"Let's stay alerted while we do."

When they neared the lane into the farmyard, a brown and white dog ran toward them, barking. Bramwell glanced at Jennara and grinned. "I guess that means the farmer is at home."

A man came out of the barn, pitchfork in hand, and stared at them. After a moment he ordered the dog back to his side.

"We're two travelers," Bramwell called, "heading south. We'd like to talk to you." He slid off Sage and walked to where the man stood. "Bramwell Sumner," he said, holding out a hand.

"Peter Moore," the balding man told him as he wiped the palm of his hand on his denim pants before shaking Bramwell's.

Bramwell turned to introduce Jennara, who'd also dismounted, but she spoke before he had the chance. "Have you heard of any Indian raids in Iowa?"

Peter shook his head. "Not hereabouts, ma'am. You can't trust a one of them redskins. We don't hold with thieving Injuns living around here, drove 'em all out a few years back. Reckon it's too far for 'em to ride to make trouble for us like I hear they been doing up Minnesota way."

"I hope you're right," she said.

"Old Towser'd give fair warning if they tried sneaking up on us," Peter said. "But I don't expect they will. The redskins know when we spot 'em around here we shoot first and ask questions later." He smiled at Jennara. "So you can set your mind t'rest. No use standing out here yawping, best come on inside. Ma'd never forgive me if I didn't invite you to have a bite to eat."

Peter and Alvina Moore were in their forties, their two daughters grown and married. "Both of them live away from here now," Alvina confided over coffee strong enough to float a spoon. "Molly's in Bruce's Crossing and Polly clear over in Sioux City. Never thought I'd see the day my girls would give up a farm to live in towns. Molly and Polly's what we named them, only lately the older one's taken on airs and calls herself Pauline." She leaned closer to Jennara. "Which reminds me, dear, I didn't catch your name."

"Oh, I'm sorry. It's Jennara Gr—"

"Jennara. Now there's a right pretty name. I got to remember it for Molly. She's in the family way." Alvina glanced toward Bramwell. "That last piece of pie's a-setting there just a-begging you to eat it."

Bramwell admitted he had room for one more slice of Alvina's blackberry pie, and while she was serving it he asked, "By any chance did another couple ride past here in the last couple of weeks? Heading south like we are?"

"The woman had blond hair, very pretty," Jennara added. "The man was blond, too, with a mustache."

"No, can't say we saw anyone like that," Peter said.

"Well," Alvina put in, "what about that artist fellow Molly told us about? The one who drew her picture 'cause she bought a bottle of the doctor's cure-all. Good likeness, he drew. She said he had a mustache."

"That was in town," Peter said.

Alvina frowned at him as if to say she knew very well it was

145

in town. "He was traveling with Dr. Phineas's medicine wagon where Molly bought that rheumatiz cure."

"How about the blond woman?" Jennara said.

Alvina's frown deepened. "Seems to me Molly mentioned a lady singer, didn't she, Pa?"

Peter shrugged.

"Men! They never listen." Alvina looked at Jennara. "Molly must've told me, otherwise I wouldn't be knowing it to say."

"Did you say your daughter Molly lives in Bruce's Crossing?" Bramwell asked. "How far away is that?"

"Town's close to a day's trip from here," Peter told him.

"When was this Dr. Phineas's medicine wagon in Bruce's Crossing?" Bramwell persisted.

Alvina thought a moment. " 'Bout a week ago, wasn't it, Pa?"

"Something like that," he admitted. "On the way to St. Louis, in Missouri, that wagon." He shot Alvina a triumphant glance, delighted to prove her wrong about him not listening. "Les—that's Molly's husband—said so himself."

"It was most kind of you to fix us supper," Jennara said. "I don't know when coffee's tasted so good to me."

"Where I come from, they don't bake blackberry pies like yours," Bramwell added. "Unsurpassable."

Alvina beamed. "No trouble 'tall. Does us a world of good to have company once in a while."

"We do have to be getting on," Jennara said.

Alvina's eyes widened. "At night? I won't hear of it! After all your camping, what you need is a night's sleep in a comfortable bed. Without the girls here, we've got a spare room nobody's using. I'd be upset if you didn't stay overnight with us."

Jennara reddened. "I don't think you under—"

"She doesn't want to put you to any trouble," Bramwell cut in hastily, realizing what had happened. In the beginning he hadn't had a chance to introduce Jennara to Peter as Miss

Gray, and later Alvina had cut Jennara short before hearing her last name. The Moores would assume any man and woman traveling together were married, and they had no reason to suppose Jennara and Bramwell weren't, hence the offer of the spare room.

"It's our pleasure having you here," Alvina said, rising. "I'll just go up and air the bed."

"But—" Jennara began.

"My dear," Bramwell said to her, "I know you won't rest until you check on the horses. Why don't we go to the barn and do that now?" As he spoke, he got to his feet and pulled back her chair, helping her up. "It'll take but a few minutes."

Peter nodded approvingly. "I gave 'em a quick rubdown, but you know your horses better than me. I'll just put the scraps together for the pigs." He left the table.

"Come outside with me and we'll talk," Bramwell said into Jennara's ear, pulling her with him toward the back door.

As soon as they were out of the house, she jerked free and turned on him. "We can't share a room," she sputtered. "Even if Alvina does believe we're married."

"Why not? We've been sleeping together for a couple of weeks now. What's to make it different if we're in the same room?"

"Camping under the trees is one thing, sharing a bed another. As you know very well."

"We don't have to actually share the bed, only the room. To sleep."

"You did this deliberately," she accused. "You allowed the Moores to think us married!"

"I tried to introduce you as soon as we arrived. Can I help it if they're a talkative pair? If you insist, I'll inform them they've made a mistake, that we're not married, and that you're a single woman. Of course I can't guarantee Alvina won't be upset. It'll certainly change her attitude toward us, especially toward you. We know what's true and what isn't, but I'm afraid no one would believe we've only been comrades-at-arms."

He was counting on Jennara's streak of practicality to assert itself and override her insistence on adhering to proper custom.

"I hope you don't think I'd force myself on you," he added.

"That isn't why I—" she paused. "I'm not worried about you!" she snapped.

"That leaves only one other person. If you intend to force yourself on me, I assure you I won't mind." Amusement crept into his voice.

"I fail to find anything funny about the situation."

"I defy you to tell me you don't look forward to sleeping in a comfortable bed."

"That has nothing to do with it."

"You'll undoubtedly wind up with the bed whether we tell the Moores the truth or not. My choice, depending on what we say, is either the spare room floor or the barn. A couple of blankets on the floor would be a damn sight more comfortable than the barn. And remember, if you insist on telling the unvarnished truth, you'll embarrass and shock our hostess . . . an unkind way to repay her for her generous hospitality."

He was arguing as though this were some important case before the bench, Bramwell thought, a case his reputation rested on winning. Why did it make so much difference? Jennara wasn't likely to allow him in the bed with her anyway.

Still, once he convinced her to share the room with him, there was always the off chance he might also share her bed. And that was something worth fighting for.

Chapter 11

The bed's too soft, Jennara told herself as she turned over for what seemed like the hundredth time. She'd stripped to her shift before lying down, but she was still too warm, despite the open window.

She'd finally agreed to share the room with Bramwell because she didn't want to cause a fuss that would distress Alvina. After all, she'd told herself, she and Bramwell had slept inside the same tepee for the past two nights.

Being closed into a room with Bramwell, she'd discovered, was not the same as sleeping inside a tepee with him and Aunt and Cub. While Alvina and Peter might be in the same house, they weren't in this room, and that made all the difference.

He lay on a quilt on the floor by the window, apparently untroubled by being in the room with her. She didn't think he'd moved once. No doubt sleep had overtaken him the minute he'd put his head on the pillow.

The bed might be too soft and the night too warm, but that wasn't why she lay awake. She kept wondering what it would be like if Bramwell were in the bed with her, his arms around her, his body close to hers. When she shut her eyes she could almost feel his lips touching hers. Almost, but not quite. Would he come to her if she called his name?

She certainly had no intention of doing that. She'd existed for twenty-nine years without desiring a man, and she meant to overcome this foolish need she'd suddenly acquired. If only she could banish every memory of Bramwell's kisses and caresses, the unwelcome cravings might disappear. Perhaps some kind of mental exercise such as naming the bones of the body would distract her enough to allow her to sleep. She'd begin with the skull.

Jennara had gotten no farther than the spinal column when Bramwell spoke.

"What are you whispering about?"

"I'm not," she said defensively.

"You are. It sounded like atlas, axis."

"I didn't know I was whispering. I'm sorry."

"Don't leave me hanging. Why those words?"

"The atlas is the first cervical vertebra—neck vertebra. It's called that because the head's above it, taken from the Greek Atlas, who supported the world on his shoulders. The axis is the second cervical vertebra."

"Why the anatomical enumeration?"

"I'm trying to put myself to sleep," she admitted reluctantly. "I think the bed's too soft. And the room's too warm."

"Strange—I was just thinking the floor's too hard."

Jennara sat up and stared at his shadowy form. "Are you suggesting we switch places?"

"Not exactly. If neither of us can sleep, we could talk for a while. It's tolerably cool here by the window."

She thought over his offer. Talking was better than tossing and turning. Undoubtedly it *was* cooler next to the window. But was it wise to be any closer to him than she was already? Especially since she was in her shift. Not that he could see much in the darkness of the room.

"I'll sit on one side of the quilt and you can have the other," he added, as though reading her mind. "I'd like you to promise me, though, you won't discuss the remaining vertebrae. Two are enough for one night."

Jennara smiled, her mind made up. There was no harm in sitting by the window talking to Bramwell. He'd outlined the rules, and from what she'd learned of him, he'd abide by them. If she did, too, it would be no different from sitting together at a night's camp among the trees.

Slipping from the bed, she walked toward the window, seeing Bramwell sit up as she approached. She sat on the opposite end of the quilt, her legs curled to the side.

"I actually feel a breeze," she said.

"That's an advantage of having the floor. You can choose the coolest spot."

"Do you think it's really Ronald and Susanna traveling with this Dr. Phineas's medicine wagon?" she asked after a moment.

"It's a strong possibility."

"Ronald does draw unusually discerning likenesses. And Susanna is a singer. I hope they're with the wagon, but I'm afraid to let myself believe they might be."

"Ronald usually lands on his feet. I won't be surprised to find him with the wagon."

Jennara, listening to what Bramwell wasn't saying, commented, "You don't sound especially pleased."

"Am I supposed to be pleased he's led me on this not-so-merry chase, at a most inconvenient time? And damn near got me killed and scalped in the bargain?"

"He could have been killed himself. They *both* could have. I've been so worried."

"Yes, I know you're fond of Ronald." He flung the

words at her.

Taken aback, she countered, "Aren't *you* fond of him? He's your stepbrother, after all."

"I prefer him alive to dead, if that's what you mean. And unmarried to married, I might remind you."

Jennara took a moment to quell her rising anger. Getting into an argument with Bramwell might keep her awake for the rest of the night. And admittedly, she had her own reasons for believing the marriage might be ill-advised. Her approval or disapproval depended on what answer Susanna gave to the question she meant to ask as soon as they caught up with the pair.

"If the two of them are with Dr. Phineas," she pointed out, "we should catch up to them before they reach St. Louis. Our horses are certain to be faster than the medicine wagon, and Dr. Phineas probably stays a day or two in each community to sell his potions." She leaned toward him. "Oh, Bramwell, I couldn't bear it if it turns out Ronald and Susanna aren't with that wagon."

Bramwell's control, frayed by his anger over her obvious concern for Ronald, snapped. He slid across to Jennara and grasped her shoulders.

"You don't want Ronald to marry your sister any more than I do. You still want him for yourself."

Outraged, she struggled, and his grip tightened.

"I'll wager you didn't fight Ronald," he muttered, pulling her to him and fitting his mouth over hers in a bruising, punishing kiss.

The feel of her warm, bare flesh under his hands banished the last remnants of his reason. Ignoring her attempts to twist free, he bore her backward until she sprawled on the quilt, his body half covering hers. Her full breasts, covered only by a layer of thin cloth, pressed

152

against his bare chest, their softness maddening.

His fingers found the bottom of her shift, pulling it up, the better to seek the secret of her womanhood. She gasped when he touched her there and then abruptly stopped struggling, but not to respond. Her body lay rigid and still under his caresses.

Bramwell, driven to a frenzy by his angry need for her, pushed her legs apart with his knee. He couldn't stop . . . he *must* have her! As he rose over her, she turned her face from him. Suddenly he knew he couldn't take her against her will. He'd never done that to any woman, and he wasn't about to start now.

Letting her go, he pushed himself to his feet, stalked across the room, and yanked open the door. At the last moment he remembered not to slam it behind him, lest he wake the Moores. Instead he closed the door with exaggerated care and descended the stairs. He'd spend the rest of the night in the barn, where he should have gone in the first place.

Damn the woman! She'd lain with his stepbrother, he was certain, the two of them alone in her house for months. She'd schemed and connived to marry Ronald for the Claridge money. She was nothing but a little bitch, a slut willing to sell herself for the promise of money, but thinking herself above lying with him. The hell with her! He had half a mind to saddle a horse and go after Ronald tonight, leave her behind.

But both horses were hers, and he'd left his boots and shirt in the bedroom. How could he go back and retrieve them? And they hanged men for stealing horses . . . not that he worried about being hanged, but it was beneath his dignity to take one of the ponies without her permission.

Well, he sure as hell didn't need anyone's permission to sleep in the barn.

As he started to let himself out of the house, Towser began to bark at him. The damn dog would wake the Moores. Bramwell cursed and retreated inside. What now? He could hardly bed down in the Moores' parlor. Everything was conspiring to force him back to the room where Jennara waited, but he was damned if he'd go. He sat on the bottom step, brooding.

How had he fallen so low as to be jealous of his stepbrother? Jealous because Jennara had given herself to Ronald and wouldn't to him. What was there about the woman that drove him to such straits?

Night before last, she'd done little to discourage him, but he had to admit she hadn't deliberately tried to entice him, either. It'd been a mistake to be alone in that room with her tonight. She'd tried to tell him so, but he hadn't wanted to listen. Now she had every right to hate him, after the way he'd behaved. If she preferred Ronald, that was her right; she'd certainly done nothing to warrant being threatened with rape.

Bramwell grimaced. There was no excuse for his behavior. If they must go on together, and he didn't see any way to avoid it, he'd have to apologize . . . the sooner the better.

He rose and slowly mounted the stairs. Hesitating outside the door, he finally knocked lightly.

"Who is it?" Jennara asked from the other side, her voice muffled.

"A most apologetic man. May I come in?"

She was silent so long that he thought she wasn't going to answer. "Jennara?"

"Come in if you must," she said at last. Begrudgingly,

154

he thought. What had he expected? To be welcomed with open arms?

He eased the door open. Jennara was a dim shape on the bed. Sitting up, he judged, with a coverlet wrapped around her. Entering, he shut the door behind him and stood beside it.

"I'm sorry," he muttered. "There's no excuse for what I did. It won't happen again."

He half expected her to snap at him, something to the effect that she certainly hoped not. But she said nothing, huddling under her cover. It struck him with horror that in his urgency to subdue her, he might have hurt her. He took a step toward the bed, intending to comfort her.

"Are you all right?" he asked, then decided that wasn't quite the way to put it. "I mean—do you need anything?" No, damn it, still not what he wanted to say.

Bramwell took a deep breath. "I didn't mean to hurt you," he said softly.

"Then what *did* you mean?" Jennara's voice sounded strained.

How the hell was he supposed to answer that? She could be the most maddening woman. "All I know is I went off my head for a few minutes," he told her. "I'll make sure I don't again."

"How?"

She was maddening and persistent. "Don't you think I have any control over myself?" he demanded. When she remained silent, he decided maybe she didn't. He hadn't demonstrated much control tonight. There was no way to prove himself to her. "I guess you'll just have to take my word for it."

"Your word." Her voice was without inflection.

Without intending to, he advanced another two steps

155

toward the bed before he managed to halt himself. She was the last person in the world he'd wanted to hurt, but he had. He longed to put his arms around her and hold her gently, to comfort her. He knew better than to try.

"I'll collect my clothes and the quilt and sleep on the landing," he said.

"That won't be necessary. I see no reason to upset Alvina by changing our sleeping arrangements. I accept your apology. I'll take you at your word. Good night." Jennara stretched out on the bed, the coverlet still wrapped about her. He wasn't sure, but he thought she had her back to the window, so she'd be turned away from him once he lay down.

He walked to the quilt on the floor by the window and eased onto it, finding nothing to say except to echo her good night.

Sleep was a long time coming.

Jennara was up and out of the room when Bramwell roused to sunlight streaming in the window. She seemed her usual efficient self as they saddled the horses after breakfast. But though she talked to Alvina and to Peter, she said only what she must to Bramwell. After taking leave of the Moores, they rode along the wagon trail toward Bruce's Crossing in silence.

"A bit cooler today," Bramwell said finally.

"September weather often is."

He blinked. August was over, summer fading . . . best to keep his mind on what he'd come west to do—find Ronald and bring him home to Philadelphia. It had already taken far too long.

"Any hostile Indians in Iowa?" he asked.

"A few Dakotas live near the Minnesota border, but we're well past there. I doubt we'll have any problem with

156

hostilities."

"Something to be thankful for."

She didn't reply.

Not many choices here, Bramwell thought. He could stop trying to start a conversation and remain as mute as she, or go on introducing subjects to tempt her into speech. Not what happened last night—he didn't want to think about that, much less discuss it.

I'm not going to talk to him unless I have to, Jennara told herself. I wish I didn't have to ride with him, but it's impossible to leave him behind.

She'd hardly slept at all. How could she after what Bramwell had done? His words hurt more than his actions. Why was he so certain she and Ronald had been lovers? Did he see her as a woman who'd take any man into her bed? Ronald had never been so bold as to try to make love to her. Perhaps he sensed she'd refuse, since he was a sensitive man . . . unlike his stepbrother.

How could she ever have allowed Bramwell to hold her in his arms and kiss her? How humiliating to remember she'd even responded to his caresses. She'd certainly never let him touch her again! The one bright spot was the possibility that they'd find Ronald and Susanna in a few days. Then she'd be rid of Bramwell once and for all. She'd never have to see him again.

Even if he became her brother-in-law? Jennara shook her head. If what she suspected was true, Susanna couldn't possibly marry Ronald. The first thing she must do when they found the pair was to take Susanna aside and confront her—away from Bramwell. It was none of his business, only Susanna's and hers.

"How do you suppose Cub's doing?" he asked, startling her from her musings.

157

"Why wouldn't he be fine?" she demanded. "He's with his people, isn't he?"

Bramwell shrugged. "I thought you might be worried about him."

"I think about him, but I don't worry." That wasn't entirely true but she didn't mean to share anything except their joint food supply with Bramwell.

"He had the makings of a champion mumblety-peg player."

"Cut's agile and intelligent. He can be anything he makes up his mind to be." Or that his dream vision allows him to be, she thought sadly. Before they were ten, most Dakota boys went off alone to fast and wait for a vision. It was close to Cub's time.

"It doesn't seem the same without him," Bramwell said. "I was even beginning to understand a little of the Dakota tongue."

Conversation languished when Jennara didn't comment, and after a while Bramwell lapsed into a gloomy silence. In time they stopped to water the horses and eat some of the cold chicken Alvina had put up for them, but Jennara was no more inclined to talk when they went on. They passed several farms and twice saw men at work cutting hay, but they met no one else on their road.

In the late afternoon, Swift Runner pricked his ears and snorted. Jennara, half drowsing, snapped to attention. Just ahead the wagon trail turned to avoid a clump of cottonwoods. Something or someone waited around that curve, hidden. Another rider? Riders?

"Bramwell," she said urgently, slowing the pony as she reached for the Spencer, "there's something on the other side of those trees."

"Indians?" He yanked the breechloader from his saddle

158

scabbard.

"Probably not. But it's best to be careful."

Bramwell urged Sage slightly ahead of her pony. Rifle in hand, he rounded the turn. By the time Jennara came up to him, he was sliding the gun back into the scabbard. She stared in amazement at the brightly colored picture on the rear of the wooden-covered wagon rolling down the road in front of them, not certain what it was meant to be.

"It seems we're about to encounter a balloonist," Bramwell observed.

Of course. The picture was a crude drawing of a hot-air balloon. "My father talked about balloons," she said, "but I've never actually seen one."

When their horses drew even with the wagon, Jennara read aloud the lettering emblazoned across the side. "Professor Alexander Taylor & His Wondrous Balloon."

The man in the driver's seat turned to watch their approach. Dressed in a gold-braided blue uniform, and wearing what looked like a navy captain's hat, he was tall and thin, with black hair and a long curling mustache that was waxed at the tips.

"Are you Professor Taylor?" Jennara asked.

He removed his top hat and sketched a bow. "In person, Madam."

"Do you really have a balloon in there?"

"But naturally. A work of art, pleasing to the eye as well as marvelously functional. Though no more pleasing to the eye than you, Madam."

Jennara smiled at him. "I'm Jennara Gray and my companion is Bramwell Sumner. Are you on your way to Bruce's Crossing?"

Professor Taylor nodded at Bramwell and returned his

attention to Jennara. "That is my destination, beyond a doubt. Once in town, I shall display my masterpiece, my beautiful balloon, for all to see. The daring, for a small fee, may ascend with me in the basket."

"Oh, I'd like to try that!" Jennara cried.

"You are courageous as well as beautiful," the professor said.

"My father believed balloons would open the higher atmosphere to scientific experiments," she said. "Have you performed experiments while aloft?"

"Alas, the scientist is ever ill-rewarded. I do what I can, but too much of my time is taken up with the need to earn a living . . . hence the tethered ascensions for a fee. Ah, but I see you're a kindred spirit of the air and wish to help with my experiments — for you there'll be no fee."

Bramwell scowled at the professor. "I was under the impression we were in a hurry to reach Bruce's Crossing," he said coldly to Jennara.

She frowned at him before turning back to Professor Taylor. "I'll be looking forward to going aloft in your balloon," she told him in farewell.

Once their ponies were well ahead of the wagon, Bramwell said, "I thought you had more sense than to be taken in by such an obvious mountebank. You can't be serious about going up in his balloon. The man's no more interested in scientific experiments than a Dakota warrior would be."

She glared at him. "Are you calling Professor Taylor a liar?"

"What he *is* interested in is getting you off somewhere alone — like aloft in the balloon."

"Every man in creation isn't like *you*," she snapped. "I'm sure I'll be perfectly safe in the balloon basket with Professor Taylor."

Bramwell's jaw clenched as he scowled at her. "If you insist on ascending into the clouds with that bogus professor, you'd better pray the Dakota thunderbird actually exists, because no one else can fly to your rescue."

By the time they reached the small farming community of Bruce's Crossing, Bramwell and Jennara weren't speaking to each other. Molly Moore Urqhardt lived across from the Lutheran church, they'd been told.

Molly, her brown hair curling to her shoulders, wore a dark blue billowing gown that tried, but failed, to conceal her distended abdomen. The Moores would be grandparents in a week or so, Jennara thought.

"Fancy Ma telling you about that artist drawing my picture," Molly said after inviting them to sit on the porch while her hired girl served lemonade. "I wish Les — Mr. Urqhardt — was here to meet you, but he's gone to Ames to pick up a shipment for the store. Maybe you can stay over till he gets back tomorrow afternoon."

"Thank you, but we're in rather a hurry," Bramwell said. "Could you describe the artist who drew your picture?"

"He was blond, like my husband. Not quite so tall, though . . . and he seemed to favor his left leg."

Bramwell glanced at Jennara and she nodded curtly. Ronald's injured left leg had been slow to heal. "Did he have a mustache?" she asked Molly.

"Come to think of it, he did."

"Could we see the picture?" Bramwell asked.

"Sure." Molly turned her head to call to the hired girl. "Helen, bring me that picture off the piano."

When it was Jennara's turn to hold the charcoal drawing in her hands, she smiled. In the head-and-shoulders

161

portrait the artist had caught Molly's friendliness, the bloom of incipient motherhood, and a hint of her pride of possession. Jennara knew it was Ronald's work before she saw the scrawled *RGC* in the right-hand corner.

"Ronald, beyond a doubt," she said aloud, returning the picture to Molly.

"The lady singer *did* call him Ronnie," Molly commented.

"Tell me about her," Jennara said.

"Her hair was more golden than his, and she had the prettiest blue eyes."

Forgetting her annoyance with Bramwell, Jennara turned to him and cried, "That's Susanna. They're alive! We've found Ronald and Susanna!"

"At least we know we're on the right track," he corrected. But he smiled and she saw his relief.

If the sun hadn't been low in the west, with the shadows of late afternoon creeping longer and longer across the dusty road, Jennara would have insisted on setting off immediately. Even the thrill of an ascension in a balloon paled next to the need to find her sister.

"I do hope you'll at least spend the night with me," Molly said. "Mr. Urqhardt would be put out if I didn't invite you. And I'd never hear the last of it from Ma."

"Only if you permit me to sleep on this porch," Bramwell put in. "I prefer being outdoors."

Molly stared at him wide-eyed. "If you say so."

Jennara, who'd tensed at Molly's offer, relaxed. There'd be no chance of a repeat of last night.

"We'll leave early," Bramwell said to her. "Unless, of course, you'd rather stay behind so as not to miss your balloon ascension."

Molly looked curiously from one to the other of them

162

and Jennara set aside her irritation at Bramwell to explain about Professor Taylor and his balloon.

Molly laid a hand on her swollen stomach. "Ooh, I'd be scared to death to go up in one of those things. Do you really mean to do it?"

"It appears I won't have the chance," Jennara said, her voice sharper than she'd intended.

To make up for her unintended rudeness, Jennara made a point of asking Molly about the coming child after Bramwell went to the barn to check on the horses.

"It's our first," Molly confided. "We think it'll be born next month. I can hardly wait to find out if it's a boy or a girl."

Jennara, eyeing Molly's huge abdomen, wondered if she wouldn't be having the baby somewhat earlier than she thought, but decided not to trouble Molly by commenting on this.

Before dark, partly to avoid Bramwell, Jennara went to the stable in the rear of the Urquardt house to groom Swift Runner. The buckskin pony was in fine condition, but in looking at Sage, Jennara noticed he seemed to be favoring his left front leg. Placing a hand on his shoulder, she ran her other hand down his leg to the fetlock. Pushing with her shoulder against his made Sage shift his weight to his off foot. She pulled up on the fetlock and bent Sage's leg to look at his hoof.

Bramwell had obviously cleaned the hoof, but when she gently ran the hoof pick around the frog, Sage snorted and tried to pull his leg from her, clearly showing the pick hurt him.

"He had a good-sized stone wedged in there." Bramwell spoke from behind Jennara, startling her. "I pried it out earlier."

"The hoof's bothering him now," she said. "He favors the leg."

Bramwell came over to examine the hoof. "I don't see any cut. Unless he was badly bruised by the stone, the hoof should be back to normal by morning."

"I hope so."

When Bramwell led Sage out of the stable at dawn, the pinto still favored his left leg and it was obvious he needed at least one more day to recover from the stone bruise. Jennara, impatient at the delay, resigned herself to waiting. At least she had the possibility of a balloon ascension to divert her, she told herself.

"If I didn't know better, I'd swear Professor Taylor put that stone in Sage's hoof." Bramwell's tone was sour. "I suppose I have no choice but to go up in the damn balloon with you."

Professor Taylor had set up his camp on the far side of town. Two half-grown boys who'd apparently been in the wagon when Jennara and Bramwell overtook it were helping the professor to inflate the balloon of varnished silk decorated with gaudy pink and silver stripes.

A small crowd gathered to watch. Catching sight of Jennara and Bramwell, the professor waved. "We are filling the balloon's envelope with hydrogen gas," he explained. "This gas, lighter than air, causes the balloon to lift from the ground."

Jennara stared in awe as the striped balloon, almost half-filled with gas, continued to rise, gradually revealing the basket that lay on the ground beneath it. Ropes stretching from the basket were tied to several trees nearby.

Bramwell left her side and approached the professor. "I'll be going up with Miss Gray," he said belligerently.

"I'd be delighted to take you aloft, sir, but, alas, I fear the basket will hold only the weight of two adults at once. I, of course, must be one of the two in order to control the rising and lowering of the balloon. Therefore, you must ascend alone with me. As must Miss Gray."

Chapter 12

Whatever is the matter with Bramwell? Jennara asked herself as Professor Taylor assisted her into the basket of the balloon. The professor couldn't be more courteous, yet Bramwell, scowling at the poor man, reminded her of an angry Dakota warrior.

Once inside the basket, she dismissed Bramwell from her mind. Going up in a balloon was an unexpected adventure and she didn't mean to miss a moment of it.

"You may wonder why I didn't completely fill the balloon's envelope," Professor Taylor said as he joined her. "It's because hydrogen gas expands in the lighter air as we go up. Have no worry about the envelope bursting, however." He pointed at the open neck of the striped balloon above them. "Expanding gas escapes from there as we go higher. Of course, because the tethering ropes remain tied, we won't rise beyond the length of the ropes, two hundred and fifty feet."

He turned toward his helpers, standing outside the baskets by the ropes. "Start unwinding," he ordered.

As the boys obeyed, Jennara felt the balloon above her tug against the ropes, eager to rise. "How can you tell how high the balloon is?" she asked.

He pointed to an instrument attached to the side of the basket. "By the altimeter. Alone, I've soared as far as twenty thousand feet, or almost four miles. That far up, the air is very thin and very cold."

"Yes, so my father explained. He said there's less oxygen in the higher elevations, making it very difficult to breathe. How he'd have enjoyed going up in a balloon!"

The professor smiled at her. "Since I suspect you inherit your father's interest in the sciences, I propose a simple experiment. I will check the difference in your pulse rate and respirations at different elevations." Without waiting for agreement, he reached for her hand, holding it while his other hand searched for the pulse in her wrist.

Although she could just as well have taken her own pulse, Jennara didn't object. She was too busy peering over the rim of the breast-high basket, gazing down at the ground. Oddly enough, the balloon didn't seem to be rising; the earth seemed to be falling away from them. Already Bramwell was reduced to a doll-sized figure.

"Eighty beats per minute," Professor Taylor announced, releasing her hand. "Near normal. Now the respirations." Before she realized what he meant to do, he laid the palm of his hand on her chest, between her breasts.

"Professor!" she exclaimed, jerking away so fast that the basket swayed.

"Easy," he warned. "It's a long way down. I didn't mean to distress you, but how else am I to check your breathing?"

"By observation," she snapped. "If I'm capable of counting a patient's respiration rate by watching the rise and fall of the chest, certainly you are. Touching is not necessary."

He swept off his naval cap and bowed. "Ah, every day I learn."

Jennara gazed at him suspiciously. Was there the slightest touch of irony in his words? She was distracted by a pronounced jerk of the basket.

"We are at the end of our ropes," he said.

The pink and silver stripes of the balloon shimmered in the sun as it quivered at the restraint, tugging to get away, to fly upward into the blue sky. How strange and marvelous it would be to drift with the winds!

"I can see you wish for more than a tethered ascension," the professor murmured.

"It must be wonderful to journey high above the earth," she admitted. "How can you bear to jounce along in a wagon instead?"

"The wagon, however slow, has one advantage—it takes me exactly where I want to go. My beautiful balloon is a wanton who refuses to be steered and goes her own way. Ah, what man can resist a wanton?" As he spoke, his hands were busy with some mechanism attached to the basket.

Jennara looked over the basket rim at the ground. About to ask if the assistants pulled the balloon down by the ropes or if there was another way to descend, she was suddenly conscious of a change in the feel of the balloon. Her eyes widened as the buildings of Bruce's Crossing, toy-tiny, drifted past below her. No, that was wrong— buildings couldn't move. It must be the balloon! She turned to stare at the professor.

"I fear we've lost our mooring," he said and reached for her.

Bramwell swore as he watched the ropes twist down

168

from aloft, freed from the balloon. He strode toward one of the boys, who, he noted, was unconcernedly winding up the fallen rope.

"He told you ahead of time what he meant to do, didn't he?" Bramwell demanded, gripping the assistant by his upper arm.

"What's it to you?"

Bramwell's grip tightened and he gave the boy a shake. "What happens now? Answer me!"

"Okay, okay. Sometimes the prof likes to sail off with a willing lady. He tells us ahead of time. Then we go and pick up the balloon . . . and him."

"Where?"

"None of your business."

"The hell it isn't."

People who'd gathered to watch the balloon ascend began to gather around Bramwell and the boy. Bramwell glared into the boy's face. "I've half a mind to kill that fake professor when he comes down. Answer me or I may include you in my plans."

"Okay, okay," the boy said. "The wind's blowing from the west, not too hard. I reckon he'll set down no more'n three, four miles away."

Bramwell flung the assistant from him and ran toward Urquardt's stables, glancing up now and then toward the drifting balloon. As quickly as he could, he saddled Swift Runner. By the time he mounted the horse, he could no longer see the balloon. He cursed and headed due east.

"A willing lady," the boy had said.

Whatever his opinion of Jennara, Bramwell didn't believe she was willing . . . not for what the professor had in mind. Damn stubborn woman! Hadn't he tried to warn her? She never listened, but always went her own way. His teeth gritted together at the thought of Jennara hundreds of feet in the air, unable to get away from that bastard.

"If you keep struggling, I greatly fear you'll tip the basket," Professor Taylor told Jennara. "Falling from this height is a most unpleasant death."

She no longer trusted anything he said, but it was true the basket swayed alarmingly as she tried to wriggle free of his embrace. The thought of plummeting from the sky was frightening enough to still her.

"Ah, that's much better," he murmured, his lips seeking hers as his hands worked feverishly to unbutton her shirt. His touch disgusted her, his smell musty, reminding her of long-stored clothes.

He tried to bear her backward onto the bottom of the basket, but she resisted without fighting, holding herself rigid, refusing to bend to fit into the tiny space. Once she was beneath him with no room to maneuver, she knew she had no chance.

Did she have any chance otherwise? Desperately she looked around. There was nothing in the basket to use as a weapon. Above her head several ropes swung. There was also a red cloth bag. Red was thunderbird's color. Red was for danger. Not daring to let herself think how dangerous it might be, Jennara freed one of her arms, reached up, and tore open the bag. Inside was a red rope and she clutched at it frantically.

Still busy trying to undress her, Professor Taylor didn't notice what she'd done.

"Stop or I'll pull the red rope," she threatened.

He gaped upward and hastily released her. "No!"

"Don't try to stop me!"

He stepped back. "You'll kill us both."

"I don't believe a word you say."

"That's the rip cord . . . for emergencies. It tears away a piece of cloth from inside the envelope so all the gas escapes at once. You don't know how to use it properly. We'll come down too fast . . . we'll crash."

"If you don't want me to pull this rope, then you land the balloon . . . *now.*"

As Jennara watched him, her fingers tight on the red rope, the professor grasped one of the uncolored dangling ropes and tugged gently.

"What does that do?" she demanded.

"It controls the gas valve at the top of the envelope. One must let the gas escape slowly, to be sure of coming down alive."

He'd begun to sound like himself once more and Jennara's eyes narrowed. She didn't trust him at all. "Maybe so, but if we don't descend faster, I'm going to pull my rope," she warned him.

He tugged harder on the plain rope and she thought she felt the balloon dip down. She hardly dared take her eyes off him to make certain he was continuing to release the gas, and she regretted missing what was undoubtedly her one and only chance to watch a balloon come to earth.

Her glances below gave her a kaleidoscope of impressions: the silver snakes of rivers, the squares of cleared and tilled fields, the brown and gold of the countryside, the trees like tiny green bouquets. She had no sensation of dropping, but she noticed the trees gradually growing larger. Suddenly the ground seemed to rush past them, coming closer and closer. Watching what the professor did, she imitated him, letting go of the red rope so she could grab the lines holding the basket to the balloon. Following his example, she pulled herself up onto the rim of the basket as it hurtled toward the ground.

She saw a blur of green, realized it must be trees, then felt a jarring, splintering crash. She lost her hold on the lines and flipped out of the basket, and that was the last she knew. . . .

Someone, somewhere in the darkness, was cursing horribly. Jennara focused on the sound. The voice was remarkably like Bramwell's. She opened her eyes. His anxious face loomed over her. He stopped in the middle of a "damn."

"I thought you'd never come to," he said. Her head was so fuzzy she couldn't make out whether anger or worry tinged the words.

She tried to raise her head and winced as pain ricocheted inside her skull. Something had hurt her. What? Glancing from side to side without moving her head, she saw she lay on the ground, a canopy of green leaves above her.

"Don't worry, he's long gone," Bramwell assured her. "If I'd had my way, he'd be gone forever."

Jennara hadn't the slightest notion what he meant, and her puzzlement must have shown.

"The great Professor of Fakery," he added.

Professor . . . the balloon . . . she'd been in the balloon with Professor Taylor and he'd made it slip its tether. He'd . . . everything that had happened flooded into her mind and she closed her eyes, wishing she hadn't been forced to remember. Her head pounded painfully.

Bramwell's hand touched her forehead. "Are you all right?"

Reluctantly she opened her eyes. "No," she said. "I'll doubt if I'll ever be all right again."

"Damn that man!"

"It wasn't him. I mean, he didn't—that is, I made him land the balloon . . . too fast. When I got thrown from the basket, I must have hit my head."

To her amazement, Bramwell began to laugh. When he could speak again, he said, "I always underestimate you. I should have known you'd prove to be more than a match for him."

"You were right about Professor Taylor," she conceded.

"A lawyer's bound to be correct once in a while."

Bramwell helped her to sit up, then stand. She leaned against him, her head throbbing. "Your shirt's undone," he said gruffly. Flushing as she recalled why, Jennara quickly fastened the buttons.

With Jennara on Swift Runner and Bramwell walking, it took an hour to get back to Bruce's Crossing, where Molly fussed over her, insisting she must rest. Jennara didn't argue.

She woke to a flash of light and a roll of thunder. The darkness of the bedroom left her unsure whether she'd slept through the evening meal or whether it was afternoon, with storm clouds accounting for the gloom. Cautiously she raised her head and, though it still ached, the pain was markedly less. She sat up just as someone tapped on the closed door.

"Yes?" she asked.

"I brought you something to eat," Bramwell said, easing the door open.

Seeing the bread, butter, and cheese on the plates he

173

carried made her realized she was hungry. "Thanks," she said.

"I couldn't find a tray." He placed the food on the stand beside her bed. "Helen's gone off on an errand and Molly's resting in her bedroom. She complained of a backache earlier."

"Molly's husband's not back?"

He shook his head. "She's worried that he's had an accident along the way. When I passed her room just now, I thought I heard her crying."

Rain spattered against the windows as Jennara, noting that Bramwell had neglected to bring any eating utensils, broke off a piece of cheese and wrapped a slice of bread around it. "I hope Mr. Urqhardt isn't trying to get home in this storm," she said.

Though she was concerned about Molly's husband, he wasn't foremost on her mind—the way she looked was. Her clothes were sadly rumpled and her hair untidy. She wished Bramwell wouldn't stare at her so.

He reached down and touched her right cheekbone with careful fingers. "You have a bruise there."

She sighed. Bruised, rumpled, and untidy . . . not a pleasant sight for anyone. "I'd give anything for a bath," she said without remembering that Helen was gone.

Bramwell grinned. "I don't mind bringing up the tub or heating the water, but I'm afraid you'd draw the line when it came to me scrubbing your back."

Hoping she hadn't blushed as much as she deserved to, Jennara answered coolly, "Thank you, I believe I'll wait for Helen." What was the matter with her, blushing like a silly young chit at his teasing? And why should the idea of Bramwell washing her back sound so appealing?

"I do appreciate you bringing me food," she told him.

174

"But I'm remaining too long in milady's boudoir?"

She blinked. He was always a step ahead of her.

He reached to her again, tilting up her face with a finger under her chin. He bent and brushed his lips across hers, turned and walked from the room.

Jennara sat for long moments without moving, savoring the kiss, battling a storm inside her that rivaled the one outside. She shook her head and immediately wished she hadn't, since the aching increased. Never mind, it was time she stopped mooning, washed, tidied herself, and made some effort to comfort poor Molly.

Standing outside Molly's door some minutes later, Jennara frowned. The sounds from the bedroom were more like moans than sobs. And Bramwell had said Molly complained of a backache. In her experience as a midwife, storms had a strange way of bringing on births. Was it possible—?

Jennara pushed open the door, entering without knocking. She marched to the side of Molly's bed and sat on the edge. "Does your back hurt worse?" she asked.

"Oh, it's a dreadful pain," Molly gasped. "It just seems to grind me down."

Jennara lay a hand on Molly's swollen stomach and, feeling its hardness, bit her lip. The woman was in active labor. Before she told Molly, she'd best get things ready for a birthing. "I told you I doctor my neighbors in Minnesota and I'd like to help you," she said, careful to keep her voice calm and even. "First of all, where is Helen?"

"I sent her to Pender's farm for eggs and milk," Molly said, her words emerging in little gasps. "The storm—"

Jennara agreed that Helen would probably wait out the storm at the farm. That left Bramwell. "I'm going downstairs to get a few things, but I'll be right back," she told Molly.

Bramwell was in the kitchen, struggling with a coffee grinder. "Never mind making coffee," Jennara ordered. "I need two basins, one empty, one half full of hot water; clean cloths—sheets and towels are the best; a clean knife or large scissors; and a clean piece of string or twine. Coarse cotton thread will do."

"What for?"

"Molly's going to give birth."

"Right now?" Bramwell's shocked expression would have amused Jennara if she hadn't been so preoccupied.

"Within hours. I must go back to her. Do you think you can get—?"

"I'll find everything you mentioned and bring it up."

"Start by heating some water," Jennara suggested as she left him.

Sitting on the bed next to Molly again, Jennara picked up her hand and held it. "Those pains you're having mean you're going to be a mother sooner than you thought," she said gently.

Molly's hand tensed, clutching hers. She burst into tears. "Where is he?" she sobbed. "Where's Les?"

"He's perfectly safe, waiting out the storm somewhere," Jennara assured her. "And you have work to do before he arrives." She had no notion of where Les was, but she wanted Molly's mind to be as free from worry as possible. "Let me tell you what to expect."

Jennara had begun counseling expectant mothers some time ago. She'd reasoned that she'd want to know what was going to happen to her if *she* were giving birth. She'd been pleased to find her teaching calmed the mothers during the birth and made the delivery of the baby easier

176

for everyone.

" . . . So the baby's head comes out first, then the shoulders and the rest of the body. Don't worry if the baby cries — it means he or she is healthy. After the baby is birthed, the hard pains are over, but your work isn't quite finished. There's the afterbirth yet to come. Once that pushes out, your part is over. All you have to do is rest and nurse your new baby."

As Jennara talked, she helped Molly undress and put on an old nightgown. Some of the immigrant farm women in Minnesota used birthing stools, but Molly hadn't one, so she'd have her baby in bed.

Jennara had brought a lamp from the kitchen to lighten the storm gloom. While the rain slashed against the bedroom windows, she felt Molly's abdomen between pains to try to tell if the baby was positioned properly. Surely that was the infant's head low in the pelvis. But then, what was the firm, round object to the left of the mid-abdomen? Jennara's eyes widened as she understood: two heads. Twins.

Remembering how she'd lost one of the last twins she'd helped birth, Jennara's heart sank. It was often difficult to save both, especially when they came early, as twins often did, but she was determined to try her best. At least the two babies explained why Molly was so large even a month before her expected birth time.

Bramwell brought up everything she'd asked for, but was careful not to step inside the room. In Jennara's experience, men, unless they were doctors, never did want to be at the bedside when a baby was born . . . not even husbands.

"Leave the door ajar and wait in case I need you to fetch something," Jennara told Bramwell.

"Is she all right?" he whispered.

"Les, is that you?" Molly demanded.

"No," Jennara said. "It's Mr. Sumner."

"Oh, where is Les? Where is he?"

Bramwell spoke through the slightly open door. "I'm watching for him, ma'am. Don't worry, I'm sure he's taken shelter during the storm. I know I would."

Bramwell's assurance seemed to ease Molly's mind, though she still clung to Jennara's hands with every pain. When Molly began to push, Jennara twisted a sheet around the footboard of the bed and brought the tied ends up for her to grasp.

"When you bear down, pull on these," she said. Looking between Molly's spread thighs, she saw the head of the first baby ready to ease through. "Push!" she commanded. "Push hard!"

Moments later a tiny boy slid into Jennara's hands, small for a newborn but healthy, as his lusty cries proved.

"You have a fine boy," Jennara told Molly. "I didn't want to upset you earlier, so I didn't say anything about the second baby. There's another yet to come."

"Twins?" Molly gasped. "Oh, dear God."

"Don't worry, everything's all right." The worried Jennara hoped Molly believed it.

After the boy's afterbirth came out, Jennara tied and cut his cord before wrapping him in a baby blanket and laying him in the oak cradle beside the bed. Nothing more happened for a few long minutes, though Molly continued to grunt in pain. When at last Jennara saw another head at the entrance to the birth canal, she sighed in relief: no breech delivery this time. But she'd relaxed too soon . . . the baby, a girl, slipped limp and

178

blue-skinned into her hands.

Jennara did her best to clear the phlegm from the baby's throat. Then, desperate, she blew her own breath into the infant's mouth and nose. *Breathe!* she cried silently. *Live!*

"Did it come?" Molly asked.

"A girl," Jennara temporized between breaths.

"She's not crying."

The little body jerked convulsively. Had the baby taken a breath? Jennara wasn't sure and continued to blow air into its mouth and nose.

"Why isn't she crying?" Molly asked.

Jennara, watching as the tiny girl finally gasped and then coughed, said, "The second baby often doesn't." Which, sadly, was all too often true. The second baby didn't cry because it was dead. *Not you,* she told the little girl silently. *You're going to live.*

Taking a breath on her own, the girl twin whimpered, a sound no louder than a kitten's mew, but Molly heard it. "That's her, isn't it? I can't get over there being two of them. A boy and a girl. The Lord's been good to us."

By the time Jennara cut the girl's cord, the baby's skin was as pink as her brother's and her cry nearly as loud. Wrapping her carefully into a basket, Jennara laid her in the curve of her mother's arm. She lifted the boy from the cradle and placed him beside his sister so their mother could admire them while Jennara cleaned away the mess.

Molly, beaming, said, "Goodness, they're small!"

When Les, soaked to the skin and frantic, burst into the room, Molly was trying to nurse the boy. "There's a man here who says you had the baby," he gasped. She pointed to the cradle, and Les stared in total disbelief

179

from the boy his wife held to the bundled girl in the cradle. "My God, there's two of them!"

After a belated evening meal, Bramwell and Jennara sat in two rocking chairs on the front porch. The storm had passed over, and the cool breeze ruffled Jennara's hair and made her huddle into the shawl Molly had given her.

"I think I'm as tired as poor Molly," she said.

"With good reason." He spoke gruffly, resisting his impulse to pull her to her feet and warm her in his arms, for she'd only misjudge his intent. He'd watched through the partly open door while she'd breathed life into a child he'd thought dead. He'd seen a woman who wouldn't give up, who fought her damnedest against death . . . a true healer.

The longer he knew Jennara, the less he understood her. Why was it when he put all the pieces of her together, they formed a picture at odds with what he knew? How could he equate the strong and admirable woman he'd watched a few hours ago with the schemer who'd tried to trap Ronald into marrying her? Was it possible his judgment of her was wrong?

Bramwell shook his head, uncertain of just *what* to believe. How could an intelligent woman, and he knew she was, ever have been fooled into trusting that mountebank with the balloon? Yet show her a sick child, an injured man, or a woman about to become a mother, and Jennara not only knew exactly what to do, but did it with quiet efficiency. On the other hand, he himself was alive because she'd killed a man to save him.

When he'd found her crumpled on the ground this

morning not far from the deflated balloon, he'd first believed she was dead. For a moment he felt as though the life had drained from him as well, nothing remaining but a strange and terrible emptiness. When at last she'd stirred and he realized she lived, his relief staggered him. For good or bad, Jennara had somehow become a part of him. What in hell he was going to do about it he had no idea.

Chapter 13

Molly's hired girl, Helen, had washed and dried both
Bramwell's and Jennara's clothes while they slept in night-
clothes loaned by the Urqhardts. Molly also gave Jennara
a new green gown and jacket fashioned of fine wool,
saying, "I'll never again be thin enough to wear this. It's
not à la mode, my dressmaker's kind of old-fashioned, but
she does sew well."

Les, profoundly grateful to Jennara for the safe delivery
of his twins, insisted that in addition she accept a horse
from him so she and Bramwell could travel on. "Now this
is a gift, pure and simple, not a trade for your pinto," he
told her. "I'll tend to your pony and get him back into
shape for you to pick up on your return."

Late the next morning Jennara and Bramwell set off
again, toward Ames, since Les told them that had been
the destination of Dr. Phineas's Medicine Wagon.
Bramwell rode the gift horse, a bay gelding.

They reached Ames on the afternoon of their second
day of travel only to find that the wagon had come and
gone. After inquiring, they were shown several charcoal
drawings signed with Ronald's initials and were told Dr.
Phineas and company were on their way to Jackson
Heights.

"We should be in Jackson Heights by tomorrow night,"

Bramwell said, consulting one of the maps he'd purchased in Ames. "With luck the wagon will still be there."

They left Ames and by mutual consent decided to camp out as they'd done the night before. Sleeping in the open with Bramwell didn't present the same problems as being in a house at night, but Jennara hadn't been completely at ease. She'd been so aware of him lying nearby that she'd had trouble falling asleep.

Not that she was afraid of him . . . that night in the Moores' spare room had been like a fever crisis—a fearful, frightening peak heralding the passing of an illness. She knew he wouldn't touch her again unless she wanted him to, and she had no intention of ever giving way to her longing to feel his arms around her. Once her temperature came down, her illness was in check. She might not be completely cured, but she'd see to it she didn't have a relapse. Unfortunately, the only sure cure for what ailed her was for Bramwell to return to Philadelphia.

Near sundown he nodded toward a wooded knoll. "Camp?"

She agreed. Now that they had no hostile forces to threaten them, their journey seemed ordinary enough . . . if it could be considered ordinary for an unmarried man and woman to travel together—or if *any* journey with a man like Bramwell could *be* ordinary. Certainly not for her!

"I keep thinking about Cub," he said as they set up their night's camp. "Remember how he enjoyed the cow?"

Jennara nodded. "And how he tried to imitate every move you made."

"He did?"

"Shooting the deer made you his hero."

"A fluke, that deer. I miss the boy. If I'd thought he

183

could be happy in a city . . ." His words trailed off and he shook his head.

"It's always painful to give up something you want very much." She sighed. "Even when you know deep down it's the right thing to do."

He smiled one-sidedly. "Are we still talking about Cub?"

Damn the man. He had her off balance again. She couldn't think of a quelling reply, so she changed the subject. "I've been meaning to ask you what Philadelphia women are wearing these days."

"Wide skirts." He spread his hands to indicate a hoop. "I've noticed the width makes it difficult for them to go through doorways."

"Maybe so, but what do the gowns look like? And the hats?"

He shrugged. "I don't really pay that much attention to ladies' fashions. Large brimmed bonnets, I think, bedecked with bows and flowers. The gowns mostly come to a vee—" he put a hand to his stomach—"then the skirts all fluff out in ruffles and such."

"I'd like to see them."

"What for? You'd have little use for such folderol, living as you do."

Was he implying she couldn't be fashionable even if she tried? He might be right about her having no use for hooped skirts, but that didn't mean she wouldn't like to try one on to see how she looked. "We do have an occasional social event in Minnesota," she said frostily.

"I beg your pardon." He sketched a bow. "Would milady give me the pleasure of the next waltz?"

Before she realized what he meant to do, he grasped her hand, turned her toward him, and placed his other hand at her waist. "Hark, 'Dreams on the Ocean' is playing," he said. "One of my favorites." He began to hum the melody and swung her into a dance.

Jennara stumbled, caught herself, and determined to show him she could waltz, followed his lead. They spun over the grass, between the trees, and around the horses. If she closed her eyes she could almost imagine they were in a ballroom with an orchestra playing and that she wore a green satin ruffled and hooped gown. She looked elegant, she knew, and when Bramwell smiled down at her . . .

Bramwell stopped so suddenly that she fell against him. He straightened her absently, head up, listening.

"I keep hearing this snuffling whimper," he said, looking around.

Jennara, wrenched from her romantic reverie, cocked her head to listen; he was right. She frowned as she tried to identify the sound. "An animal in distress," she said finally. "A young animal."

Without discussing it, they began looking for whatever was making the noise, locating the direction and narrowing their search circles. She was the first to see the half-grown bear cub.

"The poor thing's got his back foot caught in a trap," she said, halting a safe distance away. She caught at Bramwell's arm as he went past her. "Wait . . . he's dangerous."

Bramwell paused, his eyes on the animal. "We can't just leave him there like that."

Jennara bit her lip. "The kindest thing would be to shoot him."

Bramwell shook his head. "He's only a cub, we can't kill him. I'm going to spring that trap."

"You're crazy! He'll go wild if we get anywhere near

185

him. He may not be full grown, but he's big enough to do plenty of damage."

"There has to be a way. You could distract him with food while I sneak behind him—"

"No! You told me yourself how when you were a boy that cub clawed your friend's eye out. This one's hurt and scared, and a hundred times more dangerous than a tame cub."

"I mean to set him free of that trap . . . and not by killing him."

"You're being unreasonable. I don't like the idea of shooting him either, but it's that or leaving him to suffer."

"No. Get some food."

Jennara saw he was determined. If she didn't help him, he might decide to go it alone. Yet she was sure nothing they tried would work. What should she do? "I'll bring the food if you promise not to go any closer while I'm getting it," she said finally, not telling him she meant to bring the Spencer, too.

"Hurry."

When Jennara returned with several slices of ham and the rifle, the bear, on all fours, was snarling at Bramwell, who'd advanced several steps toward it.

"Get back!" she cried.

"He can't reach me." Bramwell turned to glance at her, saw the Spencer, and scowled. "I won't have him shot!"

"The rifle's just in case of an emergency," she soothed. "I brought the rest of the ham."

They decided Jennara would hold the ham out so the bear could see as well as smell it, and circle the animal in hopes the bear would keep turning to follow the meat.

Apparently the bear's hunger was at least as great as his pain, because the first part of the plan worked, the bear turning until his back was to Bramwell. Jennara draped one slice of ham over a long branch and poked it at the bear. He swiped at the ham, knocking the branch from her hand, then bent his head to gobble up the slice.

Hastily she reached for her end of the branch, retrieved it, and arranged another piece of ham for the bear. Bramwell was directly behind the bear now, reaching for the trap. Holding her breath, Jennara thrust the ham-laden branch at the bear again. "Here you are," she encouraged, her voice shaky.

The bear swiped again, hooking the ham slice onto a claw this time. Jennara continued to talk, desperate to keep the animal's attention focused on her, while she fixed a third ham slice onto the branch.

Bramwell, down on one knee, had both hands on the trap. The bear gulped down the second piece of ham. Jennara offered the third, chattering away, not even aware of what she was saying. She reached for the Spencer with her free hand. As the bear grabbed the third slice, Bramwell forced the jaws of the trap apart and yanked it off the bear's foot. He flung the trap from him and it snapped closed with a clang of metal. Jennara, with no more ham, aimed the Spencer.

The bear, chewing on the last of the ham, turned on Bramwell and rose to his hind feet. Though not fully grown, he was almost as tall as Bramwell. Before Bramwell could scramble out of reach, the bear lunged at him, raking him across the chest and right shoulder and knocking him back. At the same time, Jennara fired, purposely high, for fear of hitting Bramwell.

The blast of the rifle startled the bear. He dropped to all fours again and fled deeper into the woods. Jennara, gun in hand, ran to Bramwell and knelt beside him. Four

187

ugly gashes shredded his shirt, flesh wounds. Blood oozed up in them and trickled to the ground. Thank heaven it wasn't spurting—the bear had missed vital arteries.

Praying the bear's claws hadn't gone deep enough to damage Bramwell's lung or reach his heart, Jennara said, "If you can get up I'll help you back to camp."

"He get away?" Bramwell asked as he struggled to his feet.

"I didn't shoot the bear, if that's what you mean." She draped Bramwell's left arm around her neck. "Lean on me."

As they stumbled back to the horses, Jennara supported more and more of Bramwell's weight until finally, almost there, his legs buckled and she was forced to ease him to the ground.

Kneeling beside him, Jennara tried to examine his injuries, but the oozing blood made it impossible to gauge the depth of the gashes. When she slid off his slashed and bloodied shirt, she noticed with relief that he could move his right arm—no muscle or tendon had been severed. Wadding up the shirt, she pressed the cloth against the gashes to staunch the blood. Both No Cloud and her father had given her the same advice. "Keep a wound clean." She laid his arm across the wadded cloth to hold it in place and hurried to the stream for water.

Later, the gashes thoroughly rinsed and the bleeding slowed, Jennara wrapped her clean shirt across Bramwell's chest as a makeshift bandage and helped him put on his other shirt and his jacket. After losing so much blood, it wouldn't do for him to get chilled. She rinsed the torn and bloody shirt in the creek and hung it on a branch to dry.

"How do you feel?" she asked on her return.

"Sore. My arm's stiff."

"You'll have some interesting scars when those gashes heal." Jennara hoped the wound would heal promptly, that there'd be no suppuration with its accompanying fever.

"Stupid, what I did—as you said. But he was only a cub, he deserved a chance."

"You're as stubborn as they come."

He half smiled. "Takes one to know one."

Jennara blinked. He thought *she* was stubborn? "You're lucky to be alive," she said sternly.

"You didn't want to shoot that cub."

For one heart-stopping moment she'd thought the bear was going to kill Bramwell, and she'd known then she couldn't stand to lose him. "When it came to choosing between you and the bear, though, I have to admit to a slight prejudice in your favor." She spoke lightly so as not to betray her deeper feelings.

She must have succeeded, for he said only, "I ought to be able to travel by morning."

Jennara, noticing how the healthy tan of his face had faded to sallowness, wasn't so sure. While the gashes hadn't cut deep into the underlying tissue, he had lost a lot of blood and was bound to be a bit weak for a few days, if nothing else. Still, the bay gelding was tractable and she supposed Bramwell could manage to stay on him for part of tomorrow at least.

But by morning Bramwell was burning with fever. When Jennara washed his wounds, she shook her head at the redness of the skin around them, a sign she recognized as impending infection. There'd be no traveling today. When she told him, he didn't argue and she bit her lip in anguish. That meant he must feel even worse than he looked. And she had no more pulverized bark for a

189

febrifuge. White poplar grew in Minnesota, surely there'd be some in Iowa. Cottonwood was a kind of poplar, but would its bark be effective? Willow grew near the streams here as it did in Minnesota, and her father had sometimes used willow bark to reduce fevers. Perhaps she should try that instead.

It took Jennara a few minutes to locate a small willow tree. As quickly as she could, she scraped a quantity of the whitish bark into a pan and hurried back to the camp, where she'd kindled a small fire. Adding water to the bark in the pan, she placed it among the coals so the contents would boil. When the water had nearly evaporated, she removed the pan, added an ounce of brandy to the concoction, and stirred.

Bramwell grimaced when she insisted he swallow a dose of her brew. "Bitter," he complained. Afterward he seemed to rest more quietly. By evening, though, he was not only tossing restlessly, but babbling nonsense, delirious with fever.

Jennara did her best to try to coax another dose of the willow bark down him, but he fought her.

"Poison!" he muttered.

"Nonsense," she said firmly. "You know who I am . . . Jennara. You can trust Jennara."

"Trust Jennara," he repeated, not looking at her, his eyes glazed with fever.

"Yes, trust me . . . I want you to get better. I'm trying to help you."

"Jennara." Her name was a whisper of sound. "Jennara. Help me, Jennara."

"Bramwell, you must drink this."

With his left hand, he caught at her right hand and she hastily transferred the cup to her other hand. As he

190

brought her fingers to his hot, parched lips, he sighed, *"Jennara."*

She freed her hand, set the cup aside, and eased his head onto her lap. She held his hand firmly in hers and with her free hand lifted the cup. "Be good," she said softly. "Drink this nasty-tasting medicine so you can get well. For Jennara."

She held the cup to his lips. "Drink it up like a good boy."

"Mama?" he whispered, opening his mouth.

Jennara tilted the cup so the medicine filled his mouth. Bramwell swallowed, gagged, then swallowed again. She hugged him to her. "That's my boy," she murmured. She held his head in her lap until he drifted into a feverish sleep.

In the morning, though still sick, Bramwell had returned to his senses. Jennara cleaned the claw gashes, now beginning to suppurate. The skin around them, though red and puffy, looked no worse. She returned to the willow tree and scraped the rest of the bark from its small trunk and from all the branches she could reach, knowing it would kill the tree. Remembering how No Cloud always spoke to the trees and plants when he collected his medicines, she whispered, "I'm sorry you must die to help another to live."

By nightfall Bramwell was able to sit propped up against a tree trunk. "I think I lost a day somewhere," he said.

"Two," she told him.

He groaned. "We were *so* close to Ronald. Now the medicine wagon's at least three days ahead, maybe four, depending on how long they stayed in any one place. Tomorrow I can—"

"I don't care if the wagon's a week ahead of us," she snapped, "you're not moving from here until your fever's gone and those gashes have started to heal."

He started to argue, then gave in. "I still feel rotten," he admitted. "And it's my own fault, I know. I guess I got saving that damn bear mixed up in my mind with losing Cub, if that makes any sense."

"Not much."

He shrugged and immediately winced. "When will I learn to control these crazy impulses?"

She smiled. "Probably never. My father said people were pretty well set in their ways by the age of thirty, and my experience leads me to believe he's right."

"I'm over the hill, so I guess I'm helpless. But you have a year to go before you're frozen into your present mold for all time." His eyes held the hint of a challenge.

Jennara's heart lifted at this sign of improvement in the way he felt. At the same time, she felt a frisson of despair. She actually had less than a year to break out of her mold, if that's what she meant to do. And there was even less time before she and Bramwell would part forever.

If those bear claws had gone one inch deeper, I'd have lost him then and there, she thought . . . he'd be dead.

"Why so sad?" he asked.

"I was thinking how close you came to dying."

"There was a time you wished me dead."

"Not really. Well, maybe for a fleeting instant, once or twice."

"And now?" His eyes held hers.

Why not admit the truth? "I feel differently," she temporized, unable to go further.

"Why?"

"Because I—" the words stuck in her suddenly dry

192

FREE

BOOK CERTIFICATE

ZEBRA HOME SUBSCRIPTION SERVICE, INC.

YES! Please start my subscription to Zebra Historical Romances and send me my free Zebra Novel along with my first month's Romances. I understand that I may preview these four new Zebra Historical Romances Free for 10 days. If I'm not satisfied with them I may return the four books within 10 days and owe nothing. Otherwise I will pay just $3.50 each, a total of $14.00 (a $15.80 value—I save $1.80). Then each month I will receive the 4 newest titles as soon as they come off the press for the same 10 day Free preview and low price. I may return any shipment and I may cancel this arrangement at any time. There is no minimum number of books to buy and there are no shipping, handling or postage charges. Regardless of what I do, the FREE book is mine to keep.

Name _____

(Please Print)

Address _____ Apt. # _____

City _____ State _____ Zip _____

Telephone ( ) _____

Signature _____

(if under 18, parent or guardian must sign)

Terms and offer subject to change without notice.

6-89

throat, but she forced them out — "because when I almost lost you, I discovered I couldn't have borne to."

He leaned toward her, reaching with his left hand. "Jennara?"

She knew what he was asking and she answered by taking his hand in both of hers and bringing his fingers to her lips. Her heart hammered in her chest as she felt him stroke her lips, her cheek, along her jawline to her neck before he took his hand away. She waited breathlessly for him to say something.

"You picked a fine time to tell me," he muttered.

She stared at him a moment. Though she knew better, she'd half-expected a romantic declaration. What he'd actually said was so typical of him that it amused her. Unable to help herself, she burst into laughter.

He raised his eyebrows. "I warn you, you've given me a powerful incentive to heal quickly."

That sobered her. In his own way he'd made a declaration, one of intent, a declaration that both excited and frightened her. He meant to lead her into a strange, new territory, a place she'd never thought to enter, much less explore. On that journey he'd lead the way because she had no map, no compass, no landmarks. She'd have to place herself in his hands, to trust him.

But could she really trust Bramwell? She didn't know.

"I think this pact ought to be sealed with a kiss," he told her. "Under the circumstances, you'll have to do the honors."

Jennara, feeling awkward and shy, leaned to him and touched her lips to his. His hand came up to hold her head as he deepened her tentative kiss. The touch of his tongue inside her mouth set up a quivering warmth within her. When he finally released her she was trembling, both from her innermost feelings and from the sense that she'd committed herself to an unknown future, one in which she'd have no control.

He smoothed her hair, saying softly, "Don't be afraid. I'll never hurt you."

She thought of how they'd waltzed as he hummed "Dreams on the Ocean." The song had been appropriate. When he held her she felt as though she was being carried away by soft and dreamy waves, drifting over endless seas of wonder. It was fine as long as she remembered that the ocean was deep and dangerous as well. Drawing away from Bramwell, she made an effort to bring them both back to reality.

"Do you like music?" she asked, choosing a topic at random.

"Moderately."

"I'm not the musical one in my family. My mother was and so is Susanna."

"Your gift is healing—and compassion. I don't know if I have a particular talent, unless it's for reason. And I'd say that's a function of the intellect rather than a gift."

"I'm not so certain."

"Whether I'm good at reasoning, or whether it's a gift?"

"Exactly what do you mean by reason?"

"I was thinking of my law practice. Law is based on reason, yet most laws can be turned and twisted in the hands of a skillful attorney so reason and even justice are left by the wayside. It's a sad commentary on the legal profession."

"I don't believe you'd twist the law."

He shook his head. "I'd like to believe that, too, but I've been guilty at times and allowed my talent for reason to go astray—a betrayal of the spirit of the law. No man

194

enjoys thinking of himself as a betrayer."

"Maybe you expect too much of yourself. All too often, no matter how hard I try or what medicines I use, the patient gets worse . . . or dies. It's hard to accept, but there's no choice."

Bramwell grinned. "I count myself lucky to be one of your successes."

"You're lucky to be alive and you know it! If freeing that bear cub is an example of your reason, I'm not so sure I'd count reason as one of your talents."

"Maybe I meant persistence."

"Another word for that is stubbornness."

"As I recall, we began as two stubborn people at cross-purposes. We've come a long way."

Jennara thought to herself that the journey was far from over. They hadn't found Ronald and Susanna yet, nor had they finishing traveling their own private road . . . and where that would end was uncertain.

"You should rest," she told Bramwell.

"I seem to recall lying with my head in your lap," he said. "Was I dreaming?"

"No."

He said nothing more, but continued to look at her until she realized he was waiting. She could think of no reason not to offer her lap as a pillow once again.

Jennara soon discovered it was far different now that Bramwell was awake and in possession of his senses. She found having his head in her lap far more intimate as the warmth of him seeped through her skirt to tingle along the flesh of her thighs. His eyes were closed and she longed to trace his features with her fingers but held back, afraid to touch him. At last, unable to resist, she smoothed his hair back from his forehead.

"I think I got you mixed up with my mother when I had that fever," he said drowsily. "Not that you remind me of her — except for that awful-tasting medicine you forced down my throat. She believed the worse medicine tasted, the better it was for you."

"You called me 'Mama' once."

Without opening his eyes, he reached for her hand and brought it from his forehead to his lips. "That's not what I want, Jennara," he murmured, his breath warm against her fingers. "I don't need mothering from you. But you know that, don't you? You know what I need. . . ." His words trailed off, his breathing deepened, and he slept, still holding her hand to his face.

She watched him, her own thoughts in turmoil. Had she only imagined they'd exchanged a promise? No, for he'd insisted on the kiss to seal it. What exactly had she promised, other than to trust him?

She realized now that her tumultuous emotions resulted from more than the simple combination of a man and a woman alone together. She could have made a similar journey with, say, Ronald, and never felt this way. In fact, she didn't believe any man except Bramwell could unsettle her senses so that she wasn't sure of what she was doing.

Everything about him fascinated her, even his faults. She eased her hand from where he held it against his lips and gently touched his hair. What, she wondered fearfully yet eagerly, would happen between them next?

Chapter 14

Bramwell roused to hear the chatter of birds. He opened his eyes to predawn gloom and the flurry of wings as a flock of gray-brown birds fluttered from one tree to another, apparently without purpose. Gathering to fly south, he thought, feeling for the first time an early-morning chill to the air. The flocking birds and the changing weather were two warnings that fall was close at hand.

He eased to a sitting position and turned to look for Jennara, wincing when he moved his right shoulder. She lay on her side facing him, a blanket over her, still asleep. With her hair half unbraided, she looked like a girl, young and defenseless. Conflicting impulses warred within him. He wanted to gather her into his arms and hold her protectively, keeping her from all harm. At the same time passion rose in him, the desire to make her his, here and now.

He leaned to her, his fingers touching a strand of her hair. Her eyelids fluttered and opened. She blinked, then smiled. He smoothed her hair, his fingers undoing the rest of her braid, then combing though the long, silky tresses. Her hair clung to his hand.

197

Moving closer, Bramwell stretched out on his left side next to her. At close range her eyes were neither green nor brown, and he marveled at how her irises were intricately flecked with both colors. Fascinating eyes, changing with her moods, they gazed into his without shame, clear and honest. Forgetting about the stiffness in his right shoulder, he reached for her and winced, cursing inwardly. Would this damned injury ever heal?

Jennara reached a hand to touch him and he caught it, pulling her to him. Encircling her with his left arm, he rolled onto his back so that she lay partly atop him, her face poised above his.

"Kiss me," he murmured.

The hesitant touch of her lips on his sent a thrill through him. Jennara retained an innocence that both aroused and frustrated him. Why couldn't she give him what he so desperately wanted?

He deepened the kiss and felt her quiver in his embrace, her breath quickening. Her response fired his passion and he tightened his hold, feeling her soft breasts press against the side of his chest. He tasted the sweetness of her skin, trailing kisses along her throat to where her shirt opened in a vee. He eased his hand to cover her breast and her moan made the breath rasp in his throat.

"You taste so good," he whispered into her ear, touching his tongue to its delicate whorls.

She shivered, clinging to him, her fingers stroking through his hair.

"I want to touch you, Jennara," he murmured. "Help me. Take off your shirt."

She pulled away so quickly he thought he'd frightened her into flight, but she stayed next to him, sitting, her eyes wide and questioning. He sat up and gently caressed her breast. When he felt her nipple peak under his palm, he said, "You do want me to touch you. Take off your shirt."

Slowly she reached for the buttons. When they were undone she pulled the shirt over her head and dropped it on the grass. Her erect nipples were clearly visible through the thin fabric of her low-necked shift. "You're so beautiful," he breathed.

When he slid the shift from her shoulders and brought his mouth to her bared breasts, she arched against him, holding his head to her. He was fully aroused, the taste and feel of her stoking him almost past endurance.

At the moment he didn't care what had happened in the past. This was now, Jennara was here with him, her soft sighs and moans told him she wanted him as much as he wanted her, and he was determined to make love to her.

Jennara, her fingers tangled in Bramwell's hair while his lips and tongue caressed her breasts, thought she'd die from the intense pleasure. At the same time she felt an ever-mounting inner tension that demanded release.

When he tried to undo the buttons of her skirt, she willingly helped him, wriggling free of the skirt and her undergarment, pressing against him, kissing him, holding him to her. His hands stroked her back, her hips, along her thighs, his fingers probing between, making her gasp in need.

The coiling inside her grew ever tighter until she ached for fulfillment. *"Please,"* she whispered, *"please."*

He pulled free to remove his trousers, his movements awkward because of his stiff shoulder, and she reached to help him, trembling with anticipation when she felt the hot strength of his manhood under her fingers. She heard Bramwell draw in his breath at her touch and she took her hand away, afraid she'd hurt him.

"Don't stop," he said hoarsely.

His body, so different from hers, fascinated her. Though she'd seen naked men before, they'd been ill and in need of doctoring. Bramwell, throbbing under her hand, wasn't the same, not the same at all. She urged him to her, needing the man-woman joining she knew about but had never experienced, wanting it, wanting him because she loved him. Wrong or right, it didn't matter . . . love gave you no choice.

She felt his hardness gently probing into her own warm moistness and his touch dazzled her. When she opened to him, he drew back and probed again and again, driving her wild with need until at last she felt the full wonder of him. She gasped, tensing for an instant, unsure. He stopped abruptly and started to withdraw, but she held him to her with all her strength. Her uncertainty was replaced with an overwhelming desire to meld herself to him completely. Instinct showed her how to begin moving in a fervent, timeless rhythm, a rhythm he matched, making her feel as she'd never felt before, taking her to a strange, tantalizing place.

She couldn't think, nothing existed but what was happening inside her, nothing but her body, joined to Bramwell's in love and passion. Then, suddenly, in a wonderfully tender explosion, she was whirled away, higher than any balloon could go, out of herself, out of time.

When she came back to earth, she lay in Bramwell's arms, her head on his shoulder, content with herself, with him and with the world.

"You didn't tell me," he said.

She hated to speak, to break the spell.

"Why didn't you?" he persisted.

Sighing, she asked, "Tell you what?"

"That I was the first man to make love to you."

Jennara considered. It seemed to her she had, in so many ways, but evidently Bramwell had needed a more tangible statement. "Would you have believed me?" she countered.

He was silent for so long that she stirred, wanting to look at him. He held her so she couldn't move.

"Stay still," he said. "For a man of reason, I admit to being unreasonably dense at times. In your own way you told me. I refused to listen."

"I have my faults, but I'm not a liar."

"At this moment I can't believe you have a single, solitary fault. You're a flawless woman—beautiful, desirable, and mine."

A thrill shot through her at his words. She could hardly believe he thought her beautiful, but she couldn't deny he'd made her feel that way. And she *was* his, as much as any person could belong to another.

He hadn't said he loved her. But then, she hadn't told him in so many words, either.

"No Cloud would say I dosed you with love medicine instead of willow bark," she told him.

"Whatever it was, you don't hear me complaining," he said drowsily.

She wanted to stay where she was and never move from his arms, but after a time he fell asleep and she remembered how sick he'd been. He needed rest. Carefully easing away, she stood and sought her clothes, preparing to bathe in the stream. She looked down at him and smiled. How different this bearded Bramwell looked compared with the man who'd accosted her in her house last month!

Her smile faded as she realized how pale he was, with shadows under his eyes. He hadn't fully recovered from his injuries yet, and needed more time to rest. She made up her mind they wouldn't travel today, no matter how much he insisted. She knew what was best for him and determined to see that he got it.

After her bath, she put on the white gown and washed her other clothes in the stream. Quietly retrieving Bramwell's trousers, she washed them along with his underclothes, knowing he was stranded here until they dried. Finding his wide leather belt unusually heavy, she took care to leave it next to him, suspecting he carried money inside a secret compartment.

When her hair was dry, she brushed it and was gathering up strands to braid when she paused. Not yet, she told herself . . . Bramwell likes to see my hair loose. She ran her hands through it and sighed, remembering how she'd tingled to his hands in her hair, on her skin. Just thinking about his touch was enough to start tingling all over again.

Returning to the camp, she started a small fire and heated some water for tea. Breakfast would be tea, cheese, and the rest of the bread they'd bought in Ames. They couldn't afford to stay here for more than one day, because they'd run out of food. But that one day of rest would speed Bramwell's recovery, she was sure.

When the water was hot, she woke him. He glanced around, didn't see his clothes, frowned, and wrapped the blanket closer around his waist.

"I washed your clothes," she said.

He nodded, accepting the cup of tea she handed him, his gaze so intent that she grew suddenly shy.

"You look about sixteen in that gown and with your hair down," he told her.

"I feel about sixteen," she admitted. *Because of you,* she wanted to add. *You've banished the almost-thirty spinster, you've changed me, and I don't yet know what to make of the transformation.*

After the meal, they walked to the stream so that Jennara could help clean his wounds. When she removed his bandage, she was pleased to find the gashes no longer draining and the surrounding redness gone. Bramwell glanced at his chest. "Can't we omit the dressing?" he asked.

"It's warm enough to keep off your shirt, too, and leave those gashes exposed to the air," she said, deciding now was the time to pass on the rest of her news. "By tomorrow you'll be fit to travel." She waited for the explosion.

He half-smiled. "I'll find something or other to occupy my time until then."

"You'll rest!"

He grinned. "Do you really think so?"

Her eyes widened as he unwound the blanket from his waist, dropped it to the ground, and stepped into the stream. She watched in fascination as he sluiced water over his naked body. What a magnificent male he was, tall and strong, with a healthy, well-built body.

He slanted a wicked glance her way. "Join me?"

Despite what had happened between them already, Jennara blushed. He noticed and chuckled.

"I've already bathed," she said hastily.

"I guarantee you won't melt if you bathe again," he

said.

That depended on how you defined melting, she thought. The water wouldn't melt her, true—but Bramwell certainly could. Her knees already felt weak at the thought of removing her clothes and splashing into the stream where he waited.

"Double-dare you," he said grinning.

She frowned at him while her heart pounded in her chest. How could she take off her clothes with him watching her? Yet the idea excited her almost beyond bearing.

"I'll bet you were a boy who always took a dare," she guessed.

"I'll wager you were a girl who did, too."

Remembering how she'd been thrown off an Indian pony when she was eight because she'd tried to ride bareback like the Dakota boys, Jennara smiled . . . Bramwell was right. Turning her back to the stream, she undid the fastenings of her gown. When all her clothes lay in a heap on the grass, she hesitated.

"Do you mean to back into the water?" Bramwell's words were laced with amusement.

Jennara elevated her chin and whirled to face him. Without meeting his gaze, she marched into the stream, careful to keep her distance.

"You're a beautiful woman." There was no amusement in his voice now. "So lovely."

His words gave her the courage to look at him. Something more than admiration showed in his expression. She wasn't certain what, but it thrilled her.

"Jennara." His voice was husky as he reached for her.

Bramwell's hand trembled as he touched her rosy-tipped breast and ran his hand down over the enticing curve of her hip. No other woman could compare to her. He'd never felt like this before, almost worshipful. The water of the stream whirled around his knees as he pulled her into his arms. Overhead, the trees on either bank interlaced their branches to form a green canopy. Birds chirped and in the golden grass insects sang their end-of-summer song.

"Remember the waltz?" he murmured into her ear.

" 'Dreams on the Ocean,' " she said softly.

"Dancing was an excuse to hold you. I wanted so desperately to touch you. Now we'll make our own dreams."

He'd been so wrong about her. She'd repeatedly told him Ronald hadn't so much as kissed her, and he hadn't believed her because he'd known damn well what would have happened if she'd taken him in instead of Ronald. How could any man stay in her house alone with her for months and not go mad if he couldn't have her?

It was clear neither Ronald nor any other man had ever made love to her. He'd been the very first. Despite the way he'd behaved since they'd first met, she'd given herself to him wholeheartedly, an overwhelming gift. More than he deserved, but who was he to refuse a gift from the gods?

He'd never wanted a woman as much as he wanted Jennara at this moment. It was as though he'd never touched her before, never caressed her loveliness, never lost himself with her. He'd die if he couldn't have her.

When she opened her lips under his and he tasted the sweetness of her mouth, he could hardly control himself. Slow down, Sumner, he warned . . . take it slow and easy—don't rush her. Somewhat to his surprise, he realized that more important to him than his own satisfaction was his need to have Jennara experience all the wonder and pleasure he was able to give her.

Her skin was silken cool under his hands and the gossamer strands of her hair, blown by the breeze, floated against his bare flesh, setting his skin tingling wherever they touched it. The warmth of her lips and her enticing woman scent sent his blood racing. The shy yet eager way she offered herself to his caresses drove him wild.

"Jennara, Jennara," he murmured, holding her close against him. "If we don't leave this creek right now, we're liable to fall into the water, and since I won't be able to let you go, we'll both drown."

He felt rather than heard her amused quiver of response. Lifting her off her feet, clasping her tightly, he waded from the stream and eased her down on the grassy bank.

"I wouldn't have noticed if I did drown," she whispered, clinging to him. Did she know, he wondered, how her changing eyes, golden as the sun, promised him delights beyond compare?

He touched his lips, his tongue to each of her breasts and her gasp of pleasure added fuel to the fire already raging within him. He explored her with kisses, tasting the secrets of her body, and she moaned, her hands holding him to her.

"Bramwell," she breathed. "Oh, Bramwell, please."

He wanted to give her more, to go on and on until she learned every delight of passion but finding how ready she was for him, he wasn't altogether sure he could wait. Then she touched him and he groaned, pulling away and rising over her. She rose to meet him and because he'd already made her his, this time he found no barrier.

Joining with Jennara was like nothing he'd ever experienced. He was no longer apart; he belonged with her, together they soared to heights he'd never before experienced.

Afterward, he refused to let her go, holding her in his arms. Her contented sigh and the way she cuddled against him rewarded him more than he'd ever have believed possible.

How long would it take him to have enough of this amazing woman? A premonition ran through him as chill as the morning's warning of summer's end. What was he letting himself in for?

Jennara snuggled against him. Though she'd never before been aware of feeling incomplete, she knew now that she had been. With him she was whole, entire, completely a woman. She could understand what she'd never had before—why women stayed with their men no matter what. If she had her choice, she'd never leave Bramwell.

He still hadn't spoken of love, but she refused to let it trouble her. As long as she was with him, she'd live each moment as it came and not anticipate the next.

They both slept until afternoon. The clothes she'd washed were dry by the time they woke, so Bramwell dressed. She pulled on the white gown again and started to brush the tangles from her hair. He took the brush from her.

"I did this before," he said gently pulling the bristles through her hair. "From the beginning I wanted to touch you."

"From the beginning I wanted you to," she admitted. "Not that I would have let you."

"Who fell on whom in the barn?" he demanded. "As I recall, you attacked me."

"It was just plain fury and nothing else!"

Bramwell laughed. "You've spent much of our time together angry with me . . . not without justification. I seem to rile people easily. The only person who's never annoyed with me is Ronald."

"Ronald's very sweet-tempered."

Bramwell nodded, pausing in his brush strokes. "As a baby he was always smiling."

"You two have been together a long time, then."

"I was twelve and he was two when my mother married George Claridge. Mother needed security. We'd been on the edge of poverty since my father had died three years before, and she dreaded seeing me quit school to work in order to support us. George needed a mother for Ronald, a sensible woman to run his house and an attractive hostess for social occasions."

Jennara glanced at him. "You make the marriage sound so calculated."

"I think it was. Both were level-headed people, and each realized the other could provide what was lacking. It turned out well, particularly since they grew to be fond of one another. Even I came to respect George after a time. He, in turn, paid for my education . . . not that he didn't expect something in return."

"What was that?" she asked when, instead of going on, he silently resumed brushing her hair.

"I'm Ronald's guardian," Bramwell said. "Legally and in every other way. He was a disappointment to his father, who'd hoped to sire a businessman. After I finished law school, George told me how he depended on me to look after both Ronald and the business if anything happened to him. He died six months later, along with my mother, in a railroad accident."

She turned and clasped his hand, saying nothing. How difficult it must have been for him at twenty-four to assume responsibility for a business *and* a fourteen-year-old stepbrother while coping not only with his own grief but Ronald's as well. Watching over Ronald even at the best of times must have been a chore.

Ronald didn't seem to live in quite the same world as everyone else. In his world, he was so busy trying to sketch and paint the beauty surrounding him, he didn't have time to notice malice or danger—no evil existed as far as he was concerned.

"How did Ronald ever get through school?" she asked.

"I hired a tutor. Even then Ronald had to be coerced into learning. The tutor and I finally agreed on a program where Ronald was allowed to paint only after he completed other courses of study satisfactorily. Believe me, I often felt like a tyrant. I still do at times—an exasperated tyrant."

Jennara smiled, knowing the feeling. She'd sometimes scolded Ronald as though she were his mother. "Still, he has to take responsibility for his own decisions sometime," she said.

Bramwell shook his head, obviously dubious, and she was reminded of the reason for their being here, the elopement of Ronald and her sister. Chances were, they wouldn't have a meeting of minds on that. Taking the brush from his hand, she began to divide her hair for braiding.

"Must you?" he asked.

She paused, looking at him and seeing the glint in his dark eyes. Doing her best to ignore the warmth spreading through her, she said, "Bramwell, we have to think about moving on. For one thing, we're running out of food."

"Who wants to eat?"

"You will, and very soon," she returned tartly.

"I can always nibble on you." He pulled her backward, his arms sliding around from behind to cup her breasts. "Mmm, delicious," he murmured, nipping at her ear.

She leaned against him, forgetting everything else in the world.

The bay's snort, followed by Swift Runner's whinny, startled Jennara. Bramwell's arms fell away and they both sprang to their feet. Their camp was well into the woods, far off the road, and nothing had disturbed the horses until now.

"It could be the trapper coming by to check his trapline," she said.

"That trap I sprung was a good half-mile on the other side of the stream."

"He could have set others closer to us."

Bramwell strode to their belongings and hefted the Spencer. "Just in case it's not the trapper," he muttered.

Swift Runner whinnied again and another horse answered him. Jennara swung around to face the sound.

"Who goes there?" Bramwell demanded.

"Llwellyn Jones, a lone and weary traveler," a man's voice called. Moments later Jennara caught a glimpse of the horse and rider through the trees, coming from the direction of the road. Looking for a stream, perhaps, she thought.

As soon as he came near their camp he halted his bony, swaybacked sorrel and dismounted. Sweeping off his widebrimmed hat, he bowed. "Madam and sir, Llwellyn Jones salutes you."

Jennara opened her mouth to introduce herself, but before she got a word out, Bramwell, rifle still in his hand, stepped in front of her. "Bramwell Sumner," he said.

"And your lovely wife, I presume," Mr. Jones remarked.

Bramwell reached back for Jennara's hand, pulled her next to him, and put an arm around her shoulders. When she started to correct Mr. Jones, Bramwell squeezed her shoulder hard and she realized he wanted the stranger to believe they were man and wife.

"Where are you headed?" Bramwell asked, his tone definitely unfriendly. She wondered why. In Minnesota, travelers were invariably welcomed.

"To Missouri," Mr. Jones said.

"There's a road out there leading south." Bramwell was challenging the man for some reason she couldn't understand. Llwellyn Jones appeared harmless enough. A fair-sized man, though not as large as Bramwell, he was ordinary looking, with dark hair and eyes. His clothes were as nondescript as his horse and as far as she could see, he had neither rifle nor pistol.

"I thought I'd water old Hank here and rest for an hour." Mr. Jone's tone was ingratiating. "It's hot for September."

"We'd ask you to share a meal with us," she said, trying to make up for Bramwell's inexplicable enmity, "but we haven't enough food."

Bramwell frowned at her and she eased away from him. Did he suspect she was going to be lured off in a balloon again? He couldn't imagine she needed to be protected from every man they met. What was the matter with him that he couldn't offer simple courtesy to a fellow traveler?

Llwellyn Jones smiled. "I just happen to have two newly purchased chickens I was planning to cook. Please do share them with me."

"That's kind of you," Jennara said quickly, before Bramwell had a chance to refuse. "We accept." Facing Bramwell's angry scowl, she grasped him firmly by the hand. "We'll see to the fire while you take care of your horses." She all but dragged Bramwell with her.

When they were out of earshot, she said, "I don't know about Philadelphia, but where I come from, we're courteous to travelers. What do you find so wrong about poor Mr. Jones?"

He cast a dark look back toward the man. "I don't trust him."

"You didn't trust him before you saw him, and that I can understand. We didn't know who was approaching. But he's perfectly ordinary."

Bramwell shook his head. "There's something about him I don't like."

Suddenly Jennara thought she understood. Bramwell had called her "his." She'd observed how possessive some men could be, like male animals guarding their mates. Evidently Bramwell was one of them, because he certainly had no other reason for mistrusting poor Mr. Jones. The idea both pleased and irked her: it was heartwarming to think she meant so much to him, but on the other hand, she wasn't his possession. She wasn't even his wife.

"What harm can it do to share a meal with him?" she asked. "We have tea left and some of Molly's sweet pickles, that'll be our contribution."

"I'd rather not. The man doesn't sit right with me. I can't put my finger on exactly why, but he's somehow wrong. I'll lay odds those chickens were stolen."

Jennara rolled her eyes in exasperation. "You're bound to think the worst of him, aren't you? Maybe it comes from being a lawyer. I see no harm in the man. I've accepted his offer and I see absolutely no reason not to eat with him."

"You didn't see any reason not to go up in the balloon, either."

"For heaven's sake, Bramwell, this man isn't pretending to be a professor or anything else. He's simply a traveler . . . as we are—and frankly, I'm hungry."

Bramwell threw up his arms in defeat. "All right. We'll have the meal, but that's it. We part company immediately afterward. The sooner I see the last of Llewellyn Jones, the better."

Chapter 15

Llwellyn Jones sat with Bramwell and Jennara as the three of them made a late afternoon meal of the roasted chickens.

"You say you're from Missouri, Mr. Jones?" Bramwell's tone was skeptical.

"Where I was born and raised in good old Missouri, folks called me Lew," he said. "Going back there, yes I am. Been away too long."

"Doing what?" Bramwell asked.

"Never was a man to turn down honest work. A little of this, a little of that, enough to keep body and soul together. Anything I can do for you folks, I'd be right happy to."

"We appreciate the chickens, Mr. Jones," Jennara put in.

He nodded, busy with a drumstick, his eyes darting from her to Bramwell to the tethered horses and back again.

"That looks to be an Indian pony," he said when he'd chewed down to the bone.

"Yes." Bramwell clipped the word short.

Jennara glanced at him. She couldn't understand why he didn't trust Llwellyn Jones.

"For all you can't trust an Indian, they do raise tough little horses," Llwellyn remarked. "The Pottawatomis down by Old Muddy—pardon, ma'am, the Missouri River—do right well trading in horses."

"I imagine you know the best route from here to St. Louis," she said, ignoring Bramwell's frown. Didn't he realize travelers always exchanged information?

Mr. Jones nodded. " 'Course, the best route's to take a boat down one river or t'other, but the fracas between the Rebs and the Union's more or less shut off the Mississippi. Old Muddy, though, that's another story—'specially if you got your own boat. Traveling overland's longer, but I sure do know all the shortcuts. Be willing to show 'em to you, yes I would."

"I don't think—" Bramwell began.

"That's most kind of you," Jennara said, overriding what she knew would be Bramwell's refusal. What *was* the matter with him?

After a wary glance toward Bramwell, Llwellyn directed his words toward Jennara. "Don't know if you've heard, but Missouri's kind've unsettled on account of the war—'specially in the northern part of the state. Some of the fire-eating Rebs in Missouri have banded together, raiding and what-all to hassle the Yanks. There be more'n one band—maybe you've heard of Quantrill? The Union Army keeps on trying but they can't put 'em down. Leastways, not yet. I'd be careful, ma'am, traveling through those parts."

"I believe I've heard of Rebel raiders led by a man named Quantrill," she said.

"The one and only Major William C. Quantrill, ma'am. He shoots first and asks questions later. Wouldn't want to come up against him and his men."

"We're not soldiers." Bramwell's voice was sharp. "Why should we be in any danger from a Confederate officer and his troops?"

"The major, he suspects every stranger of being a Union

215

spy, damned if he don't. Excuse my language, ma'am. No offense meant, sir, but on account of the way you speak, it's easy enough to tell you're a Yank, and that might make for trouble."

"Me, a spy? That's ridiculous!"

"Course it is. I can see that right away. But I ain't the major. He's right prejudiced, he is."

Bramwell eyed Llwellyn narrowly. "You seem to know this Quantrill well for a man who hasn't been in Missouri for some time."

"Well, sir, I was working in Kansas not so long ago, and the major, he makes these raids across the border into Kansas. I learned all about the man there, yes I did. Even caught a glimpse of him once. You heard last month how the Rebs took over the Mississippi from Baton Rouge in Louisiana to Helena in Arkansas? Major Quantrill boasts that by October he and his troops'll have control all the way upriver to St. Louis."

Jennara, who hadn't heard the Confederates had wrested control of any part of the river from the Union forces, glanced at Bramwell to see if he was as surprised as she was. He might look impassive to a stranger, but his slight frown told her he didn't know any more about the present situation on the Mississippi than she did. She also suspected he didn't believe Mr. Jones. But what would be the man's point in saying such a thing if it wasn't true?

Llwellyn finished the last of the chicken, licked his fingers, and stood up. "If you folks don't mind, I'd like to take me a wash in the creek."

Bramwell merely shrugged so Jennara felt she had to say something for the sake of politeness. "The stream belongs to no one, Mr. Jones," she told him. He nodded to her and strolled off.

"Did you listen to that man pile one lie atop another?"

216

Bramwell demanded so loudly that she shushed him, afraid Llwellyn would overhear.

"We don't know he's lying," she protested. "We've been on the road so long we're out of touch. The Rebs could have regained control of part of the Mississippi River."

Bramwell waved a dismissing hand. "I don't doubt that part so much as I disbelieve what he said about Quantrill. Jones—if that's really his name—is up to something, I know it. There's a saying in the Pennsylvania countryside: 'If a sorrel isn't tricky, its owner is.' I've never seen a less tricky horse than Jones's tired old sorrel. The owner's another matter. As a lawyer, I've developed an acute sense of when a man's lying to me—and Jones is."

Bramwell motioned her to follow him over near the horses. There, hidden by the big bay gelding, he unbuckled his belt and slid it off. Unfastening a hidden pocket on the inner side, he removed five gold coins and handed them to her. "Hide these somewhere in your clothes."

Staring from the gold to Bramwell, she asked, "Why?"

"Because I don't trust the man. Whatever happens, this way you'll have money. Don't argue—do as I say."

Opening a saddlebag, Jennara eased out the green wool gown Molly had given her. One by one she forced the gold coins between the fine stitches of the skirt's hem, wondering the entire time what calamity Bramwell had envisioned.

"Even if we should encounter Major Quantrill in Missouri," she said, "surely he won't think you're a spy."

Bramwell shook his head. "I keep telling you, Jones is lying."

Lawyer or not, how could Bramwell be certain? she asked herself. Goodness knows he'd accused her of lying often enough when she was telling the pure and simple truth. Perhaps the practice of law encouraged distrustful-

217

ness. But rumors of Quantrill and his raiders had filtered into Minnesota. He was ruthless and cunning, people said . . . clever and quick-tempered. Jennara's fingers smoothed the fur of her medicine pouch, temporarily stored in the saddlebag because she was wearing the white gown.

If Bramwell thought it necessary to take precautions, it might be wise for her to do the same. Quickly removing from the pouch the twists of medicine that were as precious as gold to her, she eased them under the lining of the green jacket that matched the gown.

The more she thought about Quantrill, the more apprehensive she grew. There was no way Bramwell could hide his eastern origins. He gave himself away with every word he spoke. Ronald, too, had the eastern manner of speech. But Ronald was traveling with a medicine wagon, and surely that would disarm Quantrill. Besides, no one in his right mind could possibly believe Ronald was a spy—he was too transparent.

Bramwell, with his brooding dark eyes and shuttered face, was another matter. Though she well knew he wasn't one, she had to admit he looked like she imagined a spy would. Unforthcoming, saturnine . . . and Quantrill was a man who shot first and asked questions later.

She'd had dreams of the wonderful nights ahead when she and Bramwell would be camping together, just the two of them, all peril passed. Instead, more danger lay ahead . . . not for her, but for Bramwell. If he was killed, she'd want to die herself. What was giving up traveling alone with him if having Mr. Jones along might save Bramwell's life? Mr. Jones knew the country, he could show them the byways and avoid the main roads, avoid any Reb raider camps. She'd do anything, give up everything to keep Bramwell from harm.

"We'll leave as soon as we're packed," Bramwell said. "I

want to get as far away from Jones as possible. I wish you hadn't let on we were heading for St. Louis."

Llwellyn returned to their campsite as they were buckling the saddlebags. "I'm glad you decided to move on," he said, smiling from one to the other of them, apparently oblivious to Bramwell's scowl. "I'm sure you won't regret traveling with me. Believe me, once we reach Missouri, I'll save you time and trouble . . . especially trouble. Yes, I will, I surely will."

Bramwell took a deep breath, preparing, Jennara knew, to blast Llwellyn. She put a restraining hand on his arm. If they were unfortunate enough to meet Major Quantrill and Mr. Jones was with them, he might be able to convince the major that Bramwell was not a spy, but a perfectly innocent civilian in search of his stepbrother.

"I'm curious," she said to Llwellyn. "Would you recognize Major Quantrill if you saw him?"

"Yes, ma'am. That's not to say I want to see him. Truth is, he's a man to steer clear of."

"I agree." She turned to Bramwell. "Mr. Jones is familiar with Missouri and we're not," she pointed out, ignoring his angry gaze. "He's as eager to avoid Major Quantrill as we are. Traveling with him could well keep us out of trouble, besides getting us to St. Louis quicker."

"I told you—" Bramwell began.

She cut him off. "I know what you said, but what about me? Have you thought how *I'd* feel if Quantrill shoots you for a spy? How *Ronald* would feel? Mr. Jones is willing to help us, and I think we should take him up on his offer."

Bramwell clenched his jaw, biting back his fury, she was certain. He shot a dark glance at Llwellyn, then muttered, "At least I'll know where he is."

Jennara interpreted this to mean Bramwell had accepted the sense of her argument and capitulated. Before he could change his mind, she said briskly, "Well, then, Mr. Jones, shall we be off?"

In the three days it took the trio to reach the Missouri border, Jennara doubted that Bramwell got any rest. She might have known he'd be too suspicious of Llwellyn to sleep at their night camps. He'd sit up with the Spencer, keeping watch until she woke each dawn. What he expected the man to do, she had no idea. All Llwellyn actually did was sleep soundly.

By the time they crossed into Missouri, the weather was markedly cooler, and for warmth Jennara wore the green wool gown, luckily a trifle large, over her divided skirt. The green jacket came in handy, too, for the morning and evening chill.

Early on their second day in Missouri, Jennara woke to darkness. Bramwell sat propped next to her. She eased up and plucked the Spencer from his hand, whispering, "Sleep . . . I'm awake now." She didn't agree they needed to stand guard against Llwellyn, but there was no arguing with Bramwell's stubborness. The only thing she could do to see he got a few hours' sleep was to stay awake herself.

She soon realized it was closer to dawn than she'd thought. A dense overcast accounted for the gloom, and the chill, damp breeze hinted of rain. She hoped the rain would hold off until later, after they'd found shelter in some hamlet. They hadn't passed any good-sized towns yesterday—true to his word about shortcuts, Llwellyn had led them along seldom-traveled roads.

The last they'd heard, the medicine wagon had been in Iowa, and at that time Dr. Phineas was at least four days ahead of them. "Going to Trenton in Missouri, so the doctor said," an Iowa villager had told them, after proudly showing them his portrait drawn in charcoal and signed with Ronald's initials. "Then on to St. Louis."

Llwellyn was still sleeping. Jennara hadn't admitted it to Bramwell, but the longer she knew the man, the less she liked him. It wasn't that she didn't trust him, exactly, but there was something reptilian about him. For all his seemingly frank answers to questions and his glib talk, he glided away like a snake from anything specific.

Yet he'd done nothing to provoke alarm. Unlike Professor Taylor, he paid no particular attention to her, though he was courteous enough and always willing to talk. He was polite though wary with Bramwell. Yesterday, in lieu of conversation, he'd begun to whistle the same tune over and over. Poor Bramwell, half-asleep in the saddle, hadn't noticed, but the repetition had grated on her nerves. If Llwellyn started whistling again today, she'd ask if he knew another melody.

She glanced at Bramwell's sleeping face and sighed with longing. Llwellyn was with them at her insistence, so she could hardly complain; but she longed to be alone with Bramwell again. She fought her urge to touch him now, to smooth the hair from his forehead, to kiss him. He needed to sleep. The annoyance of having a third person with them, she told herself firmly, was a small price to pay if Llwellyn's presence kept Bramwell from danger.

Another week and they'd be in St. Louis. Then what? They'd be rid of Llwellyn, but intent on finding Ronald and Susanna. Would there be time for her and Bramwell? Jennara sighed again, shaking her head. If only she could be certain one way or the other about Susanna!

It was true Susanna had looked terribly peaked when she'd first arrived home from St. Louis. It was also true that she'd had spells of nausea and several incidents of morning vomiting, and had fainted once. All those symptoms didn't have to add up to pregnancy, though certainly they could. If only Jennara had confronted her sister! Instead she'd kept hoping it wasn't true, or that if it was, Susanna would confide in her.

Susanna might tend to gloss over unpleasantness, but surely her sister wouldn't be so deceitful as to marry Ronald if she were carrying another man's child — not without telling him . . . or would she?

She no longer knew Susanna well enough to be sure, Jennara thought in dismay. She could only hope she was wrong in thinking Susanna was with child. But even if she was wrong, even if Susanna was marrying Ronald for love alone, Bramwell planned to block the marriage. In that case, he and she would be at odds, adversaries again.

She'd known this from the beginning, known it wasn't wise to give way to her increasing desire to be in his arms. Wise or not, she'd been fool enough to fall in love with him, a man who'd leave her. Yes, she'd known that, too. Gazing down at him, still sleeping, she smiled sadly. If No Cloud had known what he was letting her in for when he brought Ronald to her for care, the old medicine man would never have done it.

Jennara shook her head. She was wrong . . . No Cloud, like most other Dakotas, was a man who believed in omens, in visions, in beneficent and malevolent spirits. He'd had a dream vision of a dying white man, coupled with the bad omen of a dead eagle — death among his people. He'd interpreted finding the badly injured Ronald as part of the vision and had brought him to her in an attempt to avert the evil to come, hoping that saving Ronald would save his people. Whatever happened to her as a result made no difference since she wasn't in his vision dream.

Bramwell was what happened, and she wouldn't wish

any of it undone, not the fighting, not the making love. As Cervantes said, "There's no striving against the stream." Like a river in full flood, love had taken her by surprise and swept her away. She'd had no choice.

Movement caught her eye. She turned her head and saw Llwellyn rise to his feet, yawn, and stretch. Though the sky remained a sullen gray, she knew it was well past dawn . . . time to move on. Reluctantly, hating to disturb him, she leaned down and woke Bramwell.

As they rode into the morning, Llwellyn began to whistle the same dreary tune. Jennara's lips tightened as he continued on.

"It's not your whistling that bothers me," she said, "but that one tune, over and over. Don't you know any other songs?"

"This here's my favorite," he said. "My mama used to sing it to me when I was a tad. I ain't much for singing, so I got to whistle it. Don't know as I recollect any other tunes."

Bramwell spoke up, startling her. He'd not said more than two words since she'd roused him. "I'll teach you one. Listen." He smiled at Jennara and began whistling the melody to "Dreams on the Ocean."

"That's kind of fancy for me," Llwellyn said when Bramwell finished.

"Give it a try," Bramwell urged.

Llwellyn failed dismally. After that, they rode in silence through the misty morning until, eventually, Llwellyn took up whistling again, the same old tune. Jennara gritted her teeth.

"Turn it off." Bramwell spoke quietly, but there was an undertone to his voice that boded ill for Llwellyn if he refused to obey.

The whistling stopped.

"If you whistle again," Bramwell warned, urging the bay up even with Llwellyn's old sorrel, "I'll be sure you're doing it for a purpose. Like Don Quixote, 'I begin to smell a rat.'"

Jennara blinked. Earlier this morning she, too, had recalled a line from Cervantes. Did Bramwell mean he thought Llwellyn was trying to signal someone by his monotonous whistling? Who?

Llwellyn stared sullenly at Bramwell. "I was only whistling, nothing more."

"That's exactly what I expect to hear—nothing more. I don't trust you, Jones."

As the two men scowled at each other, Jennara noticed Swift Runner's ears prick forward. She glanced ahead and caught a flicker of motion from the trees bordering one side of the trail.

"Bramwell!" she cried.

When he turned to her she jerked her head toward the trees ahead. He reached for the Spencer and froze with his hand on the stock as riders poured out from the cover of the trees to surround the three of them. Jennara counted twelve men.

"Raise that rifle and you're a dead man," one of them, obviously the leader, said.

Jennara stifled a gasp. The man wore a gray-brown uniform with a major's oak leaf on the shoulders. A black slouch hat covered his dark hair. Eyes as cold as Minnesota icicles flicked from Llwellyn to Bramwell and back, dismissing her as unimportant.

Slowly, carefully, Bramwell eased back in the saddle, lifting his hand from the Spencer. "Why have you stopped us?" he demanded.

"What's your business here?" the major shot back.

"Mr. Sumner and I are searching for missing relatives,"

Jennara put in before Bramwell could make an angry retort. "We hope to find them in St. Louis." She greatly feared the man she spoke to was Major Quantrill, and she prayed Bramwell would keep his temper.

"You may be looking for relatives, ma'am," the major said, sparing her a glance, "but from the description I got, I doubt these men you travel with are. One of them anyway."

"Mr. Jones joined us in Iowa," she informed him.

"Llwellyn Jones, sir. It's true, what the lady says about me meeting up with them in Iowa, but it may be the only truth she tells you. What I'm doing is coming home to Marthasville to see my old mama. I got word she's doing real poorly. These folks asked me to ride along with them, so I did. Didn't see no harm at first, but later on I got to thinking. 'Specially when I noticed him hiding something, a paper I think it was, in his saddlebag. I'm glad we met up with you and that's a fact. He says he's named Sumner and she's his wife, but I wouldn't go believing him, no sir."

Jennara gasped at Llwellyn. What on earth was he talking about?

"He's lying." Bramwell spoke flatly. "If any papers other than maps are in my saddlebags, it's because he put them there."

"Let's have a look at those saddlebags before there's any more talk." The major stabbed a finger at Bramwell, then Llwellyn, and snapped, "Dismount and step away from your horses." Without taking his eyes from them, he added. "Ma'am, I'd appreciate it if you'd kindly dismount also."

As Jennara complied, she decided she could no longer bear the suspense of not knowing. "Are you Major Quantrill?" she asked.

He nodded toward her. "I am." Motioning to the soldier nearest him, he ordered, "Search the bay's saddlebags. Remove the rifle first."

At least he hadn't shot first, she thought, attempting to reassure herself. Llwellyn had lied about that as well. Jennara watched apprehensively as the soldier dismounted and yanked the Spencer from its scabbard, handing it up to another trooper. He unfastened Bramwell's saddlebags, then flung one item after another onto the ground until he came to what Jennara recognized as the maps. The soldier offered them as well as a slim leatherbound book to Major Quantrill.

As the Major opened the maps, a folded paper fluttered out, spinning to the ground. The soldier retrieved it for the Major who opened the paper and studied it intently. No one spoke. Only the shifting of the horses and the creak of leather broke the lengthening silence. The sudden raucous caw of a crow made Jennara start nervously.

Major Quantrill finished perusing the paper and opened the thin book. He leafed through it, found a loose paper, unfolded it, and immediately glanced at Jennara. Nodding, he refolded it, returning the paper to the book.

"You claim this—" Major Quantrill waved the first unfolded paper—"isn't yours?" He addressed Bramwell.

"I had no paper folded inside my maps," Bramwell stated. "The one you returned to my notebook is mine, yes."

"That's not an answer. Is this yours?"

"To my knowledge, no."

"Yet it appears to have been torn from your journal. Do you deny this is your journal?" He held up the slim book.

"I don't deny the journal." Bramwell's voice was taut, controlled. "I tore no page from it."

The Major's gaze flicked from him to Llwellyn. "Where did you come from, Jones?"

"Born and raised in Marthasville, sir. You just ask anyone in town, they all know my folks and me, too."

"I meant where have you been living? You said you were returning to Missouri."

"Been helping with the harvest in Iowa, sir. There's this girl lives up near Des Moines. Her daddy don't care much for me on account of my being from Missouri, so I figured maybe—"

Major Quantrill cut him off with a quick motion of his hand. "You've been living in Iowa how long?"

"Just for the harvest, like I said, sir. A tad over two months."

Jennara frowned at him. "That's not what you told us, Mr. Jones," she snapped. "You said—"

"Ma'am, be so kind as not to interrupt." The Major's tone was sharper than his words.

He glanced once more at the paper he held, then at the two men. "According to what I see here, one of you is lying. Since I haven't yet made up my mind which, you're both under military arrest."

"I can tell you Bramwell Sumner's not a liar!" Jennara cried.

"Ma'am, I'm afraid your opinion doesn't matter to me one way or the other."

Jennara started to protest hotly when soldiers bound Bramwell's arms behind him, but a slight shake of his head stopped her. She bit back the words, telling herself he was right. If she carried on too much, the Major might decide to place her under arrest as well. As long as she remained untied, there was always the chance she could somehow set Bramwell free, though at the moment she couldn't think of a way.

She took some satisfaction in watching them tie up Llwellyn. If anyone deserved it, he did. Without a word, she allowed a soldier to help her remount Swift Runner.

When Bramwell and Llwellyn were back in the saddle, their horses led by mounted soldiers, they began following Major Quantrill along the trail.

It took over an hour to reach his camp, an assemblage of tents in the woods beside a stream. Bramwell and Llwellyn were pulled off their horses and shoved into one of the tents, with a guard at the entry. The Major himself led Jennara away.

"Rest assured that no one will bother you, ma'am," he said.

"You must listen," she told him. "Mr. Jones is lying to you. Bramwell doesn't lie, he's a lawyer from Philadelphia, he came to Minnesota to—"

Major Quantrill held up a hand. "You can't deny being prejudiced, ma'am, so save your breath." He gestured toward the tent. "This is the cook house, where you'll stay."

She stared at him, taken aback.

"You'll be alone here," the Major added, lifting the tent flap and ushering her inside. "We had to leave our cook behind after he took sick. I see no reason you shouldn't make yourself useful by taking his place." He strode away without waiting for her to agree or disagree.

She scowled after him, determined no one was going to force her to cook if she made up her mind not to. Why should she feed these Rebs who'd taken Bramwell prisoner? They could starve to death for all she cared.

It was plain the Major would refuse to listen to any of her pleas, believing she'd lie for Bramwell. She would if she had to, but what she'd tried to tell the Major was the truth. How could she convince him when he wouldn't even hear her out?

I won't let him stick me in this tent to get me out of the way, she fumed. I'll find Major Quantrill and stick to him like a burr until he's forced to listen to me. She stalked

228

through the open flap and came face to face with a grizzled older man, a soldier.

"Orders was for you to stay in the tent, ma'am," he said in a gravelly voice.

"I don't choose to." She tried to edge around him.

He blocked her passage. "Reckon it'd be a good idea to do what the major says and stay inside, quiet-like." He met her furious gaze mildly. "If you don't, the fact is I been told to tie you down, and as for me, I never question Major Quantrill's orders."

Chapter 16

Jennara sat on a folding stool inside the cook tent, her anger eclipsed by fear, though it was not for herself. Whatever else she thought about him, Major Quantrill had not harmed her, nor did she think he would.

Corporal Menck, the grizzled soldier who stood guard at her tent opening, had told her the major was questioning Bramwell and Llwellyn. Surely he'd come to recognize Llwellyn for the liar he was.

The Corporal had also mentioned that a Captain Younger, leader of a different group of Rebs, had caught a Yankee spy last month, but the spy had escaped. Quantrill and other Reb raiders had been searching for the spy since then. Was Llwellyn actually a spy for the Union? It seemed unbelievable. If he was and he had escaped, why would he ride back into danger? Maybe he hadn't fulfilled his assignment in Missouri.

Maybe he hadn't intended to return at first. Maybe he'd actually been heading north when he'd met her and Bramwell. Once he'd discovered they were traveling south, had he decided to take a chance and go with them, planning to denounce Bramwell as the spy if challenged by the Rebs? What a traitorous man! But then spies were, weren't they?

Bramwell had insisted all along that something was

wrong with Llwellyn, that he didn't trust him. In disagreeing, in treating Llwellyn as she would an other ordinary traveler, she'd played right into his hands.

The folded paper in the map was obviously incriminating evidence of espionage. Once he found that paper, the Major was bound to believe one or the other of them guilty. What if Llwellyn actually was from Marthasville? The town must exist, because Major Quantrill seemed familiar with the name. What if he really *was* who he said, and neither his family nor anyone else in Missouri knew he spied for the Union? Jennara bit her lip. In such a case, the Major might decide that Bramwell, with his eastern manner of speaking, had to be the spy.

These Reb raiders weren't likely to go to the trouble of bringing a spy to trial. They'd want to kill him then and there. Jennara shuddered, imagining Bramwell before a firing squad or with a rope around his neck. She had to do something. Now! Desperately she searched her brain for even a shred of an idea.

"Ma'am?" Corporal Menck called.

"What is it?" she snapped.

"The major, he said you'd do the cooking. I been cooking since old Bart took sick, so I can help you get started, if you want."

About to inform him that she had no intention of cooking for any Rebs, she paused. The cook had fallen sick. Could she use that? She'd have to lie, but someone else's lies are what had landed her here. Why shouldn't she lie in an attempt to free herself?

"In Iowa, we were warned that there was some cholera down in Missouri," she said, choosing her words with care in order not to say too little or too much. "I do hope poor Bart doesn't have cholera."

The silence outside the tent told her that even though she'd shot blind, she'd made a bit. "He was puking some,"

231

the corporal admitted finally, "but we figured it was from the rotgut he swigs."

"I'm sure it was." She made her words sound uncertain. "Just because a man vomits doesn't mean he has cholera."

"Course not." The corporal's voice was overly hearty.

Even the mention of cholera was frightening. Most people remembered the last epidemic along the Missouri River, several years ago, when hundreds died before it ran its course, and most also knew there was no cure for the disease. Cholera could kill a strong, healthy man in the prime of life within two hours of the onset of symptoms — diarrhea, painful cramps, and violent vomiting. Or it could make him miserable for several days and then kill him, or, less often, miraculously spare him.

She remembered her father telling her how the dreaded scourge had originated in Asia and traveled in all directions, reaching New York in 1832 and spreading across the United States. "Despite the epidemics that have occurred," he'd said, "cholera isn't contagious, as we normally use the word. In hospitals, few physicians or nurses who treat cases ever fall ill. Does it come from the air, or from decaying vegetable or animal matter? No man knows."

Indians had also died of cholera, but No Cloud insisted it was a white man's disease and therefore outside his range of cures.

Jennara had never seen a case and hoped she never would. She ran a hand along the lining of her green jacket and smiled thinly. Though she couldn't cause cholera, she had the means to mimic its symptoms.

"Corporal," she said as pleasantly as she could, "if you'd care to come inside, I'd truly appreciate your help in planning the evening meal."

When he ducked under the flap, she put a finger to her lips. "Perhaps you ought not to mention to anyone that Bart might have cholera," she said. "I wouldn't want to upset the men."

He nodded solemnly, but she knew he could no more keep from whispering the news to a comrade or two than Swift Runner could help nickering when he came near another horse.

Finding a crate with five live chickens at the rear of the tent, she decided to make chicken stew. The corporal called for a mate to fetch water and bring more wood while he built up the fire in the pit near the tent door. Then he killed the chickens for her and helped her pluck them. She couldn't help remembering how amused she'd been last month, observing Bramwell as he'd plucked his first chicken. Thinking of him as a prisoner made her more determined then ever. Unless Quantrill freed Bramwell, nothing would stop her from going through with what she planned to do. She peeled potatoes, cut up carrots, and dropped whole onions into the large pot. Spotting a bottle of powdered sage, she sprinkled in a generous amount.

The mouth-watering aroma from the simmering pot on the tripod over the fire soon caused soldiers to drift casually past the cook tent to see what was being prepared for supper and to gawk at the woman preparing it. Corporal Menck spoke in low tones with each one, spreading, she hoped, the cholera rumor.

"Dumplings would go well with the stew," she told corporal as the afternoon wore on. "Where do you keep the flour?"

"You're a right good cook, ma'am," he said, fetching a bowl full of flour from a huge sack. "I sure ain't, don't think it's a man's business anyways. It was having to cook drove old Bart to the rotgut, that's what I believe. Good whiskey never hurt a man, but rotgut can eat the bottom out of a tin pail. Stands to reason it might leave a man open to catching cholera."

"I do hope cholera's not Bart's trouble," she said fervently and honestly. She wouldn't wish cholera on anyone.

As she stirred together the dumpling mix, she thought about what she had inside the lining of her jacket to help her carry out her plan. Ground black root, ground blood root, and pulverized leaves of black locust all used together would be a powerful emetic as well as a more-than-effective purgative. Luckily none of the three medicines had such an unpleasant taste that the sage in the stew wouldn't mask it.

The mix for the dumplings ready, she carried it from the tent and stopped dead, staring. Llwellyn Jones, free of his bounds, mounted on the bay gelding and leading Swift Runner, rode from the camp.

"That's my horse!" she cried, rushing after him. "And Bramwell's!"

Corporal Menck caught her arm, halting her. He grabbed the bowl of mix to prevent it from falling to the ground. "Easy, ma'am," he said. "You ain't going nowhere."

"But—but he's stolen our horses!"

"The major must've given them to him. Sort of a reward, like."

Jennara clenched her teeth to keep from screaming her protests. *Reward!* Llwellyn the spy rode free while Bramwell remained a prisoner. She took a deep breath in a effort to calm herself. She was helpless to stop Llwellyn or regain the horses. All she could do was continue with her plan and hope for the best.

"At least I hope you'll let me take some food to Mr. Sumner," she said.

Corporal Menck shook his head. "I got my orders. He don't get to eat."

Jennara's heart sank. She'd hoped to slip Bramwell a bit of the stew before she added the medicines, not wanting him to get sick. The corporal's words relieved her of that concern. If he wasn't to be fed, Bramwell wouldn't get sick—but that thought assaulted her with a worse fear . . .

they meant to kill Bramwell and saw no point in feeding someone about to die. She hoped to God they meant to have their meal before the execution.

Please let them eat first, she prayed, easing the first twist of medicine from the lining of her jacket and concealing it in her palm. How was she to dump it into the pot without the observant corporal noticing? She had to find a way to distract him.

"Time to add the dumplings." Her voice trembled with unfeigned distress as she spoke to Corporal Menck. "I'm so upset over—over losing my horse you'll have to do it. I'll tell you how."

Under cover of the bowl he held above the steaming pot as he carefully ladled it the mix, she unwrapped the twist and dumped it into the stew, stirring well. She did the same with the other two twists until the black root, blood root, and black locust leaves were mixed into the stew. The empty containers she screwed up and slid back into the jacket lining.

Every soldier in the camp partook of the stew, including Major Quantrill. Jennara waited until they'd all been served before she ladled herself a small portion.

"We'd be honored to have you join us, ma'am," the Major offered.

She ignored his gesture. "You've let the guilty man go free and condemned the innocent one. What do you mean to do with Mr. Sumner?"

He eyed her grimly. "In wartime, traitors are shot."

She glared at him. "I might be forced to cook for murderers, but I prefer not to eat with them." She turned away, retreating toward the tent with her bowl of stew. At the entrance she paused and swung around. "I hope the cholera takes you all, like it did old Bart," she cried.

Plunging into the tent, she hid the bowl of stew behind a sack of potatoes, then dropped onto the stool and buried

235

her face in her hands, her heart hammering in apprehension. What if the medicine didn't act in time to save Bramwell? What if Quantrill saw through her attempt at a cholera scare and realized she'd put something in the stew? He might be angry enough to shoot her, too.

She raised her head and stared at the open flap, waiting. A crow called and others answered. A rhyme she'd heard as a child echoed in her mind:

> One crow for sorrow
> Two for mirth
> Three for a wedding
> Four for a birth.

If the noise of the cawing was any indication, the gathering of crows in the trees near the camp far exceeded four. Crows were reputed to bring bad luck. To whom did these birds bring ill fortune? Was it her and Bramwell, or Quantrill and his men?

She'd heard some of her neighbors in Minnesota insist that crows perched in the surrounding trees to watch a house where someone was to die. Jennara shook her head. Her father had taught her not to believe in superstitions. She refused to view the crows as a bad omen.

Bramwell wasn't going to die — not today, not for years and years. Then flashed across her mind the image of him trying to coax the cow into letting down her milk by singing "Loch Lomond" to her, or Bramwell teaching mumblety-peg to Cub, of his face, tender and warm, when she came into his arms in the creek. Tears ran unheeded down her cheeks while outside the crows continued their raucous chorus.

In her distress, she missed the first sounds of retching. It wasn't until a man cried out, "Christ, it's the cholera!" that she realized what was happening.

Rushing to the flap, she peered out. Men clutched their stomachs, staggering through the long evening shadows. Some were on their hands and knees, vomiting. Jennara grasped the handle of the paring knife she'd taken from the supplies in the cook tent and eased past the flap. As unobtrusively as she could, she made her way toward the tent where Bramwell had been taken, doing her best to avoid everyone.

"Jennara!" he cried as she ducked under the flap.

He lay on his side on the ground, his feet and hands bound behind his back. She threw herself to her knees and attacked the ropes with the paring knife. Moments later he was free and stumbled to his feet, clumsy because his circulation had been cut off by the ropes.

"Llwellyn Jones rode off with our horses," she told him as she helped him from the tent.

"May he fry in hell," Bramwell muttered, looking around warily.

"Quantrill and his men are all sick," she said. "I flavored their stew with Dakota medicine."

"We'll borrow two of their horses since ours are gone. And a rifle. I imagine Jones nicked the Spencer."

If any of the retching, miserable soldiers noticed them slipping past on their way to the horses, the men were too sick to do anything about it. Bramwell took a second look at one of the soldiers sprawled face down, stopped, and knelt beside him. Reaching into the man's pocket, he pulled out something, smiled, and tucked it away in his own pocket.

His clasp knife . . . the man must have taken it when Bramwell was searched for weapons. She picked up the soldier's rifle, a breechloader.

They grabbed two saddles from the tack tent, and once they reached the horses, Jennara chose a dappled gray, Bramwell shouted, "Get down!"

As Jennara flung herself sideways to avoid falling under the horse's hoofs, a shot rang out. She twisted her head toward the sound. Major Quantrill, leaning against a hickory trunk, his rifle cracked open, was reloading. She scrambled to her feet, and together with Bramwell pushed among the horses until the animals shielded them.

As Bramwell stooped to peer under the horses' bellies to keep an eye on Quantrill, Jennara began to untie them, crooning softly to try to soothe the snuffling, disturbed animals.

"Can you ride with only one leg over a horse's back and the rest of you hanging off to the side?" she asked. "I learned when I was a child. It's a Dakota trick to use a pony's body to shield yourself from enemy arrows and bullets. The Dakotas hang onto the mane with one hand to keep from falling, but if we can get to the saddled horses, we can use the saddle horn."

He glanced at her. "I don't have any choice but to try. Quantrill's none too steady on his feet but he's circling, trying to get a shot at us. I get the feeling we'd have to kill him before he'd give up."

And they didn't have ammunition for the rifle handy.

Bramwell plunged between the nervous horses and grabbed the bridle of the dun. "The gray's behind you," he said. "Can you get him?"

Jennara untied the last horse and led him through the others until she reached the gray. "Where's the major?" she asked.

Bramwell pointed to her left.

"We'll drive the horses off at a right angle to him," she said. "In the confusion he might not realize we've escaped. Mount!" As she spoke, Jennara leaped, got a foot in the stirrup, and swung her other leg over the gray's back, grabbing the saddle horn at the same time. She kept her head and body alongside the gray's body, not rising up into the saddle.

Gathering air into her lungs, she did her best to imitate the earsplitting Dakota war whoop. Whether it would have fooled an Indian or not, her shout scared the horses. They bolted, with her at the rear driving them onward and Bramwell to the side to keep them headed in the right direction.

With the thunder of the horses' hooves in her ears, she wasn't certain whether she heard a shot. Her horse wove between trees, and she pulled herself onto the saddle, afraid of hitting a trunk. Bramwell, she saw with relief, was riding upright, apparently unhurt.

With Jennara in the lead, they circled away from the other horses to the southwest, riding into the blue evening. She glanced skyward and, between the branches, was pleased to see the glimmer of early stars in the darkening sky. As long as the sky stayed clear they could, by using the Big Dipper as a guide, keep a southwesterly course, and sooner or later they'd reach Big Muddy.

"I take it we're heading for the Missouri," Bramwell said. "If we don't find a stern-wheeler waiting to take us aboard, what do we use for a boat?"

"We don't *dare* keep the horses, so we'll trade them to the Indians for anything that floats. I've heard about several Pottawatomi villages along the river."

"When Quantrill decided I was the Union spy," Bramwell said, "I thought I'd used up the last of my luck . . . but I underestimated again."

"I wasn't going to sit back and let those Rebs kill you," she told him. "I only wish Llwellyn could have had a taste of my chicken stew before he left."

"You dropped poison into the stew?"

She shook her head. "Just a few strong emetic and purgative medicines. They might wish they were dead for a while, but it won't kill them. The major must have an iron constitution to be able to stay on his feet and track us like he did."

"He went for the horses. He knew we'd head there. I wonder how he feels, being duped by a couple of Yankees—one of them a woman."

She raised an eyebrow. "I've never thought of myself as a Yankee."

"If you're not a Reb or a Yank, what are you?"

"A Minnesotan who favors the Union." She smiled ruefully. "I despise the man, but it's true that Llwellyn Jones also fooled the major. Llwellyn must be a spy for the Union. Would you call him a Yankee?"

Bramwell scowled. "What I'd call him isn't fit for your ears."

"I was angry with Major Quantrill and appalled to think he'd be fooled by Llwellyn, but I can understand how it happened. I don't understand Llwellyn at all. What kind of man would deliberately arrange for another man to die in his place?"

"I told you, I can't say it in words suitable for a lady to hear." Bramwell waved his hand dismissively. "Enough of Jones, let's flick him away like the scum he is. You didn't happen to find any food other than the infamous stew you cooked while you were at the camp, did you?"

She shook her head regretfully. "I'm sorry. I never once thought about either of us being hungry once we escaped."

He grinned at her. "Since you saved my life by concentrating on other things, I can find it in my heart to forgive you."

"We've lost everything *but* our lives," she pointed out.

"Almost . . . I retrieved my old clasp knife, a family keepsake. And though the major kept my journal, he returned what was in it when I asked him to. No doubt he felt he was granting a condemned man's last request."

Jennara recalled the paper falling out of the journal.

240

She'd thought at the time it might have been put there by Llwellyn, like the paper folded into the map, to incriminate Bramwell.

"Another keepsake?" she asked.

"Definitely. I'll show it to you sometime."

They rode from under the trees onto a road leading southwest. "Shall we risk it?" she asked. "I don't think they'll be in any shape to pursue us until morning."

"We scattered their horses—that'll delay them further. Night traveling will be easier on the road. Let's take a chance. If I remember the map right, we ought to come to the river just above St. Joseph."

Jennara recalled from the map how Big Muddy meandered across the entire state of Missouri before flowing into the Mississippi. "We'll still a long way from St. Louis."

"Being alive is what matters to me at the moment—alive and free. We'll reach St. Louis sooner or later."

Jennara blinked. What had happened to his urgency to corral the eloping couple and prevent their marriage?

"Not that I've changed my mind," he added.

After coming so close to losing Bramwell, whether Susanna and Ronald married or not seemed of little consequence to Jennara. The important thing was that Bramwell rode beside her in the darkness. Whatever happened later on, for now they were together.

Dawn brightened the sky by the time Jennara caught her first glimpse of the Missouri River. Behind her the thin layer of clouds in the east glowed rose pink, and ahead of her a heavy mist hid the bottoms of round, wooded hills to the other side of a foggy white expanse she knew must be the river. The barking of dogs warned them that a settlement was nearby.

The road they'd been following turned away from the top of the bluffs above the river and plunged down through thickets of burr oak. Through the thinning mist, Jennara caught glimpses of what she recognized as an Indian village.

Unlike the Dakota's circled encampments of tepees, here log houses and bark dwellings huddled together haphazardly along the edge of the water.

"Pottawatomi?" Bramwell asked.

"I think so."

Before they reached the village, dogs of all shapes and sizes met them and escorted them into it. Children darted from the dwellings to stare at them. Jennara stopped the gray at the largest of the log cabins. Without dismounting, she called in English, "We seek speech with the head of the village."

After several minutes, a tall, heavy Indian man stepped from the open door of the cabin. Unsure whether or not he'd understood her words, Jennara signed that she wished to speak to him.

He grunted and she chose to recognize the sound as an affirmative.

"We will trade for a boat," she said, signing at the same time.

His dark eyes traveled between her and Bramwell, shrewd and evaluating. The silence stretched and grew.

"You come in," the Indian said at last, speaking English.

Jennara relaxed a little. He was clearly willing to discuss a trade, or he'd never have invited them into his lodge. Once inside, he'd offer them food and they'd have to eat it or insult him. That was the Indian way.

"Whatever we're served, don't refuse it," she muttered to Bramwell as they dismounted.

"I'm starving. I'll swallow anything," he assured her.

She wondered if that included dog meat and sincerely hoped she wouldn't have to find out.

"Since he speaks English, you do the negotiating," she told Bramwell. "He'll lose face if he has to deal with a woman."

Inside, a young woman served them bowls of stew. By now Bramwell was used to the Indian style of picking up the meat with his fingers and drinking the juices from the bowl afterward. Though he couldn't identify the meat, it was savory enough to satisfy a hungry man. As he accepted a refill of his bowl, he noticed that Jennara, sitting opposite him beside two women, had hardly touched hers.

After eating, the brave filled a pipe with tobacco, lit it, blew smoke to the east, west, north, and south, and then up and down, and finally offered the pipe to Bramwell. He realized this was a ritual he couldn't refuse to participate in, so he accepted the pipe and imitated his host, giving it back when he finished, finding the pungent smell surprisingly pleasant.

His head wreathed in tobacco smoke, the Indian looked solemnly at Bramwell. "You trade for boat," he said.

"I trade for a good boat," Bramwell corrected, beginning to enjoy his role. It reminded him of conferring with an opposing attorney in an attempt to settle a case out of court, each lawyer angling to get the better bargain.

"Good boat, mine," the brave insisted.

"Good horse, mine," Bramwell countered.

"Take long time find good tree, long time make boat." The Indian made digging motions.

A boat dug out of a tree trunk, Bramwell interpreted, beginning to wonder just what he was bargaining for. "Takes a long time for a colt to grow into a horse a man can ride," he pointed out.

"One horse not one boat."

Ah, so that was the crux of the matter. The brave wanted both horses. In spite of the fact that he'd intended all along to offer both, Bramwell didn't reveal this by so much as a flick of an eyelash. "Need paddles," he said. "Need food. Need blankets."

243

The Indian waved a hand as if to say these were trivial.

"I need the paddles and food and two blankets," Bramwell repeated. "All maybe worth one saddle."

"Go look at horses. Saddles."

"I want to see the boat, too," Bramwell told him. Leaving Jennara behind in the lodge, he followed the brave outside and through the village to the river.

He'd pictured a birchbark canoe, but the dugout was a large, heavier kind of canoe, not nearly so graceful. It was tied to a rude dock, floating in the brown waters of the river. Bramwell stood on the dock, looked downriver, and drew in his breath: snags as high as a man's head thrust from the water, not one or two, but literally dozens of obstacles.

His shock must have shown on his face, because the Indian pointed to the snags, then at the boat. "Boat go good." He gestured to indicate how easy it was to maneuver the dugout around the obstacles.

Bramwell wondered uneasily if Jennara knew any more about dugouts than he did. If they were to survive as far as St. Louis, he certainly hoped so.

Chapter 17

"You made a better trade than I could have," Jennara told Bramwell as they loaded their newly purchased supplies into the dugout canoe.

He glanced at the buckskin shirt that replaced his worn cloth shirt and jacket, then looked at Jennara, fascinated by her appearance. Over her divided black skirt she wore an Indian woman's buckskin tunic decorated with porcupine quills and beads. Colorfully beaded moccasins replaced her old boots. Dropping the blankets into the canoe on top of her boots, he turned and pulled her into his arms, ignoring the semicircle of interested Indians, large and small.

"I've been wanting to kiss you ever since you miraculously appeared in that tent to set me free," he murmured. "We're not in quite so much of a hurry now."

No matter how many times he kissed her, the hot sweetness of her mouth fired his blood, making him realize afresh how much he wanted her.

"I wish we had time for more," he said regretfully as he released her.

She smiled. "I think we've provided quite enough entertainment for the crowd."

He settled her into the boat and climbed in himself. One of the Indian boys untied the rope from the dock, tossed it to Bramwell, and gave the dugout a shove. The current tugged at the boat, pulling it downriver and away from shore. Jennara waved to the Indians, then turned to gaze south along the muddy waters at the tangle of branches from drowned trees whose trunks scraped the river bottom.

"I see how our small boat can slip between the snags," she said, "but I don't understand how the steam packets manage to navigate this river."

"I'd as soon be on a packet with the pilot and the captain worrying about navigation instead of me."

"The women told me the big boats don't go past every day. You know we didn't dare wait around for one."

"The war's disrupted everything. If anyone had told me I'd be mistaken for a spy, I'd have called him mad." He shifted, quickly reaching to fend off the first of the snags with a paddle. "Look out, here we go."

With both of them maneuvering their paddles to push the dugout away from all obstructions, it proved easier than Bramwell had anticipated to thread through and around the forest of snags below the Indian village. Once past, the expanse of dun-colored water ahead seemed clear of drowned trees, but sandbars and tiny sand islands disrupted the flow of the river. Poplars and willows shrouded the banks with bluffs behind them, higher on the west side.

Bramwell soon discovered they couldn't afford to relax, and let the current carry them. Snags appeared at unpredictable intervals, and the sandbars seemed ubiquitous. Herons waded in the shallows, and occasionally an osprey would dive into the muddy water after a fish.

From time to time Jennara cried out as she discovered a new wonder. "Look at the size of the pumpkins in that field with the fodder tepees!

"I've never seen so many sheep in a flock!

"All those cords of wood stacked on the bank! The packet boats must stop there for fuel."

A stern-wheeler, the *Veronique*, passed them, chugging its

way upstream, and passengers waved, calling out greetings.

"We're coming to a town. It must be St. Joseph," Jennara said soon afterward.

Thinking she sounded tired—Bramwell certainly was—he asked, "Shall we stop here and find a room for the night? We might even come across a downriver packet that'll have room for us."

"Aren't you afraid we'll attract too much attention? It's not too unusual for a man to wear a buckskin shirt, but I'm not a man. If word got back to Major Quantrill, he might put everything together. Let's wait until we're farther down the river."

"We'll sail past St. Joseph and camp along the bank, then," he agreed.

Boats of all shapes and sizes, from a dugout much like theirs to a three-tiered side-wheeler, were tied up at the town docks, and the wharf was piled with crates. A boatman on a river raft called across the water to them, a crude comment that flushed Jennara's cheeks. Bramwell's brows drew together.

"Makes me sorry I gave up the rifle," he growled.

"We wouldn't have gotten the boat unless you'd thrown in the breechloader," she pointed out.

He shrugged, knowing she was right, but the incident left a bad taste in his mouth. In this country a man needed a gun, no doubt about it. He made up his mind to acquire a pistol as soon as he could.

Below St. Joseph the land flattened into a valley with wooded bluffs rising on either side. Bramwell waited until no other boats were in sight before using a paddle to steer the dugout into the shallows near the east bank. An egret flew up with a clumsy flap of wings as the dugout neared the shore. When the bottom grated on the sand, Bramwell slid out and, rope in hand, splashed to shore, pulling the boat after him.

Jennara scrambled from the dugout and helped him drag it from the water and hide it under the cover of drooping willow branches. Carrying their supplies, they walked through the tangle of willows and on into the flatland to where a stand of broad-leaved basswoods intermingled with sycamores. Not far away a stream fed into the Missouri.

"Only a few of the leaves are starting to turn," Jennara observed. Looking up, he noticed some yellow patches in the green canopy overhead. "In Minnesota they'd be further along," she added.

"In Pennsylvania, too." He listened to the frogs shrilling around them. "And the nights would be getting too cold for frogs."

The land sloped upward away from the river. Bramwell strode back to the edge of the grove to check on what could be seen. Finding he could barely catch a glimpse of the river through the trees, he was satisfied that if they camped within the grove, they'd be invisible to passing river traffic.

"We won't build a fire," he said, thinking any smoke might attract attention. He wasn't worried about Quantrill or his men finding them. What bothered him was the remark the raftsman had made to Jennara. Bramwell had no gun to protect her from such scum, and though he might prove a match for one man, he couldn't take on a whole crew. The best he could do was make certain he and Jennara were well hidden.

With the sun halfway down in the western sky, they shared the corn cakes provided by the Indians and then stretched out on a blanket under a basswood. Jennara lay her head on his chest and he wrapped his arm about her.

"I'm so tired," she murmured, nestling against him.

He'd been exhausted when he'd lain down, but the touch of her excited him and he longed to make love to her. Only her words held him back. They'd been up all night and she needed to rest. He kissed her forehead and softly stroked her hair until her breathing told him she was asleep.

When Bramwell was tied in the tent, expecting to die, it was Jennara he'd thought of, praying that Quantrill would allow her to go free. It was then he'd realized her life meant more to him than his own.

She always glowed like a jewel, regardless of what she wore or where she was. Perhaps, like a gem, she'd be even more beautiful in an expensive setting, but she'd be no more precious to him. When their journey came to an end, how could he bear to lose her? Circumstances being what they were, he couldn't tell her what was in his heart. He had obligations he couldn't ignore, obligations he'd sworn to fulfill. His eyelids drooped shut. One day, when it was all over . . .

He was in the boat with Jennara, drifting out of control on a turbulent, chocolate-colored river. The dugout spun and twisted as they fought to maneuver the treacherous current. The sky darkened, lightning jagged across the heavens, and a strong wind buffeted them. Intent on avoiding snags and sandbars, Bramwell watched the roiling waters, never looking up until he heard Jennara scream.

What he saw froze him. A gigantic bird, white-headed like an eagle, swooped down over the boat, his huge talons reaching for Jennara. Bramwell flung himself at the bird . . . but it was too late. With Jennara clutched in his claws, the thunderbird spiraled up and up, out of reach, disappearing into the clouds.

Bramwell, standing in the boat, cursed the bird and the storm and the river. The sky suddenly cleared, the rough water calmed. The boat rocked gently in a clear pool, while overhead a rainbow arced. He recognized the countryside—he was home in Pennsylvania. The storm was over and he was saved.

But it was a bitter comfort . . . Jennara was gone.

Someone called his name, over and over. He opened his eyes to darkness.

"Wake up," Jennara's voice begged. *"Wake up, Bramwell."*

His mind still dazed from the nightmare, he reached for

249

her, enclosing her in his arms, pulling her close. "Don't ever leave me," he mumbled.

"I'm here, I haven't left. You've been dreaming," she murmured, her hand caressing the nape of his neck.

"I hope this isn't a dream," he said, touching his lips to hers and whispering against their softness. "If it is, may I never wake up."

She was warm, she was responsive, she was Jennara. She was here, she was his. Nothing else mattered. She tasted better than the finest vintage wine. Her scent thrilled him as expensive perfumes never had. Neither satin nor velvet had the exquisite softness of her skin. He wanted more of her and more and more; he could never have enough.

He yearned to give her the same devastating pleasure he felt, pleasure any man would die for. He loved her with his lips, his tongue, his hands. He loved touching her, tasting her, kissing her everywhere, each secret he discovered sweeter than the last.

Her moans, her tiny cries of delight, her caresses excited him until he could wait no longer. Her gasp as he entered her told him she was as eager as he was for their joining.

Their coming together was as turbulent as the river in his dream. Out of control, they were caught in a wonderful frenzy that took them spiraling as high as the thunderbird flies before passion released them to glide down the rainbow into a peaceful pool of contentment.

"I dreamed the thunderbird took you away from me," he whispered into her ear as he held her close.

"Must be that Indian shirt you've been wearing," she teased.

"Wouldn't an Indian consider the dream an omen?"

"No Cloud believes to dream of the thunderbird can be good or bad . . . it can mean seeking the spiritual path, or it can presage war."

"I've had more than enough of war on this trip—with

Indians, with Reb raiders, and even with you."

She murmured agreement as her fingers traced the angle of his jaw. "But won't it be war again when we find Ronald and Susanna?" she asked after a moment.

"Not between us."

She sighed. "I'm not so sure."

"You said yourself that your sister's as feckless as Ronald. Even if she wasn't marrying him for his money, she'd be wrong for him. Ronald needs a wife who can take care of him."

Jennara tried to pull away from him, but he wouldn't let her. "Argue with me if you must, but don't leave me," he said.

"All right, here's how I see it. If Ronald's outside with a paintbrush in his hand and a canvas in front of him, he doesn't know if rain's pouring down or the sun's shining. Susanna *does* know enough to come in out of the rain. She can manage a household well enough. All she needs is a man who loves her."

"You're saying it doesn't matter whether she loves him or his money."

"I don't think she's aware that Ronald's wealthy. *I* certainly wasn't."

"Ever since he was seventeen, women have tried to inveigle him into marriage. I'll agree that he's charming, but not that charming." His tone took on a bitter edge. "Why are so many women in love with money?"

Jennara was silent for so long that he wondered if she'd fallen asleep. "Something happened to you, didn't it?" she said at last. "Something connected to one of those women."

He didn't want to remember, to unearth unpleasant memories, to be reminded of the gauche youth he'd once been.

"What was her name?" Jennara asked softly.

"Loretta." The word slipped unbidden from his lips.

"And you were in love with her."

251

"So I thought at the time." His own naiveté still rankled. At twenty-two he'd been old enough to know better. Loretta Peckham had been twenty, just two years younger, but a thousand years more experienced in ways that mattered.

"She must have been beautiful."

He might have thought so at the time, but now he knew better. Loretta's big blue eyes and the golden curls framing a heart-shaped face didn't add up to beauty. "She was pretty enough, but not beautiful," he said. "Beauty's a combination of inner and outer qualities. A heartless woman is never truly beautiful."

"What did she look like?"

"Why?"

"I want to know . . . tell me."

Bramwell sighed. Much as he'd rather not discuss Loretta and the past, at the moment he couldn't deny Jennara anything. He described Loretta.

"Susanna looks much the same," Jennara observed. "She's very pretty."

"But not beautiful."

Jennara stiffened in his arms. "I didn't say that! Susanna certainly isn't heartless, if that's what you're implying."

He touched his lips to her forehead. "Easy. Our battles are over, remember?"

He felt her gradually relax. "Why do you claim Loretta had no heart?" she asked.

"It's a long story, and boring."

"I've got all the time in the world, and I assure you I won't be bored."

Obviously she was not to be deterred, so he searched his mind for a way to begin. "I was still in law school when I met Loretta," he said finally. "She was a distant cousin of my best friend's fiancée. I imagine the fiancée was the one who told Loretta I was George Claridge's stepson. I didn't realize it then, but she must have assumed I'd be in line to inherit part of the Claridge estate.

"To be frank, she dazzled me. I'd been friendly with a woman or two, but none as pretty as Loretta. She flattered me, she flirted with me, she let me kiss her, she led me to believe she loved me. I was all set to propose marriage—which would be put off, of course, until I finished law school—when Ronald came on a visit.

"Loretta treated twelve-year-old Ronald as she would a younger brother. In spite of his youth, Ronald, like most other males, was taken with her. Loretta wasn't so brazen as to ask openly if Ronald and I were to share equally in the Claridge fortune, but in her clever little way, she wormed it out of me. It wasn't a secret, of course, but neither was it public knowledge.

"Suspecting nothing, I told her the facts. Ronald was the heir, and I would receive nothing. George Claridge, I said, was providing for me by paying for my education, and I considered that fair enough—which was true. I did then and I do now. Loretta promptly dropped me with a thud you could hear for miles. I was crushed, though whether my heart or my pride was the more bruised is a moot point. Eventually I recovered.

"I wasn't affected one way or the other when she turned up in Philadelphia circles later as a vivacious widow of twenty-five, not until she made a dead set for Ronald. The poor boy, only seventeen, didn't stand a chance. To him, she seemed like the goddess of his dreams. Fortunately, Ronald had been trying to talk me into letting him go to Europe. He was eager to view their art firsthand. I booked passage for him so fast that his ship was at sea before Loretta realized he was going. His tutor, a sensible chap, sailed with Ronald and brought him back a year and a half later. By then, Loretta had settled for a lesser catch and married him."

"And you never again believed a woman might be interested in you for yourself?" she asked.

"I wouldn't go that far. But I always made certain everyone knew I had no part of the Claridge money."

"In Minnesota, the Claridge name means nothing. What a man is and what he does means more than his name."

"Life here in the west isn't the same as in the east. You're nothing like any other woman I've ever known."

"Should I be pleased?"

He pulled her closer and kissed her. "What do you think?" he murmured against her lips.

He made love with her again, slowly, dreamily. Time didn't matter, for in the world he shared with Jennara, they had forever.

Bramwell woke at dawn. Jennara wasn't beside him. He sat up. She wasn't anywhere in sight. About to call her name, he heard splashing from the stream and smiled. Grabbing his clothes, he loped down the rise to the creek where she was bathing.

"The water's cold," she advised.

"At least it's cleaner than Big Muddy." He watched her as she wrung out her dripping hair and waded from the stream, avoiding his eyes, her face flushed, embarrassed because she was naked.

She had nothing to be ashamed of. Her lithe and delicately curved body was so beautiful it took his breath away. He caught her hand, stopping her.

"You know I like to watch you," he said tenderly. "Don't be shy."

"I can't help it. I'm not used to you—to anyone—seeing me without my clothes."

He bent his head and touched his tongue to each of her nipples, licking droplets of water from them.

"We'll never get to St. Louis if you persist," she murmured, arching to him.

"Who cares?" He stopped whatever else she might have said by placing his mouth firmly on hers.

With Jennara in his arms, he didn't care if they never moved from this spot. Nothing in the world was as important as the feel of her cool and damp skin against his, nothing mattered but her ardent response to his kiss. She tasted of the morning, fresh and sweet.

His hand curved possessively around her breast. He knew every part of her, yet when he touched her he found her as new and exciting as if it were for the first time. He meant to take time to savor her, but her lips were so warm and eager and her softness pressing against him so arousing that he had to fight the impulse to fall with her onto the grassy bank and drive hard and fast to completion.

But more compelling than his urgent need was his desire for her to experience every nuance of their lovemaking, to travel with him while they pleasured one another, and to join him in their final passionate release.

He put his mouth to her nipples, one, then the other, her tiny moans fueling his fire. His hands stroked her curves until she trembled in his arms. Gently he lowered her to the grass.

"Don't ever tell me you aren't beautiful," he said huskily as he eased down beside her. "Looking at you drives me out of my mind."

Her fingers tangled in his hair, then slid to his shoulders and along his back, urging him close, pulling him to her, showing him her need was as great as his. He resisted no longer. Her wild cry as she welcomed their joining released all restraint and he gave himself up to incomparable pleasure, knowing she felt it along with him.

Later, after breakfasting on the rest of the corn cakes, they retrieved the dugout from under the willow branches and loaded it up. At the river's edge, Bramwell made her get in, then shoved the boat into the water and climbed aboard. Though the sun had risen, patches of mist still lay on the brown water.

255

"I remember reading something a Missourian once said about Big Muddy," Jennara said as they eased into the current. " 'Too thick to swim in and not quite thick enough to walk on.' "

"I'll go along with that description." He felt as though he'd agree with anything she said now . . . anything anyone said. He didn't recall ever feeling quite so good, on top of the world. A day that began so well was bound to be perfect.

His high spirits continued, despite snags and sandbars. They passed Leavenworth, on the western bank, in Kansas, near midday. A fort stood on a rise beside the small city, which boasted buildings as high as four stories. A side-wheeler, the *Kansas*, was snugged up to the side of the dock.

Bramwell steered the dugout close to the packet. "Heading downstream?" he called to a boatman at the rail.

"Going on up to Council Bluffs this trip," the man called back.

"I guess we'll have to stick with the dugout a while longer," Bramwell said to Jennara.

"We should find a downriver packet in Kansas City," she said.

He added. "Ought to be there before dark."

Below Leavenworth Bramwell spotted another forest of snags near the east bank. As he eased the dugout to the middle of the river, he caught movement from the corner of his eyes and glanced toward the west bank. A raft loaded with bales and boxes, with four men poling, was pulling away from the shore. His nape prickled with unease as he gauged the raft's speed and realized it would soon be running alongside the dugout.

"Don't say anything," he muttered to Jennara, hoping if they gave her no more than a casual glance, the raftsmen might mistake her for a boy because of her man's hat and buckskin tunic.

Her eyes flicked from him to the raft and back. She

256

nodded.

As the raft drifted closer, Bramwell tried to pretend he wasn't interested in the craft. If it weren't for the snags, he'd have paddled nearer to the east bank the minute he saw the raft. But as it was, he was trapped between the snags and the raft.

"What've we got here?" a man called.

"Couple of Injuns," another replied.

"Naw, they ain't," a third put in. "Ya don't see Injuns with a beard."

"Breeds got beards," the second man insisted. "Seen plenty of 'em. Anyways, only one beard over there in that canoe."

"Hey, she's a squaw!" the first man shouted.

Catcalls and whistles followed. "Wait up, honey," one of the men called. "I got something I been saving just for you."

"Me first," another insisted. "I ain't had a woman in a month."

Bramwell gritted his teeth. There was hardly five feet of water separating the raft from the dugout, and the men were maneuvering closer. Soon they'd be able to reach across and pluck Jennara from the canoe, and there wasn't a damn thing he could do about it.

Suddenly she swept off her hat and glared at the raft. "I'm no Indian," she cried, "and I want no part of you. I'll kill any man who touches me!"

There was no doubt she startled the rafters, but they were far from discouraged. "I like 'em feisty," one said. "I'll take her on." He crouched at the edge of the raft, his long, hairy arms reaching out to her.

Once they dragged Jennara aboard that raft, he wouldn't be able to help her. Bile rose in Bramwell's throat as he thought of those hairy hands touching her. Desperate to save her, Bramwell reached for a snag, grabbed it, and pulled, forcing the canoe in amongst the branches of the drowned trees. Wood scraped against wood as the branches eased apart, closing behind the dugout.

The curses of the rafters rang in Bramwell's ears as he fought to find a way through the drowned forest.

"We'll be waiting for ya' downriver when ya' come outa there," one threatened.

"*If* he comes out," another said. "Them snags and sawyers ain't anything to fool with."

Their voices faded as the raft sailed on down the river.

The dead branches grated against the dugout and poked at Bramwell and Jennara. They couldn't stay where they were. He didn't think the dugout, sturdy as it was, would stand the pressure. If they fought their way through the snag forest successfully, there was nowhere to go but downriver. They could head for the bank, but then what? The rafters might well be anticipating that very move and be waiting in the shallows, ready to pounce.

Four men . . . without a gun he couldn't handle them. On the other hand, sitting here waiting to be crushed was no solution.

"I have the knife I brought from the cook tent," Jennara said. "I'm not afraid to use it."

Despite the danger they were in, he smiled. Jennara wasn't one to give up; she was a fighter. Damn it, so was he! They'd struggle through the snags and take their chances.

With Jennara helping him, Bramwell forced the canoe south and east through the branches. Limbs tore at his skin and hands and scraped along his arms and chest. More than once he heard Jennara cry out in pain, but he had no time to see how badly she'd been hurt. It began to seem as though they'd been in the deadly maze forever and would never be free.

"Storm coming," Jennara muttered, making him realize clouds had covered the sun.

When they finally eased through the last of the snags, Bramwell glanced quickly around for the raft. To his amaze-

258

ment it was nowhere to be seen. It took him a moment to realize that was because the dugout was no longer on the river. He stared at the muddy water flowing southward and realized they weren't in a feeder stream, either. They'd come into one of Big Muddy's split-offs, where the river took a new, small path that would either widen until eventually the entire river followed this new course, or dwindle and dry up.

"We're in luck," he said, "they'll never find us here. We'll go down a ways and stop before this split-off returns to the main river again." What they'd do then he wasn't certain. They'd have to decide when the time came.

Glancing at Jennara, he was appalled to see her face and hands crisscrossed with bloody scratches. "Are you all right?" he demanded.

"Thanks to you, I am." She touched his cheek. "You're all bloody."

Thunder rumbled in the west. A drop of rain struck his other cheek.

"For a day that began so well," he said, "this one can't get much worse."

Lightning zigzagged across the darkened sky as they drifted down the split-off, watching for any sign of a cutback to Big Muddy. Instead, the way grew ever shallower until the canoe scraped on sand and stopped. The rain began in earnest, drenching them in minutes as the thunderbird's fiery arrows continued to sizzle across the heavens, followed by the roar of his wings. Jennara and Bramwell huddled in the dugout, helpless.

Some time later, Bramwell felt the canoe lift and move forward. They were afloat again. He didn't know whether a tiny creek, swollen by rain, had fed enough water into their split-off to deepen it, or the storm itself had caused the water to rise. He didn't much care. Anything was better than being stuck in the mud. Even if they drifted into the river again, he thought they'd be all right. He was almost certain the storm would discourage the rafters.

Suddenly a great swell of water broke over the dugout, all but swamping it. Willy-nilly, the boat spun out of control, rushing down an ever-widening, turbulent stream. "Hold on!" he called to Jennara, grabbing a tin cup to bail with.

The snags, he thought . . . some must have been washed across to block the river, forcing Big Muddy's waters along this secondary pathway creating a new channel. They had no choice but to ride it—if their waterlogged boat stayed afloat.

Chapter 18

Wind-whipped rain lashed at Jennara's face and head. Clinging to the dugout with one hand, she used her hat to bail water from the bottom of the boat. Despite her efforts and Bramwell's, the canoe settled lower and lower into the water.

"I'll try to beach her before we're swept back into the river," he shouted, abandoning the cup for a paddle.

Jennara, remembering the snags, knew that once they reentered Big Muddy, their chances for survival were almost nil; but she feared Bramwell's efforts to reach the bank would prove useless against the storm and the waterlogged boat. In desperation she stopped bailing for a moment, peering through the rain in the hopes of seeing something that would save them.

She gasped. Dead ahead was a dock torn away from its moorings, a victim of the rushing water. Instead of breaking up and being swept downstream, the pieces held together so the dock blocked almost half of the channel.

"Bramwell!" she cried, pointing.

"Can't avoid hitting it," he called back. "Brace yourself."

The dugout crashed broadside into the ruined dock. Wood splintered and the boat tipped, overturning, spilling Jennara into the water. Bramwell's hand clamped around her wrist as she failed to stay afloat. Coughing from the water she'd swallowed, she clung to him. The canoe was gone and she saw he held onto a post that was part of the broken dock.

The turbulent water tugged at her, trying to separate her from Bramwell and Bramwell from the post he clutched. Pieces of wood split away from the dock and swept downriver. She feared it would only be a matter of time before the entire dock was gone.

The nearest bank was yards away, impossible to swim to in these turbulent waters. She couldn't even see the other bank and realized with dismay that it was because Big Muddy raged just beyond them. Their channel rejoined the main river about where the dock must have been.

The clouds overhead weren't as dark and the storm was passing to the east. The rain lessened, improving visibility and making their desperate plight all the more clear.

"Ho!" came a call from the bank. A man stood staring across the brown water at them. A black man, a Negro.

"Help us!" Bramwell shouted.

"Ain't got no rope." The Negro turned and loped away.

The post Bramwell held to quivered as a large section of the dock broke off and disappeared into the churning river. Jennara closed her eyes in despair. Would the black man come back? Even if he did, would it be in time?

"Has he gone clear to St. Louis to fetch that rope?" Bramwell muttered after a time.

As he spoke, the clouds over the river parted briefly, enough for a thin shaft of sunlight to illuminate the choppy brown water for an instant. Jennara thought that No Cloud would probably accept this as an omen for the good. Why shouldn't she? Hope was always better than despair.

Looking toward the bank, she saw nothing but a few scraggly willows still clinging to the mud, though half their roots were exposed by the new channel as the water washed away more and more earth. Another day or two, and the willows would be snags instead of living trees.

A faraway motion caught her eye and she held her breath: was it the Negro returning? As the figure came closer, she saw that it was and sighed in relief at the rope coiled over his shoulder.

"Y'all got to catch the rope," he called to them.

"I'll hang on to the post myself," Jennara told Bramwell.

"No—you let go of me while I keep hold of you. That way you can use both hands to catch."

She didn't waste time arguing. Bramwell shifted her so she faced the bank, his arm tight about her waist.

"Throw the rope!" he shouted.

The black man swung his arm, flinging one end of the rope out over the water. Jennara grabbed for it and missed. The Negro dragged the rope from the water and tried again. When she missed on the second try, tears filled her eyes. She blinked them away—this was no time to cry.

She failed again and again. On the fifth toss, she stretched as far as she could and grasped the looped end. The post Bramwell clung to groaned ominously.

"Put the loop around your waist," he ordered. "Hurry."

"Can't we both—?"

"Do as I say!" Bramwell's tone was insistent. "He's got the current to fight. We go one at a time—you first."

Jennara bit her lip as she eased the loop wider and slipped the rope over her head and down to her waist, then tightened it. What if the post gave away before the Negro could toss the rope to Bramwell?

She wanted to fling her arms around him, to kiss him and tell him she loved him, that she'd love him forever, but she had no time.

"Pull!" Bramwell shouted to the Negro at the same time he shoved Jennara toward the bank. Water swirled against her face and into her mouth and she bobbed under and up again, sputtering, her hands clutching the rope, now so tight about her waist that she thought she'd be cut in two.

Suddenly she was out of the water, being hauled onto the bank, where she lay on her side, helpless, gasping and retching. Large dark hands eased the rope over her head and off. When she finally regained her breath, she sat up and stared toward Bramwell.

He and the post were gone!

She staggered to her feet and lurched toward the edge of the bank.

"Easy, Missy," a deep voice warned.

She stopped to look at the Negro, a giant of a man, and saw the rope taut in the water. His muscles strained as he pulled it in, hand over hand. But where was Bramwell? Underwater? Drowned? She clutched her hands together.

"Here he come," the black man muttered. Bramwell's head broke the surface of the water, and the Negro reached for him, dragging him onto the bank. "Reckon he gonna need some pumping," the man said, flipping Bramwell's limp body over so he rested on his stomach, his face to the side.

Kneeling astride him, the big man pressed the heels of his hands hard into Bramwell's back. Water gushed from Bramwell's mouth. Again and again the Negro pressed on him until no more water came.

In a distant corner of her mind, Jennara realized the water had been pushed from Bramwell's lungs. But if he'd breathed in that much water, how could he live?

The Negro picked Bramwell up by his ankles, lifted him off the ground, and gave him a vigorous shaking. More water oozed from Bramwell's mouth and nose. When the black man eased him down onto his back, Jennara dropped to her knees beside Bramwell and put her hand on his chest. Did she feel the lift of air being drawn in, or was it wishful thinking?

Bramwell grunted and gagged, and her heart lifted.

"He gonna puke," the black man warned.

264

Jennara shoved Bramwell onto his side so he wouldn't choke on what came up and stayed by him until he'd rid himself of the water and everything else left inside his stomach.

Later, when he'd recovered enough to sit up, he looked from her to the big Negro and shook his head. "I feel as though somebody tried their best to stomp me to death."

The black man grinned. "Y'all done got a might of pumping."

"Water ran out of you like you *were* a pump," Jennara said. "He saved your life twice over." Looking up at the Negro, she said. "I can never thank you enough for what you've done."

"I hears the dock go, so I comes to see how bad it be and this boat goes a-bobbing by, bottom-up. I looks in the water for who be in it. Kinda surprise me y'all don't be drownded."

"I'm surprised myself," Bramwell said, struggling to his feet. He held out his hand. "My name's Bramwell Sumner. The lady is Jennara Gray."

The black man gazed at him a moment, then reached out and took Bramwell's hand in his. "I be Logan."

Bramwell shook Logan's hand. "You saved us from certain death, and I agree with Miss Gray that our thanks can never be enough. But I do thank you, twice over for my life, and more than that for hers." He smiled at Jennara, a smile of such sweetness it pierced her heart.

"Mr. Logan, you're a good man," she said. "As well as strong and brave."

"Just be Logan," he corrected. "I be free, but I don't be no mister. Me, I did no more'n what be right, Missy."

"Was that your dock?" Bramwell asked.

Logan nodded. "I sells wood for the packets to burn. The captains, they calls us wood hawks."

"Do you happen to have a horse?"

"Horse and wagon, both." Logan spoke so proudly that Jennara realized it must be unusual for a free Negro to own

265

such things.

Shivering in the cool breeze that had sprung up in the wake of the storm, she said, "Do you have a place nearby where I can dry off?"

Logan led them to his small cabin, made of logs and set in a grove of cottonwoods against a bluff rising to the east. Though he had no extra clothes, he built a fire in the stone fireplace so Jennara could warm herself and he fried some catfish he'd caught before the storm broke.

After they'd eaten, Bramwell excused himself and went outside. When he returned, he held out a twenty-dollar gold piece and Jennara realized he must have taken the money from his belt. At the Pottawatomi village, she'd shifted the five coins he'd given her from the green skirt to a small pocket in the buckskin tunic, a pocket that she'd had one of the Indian women sew shut afterward.

"We'd like to hire you to drive us to Kansas City," Bramwell told Logan.

Logan's startled gaze clung to the gold coin, but he made no move to take it. "Reckon y'all can hire me and my wagon for less'n that," he said at last.

"This is what I'll pay, no less."

Jennara smiled at Logan. "It's no use to argue with him. Once Mr. Sumner makes up his mind, no one in this world can change it."

By the time Bramwell convinced Logan to accept the coin, evening shadows darkened the unglazed windows of the cabin. "Reckon we ain't gonna leave before dawn," Logan said. "I ain't got much of—"

Before he could mention his sleeping arrangements, Jennara interrupted. "If you could lend us a blanket, Mr. Sumner and I prefer to sleep under the trees, as we're used to doing."

He offered them two cotton quilts, evidently prized possessions, because he took them from a small chest in the corner, handling the blue-and-white arrow-patterned coverlets with care.

"Ole Missus, she done give these here to me afore she died," Logan said, the quilts in his hands. "She done set me free after Ole Massa died. Missus, she never did hold with owning slaves. Set us all free. I done stayed there and helped her, 'long with some others, till she died."

"We couldn't use your keepsakes," Jennara protested.

"I wants you to. Seem like that be why Missus gives 'em to me, so's I got somethin' nice for y'all right now. Y'all gonna sleep cozy in Ole Missus's quilts. Nothing be bothering y'all in my trees, I sees to that."

They found a place in the cottonwood grove a ways from the cabin, and Jennara carefully laid one of the blue arrow quilts on the ground. Since her clothes weren't completely dry, she stripped to her shift before pulling the other quilt over her. When Bramwell joined her, she found he'd taken off every stitch.

"You can't sleep in that damp thing," he told her.

"It's almost dry."

"Jennara, there's no need for modesty. Have you forgotten this morning? Not that I can see you now — it's dark and you're hidden under the quilt, besides."

Jennara felt warmth gather inside her as she remembered what had happened by the stream. She knew he was right, but it was difficult for her to set aside childhood restrictions.

"Nice girls never show their bodies," her mother had insisted as far back as Jennara could remember, first to her, then to Susanna, who as a two-year-old had loved to strip off her clothes and run about in the nude.

"Dakota girls don't wear any clothes when they're little like Susanna," Jennara had told her mother.

"You and Susanna are not Indians! You will do as I say and learn proper ways. Sometimes I think your father and his affinity for those heathens will be the ruination of us all!

I want you to know that no one has seen me completely unclothed since I was a wee girl—which is right and proper, and don't you forget it!"

Lying under a cottonwood tree with a naked man, Jennara smiled a bit sadly. If her father had never seen her mother unclad, then they'd both missed one of life's wonders. She'd never forget the glow in Bramwell's eyes when he'd looked at her by the stream this morning. His gaze had told her without words how beautiful he thought her.

Sitting up abruptly, Jennara pulled off her shift.

"Mmm," Bramwell said, gathering her to him, "that's better . . . much better. In fact it's so good I'll have to postpone falling asleep. Indefinitely . . . "

Much later, as they lay content in each other's arms, he said drowsily, "I can recommend today's beginning and ending, but I wouldn't care to repeat the middle ever again."

Would he be so comfortable and at ease with me, she wondered, if I'd told him there in the water how much I loved him? She wished she knew. He trusted her, he desired her, he enjoyed her company, but did he love her? He never spoke of a future together. No matter what the outcome with Ronald and Susanna, would there be any future for Jennara and Bramwell after St. Louis?

Cherish what you have, she admonished herself. You almost lost him beyond all recall. Isn't it enough that Bramwell's alive and in your arms?

At first light, Jennara woke to the fragrant aroma of coffee. Nothing, she decided as she retrieved her clothes from low branches, had ever smelled so good.

"I can't make up my mind which I enjoy more," Bramwell said as she shrugged into her shift. "Watching you putting your clothes on or watching you taking them off. Though I admit to a slight preference for the latter."

I won't blush, she told herself firmly, feeling the heat rise in her cheeks. His chuckle told her she'd failed.

She glanced over her shoulder. "Laggards always suffer. If you don't hurry and dress, I may drink all the coffee before you get there."

" 'Reproved before breakfast,' " he said, smiling, " 'improved by dinner.' Or so my mother claimed. I'm afraid I was an exception to that rule."

"I've noticed you're an exception to more than one rule."

"Admit it, you wouldn't have me any other way." He sprang up and pulled her into his arms, causing her to drop the buckskin tunic she'd been about to pull over her head.

"Bramwell, you're naked!" Her protest was muffled by his kiss.

"I wish *you* were," he murmured against her lips.

Each time he kissed her was as thrilling as the first. She melted against him, unable to control the eager excitement rising within her.

"Still set on that coffee?" he whispered into her ear, nipping her ear lobe gently.

"W-e-l-l—" she drew out the word—"I suppose the coffee can wait. . . ."

As it turned out, Jennara wound up having to dress all over again. When they finally arrived at the cabin, Logan had buckwheat batter waiting and a cast-iron spider sizzling on the fire. He poured the batter into rounds on the spider and soon was heaping pancakes onto tin plates. A pitcher of honey waited in the middle of the deal table.

"Set you down," Logan invited, waving at two stools drawn up to the table. "I done ate afore ole sun come up."

"Logan, you're an excellent cook," Jennara told him after a bit, waving away another serving of pancakes, "but if I eat another I'll surely burst." In the light of morning, she realized Logan was older than she'd thought at first, probably somewhere in his forties.

He had his horse, a sturdy dun, already hitched to the wagon. Jennara noticed the small barn in back of the cabin, where chickens wandered in and out. From inside, a cow lowed mournfully.

Logan shook his head. "Ole Crookhorn, she be mad 'cause she got to wait. I takes her to pasture in a field down the road every morning 'less I be going somewhere. She figure I got nothing else to be doing 'cept tend to her."

Noting the remnants of a vegetable garden next to the barn, Jennara said, "You have a nice little farm here."

"It pleases me, Missy, it sure do. Only thing I ain't got's a woman. I got one picked out, been saving up to buy her, make her free, then we gonna get married."

"Buy her?" Jennara asked.

"She's a slave. Got to work in her massa's house till I has the price for her. They don't be letting slaves marry free men."

"How much is her master asking?" Bramwell put in.

"Eighty dollars. Take me a time, but I gonna do it. Rissa 'n me, we be happy here someday."

Anger mixed with sadness brought a lump to Jennara's throat. She glanced at Bramwell and saw that he too had been moved by Logan's calm acceptance of the way things were in Missouri.

"Logan," Bramwell said, "President Lincoln's fighting a war because of slavery. The Union plans to put an end to slavery when we win."

"I done heard 'bout Mr. Lincoln, but I ain't countin' on no man or no war. Gonna set Rissa free on my ownsome." Logan turned to the wagon. "Reckon Jack 'n me, we be ready to go if y'all are."

Bramwell lifted Jennara into the wagon and climbed in beside her. Logan had fixed a second board across the wagon bed to provide a seat for her and Bramwell.

"Gonna be jouncy, Missy," Logan advised as he climbed in himself. "Best you hold on."

She assured him she would.

270

Bramwell seemed deep in thought as the wagon pulled away from the cabin, and he didn't speak for some time. Finally he leaned forward to speak to Logan. "Do you know what a cabin passage would cost from Kansas City to St. Louis on a packet?" he asked.

"Reckon no more'n the gold piece y'all give me."

"Twenty dollars for the two of us?"

"They do be asking five for deck passage all the way from St. Louis to a place called Sioux City. That be a far piece. Cabin costs more 'n deck, only y'all be making a shorter trip."

When Bramwell sat back, Jennara said, "I don't think I told you that I'd shifted what you gave me from the green gown to this tunic. So it wasn't lost along with everything else in the river."

He stared at her for a moment. "You have the rest of the money?"

"Yes."

"I underestimated you once more. When will I learn?"

"It seemed practical to—"

"I know you're practical. What I've enjoyed discovering is that there's more to you than the no-nonsense, practical woman you present to the world."

"But that's how I am. That is, usually."

"Until you met me, you mean?"

She smiled. "You do have a tendency to distract me." Didn't he know when he touched her she forgot everything else?

"That makes two of us," he told her. "Two distracted wanderers—"

"About to complete their journey to St. Louis," she finished.

"We're not there yet."

If she could believe the warm glow in his eyes, he wanted their magic time together to last, just as she did. Wanted it never to end.

But, of course, it had to.

They arrived in Kansas City well before sundown and drove immediately to the docks. Luck favored them. The *Prairie Queen,* a stern-wheeler, was leaving for St. Louis first thing in the morning and had a cabin vacant. Twenty dollars covered all charges as far as St. Louis, and Captain Dowd, though he looked askance at their garb, was amenable to having them sleep aboard that night.

"We've time to outfit ourselves a trifle more convention-ally," Bramwell said as they returned to where Logan waited in the wagon. "Would you drop us off in the center of the city?" Bramwell asked him. "Near the stores."

"Anywheres y'all wants."

When Logan stopped the wagon beside a general store, Bramwell jumped down and lifted Jennara out. "Good-bye, Logan," she said. "I'll never forget what you did for us and I hope you come to have everything you want."

Bramwell reached up to shake Logan's hand, then gripped his wrist. "For Rissa," he said, placing four coins in Logan's palm and forcing the Negro's hand closed around them. "You gave me back what I'd thought I'd lost. This isn't in payment—I could never pay you enough. It's rare a man can buy happiness, and I want you to have the chance."

Bramwell's generosity and Logan's heartfelt gratitude brought tears to Jennara's eyes. With her vision blurred by them, she clutched Bramwell's arm, letting him lead her into the store.

He instructed her to choose several brushes and some scented soap while he decided on what he needed. After paying for his purchases and having them wrapped, except for a broad-brimmed black hat, which he put on, Bramwell asked the clerk to recommend a place where he might purchase "a gown for a lady."

Up the block, it turned out, was a seamstress named Mrs.

Vellor who supplied ready-to-wear women's dresses and other garments.

Two of Mrs. Vellor's finished creations, a gold taffeta gown made to wear with crinolines, and a lady's riding habit in tobacco-brown, fit Jennara tolerably well. The only reasonable choice was the riding habit, and she persuaded the rather reluctant seamstress to alter the skirt so it was divided.

While Mrs. Vellor busied herself with the sewing, Jennara unpicked the stitches from the pocket of the tunic and tried to return the coins to Bramwell.

"We're in no danger now, you must take them back," she told him.

"We're not in St. Louis yet. Humor me and keep them until we arrive."

"If you insist, I suppose I must. As for the riding habit, I can't pay you back immediately, but as soon as I return to my—"

"No! I've given you nothing but trouble till now. The clothes are a gift. Please accept them."

"We'll see." Jennara had no intention of doing so, but she didn't mean to argue about it in public. "I do appreciate your kindness," she added stiffly.

He tilted up her chin and gazed into her eyes. "Don't go formal on me," he threatened. "Unless you want me to see if a kiss will bring back the Jennara I prefer."

Flustered, she pulled away, aware he was capable of carrying out his threat. She was relieved when Mrs. Vellor finished and she was able to hide behind a screen and change into the riding habit. Adjusting the matching brown hat in the pier glass, she paused to look at herself, amazed at the change in her appearance. The seamstress's clever stitching concealed the fact that the skirt was divided, the warm brown color complemented her unfashionably tanned face, and the fit showed off her figure more than she was accustomed to. All in all, she looked not only respectable but moderately attractive.

Would Bramwell think so?

By the time she emerged from the dressing cubicle, he was waiting impatiently by the door, evidently having paid the woman, because he held a large wrapped bundle she assumed contained her old clothes.

She couldn't dissuade him from buying ready-made shoes for her, a sturdy pair for riding and a pair of totally impractical slippers.

"You'll wear the slippers on the boat," he informed her.

Shrugging, she accepted with grace. She didn't need the slippers, but she'd grown wary of disagreeing with Bramwell in public. Who knew what he might decide to do?

Bramwell hired a carriage to drive them to the boat. Jennara, who'd expected a tiny cubicle, was pleasantly surprised by their cabin, an enclosed room about six feet square, with doors on both sides. Oil lamps provided illumination.

Bramwell frowned at the built-in berths, one over the other, each unpromisingly narrow. "It seems they mean to separate us," he muttered. He swung around to face her. "What do you think?"

"I can sleep in the upper if you'd rather not," she offered.

He grasped her arm and sat on the lower berth, pulling her down with him. Before she knew what he intended, he stretched out, turning onto his side. She gazed at him with raised eyebrows.

"Come here," he said, "next to me. I want to try the fit." She shrugged, took off her hat, and eased down beside him.

"We'll manage," he told her, smiling, his face only inches away. Shifting onto his back, he lifted her atop him. "Even if we have to sleep like this. It's not so bad, is it?" His arms closed around her, holding her to him while he kissed her long and deeply.

274

As a delicious tumult began inside her, she thought he didn't know very much about her if he didn't realize she'd be willing to sleep on the floor to have him next to her. The close confines of the narrow berth meant that all night long they'd be touching one another, even in their sleep, and the knowledge warmed her.

"We'll miss dinner if we keep this up," he murmured, releasing her. "Up with you . . . we must dress."

Jennara scrambled to her feet. "I *am* dressed."

"Not for dinner." He reached to the upper berth where he'd laid the packages. Unwrapping the large one, he unfolded the taffeta gown and the crinoline petticoat that held out its skirts. Bowing, he said, "I believe this goes with milady's slippers."

Chapter 19

The dining room for the officers and cabin passengers of the *Prairie Queen* was the main cabin, where long tables were set up. Two brass chandeliers with glass globes over the candles illuminated the room, casting a soft glow over the white linen tablecloths and silverware on the long tables.

Jennara entered the room on Bramwell's arm. He was once more a proper Philadelphia gentleman in a black sack coat, a new white shirt, and a black tie. She wore the gold taffeta gown, its skirt held out stiffly by a crinoline petticoat, and the new fawn kid slippers. Unused to the wide skirt, Jennara felt exceedingly self-conscious, especially since the taffeta rustled when she moved, inviting attention.

When several of the men who'd gathered in the dining room gave her more than a casual glance, she wasn't certain why. Though Bramwell had enthusiastically insisted she was a veritable fashion plate, the tiny mirror in their cabin had given her no more than a glimpse of herself.

I won't dwell on my appearance, she told herself firmly. If other women learn to manage these ridiculous skirts, so can I.

Bramwell pulled out a chair for her, then seated himself to her right. A new worry troubled Jennara: judging by the décolletage of the other woman in the dining room, her neckline was not unusually low, but she had to resist the urge to tug at it, wanting to pull it higher. She yearned for an old-fashioned fichu to cross over her neck and chest.

"I feel quite bare," she whispered to Bramwell.

"You look irresistible," he assured her. "But if that fellow in the striped trousers doesn't stop staring at you, I swear I'll forget my manners and challenge him."

Her eyes widened. "To a duel? Are you mad?"

He grinned at her. "Why not to a duel? I've never fought one, never fought at all over a lady fair. In Philadelphia we generally settle our differences otherwise. Of course, I never before met a lady fair enough."

"You're teasing me."

"Don't be too sure." He scowled at the man in the striped trousers. "I suspect he's a gambler, the riverboats are reputed to be rife with the breed."

"I certainly hope you have better sense than to involve yourself in a duel with a gambler," she said tartly.

Bramwell chuckled. "My colleagues in the east wouldn't acknowledge that such a thought even crossed my mind. I'm generally viewed as a bit stodgy."

Jennara stared at him. "You? Stodgy? I can't believe it! They must not know you very well."

"Perhaps the wild west has changed me, or maybe it was meeting a woman like you." His eyes lingered on her décolletage for a moment before meeting her gaze. She caught her breath.

Desire glowed in the dark depths of his eyes, hot and unmistakable, triggering an answering need in her. She couldn't look away, she couldn't breathe. At the same time she suddenly felt beautiful, irresistible, exactly as he told her she was.

I've changed too, she thought. Who'd ever recognize the dowdy and sensible Miss Gray as this siren wearing a gold taffeta gown who shamelessly shares a man's cabin? Not to mention his embrace.

Waiters serving the first course distracted her. The turtle soup, which she'd never before tasted, proved more palatable than she'd expected. The fish was sheepshead, quite edible. Then came a variety of entrees, meats of all kinds, turkey, pigeon, and stuffed crab. She chose the crab and discovered it to be delicious. Various wines accompanied the food and she found herself having her glass refilled without realizing how much she'd drunk.

Roasted potatoes and corn were the vegetables, followed by a dessert menu that included a variety of pies and puddings. She decided on coconut pie, with coffee. How marvelous to have such a sumptuous meal after so many weeks of catch-as-catch-can food!

Almonds, raisins, and oranges were served last.

"If I traveled by boat often, I'd grow fat and lazy," she told Bramwell as he helped her from her chair.

"Not you. More likely you'd wind up running the boat . . . and better than it had been done before."

"But all this food! And wine, I'm not used to wine—my head is spinning."

"The best remedy for a spinning head is a walk on deck," he said, leading her to the door. "Then early retirement."

Men's eyes followed her as she left the room, she realized, but she no longer cared. Bramwell was the only man who mattered.

"Yes, I do feel sleepy," she told him.

His glance told her that sleep wasn't what he had in mind, and she smiled at him in complete agreement.

"You're the most beautiful woman on board," he told her after they reached their cabin.

"I thought the redhead in the blue gown—"

"She looked like a fox."

"The blonde dressed in pink was pretty."

"Candy floss for children."

"You were definitely the most handsome man." Jennara touched his beard with loving fingers. "I quite like this. Have you decided to keep it?"

"For now."

His words were spoken lightly, but for some reason they seemed to echo with a deeper meaning. Am I also "for now," Jennara wondered.

The wine's dazing me, she told herself, making me hear echoes that don't exist. But until she was undressed and in the lower berth in Bramwell's arms, her unease persisted. Whether she wished to think of the future or not, it was near at hand.

The next morning, the *Prairie Queen* pulled away from the Kansas City dock before Jennara and Bramwell rose. After they'd eaten, they promenaded on the deck, Jennara comfortable in her riding habit. As the river turned to the east, the stark bluffs gradually evolved into more rounded hills. The incidence of snags decreased, but by no means disappeared. Other steam packets churned upriver while a side-wheeler chugged downriver ahead of them.

They passed Lexington before noon and tied up at Brunswick overnight. The next day took them to Jefferson City, where the domed capitol building, on a hill above the wharf, dominated the town.

"We'll be in St. Louis tomorrow evening," Bramwell remarked as they strolled on deck before retiring.

"The end of the journey."

"You sound sad."

"Endings sometimes can be."

He gave her a measuring glance, but when he spoke he avoided facing the issue. "This comfort is quite a contrast to the way we set out—in constant danger of marauding Indians, usually hungry, and at odds with each other. All that ended, too."

"I agree we're not likely to become targets for Dakota warriors in St. Louis, and I've never been so well fed in my life. But whether or not we'll be at odds again depends on the circumstances. What if we find that Ronald and Susanna have married already?"

Bramwell's face darkened. "I don't care to discuss what may

not have occurred. In fact, I don't want to discuss the matter at all until I have to."

She shrugged and remained silent. If he wouldn't talk about it, neither would she. But the silence brought a touch of coolness between them, forgotten in bed but there again in the morning when the *Prairie Queen* resumed her journey downriver.

In the afternoon, as they watched the passing scenery, Jennara began a conversation with an elderly gentleman who used a cane, a Mr. DuBois, who'd spoken to them several times before.

"We're approaching St. Charles," he told her. "Charming town, originally French, you know, the first permanent settlement on the Missouri River. 'Les Petites Cotes' is what they named the place."

Most fitting, she thought, noting the many rounded hills dotted with buildings.

"The Spanish came in and changed the name to San Carlos," Mr. DuBois continued. "Thus it became St. Charles when America bought the Territory. It was, you know, the first capital of the state." He pointed to a large and long brick building, easily visible from the boat. "That was the capitol."

As the *Prarie Queen* pulled to the dock Jennara noticed, beyond and behind the one-time capitol, spires and domes thrusting into the air, one spire part of a massive stone church. Near the water, old log houses chinked with plaster moldered into ruin.

"German settlers have well nigh taken over the town," Mr. DuBois went on. "How times change."

Glancing at Bramwell, Jennara noted he wasn't looking at St. Charles but staring gloomily into the brown water of Old Muddy. *He'd* certainly changed, she thought.

She went on chatting to Mr. DuBois while several passengers debarked and black loaders heaved freight off and onto the boat. A piercing whistle announced the imminent departure of the *Prairie Queen* and Jennara sighed, knowing they'd be in St. Louis in less than an hour.

As the stern-wheeler churned into the channel, Jennara looked back at St. Charles. She tensed. It couldn't be! Shading her eyes from the sun with her hand, she peered at the gaudily painted wooden-covered wagon jolting along a road near the wharf, two horses tethered to the back. No, she wasn't mistaken.

"Dr. Phineas, Medical Miracles" was painted in bold black letters across the side. And if the horses were any indication, Ronald and Susanna were still with the wagon.

"Bramwell!" she cried, grasping his arm. "Look!"

Together they stood at the rail, staring at the medicine wagon. After so long a time and so many weary miles, Jennara could hardly believe they'd finally found Dr. Phineas.

Except they hadn't, quite. It was too late to ask to be set ashore here; they'd have to wait until the next stop—and that was St. Louis.

It seemed to take forever for the boat to reach the city. Then, in the bustling confusion of the St. Louis wharf, Bramwell had difficulty finding a carriage willing to drive them to St. Charles. When they finally got underway, the shadows were lengthening into evening.

"If they're not with Dr. Phineas, he ought to know where they are," Jennara said for what she knew must be the fourth or fifth time. She wouldn't keep repeating herself if Bramwell would answer with more than a grunt. What was the matter with him? They'd finally found what they'd come all this way to find. Wasn't he pleased? Couldn't he say something?

She was tense with excitement. Soon she'd be reunited with her sister. Despite her suspicions of Susanna, she truly loved her and had long feared for her safety. And she'd worried about Ronald as well, for she'd grown fond of him.

"You said we'd catch up to them before they reached St. Louis and you were right," Jennara went on, unable to stop talking. "Not by much, but right."

"Uh," Bramwell muttered.

She felt like kicking him. Instead she stared out the carriage window at the darkening sky. What would happen when he confronted his stepbrother? She longed for it to be over. She couldn't stand the suspense and anxiety.

By the time they reached St. Charles, night had fallen. There was no sign of the medicine wagon along the main street of the town. Bidding the carriage driver to stop at a hostelry called the Tayon House, Bramwell left her to go inside and inquire.

"Dr. Phineas moved on today," he said when he returned. "To Marthasville, of all places. I can't understand why, the town's away from St. Louis rather than toward the city."

"Never get there afore midnight," the driver put in. "Anyway, I reckon my horses need a rest. Be you wanting to go on, I can take you first thing in the morning."

Since they were unlikely to find anyone else to drive them to Marthasville tonight, Bramwell reluctantly agreed to wait. They stayed in a room at the Tayon House overnight. Jennara, annoyed by Bramwell's dark mood, turned away from him when he tried to kiss her. He didn't try again. Though they shared the same bed, they might have been oceans apart.

She woke at dawn after sleeping poorly. Bramwell was already up and dressing. If he didn't wish to talk to her, then she'd say nothing to him, she decided. Downstairs in the inn, they ate bread and drank coffee in silence. The driver was waiting with the carriage when they finished.

Marthasville was near the Mississippi River, a small community scattered along the slopes of the bluffs. It proved easy enough to find the medicine wagon, parked near a large log cabin which housed a store. Why the wagon had turned back rather than gone on was a mystery, but at least they'd caught up to it at last, even if no one was in it.

"Those wagon folks went to see a minister," Mr. Grabs, the storekeeper, told them. "Seems the Reverend Jones is an old friend of Dr. Phineas. Calls himself Father Jones on account of being Episcopalian."

"Jones," Bramwell echoed. "Are there many by that name around here?"

Mr. Grabs nodded. "Most aren't related to the minister, though. He's a newcomer, only been here ten years."

After describing the "wagon folks" to them, he told them how to reach the Episcopal manse. The carriage driver was eager to return to St. Louis, so Bramwell, satisfied he'd caught up with Ronald, paid the driver and dismissed him.

Jennara fought to hold her tongue. She was bubbling over with questions, but she'd made up her mind not to speak to Bramwell unless he spoke to her. At the last moment she turned back to Mr. Grabs.

"Did you ever hear of a Llwellyn Jones in Marthasville?" she asked.

"We've had three or four by that name, son after father, you understand."

"Have any of the Llwellyns come back to town recently?"

Mr. Grabs pondered. "Don't recall as any of them ever left, except for the one who joined up with the Rebs. Seems to me I heard something about him just the other day. Let me see, now—"

Bramwell, who'd started off down the road, stopped to look back impatiently. Jennara thanked the storekeeper and hurried to join Bramwell. Susanna and Ronald were far more important than tracing down the traitorous Llwellyn.

Bramwell, his brows drawn together, said not a word as he strode along so fast that Jennara found herself trotting to keep up with him. She wanted to speculate aloud on why Ronald and Susanna had suddenly gone looking for a minister. The only possible reason would be to get married. Why was it so urgent for them to marry before they reached St. Louis? But if Bramwell was determined to shut her out, she'd keep her thoughts to herself.

The Episcopal church was red brick, a solid structure with a slate-roofed steeple. Next to it was the manse, a modest two-story house painted white, with rose-of-Sharon bushes at either side of the steps. A few late pink blooms glowed amidst the green leaves. Following Bramwell, Jennara hurried up the stairs onto the porch. He grasped the brass knocker and banged it against the front door.

After a moment a plump, middle-aged woman opened the door and peered out at them.

"Is a wedding going on here?" Bramwell demanded before she had a chance to open her mouth.

The woman blinked, obviously taken aback by his abruptness. "I'm Mrs. Jones," she said. "Do you know the young couple?"

Bramwell, reminded of his manners, introduced himself and Jennara. "We're related to the couple," he added in a milder tone.

"Then of course you must come in," Mrs. Jones said.

Perfunctorily he ushered Jennara inside, and they followed Mrs. Jones to a large parlor where a white-haired man with a long drooping mustache was talking to a clergyman. Evidently, they were Dr. Phineas and Father Jones.

Jennara glanced quickly around. Ronald and Susanna stood by three large bay windows, holding hands and looking at one another. Neither turned to see who'd come into the room. From the corner of her eye, Jennara saw Bramwell glower at them.

Remembering her suspicions, she focused on her sister and drew in her breath in dismay at what she saw. There was no time to waste, she must take Susanna aside immediately and talk to her. She started to call her sister's name.

Before the word was out, Bramwell's voice cut across hers. "For the love of god, Ronald," he said angrily, "have you no eyes? You haven't known the woman long enough for the brat to be yours."

Ronald and Susanna whirled to face them, their hands still together.

"And you, Miss Gray," Bramwell went on. "Have you no shame? Or did you plan to pass the child off as Ronald's. He's

284

naive enough to believe you, but it's obvious to anyone with half an eye you're too far along."

Susanna wrenched away from Ronald, put both her hands over her obviously thickened waistline, and burst into tears. Jennara glared at Bramwell and hurried across the room to her sister.

"It's true," Susanna sobbed, clinging to Jennara. "But I was going to tell, honest I was." She raised her head and looked at Ronald, tears streaming down her cheeks. "You must believe me," she cried. "I truly love you. I was going to confess to you about the baby. Before the wedding. He—he didn't give me a chance."

Ronald said nothing, staring at Susanna, his face white and stricken.

"If you believe that, you're a greater fool than I thought," Bramwell said to him.

Jennara, one arm around her sister, took a deep breath. "Haven't you done enough damage?" she demanded of Bramwell, her voice trembling with fury. "Have the grace to shut your mouth."

Ronald took a step toward Susanna. "Whose is it?" he said, his voice almost a whisper.

"He—forced me," she gasped between sobs. "He beat me. I ran away. I never loved him. Never!"

Jennara, shaking with rage at Bramwell and torn by pity for her sister, watched Ronald's expression change and harden. No longer did he look younger than his age, boyish and innocent. Hurt and disillusionment gave way to anger as he turned from Susanna and walked away. Bramwell put a hand out to him as he passed, but Ronald knocked the hand away and left the room. The front door opened and closed.

"He's gone," Susanna sobbed. "He's gone."

Jennara looked over her sister's head at Bramwell. "You've ruined two lives," she said coldly. "I hope you're satisfied."

Bramwell stared at her. Had Jennara known all along that Susanna was with child? She'd obviously had misgivings about the marriage. Was that why? If it was, why the hell hadn't she told him?

Why was she so angry with him now? He'd only stated the truth. He'd done the right thing. The marriage, based on deceit, had to be stopped and he'd stopped it. Why was she looking at him as though she'd gladly see him dead?

"Sir," Father Jones said to him, "you might have found a more tactful way to break the news. I greatly fear for that young man's welfare. Someone ought to go after him."

Even the minister was against him, Bramwell thought. What in God's name did he expect Ronald to do, jump in the river? Still, he should go and find Ronald and talk some sense into him.

He turned to Mrs. Jones. "Is there a hotel in this town?" he asked.

"Mrs. Knute, three doors down, lets rooms," she said soberly.

"Jennara, I'll meet you later at Mrs. Knute's," Bramwell said. He turned on his heel and strode from the house.

To his surprise, the white-mustached man caught up to him on the path. "I'm Dr. Phineas," the man said, "and I've traveled all the way from the border of Minnesota with those two. I'm here to tell you, young man, that you've made a grave mistake. Yes, a mighty error in judgment. They would have worked this out between them, given time. You, sir, have parted two loving hearts with your unnecessarily cruel words. You'll regret what you've done, mark my words, for regret it you surely will."

Before Bramwell had a chance to defend himself, Dr. Phineas turned away from him and returned to the manse.

Bramwell shook his head. Ronald had to be told, it was as simple as that . . . so he'd told him. Did no one approve? He remembered reading that in olden times the messenger who brought bad news was often beheaded by the king, and he smiled wryly. It was fortunate for him that there were no kings in Marthasville.

He hadn't meant to be cruel to Jennara's sister or to Ronald. But how could he be expected to stand by and see his stepbrother gulled into marrying a woman who carried another man's child? Susanna certainly had no intention of saying a word to Ronald, regardless of what she'd blurted out when she knew she was trapped.

He meant to settle things once he found Ronald and calmed him down. He wouldn't leave Susanna stranded here. He'd see she got back to Minnesota; he'd put her on a train for Chicago with Jennara. From there the two of them could board one to St. Paul. As for Ronald, he'd take the boy back to Philadelphia with him. Ronald would soon get over her, as he had the other women who'd tried to trap him into marriage.

Just as he'd get over Jennara? A sense of desolation settled into him and he sighed. How he felt about Jennara would have to wait. At the moment he must concentrate on finding Ronald.

Bramwell searched everywhere . . . at the local inn, at a rundown hostelry, at the local tavern, at the medicine wagon. He went into Mr. Grabs's store and asked after Ronald there. Mr. Grabs had neither seen him nor heard anything about him.

"I'll let you know if I do hear of your stepbrother's whereabouts," Mr. Grabs told him. "Most people in town come by here sooner or later, and if he's anywhere around, I'm sure to find out."

Where the hell was Ronald? Bramwell didn't for a moment believe he'd done anything foolish. In any case, there were no public conveyances in the town, and the two horses Susanna and Ronald had ridden from Minnesota were still tied by the medicine wagon.

Ronald could have gotten some crazy notion in his head about joining up with the Rebs, though. Would he be fool enough to set off on foot to try?

At last Bramwell headed back to Mrs. Knute's. He'd make certain Jennara and Susanna were settled in before resuming his search for Ronald.

"Why, yes, I've given the young ladies a very nice room on the second floor," Mrs. Knute told him as she showed him into the parlor. "Would you like me to tell them you're here?"

Bramwell felt a thrust of pain when her words made him realize there'd be no more sharing of rooms with Jennara. "If you don't mind," he told Mrs. Knute, "would you ask Miss Jennara Gray to come down and have a word with me?"

He waited impatiently in the parlor. If only he knew where Ronald had gotten to! The boy's disappearance had begun to worry him.

"You asked to see me?" Jennara stood in the doorway, her eyes cold, her voice icy.

"I want you to stay here at Mrs. Knute's until I locate Ronald," he said.

"You mean you haven't found him yet?"

He shook his head. "It's only a matter of time until I do. After that, we can make arrangements for—" He paused, looking at her. How was he ever going to say good-bye to this woman? Somehow she'd affected him more deeply than he'd realized.

"Arrangements?"

"I presume you'll be taking Susanna back to Minnesota."

"She and I haven't discussed it yet."

He waved an impatient hand. "What choice is there? I want you to know I'll take care of the arrangements."

"How noble."

Anger kindled in him. He clenched his jaw to avoid a sharp retort. He had no time to quarrel with Jennara . . . no time to pull her into his arms, either. "If you remain here, I'll be able to find you when I return with Ronald." He did his best to keep his tone reasonable. "Is that too much to ask?"

"Since we have no place else to go and no way of going if we did, I imagine we'll be here when you return."

She spoke as though to a stranger, one she distrusted. Hated? Perhaps it was better this way, easier in the long run. Why, then, did his heart ache?

But, damn it, he wasn't wrong! He'd done the right thing. If Jennara could be honest with herself, she'd admit it. *She* was being unreasonable, not he.

"Where do you think Ronald is?" she asked.

"Somewhere about."

"In other words, you don't know. You've looked everywhere you could think of and you haven't found him."

Damn the woman. She always forced everything into the open. "I'll find him," he said curtly.

"I certainly hope so. I'm extremely worried about him."

I suppose she blames me for Ronald's disillusionment, he thought. Not the real villain, her sister. "Would you have had me remain silent?" he demanded.

"There was no cause to be cruel. I thought I'd come to understand you a little, but I realize now I was wrong. What you did today convinces me the sooner I see the last of you, the better I'll like it." She turned away and marched toward the stairs.

Bramwell took two steps after her, then stopped. No . . . if that's the way she felt, let her go. He didn't need Jennara in his life. The sooner he saw the Gray sisters aboard a Chicago-bound train, the sooner he could go about his own affairs and, forget them.

But as he strode from the house, intent on finding his stepbrother, the image of Jennara's face stayed with him. Not with the chill, haughty expression he'd just seen, but warm with love, inviting his embrace.

Love? The word, the idea, shook him. Why had he come up with such a ridiculous notion? She'd never loved him. The Gray sisters weren't capable of love, either of them. So good riddance to both of them.

Chapter 20

When Jennara returned to the upstairs room Mrs. Knute had rented to them, Susanna was no longer weeping. Instead she sat by the window, though there was nothing to see but the branches of a maple tree growing close to the house.

"The leaves are late in turning this far south," Jennara observed with forced heartiness. "At home I imagine they're all shades of crimson and gold by now."

Susanna didn't answer, continuing to stare at the leaves, but Jennara doubted she saw them. More than likely, Susanna was looking at the pictures in her own mind, reliving the unpleasantness, and it was time she stopped. Perhaps talking about it would help her get over the worst. Jennara crossed to her and rested a hand on her sister's shoulder. Susanna reached up to cover Jennara's hand with her own.

"What happened wasn't your fault," she said, her voice slightly hoarse from crying. "I'm the only one to blame."

Jennara couldn't find an answer to this. While she'd never be able to forgive him, Bramwell certainly wasn't to blame for Susanna's condition, or the fact that she hadn't admitted the truth to Ronald earlier. Ronald's shock at the news was to be expected. Jennara only hoped he hadn't rushed to do anything foolish.

As if reading her thoughts, Susanna said, "Do you think he's all right?"

"Ronald needs time to come to terms with all this," Jennara said, avoiding a direct answer.

"I didn't mean to hurt him, Jen." Tears brightened Susanna's blue eyes. "I never wanted to hurt him. He's the sweetest, kindest man in the whole world. I could never love another as I do Ronnie."

Again Jennara was at a loss for words. Was she to berate her sister for not revealing the truth sooner? To falsely console her by saying Ronald would recover? Finding no easy answer, she asked the question that had been bothering her since she and Bramwell had arrived in Marthasville.

"Why didn't you tell Ronald about the baby earlier?"

"I—I couldn't. I tried, but—" Susanna broke off and bit her lip.

Realizing her sister would begin crying again if she pushed for more of an answer, Jennara turned to another question. "But why did you and Ronald turn back at St. Charles and come to Marthasville? And why did you decide to marry here, instead of in St. Louis?"

Susanna turned in the chair, her fingers clutching at Jennara's hand. "I saw *him* in St. Charles, I know I did . . . and even worse, he saw me." Her tears dried as fear darkened her eyes. "So I wouldn't go on to St. Louis. Dr. Phineas said he had a minister friend, Father Jones, in Marthasville. That's why we came here."

Jennara stared, not having the slightest notion what her sister meant. "*Who* saw you? What are you talking about?"

"Curtis Hayes. He beat me, you know. My face was swollen for days. He's a terrible man. I'm so afraid of him!"

Putting some of it together, Jennara said, "Mr. Hayes fathered the child you carry?"

Susanna nodded, turning her face away. "I didn't want to—you know. But he wouldn't listen and I couldn't stop him. He—hurt me. I tried to run away, but I didn't have any money or anywhere to go, and he caught me and beat me." Susanna shivered, hugging herself. "Oh, Jen, he'll kill me if he finds me!"

"He can't know you're in Marthasville."

"What if he followed the wagon?" Susanna rose from the chair and clung to her sister. "I thought if I married Ronnie, then I'd be safe."

"Does Ronald know you saw Mr. Hayes in St. Charles?"

Susanna shook her head. "How could I tell him? He doesn't know Curtis exists. I couldn't speak of Curtis without telling him everything, even about my — my condition. I think Dr. Phineas suspected I was in the family way. He hinted once or twice that I should talk to Ronnie. I tried and tried to find enough courage to, but I was so afraid he'd leave me once he knew. And I love him, Jen, I really do."

Jennara patted her sister's shoulder. "Don't worry about this Curtis Hayes, whoever he is. I won't allow him to get near you."

Susanna drew back, her face pale and pinched. "You couldn't stop him. He does what he wants, no matter what. I just know he's followed me. What am I going to do?"

Jennara led her to the bed and persuaded her to lie down. "Try to rest."

Susanna stuffed the second pillow under her head and stared up at her sister. "You must be wondering how I came to be involved with such an awful man."

"It did cross my mind."

"After the acting troupe dissolved, I was on my own. I never had enough money, that was the trouble. I can sing a little and I can play the piano, and that was enough when I was with the troupe, but it's not easy to find a position playing a piano in St. Louis . . . a decent position, anyway. What else could I do? I would've come home, but I never had enough money to afford boat passage or a train ticket. I finally took a job as a cook. It wasn't a — a very nice place, and that's where I met Curtis. He wouldn't leave me alone. He followed me to my room and made the landlady so cross that she asked me to leave.

"So then I didn't have a place to stay and, well, he said I could stay with him, he'd take care of me. I didn't know what else to do, but I never should have believed him. Once he got me alone, he attacked me like a vicious animal. I thought I was going to die, I really did." Tears seeped down her cheeks. "Now I wish I had."

"No, you don't."

Susanna shook her head. "I stole some money from him to buy a ticket to St. Paul. That's how I got away. I never told him where I was from, so I knew I'd be safe in Minnesota. But when I came home I met Ronnie. . . ."

"Why on earth did you ever agree to go back to St. Louis?"

"Ronnie was set on getting married there. He'd made up his mind to join the Confederates and he has this Cousin Farrell in St. Louis who he was sure would help him join the Rebs. He wanted us to have our wedding at his cousin's house. Ronnie's sweet and gentle, but once he makes up his mind, no one can change it. *I* certainly tried. All he'd do was promise me he'd see I got safely back to Minnesota once we were married. I wanted to marry him, I didn't know what else to do but go with him. Besides, I could see you suspected about — about the baby, and I was afraid you'd never agree to me marrying Ronnie."

"If only you'd confided in me, Susie." Jennara used her old, affectionate name for her sister. "We could have worked things out."

"I was afraid I'd lose Ronnie. You've never been in love, you don't know how it is."

Jennara closed her eyes for a brief moment as pain knotted inside her. Not been in love? Her sister didn't know the half of it. How could she admit to Susanna that she'd fallen in love with a man she'd always known she couldn't trust, the same man who'd ruined Susanna's chances of happiness?

"If only I could see Ronnie just one more time," Susanna cried. "If only I could be sure he's all right. When you talked to that terrible stepbrother of his downstairs, did he say anything about Ronnie?"

"He was going to look for him. He means to bring Ronald here when he finds him."

Susanna sat up and began fussing with her hair. "I can't let Ronnie see me like this. I look a fright."

Hoping to distract her sister, Jennara found her brush and had started to tidy Susanna's hair when someone knocked on the door.

"Don't open it!" Susanna whispered fearfully.

"Who's there?" Jennara asked.

"There's a Dr. Phineas downstairs," Mrs. Knute said. "He says he has some things for Miss Susanna Gray."

"My belongings from the wagon," Susanna said to Jennara. "Tell him I'll be right down," she called to Mrs. Knute.

When Susanna returned to the room carrying a carpetbag, her face was ashen. Her hand trembled as she placed the bag on a chair. "Curtis knows where I am," she said. "He found Dr. Phineas and he asked him."

"How do you know it was Curtis?"

" 'A big redheaded man,' the doctor said. Who else could it be?"

"Dr. Phineas told him you were here, in this house?"

"No, no he didn't. He said he had no idea where I was because he didn't like Curtis's looks. But it's only a matter of time until Curtis finds me. We've got to get away before then, Jen. Please!"

"How?"

"We've got the two horses."

Jennara had forgotten all about the horses Susanna and Ronald had ridden away on. The black mare was in good condition, but the other, a chestnut, was their elderly wagon horse. It was a wonder he'd made it to Missouri, and probably he wouldn't have if he hadn't been able to walk at a slow pace behind the wagon for most of the way.

"I doubt we'd get far on old Ben," she said.

"He got Ronnie to the Minnesota border," Susanna insisted.

"Where you met Dr. Phineas?" At her sister's nod, she said, "Ben's old and he's no saddle horse. I don't believe he'd make it home to Minnesota with one of us riding him at a normal pace. I doubt he can go more than a mile faster than a walk. Anyway, that's a long and dangerous trip for two women alone, one of them in the family way. Besides—" About to say they had no money, she paused, reminded of the five gold coins Bramwell insisted she keep for him. She still had the coins, though obviously she must return them.

"I have to get away," Susanna moaned, twisting her fingers together. "He'll kill me this time. You don't have any idea what he's capable of. And now he'll be even worse because I took his money. Please help me, Jen."

Deciding she needed to find out for herself if Curtis really was on her sister's trail, Jennara pondered the matter. If it turned out Curtis was in town, any attempt by her to contact whomever Marthasville might have in the way of a law officer would most likely be useless. Even if she found such a person, she doubted he'd take any interest. If he heard about the stolen money, he might even be on Curtis's side. She'd have to solve the problem of Curtis herself.

Finally she said, "Look, Susie, there's a bolt on the inside of our door. I'm going out. I promise I won't be gone long. I want you to shoot the bolt once you close the door behind me. Don't open it until I come back and you're sure it's me. All right?"

Susanna nodded dubiously. "You will find a way to help me, won't you?" she begged.

"I promise I'll try."

Assuring herself that no matter how dangerous this Curtis might be, he didn't know Jennara Gray from the next woman, Jennara walked away from the house, apparently on a casual stroll, but actually checking her surroundings for any sign of a redheaded man.

She'd go as far as the wagon, she thought, crossing the

wooden planks of a footbridge over a stream. If she didn't find him there, she'd try the main street. She was on the alert or she'd never have noticed the tall man easing in and out of the trees along the bank of the stream, keeping in the shadows — evidently someone who hoped not to be seen. Jennara checked her stride, dawdling along so she could get a better look at him.

Pretending to drop something, she leaned down as though to pick it up, surreptitiously eyeing the man. Though his wide-brimmed hat all but concealed his hair, she could see it wasn't red. Somehow, though, he looked familiar. Why? Was he someone she'd met here in Marthasville? She caught back her gasp when she realized she was looking at Llwellyn Jones. Her Llwellyn Jones, the Union spy.

Straightening, he glanced quickly around. No one else was in sight. "Well, Mr. Jones," she said coolly, "who'd ever think to meet you again? And in Marthasville. I thought you were lying about that, too."

He stopped dead.

"Don't bother thinking up more lies," she went on, an idea forming. "I wouldn't give one cent for anything you had to say."

"Ma'am, you've made a mistake," he began.

"It's miss, not madam, and I've made no error. Don't bother trying to convince me . . . or Bramwell. He knows you're here, too. Mr. Grabs told him. I imagine you're surprised I'm alive. It must astound you to discover Bramwell is, too."

His eyes flickered slightly, but he maintained the mildly puzzled expression.

"Naturally, Bramwell's somewhat peeved with you," she told him. "I wouldn't give much for your chances once he meets up with you. As for me, I want my pony back."

He spread his hands. "What can I say to convince you — ?"

"Nothing. I know better than to believe you this time. But you're in luck . . . you met me instead of Bramwell. I'm not out for revenge. I don't want to kill you. All I want from you is my pony. You coveted him from the moment you laid eyes on him, so I know you've kept Swift Runner. I want him *now!*"

He started when she spat out the last word. When he didn't respond, she added, "Or should I speak to Mr. Grabs again? He's such a pleasant, *talkative* man."

Llwellyn held up a hand. "I admit nothing, but just supposing I was this person you take me for." He looked at her warily. "How would you get the horse?"

"By having you tie him outside Mrs. Knute's, with his saddle. I imagine it could be done quite casually. Who'd pay attention? With your capacity for stealth, I doubt anyone would even notice you come and go. Once the pony's left there, what's to prevent you from visiting friends somewhere else? St. Louis, perhaps. Of course, should you decide to visit St. Louis without leaving the pony behind, I can't guarantee what might happen. I may be on the side of the Union, but I have my limits and you've already breached them once."

Without a word, he turned his back and hurried off the way he'd come. Jennara stared after him, unsure whether he'd bring her the pony or not. Llwellyn was not to be trusted. She loathed the man. If she hadn't been in desperate need of a good horse, she wouldn't have made any attempt to deal with him. Jennara shrugged and continued on. She'd hope for the best.

Finding no sign of a redheaded man near the wagon, she started back to Mrs. Knute's, choosing an indirect route that would take her through the center of town, the most likely place to find Curtis.

Jennara almost missed spotting him. Because he was with two other men when she expected him to be alone, and because he wore a hat with an eagle feather in the band pulled low over his forehead, she didn't at first notice the color of his hair. The three men, roughly dressed and swaggering, reminded her of the raftsmen and she looked quickly away, not wanting to attract their attention. She might never have given them a second glance if one of the men hadn't muttered, as she approached, "Looka that piece of ass, Red. How 'bout her instead of your flown birdie?"

Jennara immediately fled into a nearby drapery shop and from the inside unobtrusively observed the three without their noticing. One definitely was a redhead.

Pretending to examine a bolt of flowered calico, she lingered in the shop until they'd gone. Even then she waited until she was certain they wouldn't see her before she left and hurried toward Mrs. Knute's, appalled at the kind of man Curtis appeared to be . . . for surely that was Curtis. Susanna did well to be frightened of him. He looked as though he'd stop at nothing. She had no way of knowing if the two with him were friends of his or men he'd met here in Marthasville, but he seemed to have told them about Susanna. Seeing him had convinced her that she must get Susanna away from here fast, on old Ben, if need be.

As she rushed up the stairs to Susanna's room, she slowed, struck by a thought. They could use a man's help. If she told Bramwell—? Jennara shook her head. After what he'd done to Susanna, she could no longer count on him for anything. He'd probably decide Curtis was no more than Susanna deserved.

"Pack!" she ordered after her sister let her into the room. "Take no more than can go in a saddlebag, and leave room for food and blankets. I'm going to talk to Mrs. Knute."

Susanna called after her, but Jennara didn't stop to answer questions as she flew back down the stairs.

Mrs. Knute was quite willing to pack cheese, bread, and apples for them. She parted with two good wool blankets when she saw the gold coin Jennara offered and added two tin cups and a water flask.

When Jennara went to the barn in back to check on the horses, Swift Runner nickered at her from where he was tied to an oak sapling. She rushed to throw her arms around his neck, thankful her bluff had worked. He was already saddled—she must have put the fear of God into Llwellyn. Quickly she retrieved one of the saddles Dr. Phineas had left in the barn and put it on Soot, the black mare. In less than a half-hour from the time she'd seen Curtis, Jennara and Susanna were ready to leave.

It galled her to hide the coins in her hem again. She desperately wanted to leave the rest of the money for Mrs. Knute to give back to Bramwell, but Susanna's safety was more important than anything else. She'd keep the coins for train tickets and in case she needed the money for her sister. Eventually she'd return every cent to Bramwell, if it took her the rest of her life.

Leaving a message with Mrs. Knute asking Dr. Phineas to take care of old Ben and telling her they were heading for St. Louis, Jennara and Susanna rode away from Marthasville.

As soon as they were out of sight of the town, Jennara changed direction, riding north. Susanna was in no condition to tolerate the grueling ride home, so Jennara planned to intersect the railroad she'd been told ran west to east across Missouri from St. Joseph and buy passage to Chicago, then on to St. Paul.

Anyone trying to trail them, she hoped, would be fooled by the news that they'd gone to St. Louis. Though St. Louis was closer to the railroad, Susanna had become hysterical at the idea of traveling there, afraid Curtis would surely run her down in his own city, so Jennara had altered her original plan to board the train in St. Louis.

"Is he following us?" Susanna kept asking after leaving Mrs. Knute's house.

When she asked once more, Jennara replied patiently, "There's no sign of Curtis . . . or anyone else." At least Susanna's fear of Curtis had taken her mind off losing Ronald.

If only I could forget Bramwell, Jennara thought. He lingered in her mind—his wry smile, the way his eyes warmed when he looked at her, the touch of his hand. They'd been through so much together. She counted herself well rid of him, but she couldn't help but wonder if she would ever truly be free of the memories.

"I want to name the baby Ronald Gregory if it's a boy," Susanna said after a time. "Gregory for our father. Or, if it's a girl, after Mama. I didn't want it at first, I hated carrying Curtis's baby, but now I think of it as mine. Not his, at all . . . just mine."

In years to come, what would they tell the child about its father? That he'd died in the war? Jennara shook her head impatiently. There was nothing to gain from worrying about what was to come. They weren't out of danger yet, and she'd do well to concentrate on making sure of their safety.

"If it is a boy," Susanna went on, "and I name him Ronald, it'll be almost like Ronnie really was his father." She smiled wistfully. "I wish he was."

Jennara sighed. Susanna would never be practical, and there was no use in trying to change her. She summoned an answering smile. "Ronald Gregory's a fine name."

"It has a noble sound, much more than his awful stepbrother's name — Bramwell. It sounds like a stomping boot. Harsh. Mean. Just like him. How did you ever manage to travel with such a man?"

"It wasn't easy much of the time," Jennara admitted. She had no intention of telling Susanna anything about the other times, the wonderful times. For they'd been wonderful, no matter what had happened later.

"You said you were on a Missouri River packet. Where did you catch the boat? In Sioux City, Iowa?"

"Lower down." Jennara was determined not to be specific. "Because of the Dakota uprising, we had some difficulties."

"Wasn't that a terrible tragedy? I guess we were lucky to get into Iowa without being killed. But we didn't know a thing about any Indian raids until folks in Iowa told us. At least it's over now. Dr. Phineas heard just yesterday that the Army's got four hundred Dakota warriors on trial and means to hang them by Christmas."

300

"Four hundred? That's too many!" Jennara was appalled. Hanging all those men would mean disaster for many Dakota families. With no young men left to hunt, the women, children, and old men would all starve.

"If they're dead they can't do any more raiding," Susanna pointed out. "You're as bad as Papa, you always take the Indians' side. What about those poor settlers they killed?"

Jennara remembered the murdered settlers all too well. What was the answer? To send all the Dakotas farther west, away from settled land? They wouldn't want to go. Minnesota was their home as much as it was the settlers'. It would be unfair, cruel. But wouldn't it be better than hanging so many of them? And wouldn't it prevent a "next time"?

She thought of No Cloud and hoped he was safe. The old shaman was a man of peace, but angry soldiers wouldn't bother to differentiate between a warrior and any other Dakota brave.

"It was a terrible time," Jennara admitted. "We had to keep running and hiding. I wasn't sure Bramwell and I were going to survive."

"Too bad he did!"

Jennara bit her lip to keep from defending him, finally saying mildly, "Whatever he did, he doesn't deserve to die."

"Did you actually *like* the man?" Susanna's tone was tinged with suspicion.

"At times, yes. When you're on the run, you develop a certain camaraderie."

Susanna looked dubious.

"Bramwell's not a Curtis," Jennara said a bit more tartly than she intended. Why was she defending him?

When Susanna's face paled and she glanced behind them apprehensively, Jennara was sorry she'd mentioned Curtis's name. She'd chosen a back road rather than the often-traveled one in the belief that if fewer people saw them, they were less likely to be found. Not that she expected anyone *had* followed them from Marthasville.

301

"When we come to a rise, I'll climb it and check our back trail to make sure no one we know is following," Jennara promised in order to calm her sister.

They rode in silence for a time until Susanna said, "You're riding an Indian pony. Wherever did you find one in the middle of Missouri?"

"He's mine. A Dakota woman gave him to me." She left it at that, not explaining the circumstances.

"I suppose you had to leave Sage behind when you took passage on the packet."

"Something like that, yes."

A while later Susanna said plaintively, "I'm getting awfully tired."

"Hold on a bit longer. I see a bluff up ahead. We'll stop there and you can rest while I climb it to check our back trail."

By the time they reached the bluff, rode off the trail, and halted, Susanna all but fell from the mare. Jennara removed a blanket from the saddlebag and laid it on the ground and Susanna stretched out, closing her eyes. Looking down at her, Jennara realized with dismay that her sister couldn't ride much farther, though there were still several hours till dusk. She'd hoped to reach the railroad before sundown tomorrow, but she saw now they wouldn't.

With a last look at her sister, she walked to the foot of the bluff. Trees grew on the slopes, but the rocky top was barren. She searched for a game trail to make the climb through the trees easier.

Jennara was breathing hard when she came to the top of the bluff and she paused to rest a moment. The leaves of the trees below hid sections of their back trail, so she waited and watched, giving any riders time to reach the open stretches she could see.

The view was spectacular. To the south Old Muddy snaked along, brown in the lowering sun, and to the east she caught a glimpse of water she knew must be the Mississippi River. Church spires of otherwise hidden towns showed tiny and

302

toylike above the trees. And along the trail, not so very far behind them, rode three men.

Jennara drew in her breath. At this distance she couldn't be certain, but one of them wore his hat pulled low, as Curtis had done, and she thought she saw a feather thrusting up from the hat. She didn't dare take any chances, not with men like those she'd seen on the street in Marthasville.

She flung herself down the slope of the bluff. Limbs and twigs tore at her hair and her clothes as she plunged through the trees. She was afraid to alert Susanna by shouting because sound often carried farther than you'd expect. Her sister was crouched on the blanket, terrified, when Jennara burst into the open.

"I heard the noise but I wasn't sure it was you!" Susanna cried.

Jennara, out of breath, put a finger to her lips. "Talk quietly," she gasped.

"He's coming." Susanna, huddling, whispered the words. "I knew he would. I'll never get away from him."

Jennara knew her sister wasn't fit to ride, but she didn't dare stay where they were, at the foot of a bluff with no place to hide. They had to move on quickly and search for a good hiding place.

"You can and you will escape from him," she assured her sister. "We both will."

Reaching down, Jennara pulled Susanna to her feet, all but lifting her into the saddle. Mounting her own pony, Jennara gave Soot a swat with the reins that sent the mare into instant motion.

With Soot in the lead and Swift Runner following, they broke from the brush back onto the trail. The winding of the road behind them hid them from the men.

"We've been dawdling," Jennara said, "but no longer. Now we run."

Chapter 21

After a futile search for Ronald along the roads leading from town, Bramwell trudged wearily back to Mr. Grabs's store.

"No one who's come by has seen hide nor hair of your stepbrother," Mr. Grabs told him. "Didn't the women find him either?"

"The women?" Bramwell echoed.

"The Misses Gray. They rode past maybe an hour ago. That's a nice little buckskin pony Miss Jennara has."

Bramwell stared at Mr. Grabs. Jennara on a buckskin pony? Where had she gotten it? And what was she doing riding off when he'd told her to remain at Mrs. Knute's? Of all the difficult women in the world, Jennara topped the list.

"Which way were the sisters heading when you saw them?" he asked.

"Why, down the St. Louis road." Mr. Grabs peered at Bramwell closely. "Something wrong, Mr. Sumner?"

Bramwell shook his head, wondering just what Jennara was up to . . . perhaps Dr. Phineas knew. He asked Mr. Grabs if he'd seen the doctor.

"I reckon he's staying with Father Jones and his wife. As I told you before, they're old friends."

Leaving the store, Bramwell decided to stop by Mrs. Knute's before looking for Dr. Phineas.

"Miss Jennara bought food and blankets from me," Mrs.

Knute told him. "I understood they were intending to travel to St. Louis." She hesitated, then asked, "Would you be seeing Dr. Phineas, sir?"

"Yes." Bramwell spoke absently, trying to decipher what was in Jennara's mind.

"Well, Miss Jennara gave me a message for him. It's about the old horse tethered by my barn. She wanted the doctor to take care of him."

Bramwell blinked, confused by the message. "What horse?"

"Old Ben, she called him. You see, Dr. Phineas brought the two horses here—the old chestnut and a black mare—along with Miss Susanna's belongings."

More confused then ever, Bramwell said, "But I was told Jennara rode off on a buckskin pony."

Mrs. Knute nodded. "Some man brought the pony after Dr. Phineas left. I didn't get a good look at him, but he was tall. Came out of the woods, he did, tied the pony to a sapling, and ducked right back into the trees. I thought it was strange at the time. Miss Jennara, though, she seemed to be expecting the pony. She hugged that horse like he was an old friend."

The pony could only be Swift Runner. That bastard Llwellyn Jones *was* in town, then. Somehow Jennara must have met him, but how the devil had she persuaded him to give her back the pony?

"Did Jennara leave any other messages?" he asked.

"No, sir."

Upset as she'd been with him, he hadn't really expected her to let him know where she was going, but it hurt that she hadn't. "They didn't say what they meant to do in St. Louis?" he asked her.

Mrs. Knute shook her head.

Why couldn't Jennara have waited for him? Bramwell fumed. It was the height of foolishness to rush off with no man along for protection, but typical of her stubborn nature.

He thanked Mrs. Knute and asked what he owed her for her trouble.

"Miss Jennara paid for everything, sir. You owe nothing."

Only then did he recall how Jennara had tried to give him back the coins she'd kept for him and how he'd refused. He was relieved to think she had enough money to afford train fare for herself and her sister back to Minnesota. Surely that was what she meant to do. Why else would she ride to St. Louis? He fought an urge to follow her, knowing it was impossible until he located Ronald. Damn it, he hated being stranded in this backwater without so much as a horse of his own.

"Is there a saddle for old Ben?" he asked.

"As far as I know, Dr. Phineas brought two of them and the ladies, they only used the one — for the mare. The pony came with a saddle on him, he did."

"Since I'm going to Dr. Phineas now, I'll saddle Ben and ride him there."

"That's fine with me, sir."

Mrs. Knute showed Bramwell through to the back door and walked out toward the barn with him. Halfway there, she gasped and grabbed at his arm. "Why, the old horse is gone!" she exclaimed.

Bramwell ran to the barn and found the saddle missing as well. So Ben hadn't merely pulled loose and wandered off.

"You're certain the women didn't take Ben?" he asked.

She looked at him severely. "I watched them ride away with my own two eyes and the old horse was not with them, he was still tied by the barn."

"Do you have any idea how long he's been gone?"

"I was in back taking down clothes less than an hour ago and he was here then."

Ronald, he realized suddenly. Ronald knew about the horse. He'd ridden him until he met up with the medicine wagon. Ronald had taken Ben and was probably on his way to St. Louis, too.

"Don't worry about Ben," Bramwell said. "I think my step-brother has him. I'll explain to Dr. Phineas."

306

Bramwell hurriedly made his way to the Episcopal manse. He planned to probe the doctor for any information he could glean, then ask Father Jones if he knew anyone who had a horse for sale. He was damned if he'd be left behind while everyone else rode off to St. Louis.

"Yes, Ronald did take Ben," Dr. Phineas admitted. "He saw Susanna and her sister on horseback and was determined to go after them."

"That leaves nothing for me to do but join the exodus to St. Louis."

"St. Louis?" Dr. Phineas frowned. "Why would you be going there?"

Bramwell looked at him in surprise. "Because everyone else is—my stepbrother and the Gray sisters."

"I find it strange you should think so. From what Ronald told me, I believe they were headed north."

Extracting the complete story from the doctor took a few minutes. Ronald, who'd apparently been wandering in the woods near the town, finally decided he must return and talk to Susanna. He was more or less lost by this time, but he eventually found wagon ruts and followed them, hoping to come to the town. He was approaching a road when he saw the two women ride past on it and realized one was Susanna on Soot, the black mare. He shouted but she didn't hear, and by the time he ran to the road, they'd rounded a curve and were out of sight.

"So he came to Father Brown's, knowing I was to stay here," Dr. Phineas finished. "He'd seen the other Miss Gray wasn't riding Ben, so he asked me where the old horse was and told me he meant to follow Susanna."

"I'm not completely sure Ronald knows north from south," Bramwell said.

"Ronald can be vague at times, but I'm familiar with all the roads hereabouts, and from how he described it, I think he was right this time."

Bramwell considered. If Ronald could be believed, Jennara

was on her way north, not south. He couldn't understand her reason for going north instead of to St. Louis, but it was like her to change direction in order to prevent him from following her.

It'll be a cold day in hell when she outsmarts me, he assured himself.

"I wonder, Doctor," he said, "if your minister friend might know of a horse for sale."

Dr. Phineas hesitated. "I think you should allow the young folks to work out their own destiny," he said finally.

"It isn't them I'm worried about." Bramwell spoke before he thought, then realized with a shock that the words were true. Ronald had been warned, he knew Susanna had lied to him. Surely he wasn't such a fool as to want her after that. In any case, it was Jennara that Bramwell meant to go after. If she thought she could leave him without so much as a good-bye, she was badly mistaken.

Dr. Phineas stroked his long white mustache and smiled. "Ah, so the wind blows that way, does it? In that case, I see no reason not to help you." His expression became sober. "One more thing before we try to locate a horse for you — Ronald mentioned that three men on horseback passed him before he reached town. Rough-looking customers, apparently. It's true the men were traveling in the same direction the Gray sisters had taken, but there was no reason to suspect they were following the women."

"Why would Ronald think so?"

"Susanna became extremely upset in St. Charles and refused to go on to St. Louis, as we'd planned. I'm not entirely certain just what troubled her. She babbled of a man who wanted to kill her and that he'd follow us there. Neither Ronald nor I could reason with her. Finally I decided to backtrack here to Marthasville and stay a few days with my friend Father Brown to give Susanna a chance to calm her nerves. She agreed to that, but insisted we leave secretly, at night." He shook his head. "Up until then she'd seemed reasonable, for a woman."

Bramwell frowned. "Did you see any evidence of a man following the wagon?"

"Never. Once we arrived in Marthasville, Ronald and Susanna decided they'd have Father Brown marry them."

"It was Ronald *and* Susanna's decision? Or just hers?"

"A mutual agreement." Dr. Phineas's voice was firm. "As for the man who may or may not have followed the wagon, who can say? I know Ronald believed Susanna's story and worried himself over it. No doubt that's why seeing the three men riding north troubled him."

Jennara urged Swift Runner on, hoping Soot would keep up of her own accord. Susanna was so frightened it was all she could do to cling to the reins and stay on the mare. A clearing appeared up ahead, then fields and a small farmhouse to the right. Jennara frowned. A farm meant people. Someone who might notice them and, if asked, be able to say how long it had been since they'd passed. There was nothing to do but go on and hope they might pass unseen.

As luck would have it, a man and a hound dog were walking across one of the fields. He waved at them but Jennara didn't respond. Rounding the next curve hid them from the farmer, but it was too late. He'd certainly be able to describe the two women who'd ridden past without so much as a wave. If it *was* Curtis following them, he'd know he was on the right trail and closing in.

Susanna couldn't keep riding much longer. But if Jennara took the horses off the trail to try to hide in the woods, Curtis, knowing how far ahead they were, might well find them. It wouldn't be hard to figure out what they'd done when he didn't catch up to them. And once Susanna was off the horse, she'd be too tired to run, and they'd be easily trapped.

Come, Jennara, she urged herself, you've outsmarted Dakota warriors. Think of a way to escape. But her mind seemed fogged, her thoughts sluggish. She fought to clear her head. What would No Cloud advise, she asked herself.

"Water hides scent." It was as though his words echoed in her mind.

Water. They'd forded a stream not too far back. Recalling this, an idea came to her. "Slow down," she called to Susanna. She had to repeat her words before her sister understood. "Now halt."

When Susanna obeyed, Jennara took the reins from her sister's hand. Leading Soot, she directed Swift Runner into the woods to the left of the trail, and once she was well off the road, turned south, through a heavy growth of hickories and sycamores, retracing the way they'd come. Reaching the creek she remembered, she convinced the pony to wade into the water and walk downstream. Since she held Soot's reins, the mare had no choice but to follow.

Perhaps she was being too thorough, but it paid not to take chances. Though she was almost positive Curtis would never expect them to go toward Marthasville and their tracks through the woods would be all but impossible for anyone but an Indian to follow, it did no harm to lead the horses through the water. The extra precaution might even allow her to sleep tonight instead of keeping watch.

When she finally came out of the streambed and looked for a place to camp, dusk permeated the woods. She helped Susanna off Soot, led her to the blanket, and left her there, already asleep before she returned to tend to the horses.

Later, sitting on the blanket next to Susanna, she ate bread and cheese in the increasing darkness. Deciding her sister needed rest more than food, she didn't try to wake her to eat. Easing down next to Susanna, she pulled the remaining blanket over them both.

Lying there, looking up at the stars through the leaves above her, Jennara was reminded of the times she'd camped in the woods with Bramwell, and she couldn't help but wish he were with her now.

I'll survive without him, she vowed. And I'll get Susanna back to Minnesota safe and sound.

But how? They might be hidden for the night, but what about tomorrow? Should she travel west before heading north once more? Or should she aim for St. Louis? What would Curtis and his cronies be expecting her to do?

There was the possibility the men weren't Curtis and company, but three harmless travelers who didn't know Susanna existed. Somehow, though, Jennara couldn't believe that. Anyway, she didn't dare take the chance. She doubted Curtis would kill her sister, but what might happen to Susanna in his hands didn't bear thinking about.

A far-off caterwaul caused her to tense, and the horses whuffled and stomped, obviously unsettled by the cry. A panther? She'd never heard one before. Minnesota had wild-cats and lynxes but no panthers. Whatever it was, the animal was too far away to attack the horses. She regretted not pushing Llwellyn to return the Spencer along with the pony, but it had never occurred to her she'd need the rifle. Though she doubted she'd need to shoot a panther, the men stalking Susanna were more dangerous than any wild animal.

Made uneasy by the cat's cry, she listened carefully to the night sounds — the reassuring familiarity of frog song, the occasional rustling that told of a small animal passing, the wind whispering through the leaves overhead . . . nothing alarming. Gradually Jennara began to relax and soon she drowsed.

Susanna's scream brought her upright, her heart hammering in her ears. Her sister, also sitting up, moaned, clutching at her. No one, nothing seemed to be near them. "What's the matter?" Jennara asked. Feeling her sister shiver, she put an arm around her. "Did you hear something?"

"No," Susanna whispered. "It was that terrible dream again. It gets worse every time."

Dream? Did Susanna still have the same old nightmare that used to plague her as a child?

"I'm riding old Whitey," Susanna went on. "Going to the Larsens'. It's dark and I'm scared."

It *was* the same dream.

"I'm afraid I'll fall off Whitey, afraid something will jump at me in the night, but most of all I'm afraid of what's happening to Mama. You're scared, too, I saw that before you boosted me up on Whitey and told me I had to ride by myself to the Larsens'."

"So long ago," Jennara said. "You were only seven years old. I felt terrible because I had to send you into the night, but I didn't know what else to do."

"Mama was bleeding. You didn't want me to see, but I did. Blood was all over her, and your hands were bloody from trying to help her. Papa wasn't home, we didn't know where he was."

Jennara relived the night as Susanna spoke in a hushed, quivering voice. How desperately she'd tried to staunch her mother's bleeding without really knowing what to do. How she'd tried to keep the terror-stricken Susanna from the room. How guilty she'd felt when, because she had no choice, she finally had to order little Susie into the night to fetch Mrs. Larsen, well aware her sister was deathly afraid of the dark.

Jennara hugged Susanna. "That's past and done with. We did the best we could, but we couldn't save her."

"In the dream I'm seven again and I don't know anything except how scared I am. In the past few months, though, the dream's gotten worse. It starts the same, I'm riding Whitey in the dark but suddenly I'm all grown up, I'm not Susie, I'm Mama, and something terrible is going to happen . . . to me, to her, to us. And tonight—" her voice broke.

"It's only a dream, Susie. You're awake now."

"I can't forget how horrible it was. It was dark, but in the dream I could see Whitey—remember how white she was? Like milk. While I was riding her she started to change color, slowly at first. It was scary, but I didn't know why until I realized she wasn't changing color at all, she was red because

I'm bleeding, Mama's bleeding, and blood is all over Whitey's withers and running down her sides. Blood that never stops coming . . ."

The blood stopped when Mama died, Jennara thought, tears in her eyes. Mama had miscarried and bled to death right there in front of her and she couldn't prevent it, couldn't help her. Shaken, she held to Susanna, both of them crying.

After a while Susanna pulled away and fumbled for her handkerchief. "I'm sorry about being so much trouble," she said. "I wish I could be more like you. I used to try, but I finally realized I never could be."

Jennara, touched, murmured, "You're fine just like you are."

"You're wrong. I've done something awful, I've gone and put you in danger. He's after us, isn't he? I didn't dream that."

"I think we've given Curtis the slip for the time being."

"When he finds us he'll do terrible things to you, too. Oh, Jen, I don't want you to be hurt because of me."

"He's not going to find us. Lie down and try to rest now." Jennara hoped she sounded more reassuring than she felt. Too late she realized she hadn't made certain her sister was all right physically. Not that she took dreams seriously, but Susanna *was* pregnant.

"Are you having any pain? Cramps?" she asked.

"I'm fine. Just kind of achy from riding Soot. You know what a fraidy cat I am, I'd tell you right away if—if I felt anything wrong." She found Jennara's hand and clung to it. "We're really safe from Curtis here?" she whispered. "You're sure?"

"Positive."

Susanna sighed and eased back down, but Jennara didn't stretch out beside her. For some reason it had never occurred to her that she was in as much danger as Susanna. Obviously if men such as Curtis captured them, she could expect every humiliation. She had no gun, and the twists of medicine were gone, along with the paring knife she'd threatened to use on the raftsmen, swept into Big Muddy with the rest of her belongings. She had no weapon to defend herself with, except her wits — and she'd do best employing those to stay out of the clutches of Curtis and his men.

Making up her mind, she decided she'd try to get what sleep she could, rouse Susanna before dawn, and circle back to the south and St. Louis. She shouldn't have allowed Susanna's fears to deter her from making for the city in the first place. As far as she could see, Curtis was more dangerous in this isolated spot than he possibly could be in St. Louis, where they'd be surrounded by people. And once they were aboard a train for Chicago, they'd be safe.

After a troubled and restless sleep, Jennara woke her sister in the gray pre-dawn and persuaded her to eat some cheese and the last of the bread. Jennara was finishing an apple when she heard a hound baying. Running rabbits, she thought, flinging the core into the woods. After rolling the two blankets, she packed them on the horses, moving efficiently but not hurriedly because it didn't occur to her that they were in any immediate danger . . . not until the hound's cries grew louder and louder. Then she recalled the hound dog in the field with the farmer. The farmer that Curtis was sure to have talked to and had evidently borrowed the hound from.

"That dog's not after rabbits," she warned Susanna. "He's trailing us! Mount up."

Jennara did her best to keep some order in their flight through the woods. She searched for a stream, knowing it was their one chance to put the dog off their scent, but she couldn't be positive they were heading south. The only thing she was sure of was that they traveled ahead of the hound and whoever followed him.

Previously, Missouri had seemed to be crisscrossed with streams, but this morning they seemed to elude Jennara. She lost her riding hat when a branch swept it from her head, and Susanna's silk bonnet was hanging down her back, held on only by the neck ties. When Jennara finally splashed into a creek, the hound belled so close behind them that she feared she and Susanna would be seen or heard taking to the water.

They worked their way upstream until they were halted by a rapids. There they had to leave the water too soon to suit Jennara. She worried that if Curtis had the dog scout the banks to pick up their scent again, the animal would easily find it. Still, they'd gained time . . . if they could get to a road before their pursuers caught them, perhaps they'd find help at a farm or from travelers.

Susanna's face had a taut, terrified look, reminding Jennara of the seven-year-old she'd once sent into the night, but her sister was in much better condition than yesterday, able to obey orders and to control Soot. If their luck held, they might yet get out of this.

"If we're caught, don't tell Curtis about Ronnie," Susanna said abruptly. "Not who he is or where he is or anything else. I don't want Curtis hunting him down. And he would . . . I couldn't bear it if he killed Ronnie."

Somewhat taken aback, Jennara assured her she wouldn't so much as utter Ronald's name. To be so worried about him, her sister must be truly fond of Ronald . . . perhaps even in love with him, as she claimed to be.

"And you," Susanna went on, "I know that Indian pony can outrun most horses. Soot can't, but he can. Promise me you'll try to escape if Curtis catches me."

"I'd never run off and leave you in his hands!" Jennara cried.

"You must!"

"Susie, I can't."

"But you could bring back help for me if you escaped."

Jennara bit her lip. Susanna was right . . . the two of them had no chance against three men. To free Susanna, she'd need help. She had a terrible feeling if she ever left her sister in Curtis's hands, she'd never see Susanna again.

"We're not going to be caught!" Jennara cried, as much to

herself as to Susanna.

The words were no sooner said than she heard the triumphant bay of the hound, once again on their trail. Ahead, the trees thinned and Jennara began to hope. A clearing could mean a farm, someone to help them. She urged Swift Runner through the last of the woods and into a meadow overgrown with weeds and young saplings. Her heart sank when she saw the log cabin with a door hanging askew.

An abandoned farm.

As the horses neared a giant sycamore in the middle of the clearing, a flock of strange little green birds with yellow heads and curved beaks flew from its limbs. Soot, startled by the birds fluttering around her head, checked and reared up. Susanna screamed as the mare's sudden shying flung her from the saddle to the ground.

Jennara turned Swift Runner and rode back to her sister. Halting the pony, she slid off and dropped to her knees beside Susanna. "Are you hurt?" she demanded.

She sighed in relief when Susanna, trying to sit up, gasped, "I just need to get my breath back."

The hound's baying was loud in Jennara's ears as she helped her sister to her feet. Susanna leaned heavily against her, still gasping for breath, unable to remount Soot, who stood with her head hanging as though ashamed of what she'd done.

As Jennara urged her sister to try to put a foot up into the stirrup, a tan-and-white hound broke from the trees and ran into the field. Tongue lolling, the dog raced toward them.

"Hurry, Susanna!" Jennara cried, boosting her sister up.

"I can't, Jen, I can't."

With one arm around Susanna, Jennara whirled to face the dog. He slowed, ambling toward them, his nose to the ground. When he stood beside the horses, he stopped and gave a triumphant bark, then walked over and sniffed at her and Susanna. At that moment a white horse loped into the field from the woods, its rider wearing a hat jammed down on his head, a hat with an eagle feather. Catching sight of his quarry, he yanked off the hat and twirled it in the air.

His hair was as red as a sunrise.

Susanna buried her face in Jennara's shoulder, shuddering. Jennara stared at him defiantly and saw to her dismay that he carried a holstered pistol. Would he have shot her if she'd tried to flee as her sister had begged her to? She suspected he would have.

He'd almost reached them when two more riders emerged from the woods. One shouted, but Curtis didn't turn. His eyes on Susanna, he rode straight toward the two sisters.

I'm damned if I'll let him scare me into scuttling aside, Jennara thought, and stood firm. Her heart thudded in her chest as the horse bore down on her, but she gritted her teeth and stayed where she was.

At the last possible second, so close she felt the heat of the horse's body, Curtis swerved his mount, circled, and came back to look down on them. Except for a reddish stubble, he was clean-shaven, and for the first time Jennara noticed the scar that ran from the corner of his left eye to his upper left lip, twisting his face into a permanent sneer. His eyes, a pale blue-gray, were alight with an emotion she couldn't identify. Glee? Anticipation?

"Look at me, love," he ordered.

A tremor shook Susanna, and Jennara's arm tightened around her.

"I said look at me!" Anger flared in his pale eyes.

The other two riders trotted up to them and halted, but Jennara saw them only from the corner of her eyes, her gaze intent on Curtis.

Slowly, Susanna shifted in Jennara's embrace, pulling away and turning to face Curtis. Jennara heard her draw a deep breath as she looked up at him.

"Come here," he commanded her.

Susanna, moving as jerkily as a marionette, walked across the space separating her from Curtis. He reached down and, grasping her wrists, yanked her up and onto his horse, forcing her to sit in front of him.

Jennara bit her tongue to keep from shouting at him to be careful. She doubted if Curtis had yet realized that Susanna was carrying a child, and she had an uneasy premonition that it would prove disastrous when he did find out.

Chapter 22

Once he held Susanna in front of him on the horse, the redheaded man glanced at his two companions. "Brod," he told the one with the sandy hair and beard, "lead the mare. Frenchie, you take the buckskin." He watched as they obeyed, then looked down at Jennara. "Get on the pony," he ordered.

She saw no advantage in defying him, so she remounted. There was no way to escape, not while the dark-skinned, dark-haired man called Frenchie had Swift Runner's reins, not to mention the fact that Curtis packed a pistol.

"Who are you and where are you taking us?" she demanded.

The redhead smiled, the scar twisting his mouth into a humorless grimace. "I'm Curtis Hayes, and I'll take you where I damn well please."

"Why?"

He blinked, apparently at a loss for an instant. Maybe he's not used to being questioned, she thought, wondering if she could somehow use this to her advantage.

"This here's my woman," he said, scowling. Susanna moaned as he tightened his hold around her waist.

"But *I'm* not." Jennara's words were far braver than she felt.

He grinned again. "Reckon Brod 'n Frenchie can toss for who gets you. Her sister, ain't you?"

Swallowing her spurt of frightened anger, she said, "I am."

319

"You're a heap scrawnier. What's your name?"

For the first time Jennara understood the Dakota people's reluctance to tell a stranger their names. She had the irrational feeling that to reveal hers to these louts would give them power over her. "Genevieve," she lied, choosing a name that would be safe in the event Susanna slipped and called her "Jen."

"Genevieve," the dark man echoed, giving the name the French pronunciation. His black eyes gleamed greedily as he stared at her.

"You haven't told me where you're taking us, Mr. Hayes," Jennara said.

He glanced up at the sky, now overcast, then around, his eyes lingering on the dilapidated log cabin in the overgrown clearing surrounded by woods. "Could be we'll camp here. You led us a rough chase 'n we could use some rest. You and Sue, here, you did some damn fancy running. Just happens I'm a hell of a good tracker, so you wasted your time. Yeah, a camp here sounds just fine. Sue 'n me, we got some catching up to do."

"That there dog's gone." Brod's voice had a nasal rasp. At his words, Jennara realized the hound was no longer anywhere to be seen.

Curtis shrugged. "Hightailed it for home. We don't need him. We got what we come for." He looked at Brod, then jerked his head toward the cabin. "Get over there and see if we can use the place."

With Soot trailing behind him, Brod rode to the cabin, dismounted, and tethered both horses to nearby saplings before venturing inside. Moments later he reappeared. "Got to clean it some, but the roof looks sound. Ought to keep us dry in case of rain."

"Women's work, cleaning," Curtis proclaimed. "Lucky we got us a couple."

A few minutes later, Jennara and Susanna were thrust inside the one-room log cabin while the three men lounged outside, guarding the one door that hung from a tattered leather hinge, and keeping an eye on the two unglazed windows, one at either end of the cabin.

Somewhat to Jennara's surprise, the floor wasn't dirt, but wide planks covered with leaf litter, old rags, a broken table, and other unidentifiable castoffs. A chipmunk darted from under her foot, startling her, and disappeared into a hole where the planks met the log wall. Recovering from her momentary fright, she shook her head at Susanna, who'd begun to pick halfheartedly at the debris.

Jennara marched to the door. "We need leaf brooms," she announced, not addressing any of the men in particular. "A couple of strong leafy branches to sweep the floor."

"Me, I'll get you some, Genevieve," Frenchie said eagerly. Brod, she noted, scowled at the dark man as he hastened toward a sapling.

The makeshift brooms by no means swept well, but they were an improvement over picking up the litter by hand. Susanna worked jerkily, her eyes blank, and she started every time Curtis spoke, though nothing he said was addressed to her. "Don't despair," Jennara wanted to whisper into her sister's ear, but she felt the words would be just that—mere words. She had no plan for escape. That seemed impossible.

When the floor was as clean as it could be without a decent broom and soap and water, Curtis ordered the two women to unpack and tend to their horses, then take their belongings inside the cabin. The men brought their things in, too, including three raw chickens wrapped in wet cheesecloth.

"Chimney looks sound enough," Curtis observed. "And lookee here, there's a spit in the fireplace. Brod, gather some wood afore it rains. We'll have us a cozy fire and get the women to cook up those chickens."

Brod made several trips, dumping the wood near the hearth with louder thunks each time. He gaped hungrily at Jennara as he passed her and finally stopped in front of Curtis, who was taking off his jacket. "Red, I wanna toss for

321

her now," Brod muttered.

"She ain't going nowhere. Eating comes first." Curtis didn't so much as glance at Brod.

"But I wanna—"

"You want your face bashed in? I said we eat." The menace in Curtis's words was all the more potent because he didn't raise his voice.

Was it possible Susanna could get the pistol away from Curtis? Jennara wondered. She was afraid her sister didn't have the nerve. Susanna seemed paralyzed with fear whenever Curtis even glanced at her, and it was doubtful if she could pull herself together enough to make the attempt, much less succeed.

I won't be close enough to him to try for the pistol, Jennara decided, and as long as he has the gun, we're helpless. In fact, even with the pistol in my hands I'd have trouble if all three of the men came at me at the same time . . . but I won't give up.

As she and Susanna prepared the chicken for roasting on the spit over the fire, Jennara avoided looking at either Brod or Frenchie and did her best not to dwell on what would happen after the meal. Although she found Brod more distasteful than Frenchie, the idea of either man touching her made her gag. And she feared for Susanna's reason if Curtis forced her to his will again.

Unfortunately she had no Indian medicines to sprinkle into the food this time. She could see no way to save Susanna or herself. But she meant to fight as long as she could.

A thin rain began to fall as the chickens roasted. The men gathered around the hearth, where the women turned the spit so the chickens would cook evenly. Susanna drooped, her eyes downcast.

Jennara wondered if Curtis would treat her sister more gently if he knew her condition. After all, it was his child. He apparently hadn't noticed any change in Susanna, possibly because she wore a tunic-type jacket that concealed her waistline. Jennara estimated her sister to be about five months

along, so the child would be born in February or March . . .
if Susanna survived.

Should she urge Susanna to tell him? Should Jennara tell
Curtis herself? But what if he didn't believe the child was his?
Her sister had no way of proving to him that it was. Better to
leave well enough alone than to chance making things worse
for Susanna.

By the time the chickens were ready to eat, the rain was
coming down in earnest and the afternoon was noticeably
cooler. Earlier Jennara had thought she'd heard a hound
baying, and as she toyed with a drumstick she didn't really
want, the sound came again, louder and closer. Everyone in
the cabin tensed. Curtis pushed himself to his feet and strode
to the door, his hand on the butt of the pistol. Jennara held
her breath, hoping against hope someone was coming to their
rescue.

The baying stopped. She tensed, waiting for the dog to
appear. Nothing happened. The hound neither came into
view nor barked again. Finally Curtis took his hand from the
gun and turned away. "Damn dog must've run a rabbit down,"
he muttered.

Jennara sighed inwardly, certain he was right. There'd be
no rescue, no outside help. She was almost certain the hound
that had tracked her and Susanna was the same dog she'd
seen in the field with the farmer. That had been the only farm
they'd passed in miles, so this log cabin must be fairly near it,
for all the good that did the two women.

"Keep watch," Curtis told Brod as he resumed his place by
the fire.

Grumbling under his breath, Brod took a chicken thigh
and drumstick to the door with him. He propped himself
against the jamb, and as he gnawed on the meat, the greasy
juices trickled into his beard, disgusting Jennara, who was
doing her best to make Susanna eat. Her sister refused everything she was offered with a mute shake of her head. Jennara
well understood how Susanna felt because she herself had to

force down every bite. Not eating, though, might expose her fear to the men, and she was determined not to show how terrified she was at the thought of having Brod or Frenchie force himself on her.

When the last of the chicken was eaten and the bones had been tossed through the door or a window into the weeds, Brod turned away from the door to glower at Curtis. "Nothing out there, no reason to stand guard," he said. "Where's them dice, Red?"

From a pocket, Curtis pulled two ivory cubes with black dots punched into them. Jennara had heard of dice, but had never seen a pair, and she eyed the small cubes with rising anger. She was a woman, not a trifle to be won on a toss of dice! But how could she avoid it? If only she could throw her captors off balance and use their confusion to her own advantage . . . set the men at odds with each other. A glimmer of an idea came to her, unappealing, but the only thing she'd come up with.

Before she could change her mind, she blurted, "Since I'm forced to this, I'd prefer to make my own choice."

All three men stared at her.

"You heard me!" she cried. "I'll decide, not leave it to chance."

Curtis recovered first. His grimace told her that he was smiling, enjoying the situation. "Well, boys, how about it? You game about giving her a choice?"

Brod and Frenchie glanced suspiciously at one another. Finally Frenchie nodded. Brod shook his head. "No!" he snarled. "You promised we'd toss for her."

"Not being a man to break a promise, the dice it is." Curtis flung them at Brod, who grabbed clumsily, missing one. It bounced on the plank floor and rolled, slipping through a crack between the boards and disappearing.

Curtis laughed. "Might as well give up," he teased Brod. "The ivories are against you."

"We can throw the one," Brod insisted. He crossed to their

gear, stacked at one end of the room, and spread a blanket on the floor. "High man wins, I shoot first," he told Frenchie.

The two men, glowering at one another, knelt at the edge of the blanket. Brod, his hand closed around the remaining die, shook his fist and then opened it to release the cube. It rolled onto the blanket and came to rest with four dots showing.

"Four!" Brod cried. "That's my lucky number — you'll never beat it."

Frenchie picked up the die, shook it and let it roll free.

"Three!" Brod shouted in triumph. "I get her!"

Jennara shot him a disdainful look. "Frenchie was *my* choice."

"He ain't nothing but a greasy Injun breed," Brod said scornfully, reaching for her.

Frenchie, his black eyes glittering with rage, knocked Brod's hand away from her. "Better a breed than a stinking shit-head whoreson," he cried, pulling out a wicked-looking knife with a long curved blade.

Brod jumped back, grabbed his own knife, and crouched to face Frenchie. Quickly Jennara stepped out of the way as the men began to circle one another, each waiting for an opening.

The sharp crack of a pistol froze everyone. Jennara whirled to see Curtis standing, his back to the door, his pistol aimed at the men.

"You ain't gonna cut each other over no woman," he growled. "You toss those pig-stickers out that window. Now! If any bastard has a knife in his hand after I count three, he's dead. One . . . two . . ."

Brod flipped his knife through the window first, and Frenchie followed suit.

"Three!" Curtis lowered the pistol, but kept it in his hand. "I'll go collect those knives later. You ain't gonna be needing them right away. And when you get 'em back, you ain't gonna use 'em on each other. Won't be no need, 'cause I'm gonna tell you how to handle the woman and you damn well better listen. Brod, you—"

Jennara, standing next to her sister, heard Susanna gasp. At the same time she caught a flicker of motion behind Curtis.

"Ronnie!" Susanna screamed.

Jennara stared in disbelief as Ronald, standing in the doorway, raised a long, thick stick and brought it down on Curtis's wrist. Curtis yelped in pain, his pistol clattering to the floor. Jennara dashed forward, kicked the gun, and with a sinking heart, saw it skitter across the planks toward Brod.

As Brod reached for the gun, Jennara grasped a chunk of unused firewood, a rotting branch so heavy she had to use both hands to lift it. Brod dropped to one knee, aiming the pistol at Ronald, but Curtis stood between Brod and his target.

"Red, get outa the way!" Brod yelled. Curtis glanced over his shoulder at him.

Ronald swung the stick again, but Curtis leaped to one side, the blow glancing off his shoulder. He grabbed the end of the stick and twisted it from Ronald's grasp. Brod, still on one knee, weaved back and forth, looking for a chance to fire without hitting Curtis.

Coming up behind Brod, Jennara raised the rotting branch high in the air, and with all her strength, brought it down on Brod's head. The club thudded against his skull, chunks of wood spraying onto his shirt as well as littering the planks. For an instant he remained kneeling, then slumped to the floor, the pistol still in his hand.

"Goddamn!" Frenchie cried, leaping across the room and reaching for the pistol. Desperately, Jennara yanked it from Brod's fingers and slid it across the floor to the wall, where it disappeared into the dark chipmunk hole. Frenchie hurried to kneel beside the hole and thrust his arm inside.

Ronald hurled himself at Curtis, pummeling him with his fists. Curtis thrust up with one leg, kneeing Ronald in the groin. Ronald screamed in pain and the sound of his voice seemed to galvanize Susanna. She rushed at Curtis, wrapping her arms around him from behind as Ronald sagged to the floor. Curtis shoved her away from him with such force that she slammed against the wall, moaned, and slid to the floor.

Jennara raised the shard of wood she still grasped and started for Curtis but Frenchie grasped her wrist and twisted the wood away. He grabbed her other wrist and, yanking her hands behind her, bound them together with rope, drawing the ends through one of the iron hooks near the fireplace and tying the rope tight so she couldn't move.

Ronald, she saw, had managed to push himself up from the floor and now hurled himself at Curtis, shouting, "You bastard!"

Curtis sidestepped his flailing attack, struck him in the neck with the side of his left hand, then kicked Ronald's legs from under him. Ronald fell half in, half out of the doorway. Curtis kicked him in the side. Ronald grunted and tried to roll away, slumping onto the ground outside. Curtis followed and kicked him in the head. Ronald lay still.

He's going to kill him, Jennara thought in despair, turning to see if her sister was aware of what was happening. She drew in her breath in horror. Susanna was sprawled on the floor, blood soaking through her clothes and staining the wood. She was losing the baby.

On dear God, Jennara thought, a dark mantle of hopelessness settling over her, it's like Mama all over again. Susanna's going to die and I can't do anything to prevent it. She couldn't look away from the blood seeping from her sister onto the unpainted planks, blood she knew would keep coming until death stopped the flow.

Her surroundings faded until she seemed to be seeing her mother lying on the big double bed in the room with the red roses on the wallpaper. The blood soaking the sheets was a darker, more sinister red than the roses, and her mother grew paler with every passing moment. She was too weak to talk or even to open her eyes, and still the blood wouldn't stop flowing.

Fourteen-year-old Jennara feared her mother was going to die. She blamed herself. If only she knew how to stop the bleeding, she could save her. She *should* know. Papa had been teaching her anatomy and physiology, but she didn't always pay close attention. Why hadn't she asked more questions? It would be her fault if Mama died. . . .

Jennara blinked and shook her head. She wasn't fourteen and in Minnesota. And she was no longer half-trained in medicine, she knew everything her father had known, and might even know enough to save Susanna, if she was free to try.

"Untie me!" she screamed, writhing against her bonds. "Curtis, she's dying! Susanna's bleeding to death, can't you see? It's your fault, all your fault."

Curtis, just outside the door, swung around to look at Susanna's crumpled form and stood staring, obviously taken aback.

"You made her fall and she's having a miscarriage," Jennara cried. "She's losing the baby you forced on her. Susanna will die unless you let me help her."

His shifted his gaze to her and she saw fear and uncertainty in his eyes.

"Please," she begged. "If you care for her at all, let me try to stop the bleeding."

He hesitated for so long that she almost gave up hope. Then, in a swirl of motion, he strode through the door, yanked out a pocketknife, opened it, and cut the rope binding her wrists to the fireplace hook, freeing her. Rubbing her hands together to restore circulation, she ran to Susanna and knelt beside her.

After a quick examination of the blood Susanna had expelled, Jennara realized the embryo and afterbirth hadn't yet come out. The bleeding wouldn't stop until they did.

"I need clean cloths," Jennara said, glancing up. Curtis

stood over her, his gaze on Susanna's ashen face. "Bring me the clothes in her saddlebags. And water, I must have water."

"Damn it, Frenchie, you heard her," Curtis shouted. "Fetch some water from the creek."

Curtis brought the saddlebags himself. Rummaging quickly through them, Jennara took her sister's chemises and set them aside. Laying a hand on Susanna's lower abdomen, she pushed down, feeling for the swollen womb. Susanna moaned and clutched at her hand, trying to dislodge it.

"You'll have to hold her hands," Jennara told Curtis.

"Uh, me?"

"There's no one else to help," she snapped. "Kneel down, pull her arms over her head, and grasp her wrists."

Reluctantly, Curtis did as she asked, using, she noticed absently, his left hand. Jennara pressed hard on her sister's abdomen, trying to massage the womb from the outside in the hope she could stimulate the muscles to contract and push out the afterbirth. Susanna moaned and cried out weakly, her eyes fluttering open. She didn't seem to see either Curtis or Jennara.

"It's all right," Jennara soothed. "I know it hurts, but I have to do this to help you."

By the time Frenchie returned with a small pail of water, Jennara realized the massage wasn't working. She'd have to try something else. "I need the eagle feather from your hat," she told Curtis.

He gasped at her.

"Tell Frenchie to bring me that feather, I need it for Susanna."

"Get the damned hat," Curtis growled at Frenchie.

When Frenchie obeyed, Curtis ordered him to pull off the feather and hand it to Jennara. With the feather in her right hand, she leaned close to Susanna.

"Open your mouth, Susie," she said softly. "Open your mouth for Jen, that's a good girl. Keep your mouth open until I say you can shut it. All right?"

Susanna didn't reply but slowly her lips parted and her mouth opened.

"Wider, Susie, wider."

With a quick motion, Jennara thrust the end of the feather into the back of Susanna's throat. Her sister gagged, gagged again and tried to spit out the feather.

"Keep your mouth open, Susie!" Jennara commanded.

Alternately coaxing and scolding, she finally convinced her sister to do as she asked. Again the feather tickled her throat. This time Susanna not only gagged, she began to vomit. Jennara hastily turned her sister's head to the side as Susanna retched and retched.

Blood gushed from her birth canal, followed by a small bloody mass Jennara realized was the embryo and the after-birth. Only then did she become aware that Frenchie, some-where behind her, was muttering *"Mon Dieu, Mon Dieu,"* over and over while Curtis swore in a low monotone.

The bleeding slowed, as Jennara had hoped, finally all but stopping. She pulled down her sister's blood-soaked skirt and looked at Curtis. He was almost as pale as Susanna and Jennara noticed his right wrist was swollen.

"You can let go of her hands now," she said. "And I wish you and Frenchie would go outside long enough for me to wash her and put a clean gown on her."

Without a word, Curtis rose and jerked his head at Frenchie, who needed no urging to leave the cabin with Curtis.

As she worked over her sister, she heard an outburst from Curtis.

"Where the hell did that son-of-a-bitch get to?" he yelled at Frenchie.

"When I come with the water, he was lying on his face right where you left him," Frenchie insisted, "limp as a dead eel. You beat the shit outa him, Red, he couldn't've got far."

Ronald, she told herself—they meant Ronald. Had he somehow gotten away? But how could he, badly beaten as

330

he'd been?

"When I find him, I'm gonna finish the bugger once and for all," Curtis vowed. "You stay here'n keep an eye on the women, Brod ain't good for nothing yet."

Jennara remembered hitting Brod over the head. Leaving Susanna for the moment, she crossed to where Brod lay on his back, breathing heavily. A lump had risen on the left side of his head and a dark bruise discolored his left temple and eye. Gingerly she felt the lump and found it spongy beneath her fingers. He didn't move or show any sign that he felt her touch. A brain concussion? It was even possible he had a fractured skull, but she couldn't bring herself to feel sorry for him.

Hurrying back to Susanna, she finished washing her and changed her clothes. "Frenchie," she called, "help me carry my sister."

He came inside and looked down at Susanna. "Red sure sets a heap of store by her. Like a wild man, he was, when she run out on him." He lifted Susanna as though she were made of glass, carrying her carefully to the blanket where he and Brod had tossed the die. Easing her down, Frenchie glanced over at Brod.

"Brod ain't moved at all," he said. "He gonna die?"

Jennara shrugged as she unfolded another blanket and laid it over her sister. "His head's probably too thick for him to be killed by a stick of wood."

Frenchie's eyes shifted from Brod to Susanna, to the door, then back to Jennara. He smiled. "Looks to me like he ain't gonna trouble us 'n she ain't either. Now ain't that handy?"

Jennara rose to her feet, belatedly realizing Frenchie's intentions as he reached for her. She struck at his hands.

"You're a feisty little piece," he said, grabbing her by the wrist, "but Frenchie'll tame you soon enough."

Jennara tried to wrench away, but his grip was too strong. She looked frantically around for something to use as a weapon. The firewood was too far away and she saw nothing else within reach.

"Genevieve, that's a pretty name," he said, attempting to pull her into his arms while she resisted with all her strength. "I used t'know another Genevieve. Dark as sin she was, and never needed no coaxing."

Taking her by surprise, he pushed her instead of pulling and succeeded in shoving her up against one of the log walls, pinning her so she couldn't move.

Why had she ever thought Frenchie was less loathsome than Brod? They were equally repulsive. His breath stank of rotting teeth, and the stench of his body pressed against hers was indescribably nasty. He still held her right wrist, but her left hand was free. As he pushed his face into hers, she twisted her head to the side, meanwhile scrabbling along the logs with her left hand, searching for anything she might use to defend herself.

A sharp splinter stabbed her finger. She pried at it, a long, thin sliver of wood, as his mouth slobbered along her neck. Back and forth she worked the wood, feeling nausea rise from his smell and his touch. At last the sliver broke free. Jennara shifted it in her fingers so the sharp point was foremost. With a quick motion, she raised her left hand and jabbed the splinter as hard as she could at Frenchie's neck.

He yelled as the sharp point penetrated his flesh, his hands going to the splinter and letting her go. Jennara darted toward the door. She couldn't make a dash for Swift Runner and try to escape—not if it meant leaving Susanna behind. And her sister was too weak to come with her. Yet if she didn't escape, how could she protect herself against Frenchie? She certainly hadn't injured him seriously, he'd soon be after her.

The knives, she thought. I'll find the knives he and Brod tossed from the window and use them to threaten him. She ran out the door and raced around the cabin only to come up short. A forest of brambles grew under that window, a tangle of blackberry bushes that no human could penetrate. Somewhere in the midst of those thorny brambles were the knives. For all the use they were to her, they might as well have been on the other side of the moon.

Chapter 23

When the misty rain began, the big, rawboned roan started tossing his head and sidestepping. Bramwell cursed and sawed the reins to get the roan under control once more. No wonder the horse went so cheaply. He was an iron-mouthed, spooky man-hater. Any rider who didn't pay close attention would soon be flat on his back in the dirt and lucky not to be trampled on in the bargain.

As if I don't have enough on my mind, Bramwell thought. The farther north he traveled from Marthasville, the more worried he became. Piecing together what he'd learned from questioning every traveler he'd met going south and every inhabitant of any building near the road, it was clear that three horsemen *had* been following the two women, whether or not they were actually pursuing them. Ronald rode behind the three men.

The roan's gait, though rough, was fast enough, but Bramwell's frequent stops to ask about Jennara and the others made for a slow journey. He had to control his urge to spur his mount into a gallop in the hopes of narrowing the distance between him and Jennara. Haste, he feared, might be exactly the wrong tactic. If the women had turned off to camp and something had happened to prevent them from going on, he'd be liable to ride on past and never know he'd missed them.

Slow and careful was the best strategy, but his apprehension was increasing with every delay. Was Jennara all right? She had to be! How could he have been so blind as to believe it possible to forget her? He could never forget Jennara if he lived a thousand lifetimes.

He loved her. She was as stubborn as they came, but what did it matter? She was the only woman in the world he wanted, or would ever want. In his eyes and in his heart, she could never be matched.

Why had he been such a fool as to let her out of his sight? Angry as she'd been at him, he might have known she'd pay no attention to his order to stay put. He was determined to find her, and when he did they'd settle things between them. He wouldn't let her get away again, no matter how furious she was.

If only he knew who the three men were and whether or not they'd caught up to Jennara and her sister. Ronald had described the men to Dr. Phineas as "rough-looking." Bramwell, picturing the raftsmen they'd so narrowly evaded on Big Muddy, clenched his fists. The roan, apparently sensing his distraction, sidestepped again, trying to swing his head around.

"Damn it," Bramwell said to him, "Hasn't anyone ever told you the rider's the boss?" The roan snorted as if in contempt.

They forded a creek, the roan reluctant to get his feet wet, and continued north with the trees to either side of the narrow road that was hardly more than a trail. It reminded Bramwell of his first few days in Minnesota with Jennara, when they'd hidden in the woods to avoid marauding warriors. How he'd chafed at the delay, ready to blame her for everything that happened. Bramwell shook his head. It had taken a while for the wilderness to transform the city lawyer and for the frontier woman to work her spell.

From the beginning, though, he'd appreciated Jennara's skill and courage. Each day his admiration of her had increased, until he'd begun to see how truly beautiful she was. Her beauty went beyond hair and skin and form to encompass the integrity of her character, her generosity to those less fortunate, her kindness and openness—all the things that made her Jennara, including her honest and delightful passion when they made love . . . even her stubbornness.

Was she in danger, in some trouble that even her quick wit and bravery couldn't overcome? If those three men were after the women. . . . He clenched his teeth and prodded the roan to go faster.

Ronald was somewhere ahead of him, but Ronald had never been a fighter. He wouldn't have the slightest notion of how to defend himself or how to protect the women. He'd set out to rescue Susanna like a knight errant when the truth was that Ronald himself needed protection.

It was hard to understand why Ronald would want to rescue a woman who'd deceived him as audaciously as Susanna had, a woman carrying another man's child. Did it belong to one of the three men? Bramwell frowned. Susanna, for all her dishonesty, appeared to be rather fragile, and certainly ladylike . . . not the type to involve herself with the type of men Ronald had described. Maybe there was more to this matter than met the eye. If so, perhaps he'd been too abrupt in his denunciation of Susanna—as Jennara had told him in no uncertain terms.

One of the things he'd learned since leaving Philadelphia was that he didn't know everything there was to know. When he caught up with the women and Ronald, he'd try to keep that in mind.

On this momentous and unpredictable trip, he'd also found a woman he could love. What he felt for Jennara was so intense and demanding that he now realized that his attachment to Loretta all those years ago wasn't even a good imitation of love. Why hadn't he had the sense to see all this in time to tell Jennara how much he loved her?

He snapped to attention in time to jerk the roan back into line. If it were left to the horse, he'd never catch up to Jennara.

The mist had condensed into a thin rain, not hard enough to drench him, but making the gloomy day even more dispiriting. Bramwell cursed the rain, the roan, and the events that had led him to be on the bedamned horse in such miserable weather.

Yet it wasn't really the horse or the weather that upset him, but his concern for Jennara. She would, he knew, try everything she could to save herself if trouble came. He didn't underestimate her courage or her determination, but in a struggle against a man's superior physical power, she didn't stand a chance. And there were three men, not one. Besides, she was burdened with Susanna, who he was sure lacked her bravery and determination. Susanna, like Ronald, needed to be protected.

I've got to find her in time, he told himself, growing more and more convinced that Jennara was in some great peril. If only he knew where she was! How many miles had he gone since he'd last seen a human being? Not a single traveler had passed him on this back road since the rain had started, nor had he come to any hamlet or even a farm. What if he'd missed her?

Somewhere high above him he heard the faint and lonesome cry of wild geese. Because of the low clouds, he couldn't spot their flying vee. Where they flew, perhaps the sun was shining. If anything had happened to Jennara, the sun would never shine again for him. He'd walk in perpetual gloom.

"No, damn your rotten red hide!" he shouted at the recalcitrant horse, who was trying to edge into the trees. "I'm in command here and we're not turning back."

One hill looked much like another as he climbed and descended them. The trail curved to avoid other hills, and streams to be forded were more frequent than suited the roan, who balked at each one. All the while Bramwell got wetter, at the same time feeling he was also getting nowhere.

Was it possible Ronald felt for Susanna some of the emotions that were tearing him apart? Was Ronald blaming himself for not being more understanding, for not being there when he was needed? Did Ronald simmer with the same dark need to kill any man that dared harm the woman he loved?

Bramwell started to shake his head, then hesitated. Jennara had accused him of wanting to play God, of trying to interfere with other people's lives instead of allowing them to solve their own problems. What did he really know of his stepbrother's feelings for Susanna? He himself couldn't tolerate such a woman — but he wasn't Ronald.

Was it possible he'd looked at Susanna askew? When he'd described Loretta to Jennara, she'd said, "Like Susanna." Had he seen Loretta in Susanna's blond hair and fair skin? Bramwell sighed. How could he tell? One thing was sure, he hadn't imagined Susanna was far along with child. What man could overlook such a gross betrayal in the woman he believed he loved, even if she'd been raped?

The hair rose along Bramwell's nape. He couldn't bear the thought of any man touching Jennara. But what if he had no choice but to bear it?

"I love her!" he shouted to the trees crowding close to the trail. "I'll always love her! She's mine!"

From a bluff thrusting above the trees, an echo came back, mocking him: " . . . *mine.*"

He rounded another curve and saw cleared land ahead, with fields to either side of the road. Farther along he noticed a farmhouse and convinced the roan to turn into the wagon-rutted road that led to the barn.

A tan-and-white hound, a short length of rope trailing from his collar, came around the barn to bark at him, then sniffed his trouser legs when he dismounted. He tied the roan firmly to a hitching post and started for the house, stopping when he noticed an unsaddled black mare alongside the barn, her reins dangling. She seemed to be nosing a bundle on the ground. Frowning, he stepped closer to take a better look. With a shock, he realized it was no bundle, but a man crumpled onto his side in the mud.

338

Hurrying to offer help, Bramwell eased the mare aside and crouched next to the fallen man. He drew in his breath sharply. "Ronald!" he cried.

At the sound of his name, Ronald's eyes fluttered open. An ugly dark bruise discolored the right side of his head and face. "Bramwell?" he muttered, as though not certain of what he saw.

"I'm here," Bramwell said. "What happened?"

"Men—got—Susanna," Ronald gasped.

Bramwell tensed. "And Jennara?"

Ronald nodded, then winced with pain. "Bastard kicked me . . . hurt Susanna. Mean to kill him. Help me up."

Though not at all sure Ronald could stay upright, Bramwell hoisted his stepbrother to his feet. "Where are the women?" he asked as Ronald leaned against him.

Ronald pointed across the road. "Log cabin . . . in the woods." He looked around and saw the black mare. "Soot." She ambled over to him and nuzzled his shoulder after he said her name. "Get me on her," Ronald told Bramwell.

Bramwell eyed the mare, seriously doubting that Ronald could ride her saddled in his battered condition, let alone bareback. Ronald needed care, not travel.

"Anyone home at the farm?" he asked.

"No." Ronald's face had no color, and it obviously hurt him to move. Even speaking took an effort. "Doors are padlocked," he said, holding to Bramwell. "No one home. Tried to remount Soot. Go for help. Didn't make it."

"You can't make it now, either. I'll get you into the barn and out of the rain before I go on." Bramwell half carried his protesting brother through the open doors into the barn and settled him onto a scattering of hay. Both the dog and Soot followed the two men into the barn. The roan whinnied indignantly at being left in the rain.

"How far to this cabin?" Bramwell asked. "Where is it?"

"Across the road, past the field—maybe two miles." He turned his face to keep the hound from licking it. "This dog

339

led me there. A farmer told me about three men who borrowed his dog to track. The hound was back by then, so I borrowed him, too. Trouble is, he gets excited and starts to bay when he gets close. Had to tie him and go on alone."

Bramwell pulled the hound away from Ronald by the piece of rope hanging from his collar. "He'd lead *me* there, then."

Wincing, Ronald tried to reach into a pocket. "Susanna's handkerchief's in here. I let the dog smell it so he'd have her scent."

Bramwell put his hand into his stepbrother's pocket, eased out a sadly soiled, lace-edged linen square, and put it to the dog's nose. "Is Jennara all right?" he asked, as he'd been longing to ever since he'd found Ronald.

"Don't know . . . bastard knocked Susanna down."

"Did you see Jennara?"

"Think so . . . yes."

"How long ago?" Bramwell demanded.

"Can't be sure. Hour . . . two, maybe."

"Was it raining then?"

"Yes."

Then it couldn't have been more than two hours, Bramwell thought. "Are the men armed?"

"Knocked a pistol from the bastard's hand. Don't know where it went. Nobody shot a gun."

"Who's this 'bastard'?"

"Redhead, scar on his face. He followed Susanna. He's the one she was afraid of in St. Charles. Should've made her tell me about it then." Ronald raised onto an elbow. "If you'd help me onto Soot—"

Bramwell shook his head. "You're hurt too badly to ride. If you came with me I'd be trying to take care of you and rescue the women at the same time. No, we're both better off if you stay here." He leaned down and gripped Ronald's shoulder. "I'll be back with Jennara and Susanna. Never doubt it."

Ronald's attempt at a smile failed miserably. "You're fighting my battles, just as always."

"This one's for me, too." Bramwell's voice was grim.

He turned away from Ronald and, leading the dog, strode from the barn, to the tethered roan. As he leaned to the hound to let him sniff Susanna's dirty handkerchief, the roan tried to bite Bramwell, who leaped aside barely in time. He swore at the horse as he untied him.

The hound tugged at the rope and Bramwell let him go, vaulting into the saddle at the same time. The dog trotted to the main trail, crossed it, and began to run over the field with Bramwell urging the roan after him.

Once in the woods, the roan displayed several more unpleasant traits—trying to squeeze his rider's leg between his flank and tree trunks, and attempting to scrape the rider off his back by heading for low-hanging limbs. Doing his best to stay on the horse and keep track of the hound as he threaded between the trees, Bramwell assessed his chances.

If no one had shot at Ronald, it could be that the pistol his stepbrother had knocked from the redhead's hand had never been recovered. He'd hope for that, but didn't count on it. In any case, with the odds against him, stealth was the only possible tactic.

The rain fell steadily as Bramwell followed the dog through the woods. Water dripped from the wide brim of his hat, and his clothes were thoroughly soaked. As he ducked one low-hanging branch after another, Bramwell muttered curses at the roan until he ran out of words.

They'd traveled over a mile when the hound began baying. Bramwell opened his mouth to call the dog and realized he didn't know the animal's name. He'd have to overtake the dog to stop him. Intent on this maneuver, he forgot the roan's trickery long enough for the horse to swerve toward a tree. A branch caught Bramwell across the chest, flipping him off the horse.

Stunned, his breath knocked out, Bramwell sprawled heavily to the ground, unable to do more than watch as the roan, snorting in triumph, turned and galloped back toward the main road while the hound, in full cry, raced on in the opposite direction.

Jennara stood beside the brambles at one end of the cabin, wiping the rain from her face while she tried to decide whether to find a stout stick and take her chances with Frenchie or to make an attempt to reach the horses. She settled on the horses. Once she had Swift Runner, she'd try to deal with Frenchie. She started to skirt the brambles, planning to go around the back way, when a hand clamped onto her wrist.

"Where in hell d'you think you're going?" Curtis demanded.

Before she could answer, Frenchie appeared around the corner of the cabin, a hand to his neck. Blood trickled between his fingers. Curtis glanced from her to Frenchie, then at Frenchie again.

"What happened?" he asked.

"Little bitch stabbed me."

"Where'd she get a knife?"

"All I had was a small splinter of wood," Jennara put in. "He can't be badly hurt."

Curtis's grimace told her he was smiling. "Too much woman for you, eh Frenchie? Never mind, we ain't got time for fun, we gotta get outa here. Give me the gun."

Frenchie shrugged. "Goddamn gun fell through a hole— it's gone for good, 'less you mean to tear up the whole damn cabin. How come we're on the run? You said you was gonna fix the guy for good."

Curtis shook his head irritably. "He took the black mare and got away. We're quitting here afore he comes back with reinforcements—let's get packing. I figure I'll have to carry Sue, so you—"

"You can't move Susanna!" Jennara cried. "It might kill her!"

"Live or die, she's *my* woman. I ain't leaving her here for that blond son-of-a-bitch." Curtis started for the cabin, pulling Jennara with him.

Frenchie trotted alongside, still bleeding and muttering to her, "I'll get you for this, bitch—you wait."

She was too upset over Susanna's having to travel to pay any attention to him. Pleading with Curtis wouldn't save her. He'd already said he'd rather have Susanna dead than in Ronald's hands. She couldn't change his mind. Was there any other way to stop him?

The pistol! It was true Frenchie had felt around in the chipmunk hole without success, but Jennara's hands were smaller. Maybe she could reach where he hadn't been able to. Somehow she'd have to find the chance to try without either of them realizing what she was doing.

"Tend to your sister," Curtis ordered, shoving her through the door of the cabin. "Get her wrapped up to keep the rain off'n her."

"Goddamn splinter broke off in my neck," Frenchie complained to Curtis, taking his hand away to show him. "Hurts like hell and won't stop bleeding."

"You want to stay here nursing your sliver and wait for the posse? The sliver sure as hell won't bother you after one of 'em shoots you dead."

"She can take it out," Frenchie persisted, jerking his head at Jennara. "She knows how to. Look how she worked on her sister."

Jennara, kneeling beside Susanna, said without turning around, "I'd need a knife to prize out the wood splinter. Are you sure you'd trust me with a knife?"

"Reminds me—how 'bout them pig-stickers?" Curtis asked Frenchie.

"Buried shit-deep in brambles, both mine and Brod's. Hey, Brod's still out cold. How we gonna get him on a horse?"

"We ain't, unless he wakes up afore we go. Fetch the horses, Frenchie."

Frenchie wrapped a filthy blue bandanna around his neck and then, muttering and groaning, left the cabin.

"Don't you go trying no tricks on me," Curtis warned Jennara. "I ain't no Frenchie, and I'd soon's break your neck as look at you."

She didn't doubt it for a minute. To Curtis, everyone who got in his way was expendable. He might believe he loved Susanna, but what kind of love was it when you'd rather see someone dead than give her up?

"Been looking for Sue ever since she left," Curtis went on. "Finally I heard tell of a lady singer with a medicine wagon and we trailed the damn thing for three days afore we caught it in St. Charles. She damn near gave us the slip there. Now I got her and I ain't losing her again . . . ever. Get her wrapped up good. Now!"

Jennara, having no choice but to obey, leaned close to her sister. "Susie! Wake up, Susie."

Susanna's eyes opened and she blinked at Jennara. "Oh, Jen, why did you wake me? I dreamed I was with Mama and she wasn't sick, she was fine. It was so wonderful! She sang to me like she used to, my favorite lullaby." Before Jennara could break in, Susanna began to sing:

Bye low my baby
Bye low, my bouncing baby . . .

She stopped suddenly, her eyes widening in fright as she looked past Jennara. Without turning, Jennara knew Curtis stood behind her.

"We're leaving, Sue." He spoke so gently that Jennara could hardly believe it was he. "I'll take good care of you."

Susanna clutched at her sister's hand. "Jen?" she pleaded.

"I can't stop him, Susie."

"You're damn right," Curtis said. "Ain't nobody gonna stop me."

Frenchie's return with the horses distracted Curtis enough

344

so that Jennara was able to move her sister and the blankets close to the chipmunk hole under the pretext of getting her out of the way as the men carried saddles and gear to the horses. She propped the blanket-wrapped Susanna into a sitting position against the wall next to the hole. Waiting until both men were both occupied, Jennara eased her hand into the hole. Susanna paid no attention. Now that she'd seen Curtis, she seemed in a stupor.

The hole narrowed almost immediately, becoming much too small for the gun to pass through. So where had it gone? Jennara drew her hand back until it was almost free of the hole, then probed carefully to either side. Nothing. On the wall side, the rounded log had no cracks, large or small. Her head pressed against the logs, she slid her hand under the floor planks and immediately scraped her finger on the sharp edge of a bent nail. She jerked away involuntarily, but managed not to yelp.

Feeling carefully back to the nail, she found metal under her fingers. The trigger guard of the pistol was caught on the nail! It was difficult to remove the gun without losing it, but she finally managed and was easing the pistol from the hole when Curtis yelled at her.

"What're you doing?"

Hastily, Jennara tried to withdraw her hand, and the pistol slipped from her fingers, falling under the floor. When the gun hit the ground underneath, it went off. Jennara, startled and upset, put an arm around her sister.

Curtis didn't associate the shot with Jennara. "Where'd that come from?" he hollered at Frenchie.

"Sounded like in back somewheres," Frenchie said. "Don't see nothing in front."

Curtis strode across the cabin to lift Susanna into his arms. "Get moving," he warned Jennara as he carried her sister from the cabin.

When Jennara passed Brod, he grunted and she glanced down at him. His eyes were open.

345

"Shot," he mumbled.

"Brod's awake," she called.

"Too late," Curtis snapped. "You coming, or do I come after you?"

Frenchie had Swift Runner on a lead, and Brod's horse trailed behind Curtis's. As she mounted Swift Runner, Jennara said, "You're not even leaving Brod a horse?"

"Your mouth's gonna get you killed sooner or later," Curtis warned her. He turned to Frenchie. "Let's get the hell outa here."

As they set off, the rain prevented Jennara from judging direction by the sun, but she thought Curtis was heading straight for the road.

Frenchie confirmed this when he complained about their route. "Taking a risk, ain't ya, going past that farm?"

"Shortest distance between two points. That farmer ain't gonna give us trouble 'cause he ain't home. Said he 'n his wife were off to her cousin's wedding, clear over to St. Joseph. You heard him, same's me."

Frenchie shrugged. "Where'd the shot come from, then?"

"They ain't after us yet, whoever fired it." As he finished talking, the baying of a hound came clearly through the trees.

"Ain't they now?" Frenchie asked, slowing.

Curtis cursed and reined in.

Before he could change direction, the dog bounded into view and, tail wagging, circled the horses.

"Should've shot the damn mutt when I had the chance," Curtis muttered. "No use trying to outrun 'em. Frenchie, get Genevieve up on your horse with you."

Frenchie hauled in the lead rope and grabbed Jennara from Swift Runner's back before she could decide what to do. She didn't make it easy for him, and in her thrashing she managed to loosen the rope holding the pony to Frenchie's saddle and then kick Swift Runner in the side. The pony snorted indignantly and broke away. Finding himself free, he trotted deeper into the woods and disappeared.

Curtis ignored the loss of the pony. "They threaten anything," he told Frenchie, "you tell 'em you'll kill her."

"A pleasure," Frenchie muttered, tightening his grip around her waist until Jennara could scarcely breathe.

They waited, but nobody came. The hound, tired of sniffing around the horses, wandered off.

After a few more minutes, Curtis swore. "That damn hound wasn't tracking us. Ain't no posse . . . no one's after us. C'mon, get moving."

Bramwell rose slowly. Every breath he drew hurt like hell, but at least he was in one piece, if on foot. He tensed when the hound's baying broke off and didn't resume. The dog had found his quarry. The cabin? The men from the cabin? Moments later he heard something crashing through the underbrush . . . a rider.

There was nowhere to hide, and any man on the ground was at a disadvantage against a mounted man. Bramwell looked up, saw the low branch that had knocked him off the roan, grabbed the branch, and pulled himself onto it, ignoring the pain that shot through his chest. Before he could climb higher, a horse appeared between the trees, riderless. No, a pony.

"Swift Runner!" Bramwell cried.

The pony heard the call and slowed. Speaking coaxingly, as he'd heard Jennara do, Bramwell lured Swift Runner close enough so he could reach down and grasp the dangling reins. He slid on to the pony's back, his heart hammering in dread. This was her horse—but where was Jennara?

Chapter 24

Bramwell, on Swift Runner, reined in his impatience to urge the pony through the woods toward the cabin. Instead, he kept him motionless, waiting. During their brush with Dakota warriors, Jennara had taught him to watch and listen for crows or bluejays, those telltale sentinels, instead of rushing into possible danger.

Besides, Swift Runner was saddled, and that suggested the men, with the women, were on the move. If only he knew what had happened to Jennara! The uncertainty set him on edge. Wait, he counseled himself, patting Swift Runner's neck to soothe the pony and keep him quiet.

No jay warned him, but because he wasn't riding himself, he heard the creak of leather as other riders made their way through the woods toward him. Quickly assessing the possibilities, he urged the pony into a walk.

Bramwell rode deeper into the woods, finally turning Swift Runner, then halting him. Concealed from the approaching riders by the trees and the mist, he sat waiting. The riders passed some forty feet away, indistinct silhouettes, dark against the gray of the late afternoon, two riders on one mount leading a riderless horse. His heart pounded. Jennara? Two more riders on one horse, again a man and a woman.

He eased Swift Runner forward and followed them, slowly

increasing his pace, gradually overtaking them. Time and again he wiped the rain from his face, still uncertain which woman was Jennara. The mist ahead of him swirled, lifting momentarily, and he recognized her on the horse nearest him with a short, dark rider's arm circling her waist.

Anger, hot and red, exploded inside him. Without thinking, he dug his heels into Swift Runner's flanks and the pony raced ahead. Bramwell shouted, an inarticulate cry of rage, and the dark rider turned, staring in surprise.

"Bramwell!" Jennara cried. "I knew you'd come!"

When Swift Runner pulled even with the other horse, Bramwell leaped from the pony and hurled himself on the dark rider. They fell to the ground, along with Jennara, who rolled free. Bramwell landed on top of the other man and savagely dug the fingers of his left hand into the stranger's throat while pummeling him with his right fist. The dark man screamed and flailed beneath him as Bramwell struck him again and again.

Arms encircled him. He reared back.

"Bramwell!" It was Jennara's voice. "Stop! You'll kill him!"

Looking down at the moaning man, Bramwell saw the bloodied face and the broken nose and shuddered, torn between the urge to go on beating the man who'd taken Jennara captive, and revulsion for what he was doing. He didn't want another man to die at his hands.

Slowly Bramwell rose, watching the man on the ground while his arm encircled Jennara and drew her close.

"Frenchie," Jennara said, "Curtis rode off and left you. He's gone. He left you behind just as he left Brod."

Frenchie rolled over, eyeing Bramwell warily. He scuttled a few feet away, pushed himself unsteadily to his feet, and staggered into the trees, looking around for his mount, Bramwell deduced. The horse had run off and was nowhere in sight.

"Thank God you're safe," Bramwell told Jennara. "They didn't harm you?"

Jennara shook her head. "But he has Susie — Curtis Hayes does. He's a terrible man, a dangerous man . . . we must find them."

"I'll take care of Hayes." Bramwell looked around for Swift Runner and saw a hand, Frenchie's hand, reaching for the reins. Bramwell rushed toward the pony.

"Look out!" Jennara cried.

Bramwell wasted no time looking. He flung himself to one side, grabbing his clasp knife at the same time. Glancing at Frenchie, he saw the man astride Swift Runner, a stout stick in his hand. Bramwell flung the knife, aiming for Frenchie's arm. At the same moment the dark man swung the stick at Bramwell and the knife passed under his arm, striking him in the chest. He screamed and clutched at the knife. Then, as Swift Runner reared in fright, he slumped sideways and fell from the saddle.

Jennara dashed past Bramwell to grab Swift Runner's bridle, crooning to calm the pony. Bramwell walked over and stared down at Frenchie, who lay motionless with the knife embedded in his chest. Whether or not he'd meant to kill the man, Frenchie was dead.

"Please hurry, Bramwell." Jennara said. "We must save Susie."

He mounted Swift Runner and pulled Jennara up in back of him. Though he'd rather she was somewhere safe, he was determined not to leave her alone.

"He rode that way." Jennara pointed to what appeared to be an animal trail through the trees.

Bramwell urged the pony ahead, aware of Jennara's soft warmth pressing against his back as they rode across a glade, along a creek, up a rocky incline, and down the other side. He came to abrupt attention when he felt her stiffen.

A white horse stood beneath a tree ahead of them, a woman slumped in the saddle, her arms around the horse's neck. Susanna. Jennara called her sister's name and slapped Swift Runner's flank, sending him trotting forward.

"Careful," Bramwell warned as she reined in beside the white horse, "it might be a—"

He broke off, sensing motion above him, and looked up to see a figure leap down at him, feet first. He flung up his head. Dazed, he tumbled to the ground.

Bramwell tried to focus his eyes. Trees, horses, mist seemed to all whirl about him. A red-haired man—Curtis Hayes?—knelt over him. The stranger raised his arm and Bramwell saw he held a knife, the steel blade deadly.

"En garde!"

Bramwell looked in the direction of the shout. A black horse cantered toward them, the rider leaning forward, a lance gripped in one hand. Bramwell's mouth gaped. A knight riding to save them? He couldn't be seeing right.

The rider charged, his horse at a gallop. Hayes stood, knife in hand. "Mine!" he shouted at the rider. "She's mine!"

Bramwell rolled away from both Hayes and the oncoming horseman, propped up against a tree where he watched in unbelieving fascination as the horseman, lance extended, raced at Hayes. With a fearful thud the lance struck Hayes, the blow hurling him onto his back, the shock sending the rider tumbling from his horse to crumple onto his left side on the ground.

Pulling himself up with the aid of the tree trunk, Bramwell staggered toward the fallen men. Curtis Hayes was dead, a pitchfork buried deep in his chest. Bramwell stumbled to the other man, the knight errant, and stared down at him.

Ronald smiled weakly up at him. "Didn't think I had it in me, did you?" he gasped before his eyes closed and he went limp.

Jennara hurried over and knelt beside the unmoving Ronald.

"Is he dead?" Susanna cried frantically from behind her. "Please tell me he's not dead."

"Shh, Susie, he's alive." Jennara spoke the truth, but as she assessed Ronald's injuries, she wondered if he'd survive. She'd called his name, but his eyes remained closed and he showed no sign of awareness. The bruise on his head suggested a brain concussion at the very least. She suspected several of his ribs were broken, and the laceration on his left leg went so deep she worried that the tendons might have been severed. If so, even if he recovered, it would be a miracle if he ever walked on that leg again.

Susanna eased down next to Ronald and brushed his hair gently from his forehead. Leaning close to him, tears falling from her cheeks, she whispered, "You saved my life, Ronnie. I love you, I always will. Please get better."

To Jennara's surprise, his eyes opened. Raising a weak hand, he touched Susanna's wet cheek. "Don't cry." His voice was scarcely audible.

Bramwell, on Ronald's opposite side, dropped to his knees. "You saved us all, Don Quixote," he said gruffly. "You fought your own battle and mine, too."

Ronald's eyes drifted to Bramwell and he nodded slightly, then fixed on Susanna once more. "Stay with me," he said.

"I'll never leave you," she assured him. "Never!"

Bramwell caught Jennara's eye and tipped his head toward the horses. Realizing he wanted to speak to her without the other two hearing, she rose and followed him.

"Will he be all right?" Bramwell asked.

Bramwell had to be told the truth. "I don't know. Maybe — if the broken ribs don't puncture a lung and if the head injury hasn't seriously damaged the brain. As for the leg — he'll be lucky to walk again. He certainly can't ride out of here."

Bramwell frowned at the mist surrounding them. "There's a farm not too far away. We'll have to get him to shelter before it begins to rain again."

"We'll rig a litter so the two of us can carry him. There are blankets in the saddlebags. All we need are a couple of stout poles. Susanna ought to be able to ride Soot as far as the farm."

Bramwell ran his fingers lightly over Jennara's face, as

though he were a blind man memorizing her features. Except for the one brief moment in his arms, he hadn't touched her, and the caress warmed her.

"How are you?" he asked gently.

"Not too tired to carry one end of the litter." She hoped it wasn't a lie. Being a captive, unsure of what would happen from one moment to the next, had exhausted her. She wanted nothing more than to collapse and let someone else take charge. "What about the others?" she asked. "I forgot to tell you the third man's hurt, but alive in a log cabin. He can't be left there."

"As far as I'm concerned, he can rot where he is." Bramwell's tone was grim.

"But—"

"He'll last the night. If he doesn't—all the better. I'm not wasting any sympathy on those louts."

While Bramwell scouted for suitable branches for poles, Jennara found a blanket in the saddlebags. Using rope, they wove a webbing between the two poles and covered it with the blanket. As carefully as he could, Bramwell lifted Ronald onto the improvised litter, then hoisted Susanna into the saddle, Soot leading the riderless Swift Runner.

On their way to the farm, Curtis's horse appeared with Brod's horse still trailing on a lead. Both horses followed them. Jennara thought the journey would never end. The times she had to signal Bramwell to lower the litter so she could rest grew more and more frequent, until finally she was too tired to lift, so Bramwell arranged a makeshift travois from the litter and attached it to Swift Runner. Boosting Jennara onto the pony, he mounted Curtis's big white horse.

The pony, accustomed to pulling a travois, obeyed Jennara's every command as slowly, carefully, they rode out of the woods, across the field and the road, and into the farmyard.

Bramwell smashed the padlock on the back door, carried Ronald into the farmhouse, and placed him on the floor while he rummaged in a wardrobe for dry clothes to replace Ronald's wet ones. "Ever since we met," he called to Jennara in the next room, "I seem to specialize in entering other people's houses uninvited and using their belongs without permission."

Jennara, who was helping Susanna into dry clothes, smiled slightly. The proper eastern lawyer she'd first encountered had certainly changed. And, to her way of thinking, not for the worse. Once she was satisfied that the riding hadn't caused her sister to bleed excessively, she insisted Susanna lie on the parlor couch and tucked a quilt around her.

"I don't think I've ever been so tired," Susanna said, "but I am better, I know I am."

Jennara thought she saw a question in her sister's eyes and sighed. "Susie," she said gently, "you *do* realize you lost the baby, don't you?"

A single tear rolled down Susanna's cheek. She raised a weak hand and brushed it away. After a moment she said, "Curtis is dead, he'll never come after me again. And Ronald is alive. Whether he loves me or not, I'm glad he's alive."

Jennara left Susanna to tend to Ronald's leg wound and was pleased to find a good supply of clean rags to use for bandages. She finished the bandaging just as Bramwell reentered the house after caring for the horses.

"That blasted roan is tethered in the barn," he said. "I'd hoped he was gone for good."

"What roan?"

Bramwell told her about the ornery horse he'd bought for a song in Marthasville, and how the roan had finally outsmarted him. "But I suppose I've reason to be grateful to him," he finished. "Apparently that's why Ronald came after me — because the riderless roan showed up at the barn. Not that the beast meant to do me a favor, he was either after the mare or wanted to get out of the rain. Ronald feared I was in trouble and decided there was no one else to come to the rescue. He was already hurt — how he got the saddle off the roan and onto Soot and rode to help us with the pitchfork, I'll never know." Bramwell shook his head. "I never realized how courageous the boy was. I've been underestimating him for years."

"He's a man, Bramwell, not a boy."

"A man," Bramwell echoed. "Yes, he's certainly proved himself. How is he?"

"Sleeping. I gave him some laudanum I found here. We'll owe the farmer—"

"I'll pay for everything we use, and throw the roan in as a bonus."

"Some bonus!"

Bramwell grinned at her.

"That reminds me," she said, "I used one of your twenty-dollar gold pieces to pay Mrs. Knute. I'll certainly see you're repaid as soon as—"

"No! Not now, no discussion of money now. You're still wearing those wet clothes. Find something dry."

She eyed him. He was dripping all over the kitchen floor. "How about you? I will if you do."

"And then we'll rest."

Jennara readily agreed; she was so tired she could hardly stand. She found the only garment of Susanna's that would fit her was a nightgown of white batiste threaded with blue ribbon. It was so sheer as to be shameful, but with a chemise underneath, it would do.

The only remaining bed was the four-poster that belonged to the farmer and his wife. As Jennara, groggy, stumbled toward it, Bramwell met her halfway.

"We'll share the bed," he said in a no-nonsense tone. "I'm tired and so are you. We might as well be comfortable while we sleep."

She was too exhausted to argue.

After they'd gotten into bed, Bramwell could tell from Jennara's regular breathing that she slept. He, too, was tired, but he'd come too close to losing her forever not to be aware that she lay next to him now. He wanted to wrap his arms around her and hold her close . . . not make love to her, just hold her, comforted by the feel of her against him.

As he closed his eyes, bits and pieces of the last few hours flitted across his mind — Hayes standing over him with the knife, Hayes screaming like a madman at Ronald, "Mine! She's mine!"

Bramwell recalled the echo from the bluff on his journey with the roan. He'd claimed Jennara with the same word: "Mine." The echo had mocked him, and rightly so. How selfish to claim a woman as though she were stock to be bought and sold! Even if he were selfish enough to try to claim her, he knew Jennara would never belong to anyone except herself. Unlike her sister, she was perfectly capable of living without a man . . . without him.

Had he learned too late that he didn't want to live without her? His future was too uncertain for him to make plans, but he knew he needed her.

Did she need him? How would he stand it if she didn't?

With effort, Bramwell focused his mind on their immediate problems, some difficult, but all solvable — which was more than he could say about what he felt for Jennara.

He'd have to go to the cabin tomorrow and see about the injured third man; he knew Jennara would insist the man be rescued. As for Frenchie and Curtis Hayes, he supposed someone would have to be notified that they were dead. And he'd better look for Frenchie's horse while he was at it. Maybe the hound would help him.

As soon as Ronald could travel, he'd see about renting a carriage to take them all to St. Louis. The four of them would travel by train from there to St. Paul. He'd make arrangements for Swift Runner and Soot to be transported north, too. Then it would be time to say good-bye.

No, he wouldn't think about that.

What of Susanna and Ronald? Bramwell sighed. Ronald didn't seem to realize she was all wrong for him. Despite all the evidence, the child she'd concealed from him, Ronald evidently believed he still loved her. Love was certainly blind, as the poets maintained.

In his own case, he'd been blind *to* love, a very different thing. And now that he was able to give a name to how he felt about Jennara, he couldn't be sure she'd care to hear the word.

With a groan, he turned toward her and reached out to touch her hair with his fingertips. Here was the woman he'd taken as though by right, never thinking of tomorrow or the next day, not understanding how the ties between them were weaving and interweaving until he was so linked to her that to be apart was unthinkable.

Such a beautiful woman! He gazed at her rounded breasts rising and falling under the thin white material of her gown. He yearned to untie the blue ribbons and free her soft breasts, to gaze at them, caress and kiss them. Desire began to simmer inside him.

Turn your back to her, Sumner, he advised himself, or you'll never get any sleep. Shifting position, he closed his eyes again, but he couldn't close his mind against the insidious thoughts that rose to plague him. Had any of those louts dared to touch, to abuse her? It shouldn't matter. After all, two were dead and one was so badly hurt that he might be dead by morning—but it did matter. Anger replaced his desire—at himself, at the dead man, at Jennara.

Why did she have to be so obstinate? If she'd stayed at Mrs. Knute's as he'd told her to, none of this would have happened.

So now you're blaming her, Sumner? he asked, disgusted with himself. Everything is Jennara's fault and none of it yours, or Susanna's, or Ronald's? Curtis Hayes and his obsession with a woman who hated and feared him had nothing to do with it?

He sighed, his anger ebbing. Nothing could change how he

357

felt about Jennara. Whatever had happened to her, he still loved her. Shifting once more onto his back, he reached for her hand and, holding it in his, fell asleep.

Bramwell woke to darkness. For a moment he wasn't certain where he was, then a long quavering howl reminded him. What in hell was the damned hound complaining about? Rising, he went into the kitchen to look toward the barn and caught sight of the dog, nose pointed skyward, howling. Only then did Bramwell realize why he could see so well. The sky had cleared and a full moon silvered the night.

He decided to check on Ronald as long as he was up and eased silently into the second bedroom. Moonlight streamed in through the window, illuminating not one, but two blond heads. Susanna, propped against the white-painted headboard, sat atop the covers, a quilt wrapped around her. Intent on watching Ronald, she didn't see Bramwell standing in the doorway.

Softly, gently, she brushed a strand of hair from Ronald's forehead, taking care not to wake him. The tenderness of the gesture moved Bramwell despite himself and he quietly backed away.

When he slipped back into bed, Jennara stirred and murmured his name in her sleep. Was she dreaming of him? Unable to resist the impulse, he leaned over and brushed her lips with his.

One taste of her wasn't enough, would never be enough. He didn't want to wake her, but he couldn't prevent his lips from lingering on hers until hers parted and her arms rose to encircle him. By then his good intentions were well and truly lost.

Pulling her into his arms, he kissed her, releasing all the pent-up passion he'd fought to control. He meant to be tender and gentle, but his need for her flamed through him like one of the thunderbird's arrows.

"Bramwell," she murmured, her breath warm against his ear.

Made clumsy by desire, his fingers tangled in the ribbons that held her gown closed. She put her hands over his, pushing them away to untie the ribbons herself. He eased the gown and her chemise down over her shoulders until her breasts were free.

He drew in his breath at her beauty, revealed by the moon's pale glow — her eyes dark with mystery, her hair spread onto the pillow and spilling over her bared breasts. He had no words to tell her how lovely she was. All he could do to try to show her how he adored her was to kiss and caress her.

Her sighing moans and the eager way she pressed close excited him, telling him that her desire matched his own. She wanted him — a wonder he'd never take for granted.

He longed to be able to take the time to undress her slowly and savor every moment, but his need was too urgent. He had to touch her now, hold her now, be a part of her now.

He groaned in pleasure when, all their clothes off, there was no barrier left between them. His hands caressed her, stroking the sweet warmth of her until he could wait no longer. She rose to meet him and they joined as they made the tumultous journey together along the ancient but ever-new pathway of love.

Afterward, content and happy, he held her in his arms. Words crowded to his tongue, all the things he'd wanted to say to her earlier but could not — love words he'd never uttered to anyone.

"Jennara," he murmured.

She didn't respond and he peered more closely at her. Her eyes closed, she breathed deeply and regularly. She was asleep.

As he continued to hold her protectively, Bramwell wondered if he was fated always to be too late with his declaration of love. But she could hardly escape from him here. He'd tell her when she woke.

Only it didn't work that way. When he roused from a deep, peaceful sleep to a bright morning, Jennara wasn't in his arms or in the bed—or even in the bedroom.

He found her outside, gathering eggs from the chickens that had the run of the barn. The roan slanted him an evil look as he passed, and Bramwell gave him a wide berth.

"Ronald's much better this morning," she told him as he came up to her.

"That's good news." He leaned down to kiss her.

"You'll make me drop the eggs!"

"Who cares?"

"*You* will when you go hungry."

He put his hands on her shoulders, looking down at her. She wore her old divided black skirt and a man's blue shirt, evidently the farmer's, and she'd never looked more desirable.

"There are other things beside eating," he murmured, nuzzling her neck.

"Mmm . . . I quite agree. But we have two patients to think about."

He drew back. "Two?"

"Curtis knocked Susanna down and she lost the baby—and very nearly died. She's not well yet."

Bramwell remembered how he'd seen Susanna keeping watch over Ronald during the night, and it took on new significance. Despite her own weakened condition, she'd worried about Ronald. Perhaps there was more to her than he'd thought.

"So we have to make certain they both eat a good breakfast," Jennara went on.

Still holding her shoulders, he gazed into her changeable eyes. "I hope none of those louts hurt you."

"I managed to fight them off." She spoke lightly, but he could feel her shudder.

Thank God she'd been able to. The experience, though, had clearly terrified her. He'd let her tell him when she was ready. Meanwhile, he'd pass it off as she had. "I had the feeling you might. After all, you outwitted ravening Indian warriors and laid Quantrill low. Plus retrieving Swift Runner from that miserable schemer Jones."

He was rewarded by her smile. "I truly enjoyed having the chance to bring Llwellyn to terms."

"I'll admit I wondered how."

"I told him all I wanted was my pony, and if I didn't get Swift Runner back, I'd tell you that he was in town and you'd kill him. He figured giving up the pony was a better bargain."

"I might well *have* killed the bastard," Bramwell muttered, releasing her.

Together, they walked back to the house.

While Jennara scrambled eggs, Bramwell went in to see Ronald. Susanna, sitting in a chair by the bed, looked up with both defiance and fear in her eyes, as if she expected him to order her from the room. Bramwell felt a brush of shame. He nodded to her, unable to think of anything to say.

"How're you feeling?" he asked Ronald.

"I'm afraid I'll live." Ronald's voice held a hint of humor. "And with all my aches and pains, I'm not so sure that's good news."

"It makes *me* happy." Susanna spoke so softly she could scarcely be heard.

Ronald smiled at her and it was clear to Bramwell that the two had healed the breach between them. He still didn't know the entire story of how Hayes had fathered her child, but after encountering Hayes, he couldn't believe it had been with her consent. He should never have been so abrupt when he'd interrupted the wedding in Marthasville. If he'd given her a chance to explain . . .

"Susanna and I love one another. We plan to marry." Ronald's words were level and undefiant. He was simply stating a fact. A man had spoken. The boy his stepbrother had been was gone.

Bramwell looked from one to the other, suddenly realizing what it was about Susanna that so appealed to his stepbrother: she needed Ronald. No woman Ronald had ever imagined himself to be in love with before had needed him, but Susanna did. Bramwell also realized it would be good for his stepbrother to have someone who depended on him — not for money, but for love and caring. As for Susanna, he couldn't be sure, but he thought she might well devote her life to making Ronald happy.

He smiled a bit tentatively. "I don't know quite how to say this. I credit Jennara with teaching me how to admit I'm wrong when I am, which is oftener than I like to think. I made a mistake in Marthasville. I'm sorry for the pain I caused, and I hope you'll both forgive me. I'm pleased you've decided to marry."

Susanna looked at him with open incredulity. Ronald's expression changed from surprise to cautious belief. Bramwell leaned over the bed and hugged his stepbrother's shoulders, then turned to Susanna. Before she could object, he gave her a quick kiss on the cheek. She blinked, then smiled radiantly, and he saw that Susanna, at her best, was undoubtedly an appealing woman, though she'd never have the fascinating complexity of her sister.

Jennara appeared in the doorway with a tray of food.

"You're just in time to congratulate Susanna and Ronald," Bramwell told her. "They plan to marry."

Jennara set the tray on a small table near the bed and glanced from one to the other, her gaze settling on Bramwell. He knew she was trying to decipher how he felt and hoping for the best. He grinned at her and saw her relax.

"I think that's wonderful!" she cried, hurrying to embrace her sister, then Ronald. "When?"

"In St. Louis, at Cousin Farrell's," Ronald said. "I wrote him when we were in Iowa, in Ames, about my change in plans." He turned to Bramwell. "You know, when I first wrote him from Philadelphia, I asked Cousin Farrell to help me enlist in the Confederate Army when I reached St. Louis, telling him it must be a secret because my stepbrother didn't approve. Since Farrell grew up in South Carolina, I was certain he'd be a Southern sympathizer." Ronald touched his left leg with tentative fingers. "I'm not certain either army would want me now."

"I'm afraid that leg's going to give you trouble for some time," Jennara confirmed. "You'll limp for the rest of your life."

Ronald caught Susanna's hand and smiled at her. "She'll take care of me." She nodded vigorously.

Jennara and Bramwell crossed glances. He shrugged as if to say, who knows, maybe she will.

"I never once thought of Cousin Farrell," Bramwell admitted. "I don't even believe I have his address. Ronald, you're more devious than I suspected."

"It was partly your fault," Ronald said. "You never *would* listen to me."

"Ah, well, this trip has changed me . . . you'll see."

"Breakfast is getting cold," Jennara warned.

With her rare combination of practicality, wit, and tolerance, she keeps us all anchored, Bramwell thought. Only when we're alone together does she slip the cables and soar with me. God knows, that's worth everything I own, worth the world and more.

But all too soon he and Jennara wouldn't be together, couldn't be. Unlike Ronald, he had no debilitating injury. He did, though, have an obligation to fulfill, one that would take him and keep him away from Jennara. He only wished he knew for how long.

Chapter 25

Closeted with Susanna in one of Cousin Farrell's bedrooms, Jennara fastened the last of numerous satin-covered buttons on the back of her sister's powder-blue gown. Susanna had dismissed the maid, preferring to be alone with Jennara.

"I can't marry in white," Susanna had insisted. "It wouldn't be proper."

Susanna had surprised Jennara more than once in the past few weeks. Though still not strong, she'd insisted on taking over Ronald's care, and Jennara, noticing how Ronald brightened when Susanna was near him, hadn't argued too long or too hard.

Not that Susanna shared a bedroom with Ronald. Ever since they'd left the farmhouse, all the proprieties had been observed—the two men in one room at night, the two women in another. In a way, the arrangement suited Jennara, for she felt it might make it easier when the time came to say good-bye to Bramwell.

"I can't understand why you won't come with Ronnie and me to Philadelphia," Susanna said, turning to look at her.

Jennara noted absently that the gown was the exact color of Susanna's eyes. "I have to go home, you know I do," she said.

"I don't see why," Susanna insisted. "You must know Bramwell can't keep his eyes off you. You're hardly out of his sight before he's off looking for you. He'd be more than happy if you decided to come east."

"I doubt that. Once we're apart he'll forget me. And remember, Minnesota *is* my home, after all." Jennara tucked in a stray wisp of her sister's hair. "You look lovelier than any bride I've ever seen."

Immediately distracted, Susanna gazed anxiously into the mahogany pier glass, twisting this way and that to check her appearance. "Do you think Ronnie will like my dress?"

"With you inside it, he'd like a gunnysack." Jennara spoke a bit more tartly than she'd intended. She was truly happy to be a part of their marriage ceremony, but she found it hard to be around two such happy people when she was well aware that their kind of happiness would never be hers.

"Cousin Farrell has been so nice to us," Susanna said. "He's really an old dear. You'd think Ronnie was his own son, the way he's taken care of everything for us."

Farrell Farnsworth, sixty, a childless widower, was exactly how Jennara had pictured a southern gentleman, down to his bushy white mustache. "Cousin" was a courtesy title. He was really a remote connection of Ronald's maternal grandmother, but Susanna was right, he took as much pleasure in arranging the wedding as if he'd fathered Ronald. He'd been charmingly hospitable to her and her sister as well as to Bramwell.

"I still can't get over how kind Bramwell's been to me," Susanna went on. "I can hardly believe he's the same man who said those cruel things in Marthasville."

"He's a man who admits his mistakes." Jennara smiled to herself as she spoke, remembering their long journey

365

together and all the mistakes Bramwell had made along the way—and her own mistakes as well. They'd learned a lot from one another.

"Even Ronnie's changed," Susanna said with a tiny frown.

Jennara suspected her sister found the new Ronald more difficult to manage, but that was all to the good for both of them. "He grew up in a hurry," she said. "Just like you had to do."

Susanna bit her lip. "Sometimes I think about the baby I lost and I'm sad. Mostly, though, I'm relieved. Is that so terrible of me?"

Jennara shook her head. "I'm sure you would have loved the baby, had it survived, but you'd always have feared the child might turn out like its father."

Susanna shuddered. "I don't want to think about *him* ever again."

"Then we won't. Let me put on your hat and veil, it's almost time to go downstairs."

Susanna caught her sister's hand. "Jen, do you believe Ronnie really, truly loves me?"

"If you could see how he comes alive the moment you walk into a room, you wouldn't ask me. I'm sure his rapid recovery is due to the fact that you were his nurse."

"Oh, I do love him so! Jen, you just don't know. . . ."

Didn't she? Biting back more tart words, Jennara forced a smile. This was Susanna's wedding day, and she wouldn't do anything to spoil her sister's happiness.

They descended the stairs slowly, Jennara well behind Susanna, partly because she still didn't have the knack of managing a hoopskirt, and her sister had insisted she wear the latest fashion.

The sliding doors of the double parlor had been thrown open to create one large room. Father Young stood with

366

his back to the fireplace while Cousin Farrell beamed from the doorway. Ronald, with the help of a cane, stood at the foot of the curving staircase, and his bemused expression when he saw Susanna should have settled any question in her mind of how he felt about her.

Susanna was lovely in the blue satin gown, with its high neckline and long sleeves, her fair hair curling softly to her shoulders. She had no trouble at all with the hoop skirt, moving gracefully down each step until she reached Ronald, who wordlessly held out his arm.

Jennara blinked back tears of thankfulness that her baby sister had found a wonderful man to love and marry. Ronald and Susanna had, both in their own way, earned the right to happiness.

Stepping carefully, one hand on the bannister, Jennara followed her sister. Before she reached the foot of the stairs, Bramwell strode from the foyer to stand looking up at her. Jennara caught her breath. Something more than admiration, more than desire, glowed in the depths of his dark eyes. Trapped in the spell of what shimmered in the air between them, Jennara forgot the hoop skirt. On the next to last step, her toe caught on the lowest round of the hoop and she stumbled, falling forward.

Bramwell's arms reached out and caught her, holding her close for a moment before he set her upright on the polished parquet floor. "You always do the unexpected," he murmured, his eyes gleaming with amusement as he offered her his arm.

Gathering her ruffled dignity as best she could, Jennara placed her fingers on his arm and they joined the others in the parlor.

The room was brilliant and fragrant with flowers, and its polished mahogany wainscoting gleamed beneath flocked green-and-white wallpaper. Matching crystal chan-

367

deliers hung from the ceiling, their candles unlit. No candles were necessary with the late afternoon sun lighting the room, turning Susanna's hair to gold as she passed a window.

"Doesn't she look beautiful?" Jennara whispered.

"Not as beautiful as her sister," Bramwell murmured.

His praise warmed her, as always, but she didn't look at him, afraid he'd see how she longed to be standing where Susanna stood, in front of the minister, with Bramwell next to her . . . standing there listening and responding to the old, binding words that transformed a man and woman into husband and wife.

Champagne was served afterward, and then there was dinner at the long mahogany table in the dining room. Ronald and Susanna escaped upstairs early. Because Ronald's leg still caused him trouble, there'd be no wedding trip for them except the one to Philadelphia in two days' time.

It was after eleven when Jennara bid good night to Cousin Farrell. Bramwell stayed behind to share a nightcap with their host. Retiring to her room, Jennara allowed the maid to extract her from the elegant lavender gown, but she insisted on donning her nightgown by herself. It troubled her that Ronald's money had paid for her new clothes. Wealthy or not, it was one thing for him to outfit his wife, another to provide for a sister-in-law. But he'd been so hurt when she'd protested that she'd given in, reluctant to upset him.

As she slipped into the pale pink robe that matched her nightgown, she had to admit that, whatever her reservations, she enjoyed the fine fabrics and excellent fit of the clothes. Sliding her feet into pink slippers, she drifted to the window, looking out into the dark December night, where a crescent moon peeked from behind gossamer clouds.

She'd been away from home almost six months, and wondered what she'd find when she returned. Had the house been burned or did No Cloud's painted symbols keep it safe? And what of No Cloud himself? God willing, he'd survived the uprising.

She'd heard from Cousin Farrell that President Lincoln had made the final decision on how many Dakota warriors were to hang, reducing the total from four hundred to thirty-eight. The executions were to take place in Minnesota the day after Christmas. Cousin Farrell hadn't approved of the reduction. He didn't approve of anything President Lincoln said or did since. As Ronald had surmised, he was a dyed-in-the-wool Rebel.

When the tap came at her door, Jennara knew it was Bramwell. Even though she knew she'd been waiting for him to knock, she hesitated. It wasn't proper to see him alone in her room, but she didn't care a whit about that. Her worry was if it was wise to see him alone when she couldn't conquer her longing to melt into his arms.

Vowing to remain aloof, she crossed the room and opened the door. Bramwell strode inside, kicked the door shut behind him, and reached for her. Jennara stepped aside.

"No." Her clipped refusal was far stronger than she felt.

He raised an eyebrow. "Why not?"

"Cousin Farrell—"

"The hell with Cousin Farrell, that old Reb reprobate." His words were slightly slurred, and she suspected he might have had one glass of wine too many. Port, she'd heard, could be quite potent, and port was Cousin Farrell's evening drink.

"He's been a very gracious host," she pointed out.

"He wouldn't *dare* be found guilty of not providing the

famous southern hospitality." Bramwell caught her by the shoulders. "What's this you've been telling your sister about traveling back to Minnesota alone?"

Damn. She might have known Susanna would blab to Ronald and Ronald would tell Bramwell. "I feel Ronald needs you more than I do," she said, "I'm perfectly capable of getting home by myself while he—"

"—he has a devoted wife to minister to him," Bramwell finished for her. "If you think I'd let you get on a train alone, you're badly mistaken. I intend to see you safely to your house. If the Indians burned it during the uprising, I mean to make sure you find a place to stay."

"I got along for twenty-nine years without you—" she began, intending to go on, but his angry scowl stopped her. What on earth had she said to upset him?

"I don't want to hear you tell me you don't need me." His fingers dug into her shoulders. "Is that clear?"

She blinked. Not need him? Good God, she'd never expected to need anyone as much as she needed Bramwell. But get along without him? Yes, she could do that . . . she *had* to. Jennara shifted her shoulders, trying to free herself. His grip tightened.

"You're not moving until you give me the real reason why you said no to me just now. For the love of God, Jennara, we haven't been together for weeks."

"I don't want you to touch me." Her tone was frosty. "I don't believe I have to explain why."

He glared at her then, his hands still on her shoulders, bent and kissed her, a hard, savage kiss, angry and demanding. She could no more resist him than she could fly. Helpless against the assaulting demands of her senses, she swayed toward him, her lips parting, answering his urgency with her own. He tasted of port, of passion, of himself: a potent brew.

His kiss deepened, promising everything she wanted, more than she'd ever dreamed of, wonders never before experienced. And Bramwell was a man who kept his promises.

A remnant of pride stiffened her spine, keeping her from surrendering completely. She'd made up her mind not to make love with him again, and she would not! Jennara pulled away.

"If you insist on traveling to Minnesota with me, then I suppose you must," she snapped, feeling her heart hammering in her ears. "But we will *not* be traveling as—as lovers. That's over and done with—tonight or any other night. Is that clear?" Deliberately she echoed his words.

He stared at her, the anger in his eyes giving way to bewilderment and pain. She had to force herself not to reach out to him.

"If that's your decision, I have no choice but to honor it." He spoke as coldly as she had moments before. Without another word he turned on his heel and left the room.

The train trip from St. Louis to Chicago and from Chicago to St. Paul was interminable. Jennara tried her best to enjoy the experience, a first for her, but could not. With Bramwell beside her, a cold, silent Bramwell, she couldn't fix her attention on anything but him. Neither the novelty of the train nor the passing scenery interested her. She was aware only of Bramwell and the wrongness between them.

It was her fault, yes—but his too. Or perhaps she should blame neither of them. She was what she was and he was what he was, as different as day and night, as different as a frontier healer and a Philadelphia lawyer. Circumstances had thrown them together and forged a bond strong enough to make her love him. But loving him didn't mean she had to give up every grain of pride and dignity she possessed. Didn't he understand that the longer she stayed in his arms, the less likely she'd be able to say good-bye and walk away from him without looking back? He surely didn't wish to have her sobbing and clinging to him, creating a painful scene, any more than she did.

Because he *was* going to leave her. He'd never given her any reason to believe he wouldn't. If she must bear it, she had to do so in her own fashion.

It was a tremendous relief when the train pulled into the St. Paul station. Swift Runner and Soot had traveled well in the livestock car, but were as eager as she to ride away from the city for home. Even Bramwell's mood improved when, allowing the horses to set their own pace, they left the city, traveling southwest on a road that was lightly covered with snow.

"Your trunk will be sent on by wagon, I made the arrangements," he told her.

"Thank you. But when *I'll* put on a hoop skirt again, I've no idea," she said. Under her warm coat, she wore her brown riding clothes, cleaned and pressed by Cousin Farrell's servants, and felt more comfortable than she had in weeks. Taking a deep breath of the cold, fresh air, she smiled at Bramwell for the first time in days. "Now *this* is proper December weather—none of that Missouri rain."

They stayed that night and the next two in small country inns in separate rooms. On the last day of the journey, the weather, which had been fair and moderate, turned colder, and it began to snow. By the time they neared Jennara's house, the wind had risen, blowing the snow into drifts. Traveling in such weather was dangerous, and Jennara was relieved when she saw the chimneys

372

of her house above the trees. Soot, evidently sensing she was near home, picked up her pace and Swift Runner followed.

"It's still there!" Jennara cried moments later when she saw the rest of the house through the bare trees. The barn was also intact, and Bramwell took the horses inside and rubbed them down while Jennara hurried into the house to kindle blazes in the stove and fireplaces.

Nothing had been touched inside, and there was no evidence that any Dakota warrior had even been near the place. She breathed a prayer of thankfulness to No Cloud.

The house was cold and it would take time for the chill to dissipate. Jennara was huddled in front of the parlor fire when Bramwell stomped in, covered with snow and carrying the rest of their supplies.

"Had trouble getting from the barn to the house," he said. "It's a regular blizzard out there."

She was glad they'd arrived safely, but now she had to worry about how long the storm might last. It would be impossible for Bramwell to leave until the weather improved. She'd thought he'd be staying overnight at the most, but listening to the wolf-howl of the wind, it was obvious Bramwell would be in her house longer than that. She'd known storms to last the better part of a week. And to keep warm tonight, they'd have to sleep in front of the parlor fireplace. All the other rooms would be far too cold.

"This is your customary December weather?" Bramwell asked, removing his coat and joining her in front of the fire.

"We don't always have a blizzard in December," she said defensively.

"That Missouri rain looks better and better," he said. "It's easier to get dry than to get warm."

373

"I'll wager you have snow in Philadelphia by now."

"If we do, it's a reasonable amount. This state goes to extremes. My experience leads me to believe Minnesota is either too hot or too cold, and every moment spent here is fraught with hidden dangers."

Opening her mouth to defend her state, Jennara saw the corner of his mouth twitch and realized he was teasing her. She shifted tactics, doing her best to look worried. "I only hope the food holds out. If the storm lasts over two weeks, I don't know how we'll survive unless we eat horse fodder."

"Two weeks?"

She nodded. "Sometimes we don't see the sun until March. But don't worry, they'll have the snow tunnel to St. Paul completed long before then."

He grinned at her. "I might have believed you six months ago, but I've learned a thing or two since then."

"Have you?"

His smile faded as his eyes met hers. "I've lost a few prejudices and gained—" He took a step toward her.

"That reminds me," she said hurriedly, edging away. "I've something I want to give you." She all but ran toward the stairs.

Damned if she didn't behave as though she were afraid of him. Bramwell knew it couldn't be true, what she must fear was his touch, or more precisely, her response to his touch. Why?

He listened with satisfaction to the keening wind rattling the windows as it sought entry. He put no credence in her account of two-week storms, but this one was sure to last a day or two, keeping him snowbound here . . . alone with Jennara. That was worth the risk of eating

374

horse fodder.

When she reappeared in the parlor, she reached her hand to him. On her palm rested a long, thin, horn-cased clasp knife. "This was my father's," she said. "I want you to have it . . . to replace yours."

He took it and slid the sharp steel blade in and out of the horn handle. "This is a beautifully crafted old knife, much more valuable than mine was."

"I'd like to think of you having it."

"Why?"

A flush suffused her cheeks and she glanced away from him.

He dropped the knife into a pocket and took a paper from the inside of his vest. "A month or so ago, I promised to show you this," he said, offering it to her.

Jennara took the paper and unfolded it. When she glanced at it, her cheeks grew pinker. "It's the sketch Ronald drew of me." Her voice was almost inaudible.

"I keep it next to my heart. Surely you know why."

She swallowed, then bit her lip.

Now was the time to risk everything. He grasped her hands, drawing her close, murmuring, "I think we've found our own kind of love medicine, don't you?"

Her eyes widened in surprise, then began to glow, and he knew he was right. "You *do* love me!" he exclaimed triumphantly.

"I—yes." He could hardly hear her words.

He pulled her into his arms. "For days, weeks, I've wanted to tell you how much I love you, but the time was never right." He kissed her gently, lovingly. "For a while I thought you were never going to let me touch you again," he murmured into her ear.

Jennara sighed, her fingers tangled in his hair. "It wasn't easy to stay out of your arms."

He kissed her again, long and thoroughly, then reluctantly released her. They must talk, he had to make her understand the difficulties ahead. Lifting pillows from the sofa, he arranged them on the floor in front of the fire and pulled her down to sit beside him.

"When I came here in June," he began, "I told you I was in a hurry to find Ronald. The reason was—is—that I accepted a commission in the United States Army just before I got Ronald's letter telling me he was in Minnesota. I asked for and received permission to settle my personal affairs before I entered active service." He smiled. "I may hold the record for the longest time taken settling personal affairs. The point is that I must return to Pennsylvania as soon as possible and join my cavalry unit."

She stroked his face, fingering his beard. "You even look like a cavalry officer."

He kissed her palm. "I love you more than I ever thought possible. I want you to be my wife. Tell me you'll wait for me until the war is over."

Jennara pulled her hand away. "No, I won't wait for you."

Stunned, he stared at her.

"When we first met," she said, "you accused me of conniving at marriage. You were wrong then. Now you'd be right. I love you, but either we marry immediately, so I can be with you as much as possible during the war, or you'll have to take your chances on finding me when it's over. I've done a lot of thinking on our trip here, and I've decided my duty as a healer is to help tend the war-wounded. So, you see, I won't be waiting here."

He scowled at her, knowing it was useless to argue once she made up her mind. Of all the stubborn, wrong-headed women! The last place he wanted her was anywhere near the battle lines. Didn't she realize she'd be in danger?

After a moment or two, his expression lightened. Wasn't that one of the reasons he loved Jennara, because she knew her own mind and wasn't afraid to speak it? And as usual she was right. To hell with gallantry . . . he'd be a fool to risk losing her, a fool not to marry her as quickly as possible and take her back with him so they could be together for whatever time he had left. He wanted to be with her forever.

Jennara smiled. "Besides," she said, "I've worked hard at making a frontiersman out of you. Now it's your turn to improve me by teaching me some of your eastern ways."

He put an arm around her, holding her so he could look into her wonderful, changeable green-gold eyes. "My love, no man living could improve on what you already are. The only thing I want ever to change is your last name to mine. And the sooner, the better!"

Chapter 26

From the kitchen window Jennara glanced at No Cloud's tepee under the sycamores at the edge of the woods in back of the house. When the Dakotas had been moved from their Minnesota lands to a new reservation farther west, she'd offered the old medicine man a home with her. Since she was the nearest thing to a family he had left after the uprising, he'd moved his tepee to her land. His companionship these past two years had meant a great deal to her.

Though she'd intended to follow the fortunes of war and tend the wounded, circumstances had prevented her from carrying out her vow, and she'd returned to her home in Minnesota, where she was still the only healer for the settlers in the district.

Thinking she heard something, she turned and hurried to the front porch, but nothing, no one was in sight. Stay calm, she warned herself. Everything's all right, of course it is.

She'd been flying around the house like a madwoman ever since the message had come . . . as if it made any real difference how the place looked.

It was a lovely day—thank heaven, because April could certainly be fickle in Minnesota. It could even snow! But the sun shone and the breeze was pleasant, if a bit cool.

How strange life could be! She'd thought more than once that her future was planned, only to have everything turned topsy-turvy by fate, sometimes for the worse, sometimes for the better. Why she, of all people, hadn't expected the most recent of fate's interferences, was more than she could understand. As a healer, she should have at least taken it into consideration.

Was that dust she saw rising above the trees? There'd been no rain this past week—perhaps it was. Dust meant horses, someone coming. Eagerly she ran down the front steps and out to the drive. Through the small, new leaves of the maples, she caught a glimpse of more than one horseman and frowned. Those weren't horses, they were ponies . . . a delegation of Dakotas.

They swept into her driveway, five of them—two braves, two Dakota women, and a half-grown boy.

"Little Bear!" Jennara cried, surprised and pleased. No Cloud had told her the boy had come back to live in Minnesota, but she hadn't seen him. "How tall you are!" she exclaimed as he dismounted. "I took you for a warrior!"

"We heard," he said, trying not to show his pleasure at her words. "I came with my friends."

She longed to hug him, but knew she must not. It wouldn't do to ruffle his dignity, especially in public. Her excitement at seeing Cub again made her forget for a moment why she was waiting, but the sound of hooves reminded her and her heart began to pound.

The Dakotas drew their ponies off the drive and the women dismounted to stand near Little Bear. The two mounted braves stared impassively along the drive, waiting as she did, though she was far from impassive.

A horseman rode under the arching maples, a rider with a wide-brimmed blue hat covering his black hair. He checked his horse momentarily at the sight of the Dakotas, then continued on at a slower pace.

"Bramwell!" Jennara cried, racing toward the oncoming horse.

He halted and pulled her onto the saddle, wrapping his arms around her and kissing her. For long moments nothing else existed but Bramwell.

"Is this your idea of a welcoming delegation?" he murmured into her ear. "What were you doing, trying to scare me to death?"

"They're Cub's friends," she said, so breathless she could hardly speak. "He came to greet you. I had no idea this would happen."

It would have been a grave affront to the Dakotas not to offer food. At any other time Jennara would have been happy to, but this was to have been their special time, hers and Bramwell's. After so long, almost two years, they needed to be alone together. She smiled ruefully at him. Nothing could be done about Fate.

Bramwell shook hands with Cub, then pulled him into a bone-crushing embrace. From a man, it was acceptable, and the two grinned at each other. As if taking this for a sign, the braves dismounted and came to greet Bramwell.

The formalities over, everyone entered the house. The Dakota braves and Cub sat on the parlor floor. Bramwell shrugged and joined them. The two women followed Jennara into the kitchen. They would, she knew, serve their husbands.

Cold roast beef, bread, cheese, and jelly were rapidly consumed to the very last crumb, washed down by coffee generously dosed with sugar and cream. Reluctantly Jennara brought out the pie she'd so carefully made. By serving a very small piece to everyone except herself, she made it go around.

"Butterscotch?" Bramwell asked, raising an eyebrow.

She nodded ruefully. The pie was especially for him, yet he'd gotten no more than a taste.

When the last of the pie was gone, the eldest of the Dakotas rose and made a short speech.

Jennara translated. "He says they're happy to see that the husband of their friend—that's me—has returned from battle victorious. They say that you are welcome in their tepees, and they wish that we may both enjoy good health and have many strong children."

Bramwell raised his eyebrows before nodding toward the speaker. "I'm grateful for the welcome, and I'll remember your kind wishes."

After Jennara had translated his words, one by one the Indians got to their feet and filed from the room, leaving by the front door. Because it wasn't their custom, no one said good-bye.

"How are Susanna and Ronald?" she asked Bramwell as she picked up the dishes.

"I suppose you know your sister persuaded Ronald to hang a few of his paintings in the Claridge store?" When she nodded, he said, "Susanna's business sense is amazing. Ronald can't paint fast enough to keep up with the demand for his work. They're both as happy as clams."

He sighed. "Thank God Ronald missed the war! I can hardly believe it's over and done with at last."

"I can hardly believe you're really here at last." Jennara threw her arms around him.

Hugging her, Bramwell said, "Where is he?"

Jennara took him by the hand and led him into the kitchen and out the back door, heading for the tepee at the far end of the clearing. Bramwell glanced at her quizzically before putting an arm about her so that they walked close together.

381

"I had everything so well planned," she said. "I never expected Cub and his friends to show up."

"I take it you're raising him to be another Cub," Bramwell said, eyeing the tepee as they neared it.

"No, of course not! Though he does love visiting No Cloud." Jennara stopped outside the open flap of the tepee. "We come," she said in the Dakota tongue.

"Enter, with quiet," No Cloud answered from inside.

They ducked into the tepee where she introduced her husband, who greeted the old medicine man softly and courteously, though Bramwell's attention was fixed on the small boy curled up asleep on a mat beside No Cloud.

"He looks like me," Bramwell told Jennara in a surprised half-whisper.

She nodded. "All except for the green eyes."

"When he wakes, I will bring him to you," No Cloud said, smiling. "It is well for a returning warrior to have time alone with his wife."

They ran, laughing, back to the house. "I never dreamed I'd bear a child so soon after we married," Jennara said when they reached the kitchen. "Gregory Bramwell Sumner came as a complete surprise."

"And you a doctor?"

"I mean, I had all these plans—"

"—that Gregory interrupted." He scooped her into his arms and headed for the stairs. "I know how you value Dakota advice," he said as he began climbing, "so why don't we plan a few more interruptions? Strong and healthy ones, of course." He swung her onto the bed and fell on it beside her, pulling her into his arms.

"How can I argue with a victorious warrior?" she said, as her lips met his. "Especially one with such potent love medicine."

ZEBRA HAS THE SUPERSTARS
OF PASSIONATE ROMANCE!

CRIMSON OBSESSION   (2272, $3.95)
by Deana James

Cassandra MacDaermond was determined to make the handsome gambling hall owner Edward Sandron pay for the fortune he had stolen from her father. But she never counted on being struck speechless by his seductive gaze. And soon Cassandra was sneaking into Sandron's room, more intent on sharing his rapture than causing his ruin!

TEXAS CAPTIVE   (2251, $3.95)
by Wanda Owen

Ever since two outlaws had killed her ma, Talleha had been suspicious of all men. But one glimpse of virile Victor Maurier standing by the lake in the Texas Blacklands and the half-Indian princess was helpless before the sensual tide that swept her in its wake!

TEXAS STAR   (2088, $3.95)
by Deana James

Star Garner was a wanted woman—and Chris Gillard was determined to collect the generous bounty being offered for her capture. But when the beautiful outlaw made love to him as if her life depended on it, Gillard's firm resolve melted away, replaced with a raging obsession for his fiery TEXAS STAR.

MOONLIT SPLENDOR   (2008, $3.95)
by Wanda Owen

When the handsome stranger emerged from the shadows and pulled Charmaine Lamoureux into his strong embrace, she sighed with pleasure at his seductive caresses. Tomorrow she would be wed against her will—so tonight she would take whatever exhilarating happiness she could!

Available wherever paperbacks are sold, or order direct from the Publisher. Send cover price plus 50¢ per copy for mailing and handling to Zebra Books, Dept. 2695, 475 Park Avenue South, New York, N.Y. 10016. Residents of New York, New Jersey and Pennsylvania must include sales tax. DO NOT SEND CASH.